EVERYMAN'S   LIBRARY

EVERYMAN,
I WILL GO WITH THEE,
AND BE THY GUIDE,
IN THY MOST NEED
TO GO BY THY SIDE

FRANZ KAFKA

THE
CASTLE

TRANSLATED FROM THE GERMAN
BY WILLA AND EDWIN MUIR

WITH AN INTRODUCTION BY
IRVING HOWE

EVERYMAN'S LIBRARY
Alfred A. Knopf New York London Toronto

127

THIS IS A BORZOI BOOK

PUBLISHED BY ALFRED A. KNOPF

First included in Everyman's Library, 1992

Copyright information (US)
Copyright 1930, 1941, 1954 by Alfred A. Knopf, Inc.
Copyright renewed 1958, 1968, 1982 by Alfred A. Knopf, Inc.
Originally published in German as *Das Schloss* by Kurt Wolff
Verlag, 1926, by Schocken Verlag, Berlin, 1935, and by Schocken
Books Inc., New York, 1946. Copyright 1926 by Kurt Wolff
Verlag, Copyright renewed 1954 by Schocken Books Inc.

Copyright information (UK)
Munich: Kurt Wolff Verlag, 1926; Berlin: Schocken Verlag, 1935;
New York: Schocken Books, Inc., 1946; London: Martin Secker &
Warburg Ltd., 1930; Definitive Edition 1953

Introduction Copyright © 1992 by Irving Howe
Bibliography and Chronology Copyright © 1992 by Everyman's Library
Typography by Peter B. Willberg

All rights reserved. Published in the United States by Alfred A. Knopf,
a division of Random House, Inc., New York, and in Canada by
Random House of Canada Limited, Toronto. Distributed by Random
House, Inc., New York. Published in the United Kingdom by
Everyman's Library, Northburgh House, 10 Northburgh Street,
London EC1V 0AT, and distributed by Random House (UK) Ltd.

US website: www.randomhouse.com/everymans

ISBN: 978-0-679-41735-4 (US)
978-1-85715-127-5 (UK)

A CIP catalogue reference for this book is available from the British Library

Library of Congress Cataloging-in-Publication Data
Kafka, Franz, 1883–1924.
[Schloss. English]
The castle / Franz Kafka.
p. cm.—(Everyman's library)
Translation of: Das Schloss.
Includes bibliographical references (p.   ).
ISBN 978-0-679-41735-4
I. Title.
PT2621.A26S33   1992
833'.912—dc20

92-52904
CIP

Book design by Barbara de Wilde and Carol Devine Carson

Printed and bound in Germany by GGP Media GmbH, Pössneck

INTRODUCTION

———

... who search the reason of things
Are those who bring the most sorrow on themselves
– Euripides, *The Medea*

The central figure of *The Castle* – we know him only as K. – is a land surveyor who never gets a chance to do any surveying. His job is to measure and estimate, which in the Kafkan economy suggests that he should be taken as a seeker, a man embarked on a quest for meaning. He comes to the Castle, that clouded locus of authority, not 'to lead an honored and comfortable life', but in order to gain acceptance by the higher, perhaps celestial powers and thereby to discover 'the reason of things'. In a revealing passage that Kafka deleted, perhaps because it is too revealing, K. says: 'I have a difficult task ahead of me and have dedicated my whole life to it ... Because it is all I have – that task, I mean – I ruthlessly suppress everything that might disturb me in carrying it out ...'

Where the protagonist of Kafka's previous novel *The Trial* is torn out of a sluggish routine by an unspecified accusation and then exhausts himself in a sequence of defensive probes, the K. of *The Castle* acts from his own decision, a freedom of consciousness and choice. His 'task' is self-determined, not imposed. It may be doomed by forces beyond his control or distracted through an inner confusion of desires; but to borrow a phrase Kafka used in conversation with his friend and biographer Max Brod, the effort to penetrate the Castle suggests a wish 'to get clear about the ultimate things'. Getting clear about 'the ultimate things' was the driving impulse behind Kafka's fictions, with the proviso that it is a wish quite unrealizable. The world will not yield to lucidity.

K. is hardly a rebel, certainly no more so than Kafka himself, but his wish to reach the shadowy heart of the Castle puts him in opposition to the slackness of the bulk of humanity. This land surveyor who has abandoned home and family wants, in our American idiom, to 'get the lay of the land', that is, to penetrate the structure of existence, assuming that such a structure exists and can be known. But the grey eminences of the Castle make it clear that they have little use for a land surveyor, and even if they do grudgingly admit him to the village, one obstacle after another blocks his path, whether planted deliberately by the Castle authorities or simply there, as part of the way things are. In exasperation K. concludes that 'they're playing with me'.

K.'s desire to reach and then go beyond the Castle – but what can there be beyond? – was, I believe, shared by Kafka himself, though with a keener scepticism and a sharper humor regarding the risks of the enterprise. It is this evident kinship between author and protagonist – *The Castle* was begun as a first-person narrative – that prompts the opinion that of all Kafka's fiction this is the most personal. K. is not of course a mouthpiece for Kafka – he lacks Kafka's grave intelligence and humor – but his inner conflict between a taste for ordinary life and the demands imposed by his quest were in good part shared by Kafka, who also kept wondering about 'the reason of things'. Where many of Kafka's earlier stories ('The Judgment', 'The Metamorphosis') entail a sense of plight, *The Castle* projects a greater strength of will than we have encountered in Kafka's earlier writings – an effort to overcome the muteness of existence.

Franz Kafka was born in 1883 to a middle-class Jewish family in Prague. Whatever Jewishness he experienced as a boy he later judged to be tepid and residual, a slothful routine of ritual observance. The Prague Jews, as a nervous minority, aligned themselves with a larger minority, the German-speaking population of the city, thereby experiencing a kind of doubled estrangement. Among some younger Jews in Prague, however, there was a lively cultural circle to which young Kafka was drawn. And even then, in early age, he saw himself as a writer: 'My talent for portraying my dreamlike inner life has thrust aside all other matters into the background.'

A neurotic streak runs through Kafka's entire life, manifest in his drawn-out emotional contest with his father, a somewhat coarse but energetic merchant whom he raised in imagination to the status of a fearsome authority-figure. Kafka's neurosis also came out in a repeated incapacity, except for a brief final relationship before his death in 1924, to sustain his engagements with women. But while this neurotic streak runs very deep, leading at times to something like a celebration of passivity, it does not finally control his major works, for there, through a severe discipline, the neurotic component is now a theme or subject, serving mainly as a burden to be lightened.

No other writer of our century has so strongly evoked the claustral sensations of modern experience, sensations of bewilderment, loss, guilt, dispossession. These are sensations known to millions of people quite unaware of Kafka's writings and without any claim to philosophical reflection. The aura of crisis hanging over Kafka's life and work is at once intimately subjective, his alone, and austerely impersonal, known to all of us. 'I represent,' he wrote, 'the negative elements of my age' – more accurately, the struggle to confront and perhaps keep at bay these 'negative elements'.

Kafka's stories and novels cannot be comfortably placed in any of the usual literary categories even as they share aspects of all – fable, allegory, realistic narrative, parable. His ideas are formed through images of situations 'the pathos of which' remarks Jorge Borges, 'arises precisely out of the infinity of the obstacles that repeatedly hinder' Kafka's characters. And these obstacles soon come to seem rooted in the very nature of things, a world created without regard to human needs, perhaps even in opposition to those needs.

The sense of helplessness in an ice-cold universe; the persuasion that guilt follows from consciousness, since consciousness besets us with the vision of a perfection that existence can only reject; the feeling that we are at a hopeless distance from kin and self ('in my family,' writes Kafka, 'I am more estranged than a stranger'); the press of anxiety as an index of being; the fear that humanity has lost the capacity for transcendence; the notion that 'the Day of Judgment is a summary court in perpetual session' – such sentiments are the very stuff of modern consciousness, though nowhere expressed with the force they achieve in Kafka's writings.

Quite understandably, there have followed seemingly end-less efforts to interpret Kafka's writings, and while each approach contributes a measure of understanding, there is a tendency for all of them to narrow the scope of Kafka's fiction. Psychological interpretations stress his struggle to achieve a self-sufficient way of life as presumably reflected in the pro-gress of his work. Sociological interpretations point to Kafka's gift for representing the decay of mid-European society during the early years of this century and his mordant sketches of life-denying bureaucracies ('the fetters of a tormented mankind are made of red tape'). Religious interpretations focus upon the yearning, felt to be implicit in the Kafkan texts, for a glimpse of transcendence. And still other critics see Kafka's work as strongly coloured by his Jewishness, citing the famous letter to his father in which he writes that he had grown up with 'the ghost of Judaism', a 'ghost' that would haunt his imagination throughout his life.

While there is almost no mention of Judaism or Jews in Kafka's fictions, the aura of estrangement that pervades many of them – for instance, K.'s efforts as an outsider to gain acceptance from the authorities of the Castle – may be seen as an oblique reflection of Jewish concerns. Robert Alter, one of the critics who most sensitively proposes this approach to Kafka, writes that what he sought to do 'was to convert the distinctive quandaries of Jewish existence into images of the existential dilemmas of mankind *überhaupt*, "as such" ... His stories and novels are repeatedly and variously concerned with questions such as exile, assimilation, endangered community, revelation, commentary, law, tradition, and commandment.' And certainly the late, remarkable story 'Josephine the Singer, or the Mouse Folk' invites being read as a parable of the Jewish situation. With this approach to Kafka I see no reason to quarrel, since it stresses genesis rather than bearings; I would only add that by the twentieth century one may well feel that most of the themes Alter identifies as 'the distinctive quandaries of Jewish existence' have become quandaries for all of mankind: Kafka didn't need to 'convert' them, he merely needed to recognize them. One feels, as perhaps the strongest response to Kafka's writings, that he must finally be taken as a writer of universal significance – his novels and stories lose a great deal if narrowed to the terms of a particular doctrine or theology.

Kafka's stories evoke an acute sense of a crisis of modern civilization encompassing in scope and revealing itself as a torment of uncertainty with regard to the simple question: how should we live? For this crisis of civilization we no longer have an adequate language, such terms as alienation and commodification having gone dead in our hands through misuse. One part, but only one part, of this crisis finds expression in a line from a poem by Gershom Scholem: 'Where once God stood now stands: Melancholy.' It is when we turn to the concrete images dominating Kafka's writings – the man shrinking into an insect, the hunger artist losing his vocation, the clerk searching for his accusers – that the abstractions with which we discuss his work come to trembling life. What are the grounds of our existence? By what right do we lay claim to the earth? If there is a right way for us, what might it be? And even if we know the right way, can we ever find it? Such questions occur as subterranean puzzlements, in the short fictions as parables of entrapment ('The Burrow', 'The Hunger Artist') and in the novels as narratives of blocked quest, a quest that takes place both in relation to the external world and the recesses of the psyche. 'Man,' writes Kafka in his diaries, 'cannot live without a permanent trust in something indestructible in himself, and at the same time that indestructible something as well as his trust in it may remain permanently concealed from him.' Now stands: Melancholy.

Kafka could not content himself with verisimilitude, the usual novelistic business of depicting the world 'as it is'. He wrote out of a need to 'complete' the world – by which I mean that he strove to go beyond notations of the empirical, he wished to bring fragments of perceived experience into a perceptual and moral coherence, and at times he seems to have hoped that human existence could be made to yield what he called 'the pure, the true, the indestructible'. He yearned for some principle of order that would make lucid the darkness of being. This is basically a religious desire, but in Kafka it was not sustained by a firm religious belief. He once called his writing 'a form of prayer', but it is a prayer without an assured destination – the prayer of a man with strong religious sensibilities who is entangled in a web of modern scepticism.

Now, all this has little to do with theology or philosophy in any formal sense, since Kafka was a writer of stories – stories of enigma – and if a metaphysician, a metaphysician of images. He was not the sort of writer who cherishes the surfaces of the world for their own sake. Notwithstanding his mastery of realistic detail, evident throughout *The Castle*, Kafka's aim was to penetrate, more than to represent, reality. Everything partial and unformed he hoped to 'complete' through art, even as that very art demonstrates the hopelessness of such an aim since incompleteness is the essence of our life. Which is perhaps one reason his major works remain unfinished.

The desire to apprehend order, unity, fulfilment takes the form in *The Castle* of a constant striving, what K. calls his 'task' (I see him as a very distant cousin of Don Quixote). Having left behind the life of ordinariness, K. must search without end, exhaust himself in a quest without conclusion. ('There is a goal,' writes Kafka, 'but no way: what we call way is only wavering.') If I am right in supposing this to reflect the religious yearnings of a nonreligious intelligence, it should also be said that such yearnings can constitute a kind of religious experience, perhaps the most serious of our time.

The Kafkan universe is thick with anxiety, though an anxiety strangely mixed with a self-deriding amusement. Manifesting itself in most of Kafka's major characters, this anxiety has been well described by Gunther Anders:

If a man does not know what position he is in nor where he is going, what he owes nor to whom, what he may be suspected of, or why he is being accused, or whether or not he is tolerated (if so, for how long, if not, on what authority), then all his energies will be consumed by an unremitting search for meaning, a kind of mania for interpretation.

This is pretty much the situation in which K. finds himself as he seeks vainly an entry into the Castle, and it soon becomes an experience shared by readers as they feel themselves caught up in a maze of obscure incident. One reason for the amorphousness of Kafka's protagonists, especially Joseph K. and K.

INTRODUCTION

– for their lack of the psychological density we expect from the central figures of realistic novels – is that this enables readers to 'enter' into their wanderings, not through the usual sort of identification but rather by providing interpretations in accord with their own needs and dispositions. Interpretation becomes a way of relieving the anxiety of reading – it cannot be helped: each interpretation must yield to another, there can be no end to it so long as a single mind seeks understanding, men and women cannot know and the gods do not speak. (The Castle, writes Kafka, 'was silent as ever'.) No more than Kafka can 'complete' his fictional world can we 'complete' his novels. Nor is there any reason, except perhaps human frailty, to wish to. Some interpretations do succeed in bending his fictions to one or another system of thought, but these end up as empty victories, since all they can reveal is what the critic has started with.

Might it not then be, I ask with my own complement of anxiety, that the 'true' way to read Kafka – but of course there is no 'true' way – is to stay as close as possible to the texts themselves? To strive for a phenomenological rigor in which, for example, we allow that in the dream-work of 'The Metamorphosis' Gregor Samsa does indeed turn into a giant insect – let us not allegorize this incident away and thereby deny its terror! I have in mind here a distinction, perhaps arbitrary, between a reading and an interpretation. A reading describes the text as scrupulously as possible, seeking to evoke its uniqueness; an interpretation transposes the text into a sequence of supplied meanings.

In a disciplined reading of *The Castle* we would follow K.'s blunderings through the village and share in his frustrations when trying to reach the Castle, but all the while would refrain from attaching or imposing any schema of meanings. Or perhaps more to the point, we would find the meanings within the dynamic of experiences depicted by Kafka so that we would not feel obliged to wonder what the Castle 'stands for' or what might be the 'deeper' nature of K.'s quest. Enough that there is a quest, that the man engaged in it keeps suffering frustrations, and that the distant objective remains inaccessible. These events have a weight of their own and

xi

ιequire no 'translation' into any sequence or system of ideas. At the least, this would acknowledge Kafka's extraordinary powers of invention, leaving us in that state of alertness, sometimes akin to exaltation, which is probably where, all interpretation done, we end in any case.

It might be good if we could do this. It might be good if we could simply share, without any distracting elucidation, in K.'s quest. But we cannot. To forgo interpretation seems beyond human capacity. Our anxieties, our hungers for a patch of certitude, our susceptibilities to categorical thinking – all press us toward interpretation, perhaps the 'original sin' of literary criticism. So before we too succumb to this 'sin', let us venture a few basic descriptions of Kafka's literary methods:

*In many of his fictions Kafka fuses, quite as dreams do, the commonplace and the uncanny. The reader shuttles uneasily between the realistic and the fantastic; some Kafka stories demand an opening imaginative premise – a man becomes an insect, creatures live in burrows, a hunger artist fasts in public – while the rest seems, if only at first, true to the laws of logic and nature. Very soon, however, we come to see that the laws of logic and nature are being twisted, again as in dreams, on behalf of thematic ends. What Martin Greenberg in his fine study of Kafka calls 'the stammering efforts of the humble client unconscious' make themselves heard as against the 'bureaucratic consciousness'. The disarrangement of the apparently realistic dream-material can take on coherence, in slow steps, only through the reader's (the dreamer's) active intervention. In *The Castle*, however, there is a somewhat different pattern: a greater external order more closely approximating the nineteenth-century novel of education. But again this seems true only for the overall pattern of narration, which invites the application, though it does not satisfy the requirements, of allegory. Much of the local incident in *The Castle* still follows the dream-work of Kafka's earlier writings.

* *The Castle* is a quest narrative but insofar as it deviates from traditional quest patterns in barely negotiating any progress, it could be called an anti-quest narrative. (Kafka spoke of 'marching in place'.) What is it that blocks K.'s quest? At first, we may suppose that one or another antagonist stands

in his way, but after a time we come to suspect that it is the very nature of the world, incomprehensible and perhaps malign, that thwarts him. Once this realization sinks into K.'s mind, it may account for his utter weariness at the end.

*Kafka's characters tend to be stripped to generic being, with but rudimentary physical descriptions and very little psychological analysis. ('Never again psychology,' he wrote.) It is precisely this mode of characterization that enables readers to supply multiple interpretations of the action, as if, in part, they too are 'writing' the story. It is true that the mere fact of narrative presupposes a certain minimal psychology, but only seldom does Kafka 'enter' a character. What matters about the Kafka protagonists is not their 'intrinsic being' but rather the role they must perform in narratives of enigma.

*Kafka's prose is spare, austere, lucid, barely coloured; scholars call it a 'classical German'. Whatever difficulties we encounter do not concern language. Everything in Kafka is clear – language, events, characters – everything but the world itself and the primary 'reason of things'.

* Kafka's fiction is rich in comedy, often in a biting desperate farce. (The search for ultimate meanings, as Cervantes knew, soon attains a sad absurdity.) In *The Castle* there is the farce of endless paper-shuffling, as well as the jack-in-the-box assistants who shadow K. as if they were secret agents of the id.

* Kafka is a master of a fictional genre that unites narrative and reflection (often monologue). The long speech of the village mayor (Ch. 5), while pertinent and amusing in its own right, serves also to advance the narrative. The story moves, the quest does not. Many of the monologues anticipate the reader by offering interpretations, probably mistaken ones, within the text, as when the landlady of the inn tells K., 'You misconstrue everything, even a person's silence.' It is this pattern which has led some commentators to speak of Kafka's fictions as 'Talmudic'.

*Kafka's world is cluttered with paper, the white blood of bureaucracy. This is an hierarchical world, with set places reserved for function and status, and only a few quasi-picaresque wanderers like K. can disturb its sluggish equanimity. The bureaucracy of the Castle seems totally absorbed in processes the purpose of which has become obscure or forgotten – a sort of parodic version of deism.

*It is tempting to treat Kafka's fiction as allegory, since allegory, as a stable mode of interpretation, can be reassuring, and after reading Kafka one needs a measure of reassurance. But the close parallelism between narrative and cognitive system (ideology, theology) that allegory requires is precisely what Kafka does not provide – indeed, precisely what his fictions are in search of. *The Castle* can be read as an effort by K. to discover an allegory for his journey.

*Even if we manage to provide an inclusive interpretation for a Kafka novel, it often seems difficult or impossible to 'fit' local episodes into the general scheme. Perhaps it would be best to see such obscure or difficult episodes simply as narrative segments that do not require separate elucidation, somewhat as one might respond to a local passage in an abstract dance work. But so to read *The Castle* is very hard, perhaps impossible.

*

If the local segments of *The Castle* can remain puzzling, its main narrative line seems clear. K. arrives in the village, claiming to have an appointment from the Castle as land surveyor, but neither we nor the villagers can be quite certain that he does have the appointment. Some of the villagers are sceptical: given their submission to the Castle, what need is there for a meddlesome land surveyor who keeps asking irksome questions? In the eyes of K., however, the appointment is a crucial step toward his goal of entering the Castle.

In a series of nervously amusing chapters K. learns from the villagers how inaccessible the Castle officials are, yet how absolute is their dominion – all of which leaves him depressed with the thought of 'the futility of all his endeavors'. The two prankster-assistants assigned to him, presumably by the Castle, do no work nor are they asked to – it's as if the whole idea of 'land-surveying' has become an object of mockery. All K. can achieve is to be allowed to live in the village as a janitor.

K. meets a barmaid Frieda (peace in German) who is said

xiv

to have been the mistress of a high Castle official, Klamm (tight, clamp, heavy silence in German). What we learn about Klamm is that he is a pudgy fellow who smokes cigars, falls asleep frequently, and has a taste for village girls. For a little while K. and Frieda achieve some sexual pleasure, yet this brings K. no peace, since he is determined that life's satisfactions will not stand in the way of his 'task'. 'He only and no one else should attain to Klamm, and should attain to him not to rest with him, but *to go beyond, farther yet, into the Castle*.' (Emphasis added.) In response Frieda rightly accuses K. of loving her only in order to reach Klamm:

... providing you reach your end, you're ready to do anything; should Klamm want me, you are prepared to give me to him; should he want you to stick to me, you'll stick to me; should he want you to fling me out, you'll fling me out ... You have no feeling for me but the feeling of ownership.

Frieda's accusation is damning: all of K.'s behaviour is instrumental, subordinated to his 'task'.

Meanwhile we are given several glimpses of the Castle from a distance (that 'scandalous bureaucracy,' K. calls it). These reports of the shrouded Castle and its scurrying bureaucrats, all second-hand and open to being misconstrued, are done in a style somewhat like that of deadpan silent-film comedy. Silent, about the actual or proclaimed ends of the Castle; silent, about any faint interest it may have in the people of the village (except for the sexual use of its girls). Like K., we can never penetrate the Castle, but from all that emerges it comes to seem a vast, soulless mechanism for the circulation of paper and the composition of unread reports, calling to mind Dickens' Circumlocution Office in *Little Dorrit*.

*

It was very early in the morning, the streets clean and deserted. I was on my way to the railroad station. Upon comparing my watch with a clock in a tower I noticed that it was much later than I had thought. I would have to make great haste. The panic into which this discovery threw me made me uncertain of the way. I was not yet quite familiar with this city, fortunately there was a policeman nearby. I ran to him and breathlessly asked the way. He smiled and said: 'From me you wish to learn the way?' 'Yes,' I said, 'for I cannot find it myself'. 'Give it up, give it up,' he said and turned away abruptly, as people do when they want to be alone with their laughter.

At the very heart of *The Castle* (Ch. 15) there is a long interspersed narrative which I take to be essential to an understanding of this novel – and here I diverge from most of the familiar Kafka interpretations.

A young woman named Olga, modest and thoughtful, tells K. the story of her accursed family: how the other villagers shun the Barnabas family as a nest of pariahs because her sister Amalia had rejected the sexual advance of a Castle official; how her brother keeps tormenting himself with questions as to whether he really is a messenger employed by the Castle ('he goes into the offices, but are the offices part of the real Castle?' – and for that matter, what if there is no 'real Castle?'); how her aged father keeps begging for a 'pardon' from the Castle officials on behalf of his daughter Amalia, begging even for a moment's notice, which they blandly or haughtily refuse.

Amalia, the younger sister of Olga, had been singled out by Sortini, a Castle official, who sent her a vulgar note proposing that she immediately come to bed with him. Nor is this an exceptional demand: other Castle officials have also ordered village girls to serve as mistresses. Amalia, however, tears Sortini's letter into bits. For this act of defiance, the family suffers ostracism, not directly from the Castle officials but from the pliant villagers.

What are we to make of this? One Kafka commentator has described Amalia's behaviour as 'the pride of those who will not serve' the gods; evidently mortals must obey. The Italian critic Pietro Citati, in his recent book on Kafka, writes that 'we must not draw the mediocre conclusion [from the Amalia-Sortini episode] that the divine is simply a deceit', though he fails to explain why, if there is deceit, it should be regarded as divine or if it is divine, it should not be subject to moral judgment. We must not, writes Citati, submit this incident to 'the test of reality', though what other test mortal readers can bring to bear I do not know.

I cite Citati because his views are not uncommon, and

behind them lies an assumption that piety entails abasement and faith, unquestioning obedience. Nowhere in Kafka's text, however, is this assumption supported; nowhere is it suggested that the Castle, simply because it is the seat of authority, merits absolute submission or should not be put to 'the test of reality', which is to say, the test of our judgment. Some Kafka critics, intent upon accepting the ways of the Castle as a transcendent value, fall back upon the justifying comparison between Amalia's ordeal and God's command that Abraham sacrifice Isaac, which is said to be another instance of the Kierkegaardian notion of a 'teleological suspension of the ethical'. Leave aside whether Abraham's readiness to sacrifice his son is quite the marvel of faith it is often taken to be, and leave aside, as well, the question of whether we can or should suspend 'the ethical'. Let us simply recall that in the Biblical story an angel does appear in order to save Isaac and that God does not insist upon the ultimate test of bloodshed – while under the reign of Kafka's Castle there is no reason to expect a similar intervention. Had Amalia gone to Sortini, as other village girls have gone to Klamm, he would not, we may suppose, have renounced the pleasure of taking her.*

The Amalia episode stands as an instance of moral strength and intransigence in notable contrast to K.'s manoeuvrings to find his way into the Castle, and it thereby raises the possibility of sharply contrasting positions, neither explicitly endorsed nor repudiated by Kafka, with regard to the Castle. For if the Castle is to be seen as the seat of 'heavenly authorities', as Max Brod claimed, or as the agency of 'divine dispensation', as Thomas Mann echoed, then it would seem to follow – at least the text so allows us to conclude – that we are in the presence of a coldly malevolent divinity. Is it not then possible – I would think, likely – that Kafka meant us to look upon Amalia with a certain admiration, as an unsubduable woman, defeated but still upright, who will not yield to

*The Yiddish poet H. Leivick recalls that upon hearing as a schoolboy the story of Abraham and Isaac, he asked his teacher, 'But what if the angel had been late?' This little boy was evidently incapable of a 'suspension of the ethical'.

arbitrary power, whether from on high or below? I believe, in fact, that Amalia should be seen as the heroine of the book, sustained by suffering and quiet in her resolve. She does not challenge the Castle's dominance; she does not even criticize it; she simply refuses any connection with it.

By comparison K. seems unsure of himself, obsessive in his quest and often confused in the ways he undertakes it. Pietro Citati, now seemingly ready to accept the 'test of reality', calls Amalia 'an Antigone who has fallen into Kafka's world ...' That is fine, though 'fallen' seems not exactly right, since it is Kafka who has put Amalia there, as a moral counterweight to the main narrative. In Sophocles' play Antigone says: 'What help or hope have I/In whom devotion is deemed sacrilege?' As she cares for her aged parents, Amalia might repeat these words but for her choice of silence.

There remains the Castle itself. Neither in his own voice nor through any of the characters does Kafka designate the Castle as being of this world or another, nor does he decisively comment on its order of values, whether benevolent or malignant. What the text does provide is a clear relationship between power and submission, as well as the failure of K. to break past that relationship. All of this – if I might return to the idea of a reading instead of an interpretation – could sustain a view of *The Castle* in which the question of ultimate ends would be left unanswered, the temptation to assign moral weights to the various acts would be refused, and we would then have a marvellous narrative depicting the sheer dynamics of striving and resistance, with the great likelihood that both will be thwarted by the vast indifference of the cosmos. If such a reading failed to satisfy our need for 'final meanings', it would be in harmony with Kafka's posture of doubt. Apparently, however, this is not enough, otherwise we would not have the deluge of Kafka interpretations.

Interpret, then, we must. One prevalent interpretation sees the Castle as a locus of divinity, or perhaps only its visible antechamber, and argues that K.'s fruitless campaign to attach himself to the Castle must be regarded as evidence, in Thomas Mann's words, of 'the grotesque unconnection between the human being and the transcendental'. What gives this interpretation a touch of plausibility is our knowledge that Kafka was a deeply serious man with religious aspirations he could not settle into belief. But what calls this interpretation into question is Kafka's own depiction of the Castle as a barren and soulless place, and of its officials as barren and soulless bureaucrats. The critic Erich Heller, writing as a Christian, has remarked:

I do not know of any conceivable idea of divinity which could justify those interpreters who see in the Castle the residence of 'divine law and divine grace.' Its officers are totally indifferent to good if they are not positively wicked. Neither in their decrees nor in their activities is there discernible any trace of love, mercy, charity, or majesty. In their icy detachment they inspire certainly no awe, but fear and revulsion.

As if in reply, those who hold to the view of *The Castle* first put forward by Max Brod and Thomas Mann argue in effect that the ways of God or the gods, because beyond our comprehension, cannot be subject to our judgment. They also point toward the end of *The Castle* where K., in a talk with an official named Bürgel (guarantee or warrant in German), learns that a wise passivity and a bit of luck – what this Bürgel calls 'a word, a glance, a sign of trust' – might have enabled K. to proceed toward his goal. This conversation then persuades K. toward a more indulgent view of the Castle. But neither he nor we know whether Bürgel's remark is still another instance of the run-around to which K. has been subjected by the Castle officials and, more important, K. seems no longer to care – 'he now felt a great dislike of everything that concerned him'. It is one of Kafka's most brilliantly amusing touches that K., by now exhausted in his hopeless quest, should fall fast asleep during the official's advice.

Did Kafka accept the idea that the ways of divinity, being beyond comprehension, should also be beyond judgment? I cannot say and doubt that anyone else can either, but what can be said with some assurance is that there is little warrant for such a notion in *The Castle*. He remains committed to enigma not because he wishes to engage in displays of cleverness – the last thing from his mind! – but because he found 'the reason of things' deeply inaccessible. It is not to be supposed that, finally, Kafka is in a better position than K.

Still, if we do accept the interpretation that the Castle harbors some order or similitude of divinity, there is reason to regard this as a 'fallen' or debased divinity, quite as 'fallen' as Kafka took humanity to be. Or perhaps the Castle harbors what Erich Heller calls 'a company of Gnostic devils' who have overthrown a once benign divinity, usurpers claiming an authority not rightfully theirs. The rule of things may come from the Castle, but that rule is marked by a soulless formalism, as if its makers had forever closed their eyes to human needs – or had forgotten the spark that once lighted divinity. That the reigning powers may not be friendly to humanity is an idea Kafka was neither the first nor the last to suppose. Against this background the moral resistance of Amalia comes to seem all the more impressive, suggesting that at least in *The Castle* there was a side of Kafka not nearly so submissive to fate as some of his critics have supposed.

What, then, shall we make of K.'s quest? Max Brod has written that he once asked Kafka how *The Castle* was to end and that Kafka replied:

The ostensible land surveyor was to find partial satisfaction at least. He was not to relax his struggle, but was to die worn out by it. Round his deathbed the villagers were to assemble and from the Castle itself word was to come that though K.'s legal claim to live in the village was not valid, yet, taking certain auxiliary circumstances into account, he was to be permitted to live and work there.

Yes, but not a word about reaching the Castle! Surely this constitutes one of Kafka's mordant ironies, since the 'concession' to be granted K. at the end does not measurably improve the position he was in at the outset, nor does it necessarily enable him to achieve his 'task'. Still, despite its hopelessness, K.'s quest may be seen as an authentic yearning for knowledge and truth, even if he lacks the strength, as humans do, to sustain that quest and even if there are moments when it seems he would have been better off staying with Frieda.

So there is a kind of heroism in K.'s quest, as, I think, also in Amalia's intransigence. To the quandaries posed by the

INTRODUCTION

Castle, K. and Amalia represent two 'solutions', neither of which provides any assured path to 'the reason of things'. The very negations entailed by Kafka's great work imply a steadfast refusal of certainties, a clear-eyed persistence with doubt. The world will not yield to lucidity.

Irving Howe

IRVING HOWE, who died in 1993, was Distinguished Professor Emeritus at the Graduate Center of the City of New York and co-editor of *Dissent* magazine. His publications include *The American Newness*, *William Faulkner: A Critical Study*, *Leon Trotsky*, *World of our Fathers*, *Culture and Politics in the Age of Emerson*, and *Socialism and America*. His *Selected Writings* appeared in 1990.

SELECT BIBLIOGRAPHY

————

The most authoritative biography of Kafka is that of Ernst Pawel, *The Nightmare of Reason: A Life of Franz Kafka,* Farrar, Straus, & Giroux, New York, 1984.

The extensive publication of his own letters and journals provides additional insight, especially:

the two volumes of Diaries, edited by Max Brod, and variously translated, Schocken, New York, 1948 and 1949. A single volume English edition appeared in Peregrine, 1964;

Letters to Milena, translated by James and Tania Stern, Penguin, Harmondsworth, 1963;

Letters to Felice, trans. Stern and Duckworth, Penguin, Harmondsworth, 1974; and

Letters to his Father, trans. Kaiser and Wilkins, Schocken, New York, 1966.

There is also the *Correspondence of Walter Benjamin and Gershom Scholem, 1932–1940,* Schocken, New York, 1989, an illuminating exchange of letters between two men intellectually close to Kafka.

Among contemporary commentaries, Max Brod's highly contentious and sentimental biography of his friend is worth looking at, as are *Conversations With Kafka* by Gustav Janouch, Derek Verschoyle, London, 1953, and (incomparably) the essay collected in Walter Benjamin's *Illuminations* edited by Hannah Arendt, Fontana, London, 1973.

The background to Kafka's life is covered in J. P. Stern, *The World of Franz Kafka,* Holt, Rinehart and Winston, New York, 1980.

An excellent critical work on Kafka is Martin Greenberg's *Kafka: The Terror of Art,* Horizon, New York, 1983.

And Ronald Gray's *Franz Kafka,* Cambridge University Press, Cambridge, 1973, and Anthony Thorlby's *Kafka,* Heinemann, London, 1972, are both helpful general surveys.

Erich Heller's *Kafka,* Fontana, London, 1974, is probably the most useful short study of the whole *oeuvre,* while the same author's *The Disinherited Mind,* Penguin, Harmondsworth, 1951, attempts to place Kafka in the context of earlier German literature.

CHRONOLOGY

DATE	AUTHOR'S LIFE	LITERARY CONTEXT
1883	Birth in Prague (3 July) of Franz Kafka, son of a prosperous Jewish businessman who will later insist on German schools and the German University. Franz Kafka is brought up as a non-orthodox, Western Jew.	Maupassant: *Une Vie.* Nietzsche: *Thus Spake Zarathustra* (to 1884). Death of Turgenev.
1884		Huysmans: *À Rebours.* Tolstoy's *What I Believe* is banned.
1885		Howells: *The Rise of Silas Lapham.* Maupassant: *Bel Ami.* Nietzsche: *Beyond Good and Evil.*
1886		Rimbaud: *Les Illuminations.* Hardy: *The Mayor of Casterbridge.* Tolstoy: *The Death of Ivan Ilych.* His play, *The Power of Darkness*, offends the Tsar and is banned. Henry James: *The Bostonians* and *The Princess Casamassima.*
1888		Mallarmé: *Poésies.* Strindberg: *Miss Julie.* Sudermann: *Frau Sorge.* Birth of Anna Akhmatova.
1889	Attends German elementary school until 1893. Birth of the first of his three sisters (two younger brothers die in infancy).	Ibsen: *Hedda Gabler.* Hauptmann: *Before Sunrise.* Strindberg: *The Creditors.* Birth of Jean Cocteau.
1890		Hamsun: *Hunger.* Wilde: *The Picture of Dorian Gray* and *The Critic as Artist.* Henry James: *The Tragic Muse.* William James: *The Principles of Psychology.*

HISTORICAL EVENTS

Death of Wagner, Marx, Manet. Birth of Mussolini, Webern. First Russian
Marxist revolutionary organization, the Liberation of Labour, founded in
Geneva by Georgi Plekhanov. Opening of National Theatre in Prague.
First skyscraper built (10 stories) in Chicago.

Fall of Khartoum. Berlin conference on African affairs; Togo and the
Cameroons become part of the German Empire. Death of Smetana.

Bulgarian Crisis (to 1886); Ferdinand of Saxe-Coburg becomes Prince of
Bulgaria. Formation of the German East Africa protectorate. Karl Benz
produces first car. Birth of Alban Berg.

German deputies in the Bohemian Diet leave in protest at the Czechs' not
acknowledging restricted German-language areas in Bohemia (Germans
return to Diet, 1890). Neutrality agreement between the Russian and
German Empires (1887).

Death of German Emperor, Wilhelm I. Convention of Constantinople:
Suez Canal declared open to ships of all nations. Mahler's first symphony.

Second International founded in Paris, and the establishment of 1st May as
a workers' holiday (first celebrated in Austria-Hungary, 1890). Eiffel Tower
built. Birth of Hitler.

Fall of Bismarck. Wilhelm II's personal rule begins. Death of Van Gogh
and Heinrich Schliemann.

DATE	AUTHOR'S LIFE	LITERARY CONTEXT
1891		Wilde: *The Soul of Man under Socialism.*
		Howells: *A Modern Instance.*
		Shaw: *Quintessence of Ibsenism.*
		Birth of Bulgakov.
1892		Hamsun: *Mysteries.*
		Ibsen: *The Master Builder.*
		Hauptmann: *The Weavers.*
		Hofmannsthal: *The Death of Titian*
1893	Attends German Staatgymnasium until 1901.	Fontane: *Frau Jenny Treibel.*
		Tolstoy: *The Kingdom of God is within You.*
		Sudermann: *Heimat.*
		Schnitzler: *Anatol.*
		Death of Maupassant.
1894		Hamsun: *Pan.*
		Bryusov publishes *The Russian Symbolists.*
		Heinrich Mann: *In a Family.*
1895		Hardy: *Jude the Obscure.*
		Fontane: *Effi Briest.*
		Wilde's trial and imprisonment; writes *An Ideal Husband* and *The Importance of Being Earnest.*
		Gorky: *Chelkash.*
		Birth of Ernst Jünger.
1896		Chekhov: *The Seagull.*
		Fontane: *Poggenpuhls.*
1897		Housman: *A Shropshire Lad.*
		Henry James: *What Maisie Knew.*
1898		Tolstoy: *What is Art?*
		Zola: *J'accuse.*
		Shaw: *Plays Pleasant and Unpleasant.*
		Wilde: *The Ballad of Reading Gaol.*
		Strindberg: *Inferno.*
		Thomas Mann: *Little Herr Friedemann.*
		Svevo: *As a Man Grows Older.*
		Birth of Erich Maria Remarque.
		Death of Fontane and Mallarmé.

CHRONOLOGY

Decisive election victory for liberal Young Czech party. 20,000 Jews brutally evicted from Moscow. Work begins on Trans-Siberian railway.

Panama scandal in France. Anarchist outrages in Paris. Munich *Sezession* (German artists under Franz von Stuck rebel against salon system). Diesel patents internal combustion engine.

Independent Labour Party founded in England. Omladina show-trial of radical youth movements in Prague. Death of Marshal MacMahon. Dvořák's 'New World' Symphony. Munch: *The Scream.*

Dreyfus trial begins. German–Russian commercial treaty. Beginning of Armenian massacres in Turkey. *Yellow Book* launched. Debussy: *L'Après-midi d'un faune.*

Lenin leads the St Petersburg Union of Struggle for the Liberation of the Working Class. Arrested; banished to Siberia (1897–1900). Cézanne exhibition in Paris. Lumière brothers invent cinematograph. Marconi invents wireless telegraphy. X-rays discovered. Freud's *Studien über Hysterie* inaugurates psychoanalysis. Masaryk: *Czech Question, Our Present Crisis.* Mahler: *Till Eulenspiegel's Merry Pranks.*

Establishment of Nobel prizes. Theodore Herzl, founder of modern political Zionism, publishes *Der Judenstraat* putting forward the idea of a Jewish national home in Palestine. Henry Ford produces his first car.
Badeni Language Decrees give Czech the status of 'internal official language'; implementation hampered by Germans, leading to anti-German riots in Prague with an anti-Semitic element, and the withdrawal of the Decrees. First Zionist Congress in Basel. Graeco–Turkish War. Vienna *Sezession* founded by Klimt to further modern (*Jugendstil*, Symbolist) movement. Beginning of Klondike gold rush. Electron discovered. Death of Brahms. First German Navy Law begins the arms race. Death of Bismarck. The Gautsch Language Decrees, a watered-down version of the Badeni decrees, are accepted: Czech could be 'official language' in mixed German–Czech communities. First Congress of Russian Social Democratic Workers' Party in Minsk. War between Spain and USA. British reconquer the Sudan. German fleet seizes Kiaochow; secures 99-year lease from China. Curie discovers radium. Moscow Arts Theatre founded.

DATE	AUTHOR'S LIFE	LITERARY CONTEXT
1899		Yeats: *The Wind Among the Reeds.* Tolstoy: *Resurrection.* Chekhov: *The Lady with the Little Dog.* Gorky: *Foma Gordeev.* Birth of Borges.
1900		Conrad: *Lord Jim.* Freud: *Interpretation of Dreams.* Schnitzler: *La Ronde.* Dreiser: *Sister Carrie.* Death of Wilde and Nietzsche.
1901	Studies Law at the German Karl-Ferdinand University in Prague but is drawn to the literary circles of the city.	Chekhov: *Three Sisters.* Thomas Mann: *Buddenbrooks.* Strindberg: *Dance of Death.*
1902	Kafka very quickly defines his ideal style – cool, sober and very elegant: a language 'ohne Schnörkel und Schleier und Warzen'. Meets Max Brod.	Rilke: *The Book of Pictures.* Gide: *L'Immoraliste.* Sudermann: *The Joy of Living.* Henry James: *The Wings of the Dove.* Death of Zola.
1903		Thomas Mann: *Tristan, Tonio Kröger.* Moore: *Principia Ethica.* Shaw: *Man and Superman.*
1904	Begins 'Description of a Struggle'.	Henry James: *The Golden Bowl.* Conrad: *Nostromo.* Pirandello: *The Late Mattia Pascal.*
1905		Thomas Mann: *Fiorenza. The Blood of the Walsungs* is withdrawn. Rilke: *The Book of Hours.* Gumilev: *The Path of the Conquistadors.* Wharton: *The House of Mirth.* Birth of Sholokhov.
1906	Receives law degree. Embarks on his year of practical training in Prague Law Courts.	Gorky: *The Mother* (to 1907). Hofmannsthal: *Oedipus and the Sphinx.* Death of Ibsen.

CHRONOLOGY

HISTORICAL EVENTS

Renewal of *Ausgleich* of 1867 (established Dual Monarchy of Austria-Hungary) following agitation for its repeal and (in 1897) breakdown in constitutional government and government by imperial decree. In Prague, Polná or Hilsner Affair: a Jewish vagabond accused of ritual murder of Czech girl. Boer War (to 1902). Second Dreyfus trial and pardon. Karl Kraus founds the journal *Die Fackel* in Vienna. Schoenberg: *Verklärte Nacht*. Berlin *Sezession* formed by German *avant-garde* artists under Max Liebermann.

Beginning of severe recession in Austria-Hungary. Economy does not recover until 1906–7. Czech People's Party founded (programme composed by Masaryk). Bülow becomes Chancellor of Germany. Founding of British Labour Party. Boxer Rebellion in China (to 1901). Max Planck formulates quantum theory. Birth of German composer Kurt Weill.

Death of Queen Victoria. Accession of Edward VII. Roosevelt succeeds assassinated McKinley as president of USA. Marconi's first radio communication between USA and Europe. Beginning of Picasso 'Blue' period. Dvořák: *Russalka*.

Conflict between 'Bolsheviks' and 'Mensheviks' at 2nd Congress of Russian Social Democratic Workers' Party. Death of Gauguin. King Alexander of Serbia and Queen Draga murdered. Austria-Hungary and Russia conclude agreement about their respective rights in south-east Europe. In Britain, Emmeline Pankhurst founds Women's Social and Political Union. First flight by Wright brothers.

Entente Cordiale between Britain and France. Russo–Japanese War (to 1905). Work begins on Panama Canal. Janáček: *Jenůfa*.

First Russian Revolution. 'Red Sunday' in St Petersburg. Foundation of German Agrarian Party in Bohemia. Einstein's Special Theory of Relativity. Beginning of Fauvism. Die Brücke formed in Dresden by leading German Expressionists. Richard Strauss: *Salome*.

Constitution in Russia. First Duma meets and is speedily dissolved. Conference of Algeciras; French successfully resist German attempt to gain influence in Morocco (Austria-Hungary alone supports Germany). Young Czech movement reorganized under Karel Kramář.

THE CASTLE

DATE	AUTHOR'S LIFE	LITERARY CONTEXT
1907	Writes 'Wedding Preparations in the Country'. Takes temporary position with Assicurazioni Generali, Italian insurance company.	Blok: *The Terrible World*. Rilke: *New Poems*. Strindberg: *The Ghost Sonata*. Adams: *The Education of Henry Adams*. Conrad: *The Secret Agent*. William James: *Pragmatism*.
1908	Accepts position in Prague with Workers' Accident Insurance Company, the Arbeiter-Unfall-Versicherungs-Anstalt.	Forster: *A Room with a View*. Bennett: *The Old Wives' Tale*.
1909	Eight prose pieces published in *Hyperion*. Trip to Riva and Brescia (with Max and Otto Brod). Writes *Die Aeroplane in Brescia*.	Bely: *The Silver Dove*. Gide: *La Porte étroite*.
1910	Begins to write a diary in which he relentlessly analyses his inner life. Five prose pieces published in *Bohemia*. Trip to Paris (with Max and Otto Brod). Visit to Berlin.	Tsetsaeva: *Evening Album*. Rilke: *Sketches of Malte Laurids Brigge*. Forster: *Howards End*. Wells: *Mr Polly*. Döblin co-founds the Expressionist *Der Sturm*. Death of Tolstoy.
1911	Official trip to Friedland and Reichenberg. Trip (with Max Brod) to Switzerland, Italy and France, writing travelogues. Becomes interested in Yiddish theatre and literature.	Pound: *Canzoni*. Conrad: *Under Western Eyes*. Heinrich Mann's manifesto: *Spirit and Deed*. The Poets' Guild formed (founders of Russian Acmeism). Wharton: *Ethan Frome*.
1912	Meets a Jewish girl from Berlin, Felice Bauer, to whom he will be engaged twice. The short story 'Das Urteil' ('The Judgment') is written six weeks later. Visits Leipzig and Weimar. Works on a novel to be called *Der Verschollene*, to be published posthumously in 1927 as *Amerika*.	Thomas Mann: *Death in Venice*. Pound: *Ripostes*. Heinrich Mann begins *Man of Straw*. Dreiser: *The Financier*. Hofmannsthal: *Everyman*.

CHRONOLOGY

Ausgleich again renewed. New financial and commercial arrangements made which last until the Great War. Monarchy embarks on the last stage of its foreign policy – greater influence in the Balkans coupled with closer union with Germany. Law of universal suffrage in Austria-Hungary; first elections under that law. Triple Entente of Britain, France and Russia. Failure of Hague Peace Conference to halt the arms race.

Austria annexes Bosnia and Herzegovina. By obstructive tactics, German minority (German speakers form only 30% of the electorate) succeed in paralyzing regional parliament in Bohemia. Second Slav Congress in Prague. Cubism begins in Paris. First performance in Vienna of Schoenberg's *3 Pieces* (demonstrating atonality, or keyless music) arouses vehement hostility.
Zionists found Tel Aviv. Blériot flies English Channel. *La Nouvelle Revue Française* founded. Futurist movement founded by Italian poet Marinetti.

Post-Impressionist Exhibition in London. Death of Edward VII.

Assassination of Stolypin, Russian Minister of the Interior, by a Socialist Revolutionary terrorist. Italo-Turkish War (to 1912). Strikes in Britain: dockers, miners, weavers, railwaymen. George V announces transfer of capital of India from Calcutta to Delhi. Revolutions in China: Manchu dynasty overthrown. *Der Blaue Reiter* founded in Berlin. Bartók: *Bluebeard's Castle*; *Allegro barbaro*. Amundsen becomes first man to reach the South Pole.

Haldane (British Secretary for War) visits Berlin, but fails to secure reduction of naval build-up. German Social Democratic party poll more votes in general election than any other party. German Socialists declare themselves anti-war; assert international proletarian solidarity. Formation of Balkan League – Serbia, Bulgaria, Montenegro. Serious disorder in Croatia leads to policy of repression; elsewhere in the Austro-Hungarian empire local diets suppressed and constitutional methods of government replaced by autocracy. Sinking of the *Titanic*. Schoenberg: *Pierrot Lunaire*.

DATE	AUTHOR'S LIFE	LITERARY CONTEXT
1913	Publication of *Betrachtung* (*Meditation*), *The Judgment* and *Der Heizer* (*The Stoker*). Visits Felice in Berlin. Travels to Vienna and Italy. Meeting with Grete Bloch and beginning of correspondence. (She becomes the mother of his son who dies in 1921, and of whose existence Kafka is ignorant.)	Proust: *A la Recherche du temps perdu* (to 1927). Lawrence: *Sons and Lovers.* Trakl: *Poems.* Alain Fournier: *Le Grand Meaulnes.* Apollinaire: *Alcools.* Mandelstam: *Stone.* Gorky: *Childhood.* Cather: *O Pioneers!*
1914	Engaged to Felice. Breaks off his engagement. Visit to Germany. Starts working on *Der Prozess* (*The Trial*). Writes 'In der Strafkolonie' ('In the Penal Colony').	Joyce: *Dubliners.* Kaiser: *The Burghers of Calais.* Blok: *Carmen.* Akhmatova: *Rosary.*
1915	'Die Verwandlung' ('The Metamorphosis'), an acknowledged masterpiece of precision, lucidity and grotesque implication, is published. Reconciliation with Felice.	Ford: *The Good Soldier.* Lawrence: *The Rainbow.* Woolf: *The Voyage Out.* Mayakovsky: *A Cloud in Trousers.*
1916	Resumes writing after two years' silence: the fragment of 'A Country Doctor', 'The Hunter Gracchus' and other stories later included in *A Country Doctor*.	Joyce: *A Portrait of the Artist as a Young Man.* Death of Henry James.
1917	Tuberculosis of the lung is confirmed. Relationship with Felice ends. Writes stories, among others: 'A Report to an Academy', 'The Cares of a Family Man' and 'The Great Wall of China'. Learning Hebrew.	Yeats: *The Wild Swans at Coole.* Eliot: *Prufrock and other Observations.* Pasternak: *Above the Barriers.*
1918		Joyce: *Exiles.* Kraus: *The Last Days of Mankind* (to 1922). Thomas Mann: *Considerations of an Unpolitical Man.* Spengler: *The Decline of the West* (to 1923). Kaiser: *Gas* (to 1920). Blok: 'The Twelve'. Birth of Solzhenitsyn.

CHRONOLOGY

Treaty of London ends First Balkan War. Second Balkan War
(June–August). Treaty of Bucharest; partitioning of the Balkans. Woodrow
Wilson president of USA (later a strong supporter of the dissolution of the
Hapsburg monarchy). Bohr's discovery of atomic structure. First Charlie
Chaplin film. Stravinsky: *The Rite of Spring*.

Heir to Austro-Hungarian throne, Archduke Franz-Ferdinand d'Este and
his wife, Sophie, assassinated in Sarajevo (June). Austria-Hungary declares
war on Serbia (July). World War I breaks out (August). Russia invades
Galicia. President Wilson proclaims US neutrality. Political periodicals
L'Indépendence tchèque and *La Nation tchèque* founded in Paris. Leading
politically active Czechs begin to be arrested in Austria. Panama Canal
opens. Vorticist movement founded.
Sinking of the *Lusitania*. Entrance of Italy into the war against Austria-
Hungary. Serbia and Poland overrun by Austro-Hungarian and German
troops. Gallipoli disaster. Malevich's Suprematist manifesto. Einstein's
General Theory of Relativity.

Franz Joseph I dies; Charles I's accession to Austro-Hungarian throne.
Russian troops again on Austrian soil. Murder of Austrian premier Stürgh;
growing unpopularity of the war leads to strikes and rioting. Huge death
tolls at the battles of Verdun and the Somme. Lloyd George becomes
British Prime Minister. Easter Rising in Dublin. Political strike in Berlin.
Rasputin assassinated. Tzara founds the Dada group in Zürich.
February and October Revolutions in Russia. In March, fall of the
monarchy; Petrograd riots. US declares war on Germany, 6 April. Balfour
Declaration, promising the Jews a home in Palestine. *Ausgleich* due for
renewal but proves impossible to negotiate.

Wilson's Fourteen Points (January); point 10 includes notion of self-
determination for the nationalities of Austria-Hungary. Russia accepts
terms dictated at Brest-Litovsk (March). Pittsburgh Accord on the union of
Czechs and Slovaks in a joint republic (May). Brazil declares war on
Austria-Hungary (September). Declaration of Czecho-Slovak independence
(October). German deputies from Bohemia and Moravia meet in Vienna
under leadership of Lodgman von Allen, aiming to establish a German
Land in Bohemia with its own parliament, as a province of German Austria.
To forestall the build-up of a 'greater Germany', the Allies join with the

DATE	AUTHOR'S LIFE	LITERARY CONTEXT
1918 *cont*		
1919	Stays in various sanatoria. Briefly engaged to Julie Wohryzek who inspires him to write 'Brief an der Vater' ('Letter to his Father'). 'In the Penal Colony' and *A Country Doctor* are published.	Sherwood Anderson: *Winesburg, Ohio.* Dos Passos: *One Man's Initiation.* Cocteau: *Ode to Picasso.*
1920	Meets Milena Jesenská-Pollak, with whom he later corresponds.	Lawrence: *Women in Love.* Wharton: *The Age of Innocence.* Sinclair Lewis: *Main Street.* Pound: *Hugh Selwyn Mauberley.* Mayakovsky: *150,000,000.* Čapek: *RUR.*
1921	Goes back to work with the Workers' Accident Insurance Company. 'The Bucket Rider' published.	Death of Blok and Gumilev. Thomas Mann: *Goethe and Tolstoy.* Hašek: *The Good Soldier Švejk.* Pirandello: *Six Characters in Search of an Author.*
1922	Writes *Der Schloss* (*The Castle*), 'A Hunger Artist' and 'Investigations of a Dog'. Breaks off relations with Milena Jesenska-Pollák. Retires from the insurance company because of his ill-health and works until his death in a sanatorium near Vienna. 'A Hunger Artist' published.	Eliot: *The Waste Land.* Woolf: *Jacob's Room.* Joyce's *Ulysses* published in Paris. Brecht: *Baal, Drums in the Night.* Pasternak: *My Sister Life.* Toller: *The Machine Wreckers.* Mandelstam: *Tristia.* Borges: *Fervor de Buenos Aires.* Čapek: *The Absolute at Large.* Death of Proust.
1923	Meets Dora Dymant, daughter of an orthodox Polish rabbi, and lives with her for a time in Berlin. His illness drives him to Prague before he enters a sanatorium near Vienna. Writes 'The Burrow'.	Gorky: *My Universities.* Babel: *Red Cavalry* (to 1925). Rilke: *Duino Elegies, Sonnets to Orpheus.* Cather: *A Lost Lady.*

CHRONOLOGY

Czechs to take action against the separatists. Conclusion of World War I: Armistice Day, 11 November. Abdication of Wilhelm II. Masaryk elected President of Czecho-Slovakia. In Great Britain the Suffrage Bill is passed, giving women over thirty the vote. Irish rebel Con Markiewitz elected first British woman MP. Russian Civil War. Nicholas II assassinated.

Rutherford splits the atom.

Versailles Peace Conference. Weimar republic created in Germany; a 'Soviet Republic' established in Munich and quickly suppressed. Collapse of Austro-Hungarian empire. Food shortages and demonstrations in Prague; some channelled into anti-Semitic pogroms. Social Democrats win election and ally with Agrarians to form a government. The 'Red Scare' in the US. First Atlantic flight. Death of Renoir. Foundation of the Bauhaus, teaching institution for the arts, by Walter Gropius. Marinetti's *Manifestos of Futurism*.

League of Nations meets for first time. Russians driven out of Warsaw. 'Little Entente' between Czechoslovakia, Rumania and Yugoslavia. Chauvinistic activities of right-wing Czech extremists lead to bloody clashes with German population. Jewish shops attacked. Social Democrats win convincing election victory (even winning 43.5% of the German vote); Marxist left-wing expelled. Ensuing General Strike crushed. Irish Civil War. Kapp *putsch* in Germany to effect Nationalist counter-revolution defeated by Berlin workers. Robert Wiene's *The Cabinet of Dr Caligari* – epitome of Expressionism in German cinema. Gandhi initiates campaign of civil disobedience in India.

Irish Free State (excluding six counties) founded. New Economic Plan in Russia. Communist Party of Czechoslovakia founded. Rise of Fascism in Italy. Janáček: *Katya Kabanova*.

Stalin becomes General Secretary of the Central Committee. USSR established. Fascist march on Rome; Mussolini becomes Italian Prime Minister. Creation of Czech Fascist Party. In Germany, political assassinations of Erzberger and Rathenau by right-wing extremists.

Czechoslovak Minister of Finance, Rašín, assassinated. National revolution in Turkey under Kemel Pasha. Munich *putsch* by Nazis fails. Hyperinflation in Germany.

THE CASTLE

DATE	AUTHOR'S LIFE	LITERARY CONTEXT
1924	Moves back to Prague. Writes 'Josephine the Singer'. He is nursed in his last months by Dora Dymant, in a nursing home at Kierling. Dies there and is buried in Prague. Collection, *A Hunger Artist*, published shortly after his death. He leaves a testamentary direction that his work has to be destroyed after his death, which is disregarded by his friend and executor Max Brod.	Mann: *The Magic Mountain* published. Pasternak: *The Childhood of Luvers, Themes and Variations*. Mayakovsky: *Vladimir Ilich Lenin*. Ford: *Some Do Not*. Forster: *A Passage to India*. O'Neill: *Desire under the Elms*. O'Casey: *Juno and the Paycock*.
1925	Publication by Max Brod of *Der Prozess* (*The Trial*).	Woolf: *Mrs Dalloway* and *The Common Reader*. Cather: *The Professor's House*. Scott Fitzgerald: *The Great Gatsby*. O'Neill: *The Fountain*. Dreiser: *An American Tragedy*. Stein: *The Making of Americans*.
1926	Publication by Max Brod of *Das Schloss* (*The Castle*).	Gide: *Si le Grain ne meurt*. Ford: *A Man Could Stand Up*. Death of Rilke.
1927	Publication by Max Brod of the unfinished *Amerika*.	Woolf: *To the Lighthouse*. Hesse: *Der Steppenwolf*. Brecht: *Man is Man*. Birth of Günter Grass.

CHRONOLOGY

First Labour Government in Britain, under Ramsay MacDonald. In Italy, Fascists obtain almost two thirds of votes in election amidst widespread use of violence and intimidation. Murder of Mateotti, openly opposed to Mussolini. Death of Lenin. Breton: *Manifesto of Surrealism*.

Hindenburg becomes German Chancellor. 'Monkey Trial' (Scopes), Dayton, Tennessee. Eisenstein: *Battleship Potemkin*. Trotsky's *Literature and Revolution*. Berg: *Wozzeck*. G. B. Shaw awarded Nobel Prize.

General Strike in Britain. Germany admitted to membership of League of Nations.

Socialist riots in Vienna following acquittal of Nazis for political murder. Leon Trotsky expelled from Communist Party. World economic crisis. Lindbergh's solo Atlantic flight. Invention of cinema sound.

NOTE ON THE TEXT

The present English edition is based on the definitive German edition of *Das Schloss*, S. Fischer Verlag, Frankfurt am Main, 1951, Lizenzausgabe von Schocken Books, New York. Thus it is considerably larger than the previous editions which followed the text of the first German publication of the novel. The additions – results of Max Brod's later editing of Franz Kafka's posthumous writings – are: the concluding section of chapter XVIII, the whole of chapters XIX and XX, and the Appendix consisting of a number of variations, fragments, and above all of many passages stroked through and thus deleted by the author, but deemed sufficiently interesting by the editor to be made accessible after all. Passages quoted in Max Brod's postscripts to the various German editions (some merely repeating material already included in the Appendix, and some new variations) have been given their appropriate places in the Appendix to this edition.

CONTENTS

I

IT was late in the evening when K. arrived. The village was deep in snow. The Castle hill was hidden, veiled in mist and darkness, nor was there even a glimmer of light to show that a castle was there. On the wooden bridge leading from the main road to the village K. stood for a long time gazing into the illusory emptiness above him.

Then he went on to find quarters for the night. The inn was still awake, and although the landlord could not provide a room and was upset by such a late and unexpected arrival, he was willing to let K. sleep on a bag of straw in the parlour. K. accepted the offer. Some peasants were still sitting over their beer, but he did not want to talk, and after himself fetching the bag of straw from the attic, lay down beside the stove. It was a warm corner, the peasants were quiet, and letting his weary eyes stray over them he soon fell asleep.

But very shortly he was awakened. A young man dressed like a townsman, with the face of an actor, his eyes narrow and his eyebrows strongly marked, was standing beside him along with the landlord. The peasants were still in the room, and a few had turned their chairs round so as to see and hear better. The young man apologised very courteously for having awakened K., introducing himself as the son of the Castellan, and then said: 'This village belongs to the Castle, and whoever lives here or passes the night here does so in a manner of speaking in the Castle itself. Nobody may do that without the Count's permission. But you have no such permit, or at least you have produced none.'

K. had half raised himself and now, smoothing down his hair and looking up at the two men, he said: 'What village is this I have wandered into? Is there a castle here?'

'Most certainly,' replied the young man slowly, while here and there a head was shaken over K.'s remark, 'the castle of my lord the Count West-west.'

'And must one have a permit to sleep here?' asked K., as if he wished to assure himself that what he had heard was not a dream.

'One must have a permit,' was the reply, and there was an ironical contempt for K. in the young man's gesture as he stretched out his arm and appealed to the others, 'Or must one not have a permit?'

'Well, then, I'll have to go and get one,' said K. yawning and pushing his blanket away as if to rise up.

'And from whom, pray?' asked the young man.

'From the Count,' said K., 'that's the only thing to be done.'

'A permit from the Count in the middle of the night!' cried the young man, stepping back a pace.

'Is that impossible?' enquired K. coolly. 'Then why did you waken me?'

At this the young man flew into a passion. 'None of your guttersnipe manners!' he cried. 'I insist on respect for the Count's authority! I woke you up to inform you that you must quit the Count's territory at once.'

'Enough of this fooling,' said K. in a markedly quiet voice, laying himself down again and pulling up the blanket. 'You're going a little too far, my good fellow, and I'll have something to say to-morrow about your conduct. The landlord here and those other gentlemen will bear me out if necessary. Let me tell you that I am the Land Surveyor whom the Count is expecting. My assistants are coming on to-morrow in a carriage with the apparatus. I did not want to miss the chance of a walk through the snow, but unfortunately lost my way several times and so arrived very late. That it was too late to present myself at the Castle I knew very well before you saw fit to inform me. That is why I have made shift with this bed for the night, where, to put it mildly, you have had the discourtesy to disturb me. That is all I have to say. Good night, gentlemen.' And K. turned over on his side towards the stove.

'Land Surveyor?' he heard the hesitating question behind his back, and then there was a general silence. But the young man soon recovered his assurance, and lowering his voice, sufficiently to appear considerate of K.'s sleep while yet speaking loud enough to be clearly heard, said to the landlord: 'I'll ring up and enquire.' So there was a telephone in this village inn? They had everything up to the mark. The particular instance surprised K., but on the whole he had really expected it. It appeared that the telephone was placed almost over his head and in his drowsy condition he had overlooked it. If the young man must needs telephone he could not, even with the best intentions, avoid disturbing K., the only question was whether K. would let him do so; he decided to allow it. In that case, however, there was no sense in pretending to sleep, and so he turned on his back again. He could see the peasants putting their heads together; the arrival of a Land Surveyor was no small event. The door into the kitchen had been opened, and blocking the whole doorway stood the imposing figure of the landlady, to whom the landlord was advancing on tiptoe in order to tell her what was happening. And now the conversation began on the telephone. The Castellan was asleep, but an under-castellan, one of the under-castellans, a certain Herr Fritz, was available. The young man, announcing himself as Schwarzer, reported that he had found K., a disreputable-looking man in the thirties, sleeping calmly on a bag of straw with a minute rucksack for pillow and a knotty stick within reach. He had naturally suspected the fellow, and as the landlord had obviously neglected his duty he, Schwarzer, had felt bound to investigate the matter. He had roused the man, questioned him, and duly warned him off the Count's territory, all of which K. had taken with an ill grace, perhaps with some justification, as it eventually turned out, for he claimed to be a Land Surveyor engaged by the Count. Of course, to say the

5

least of it, that was a statement which required official confirmation, and so Schwarzer begged Herr Fritz to enquire in the Central Bureau if a Land Surveyor were really expected, and to telephone the answer at once.

Then there was silence while Fritz was making enquiries up there and the young man was waiting for the answer. K. did not change his position, did not even once turn round, seemed quite indifferent and stared into space. Schwarzer's report, in its combination of malice and prudence, gave him an idea of the measure of diplomacy in which even underlings in the Castle like Schwarzer were versed. Nor were they remiss in industry, the Central Office had a night service. And apparently answered questions quickly, too, for Fritz was already ringing. His reply seemed brief enough, for Schwarzer hung up the receiver immediately, crying angrily: 'Just what I said! Not a trace of a Land Surveyor. A common, lying tramp, and probably worse.' For a moment K. thought that all of them, Schwarzer, the peasants, the landlord and the landlady, were going to fall upon him in a body, and to escape at least the first shock of their assault he crawled right underneath the blanket. But the telephone rang again, and with a special insistence, it seemed to K. Slowly he put out his head. Although it was improbable that this message also concerned K. they all stopped short and Schwarzer took up the receiver once more. He listened to a fairly long statement, and then said in a low voice: 'A mistake, is it? I'm sorry to hear that. The head of the department himself said so? Very queer, very queer. How am I to explain it all to the Land Surveyor?'

K. pricked up his ears. So the Castle had recognised him as the Land Surveyor. That was unpropitious for him, on the one hand, for it meant that the Castle was well informed about him, had estimated all the probable chances, and was taking up the challenge with a smile. On the other hand, however, it was quite propitious, for if his interpretation were right they had underestimated his strength, and he would have more freedom of action than he had dared to

6

hope. And if they expected to cow him by their lofty superiority in recognising him as Land Surveyor, they were
mistaken; it made his skin prickle a little, that was all.

He waved off Schwarzer who was timidly approaching
him, and refused an urgent invitation to transfer himself
into the landlord's own room; he only accepted a warm
drink from the landlord and from the landlady a basin to
wash in, a piece of soap, and a towel. He did not even have
to ask that the room should be cleared, for all the men
flocked out with averted faces lest he should recognise them
again next day. The lamp was blown out, and he was left in
peace at last. He slept deeply until morning, scarcely disturbed by rats scuttling past once or twice.

After breakfast, which, according to his host, was to be
paid for by the Castle, together with all the other expenses
of his board and lodging, he prepared to go out immediately
into the village. But since the landlord, to whom he had
been very curt because of his behaviour the preceding night,
kept circling around him in dumb entreaty, he took pity on
the man and asked him to sit down for a while.

'I haven't met the Count yet,' said K., 'but he pays well
for good work, doesn't he? When a man like me travels so
far from home he wants to go back with something in his
pockets.'

'There's no need for the gentleman to worry about that
kind of thing; nobody complains of being badly paid.'

'Well,' said K., 'I'm not one of your timid people, and
can give a piece of my mind even to a Count, but of course
it's much better to have everything settled up without any
trouble.'

The landlord sat opposite K. on the rim of the window-
ledge, not daring to take a more comfortable seat, and kept
on gazing at K. with an anxious look in his large brown
eyes. He had thrust his company on K. at first, but now it
seemed that he was eager to escape. Was he afraid of being
cross-questioned about the Count? Was he afraid of some
indiscretion on the part of the 'gentleman' whom he took K.

7

to be? K. must divert his attention. He looked at the clock, and said: 'My assistants should be arriving soon. Will you be able to put them up here?'

'Certainly, sir,' he said, 'but won't they be staying with you up at the Castle?'

Was the landlord so willing, then, to give up prospective customers, and K. in particular, whom he so uncondition-ally transferred to the Castle?

'That's not at all certain yet,' said K. 'I must first find out what work I am expected to do. If I have to work down here, for instance, it would be more sensible to lodge down here. I'm afraid, too, that the life in the Castle wouldn't suit me. I like to be my own master.'

'You don't know the Castle,' said the landlord quietly.

'Of course,' replied K., 'one shouldn't judge prematurely. All that I know at present about the Castle is that the people there know how to choose a good Land Surveyor. Perhaps it has other attractions as well.' And he stood up in order to rid the landlord of his presence, since the man was biting his lip uneasily. His confidence was not to be lightly won.

As K. was going out he noticed a dark portrait in a dim frame on the wall. He had already observed it from his couch by the stove, but from that distance he had not been able to distinguish any details and had thought that it was only a plain back to the frame. But it was a picture after all, as now appeared, the bust portrait of a man about fifty. His head was sunk so low upon his breast that his eyes were scarcely visible, and the weight of the high, heavy forehead and the strong hooked nose seemed to have borne the head down. Because of this pose the man's full beard was pressed in at the chin and spread out farther down. His left hand was buried in his luxuriant hair, but seemed incapable of supporting the head. 'Who is that?' asked K., 'the Count?' He was standing before the portrait and did not look round at the landlord. 'No,' said the latter, 'the Castellan.' 'A handsome castellan, indeed,' said K., 'a pity that he has such an ill-bred son.' 'No, no,' said the landlord, drawing K. a little towards him and whispering in his ear, 'Schwarzer exaggerated yesterday, his father is only an under-castellan, and one of the lowest, too.' At that moment the landlord struck K. as a very child. 'The villain!' said K. with a laugh, but the landlord instead of laughing said, 'Even his father is powerful.' 'Get along with you,' said K., 'you think everyone powerful. Me too, perhaps?' 'No,' he replied, timidly yet seriously, 'I don't think you powerful.' 'You're a keen observer,' said K., 'for between you and me I'm not really powerful. And consequently I suppose I have no less respect for the powerful than you have, only I'm not so honest as you and am not always willing to acknowledge it.' And K. gave the landlord a tap on the cheek to hearten him and awaken his friendliness. It made him smile a little. He was actually young, with that soft and almost beardless face of his; how had he come to have that massive, elderly wife, who could be seen through a small window bustling about the kitchen with her elbows sticking out? K. did not want to force his confidence any further, however, nor to scare away the smile he had at last evoked. So he only signed to him to open the door, and went out into the brilliant winter morning.

Now, he could see the Castle above him clearly defined in the glittering air, its outline made still more definite by the moulding of snow covering it in a thin layer. There seemed to be much less snow up there on the hill than down in the village, where K. found progress as laborious as on the main road the previous day. Here the heavy snowdrifts reached right up to the cottage windows and began again on the low roofs, but up on the hill everything soared light and free into the air, or at least so it appeared from down below.

On the whole this distant prospect of the Castle satisfied K.'s expectations. It was neither an old stronghold nor a new mansion, but a rambling pile consisting of innumerable small buildings closely packed together and of one or two

9

storeys; if K. had not known that it was a castle he might have taken it for a little town. There was only one tower as far as he could see, whether it belonged to a dwelling-house or a church he could not determine. Swarms of crows were circling round it.

With his eyes fixed on the Castle K. went on farther, thinking of nothing else at all. But on approaching it he was disappointed in the Castle; it was after all only a wretched-looking town, a huddle of village houses, whose sole merit, if any, lay in being built of stone, but the plaster had long since flaked off and the stone seemed to be crumbling away. K. had a fleeting recollection of his native town. It was hardly inferior to this so-called Castle, and if it were merely a question of enjoying the view it was a pity to have come so far. K. would have done better to visit his native town again, which he had not seen for such a long time. And in his mind he compared the church tower at home with the tower above him. The church tower, firm in line, soaring unfalteringly to its tapering point, topped with red tiles and broad in the roof, an earthly building – what else can men build? – but with a loftier goal than the humble dwelling-houses, and a clearer meaning than the muddle of everyday life. The tower above him here – the only one visible – the tower of a house, as was now apparent, perhaps of the main building, was uniformly round, part of it graciously mantled with ivy, pierced by small windows that glittered in the sun, a somewhat maniacal glitter, and topped by what looked like an attic, with battlements that were irregular, broken, fumbling, as if designed by the trembling or careless hand of a child, clearly outlined against the blue. It was as if a melancholy-mad tenant who ought to have been kept locked in the topmost chamber of his house had burst through the roof and lifted himself up to the gaze of the world.

Again K. came to a stop, as if in standing still he had more power of judgment. But he was disturbed. Behind the village church where he had stopped – it was really only a chapel widened with barn-like additions so as to accommo-

date the parishioners – was the school. A long, low building, combining remarkably a look of great age with a provisional appearance, it lay behind a fenced-in garden which
was now a field of snow. The children were just coming out
with their teacher. They thronged round him, all gazing up
at him and chattering without a break so rapidly that K.
could not follow what they said. The teacher, a small young
man with narrow shoulders and a very upright carriage
which yet did not make him ridiculous, had already fixed
K. with his eyes from the distance, naturally enough, for
apart from the school-children there was not another
human being in sight. Being the stranger, K. made the first
advance, especially as the other was an authoritative-looking
little man, and said: 'Good morning, sir.' As if by one
accord the children fell silent, perhaps the master liked to
have a sudden stillness as a preparation for his words. 'You
are looking at the Castle?' he asked more gently than K. had
expected, but with an inflection that denoted disapproval of
K.'s occupation. 'Yes,' said K. 'I am a stranger here, I came
to the village only last night.' 'You don't like the Castle?'
returned the teacher quickly. 'What?' countered K., a little
taken aback, and repeated the question in a modified form.
'Do I like the Castle? Why do you assume that I don't like
it?' 'Strangers never do,' said the teacher. To avoid saying
the wrong thing K. changed the subject and asked: 'I suppose you know the Count?' 'No,' said the teacher turning
away. But K. would not be put off and asked again: 'What,
you don't know the Count?' 'Why should I?' replied the
teacher in a low tone, and added aloud in French: 'Please
remember that there are innocent children present.' K. took
this as a justification for asking: 'Might I come to pay you a
visit one day, sir? I am to be staying here for some time and
already feel a little lonely. I don't fit in with the peasants
nor, I imagine, with the Castle.' 'There is no difference
between the peasantry and the Castle,' said the teacher.
'Maybe,' said K., 'that doesn't alter my position. Can I pay
you a visit one day?' 'I live in Swan Street at the butcher's.'

That was assuredly more of a statement than an invitation, but K. said: 'Right, I'll come.' The teacher nodded and moved on with his batch of children, who began to scream again immediately. They soon vanished in a steeply descending by-street.

But K. was disconcerted, irritated by the conversation. For the first time since his arrival he felt really tired. The long journey he had made seemed at first to have imposed no strain upon him – how quietly he had sauntered through the days, step by step! – but now the consequences of his exertion were making themselves felt, and at the wrong time, too. He felt irresistibly drawn to seek out new acquaintances, but each new acquaintance only seemed to increase his weariness. If he forced himself in his present condition to go on at least as far as the Castle entrance, he would have done more than enough.

So he resumed his walk, but the way proved long. For the street he was in, the main street of the village, did not lead up to the Castle hill, it only made towards it and then, as if deliberately, turned aside, and though it did not lead away from the Castle it got no nearer to it either. At every turn K. expected the road to double back to the Castle, and only because of this expectation did he go on; he was flatly unwilling, tired as he was, to leave the street, and he was also amazed at the length of the village, which seemed to have no end; again and again the same little houses, and frost-bound window-panes and snow and the entire absence of human beings – but at last he tore himself away from the obsession of the street and escaped into a small side-lane, where the snow was still deeper and the exertion of lifting one's feet clear was fatiguing; he broke into a sweat, suddenly came to a stop, and could not go on.

Well, he was not on a desert island, there were cottages to right and left of him. He made a snowball and threw it at a window. The door opened immediately – the first door that had opened during the whole length of the village – and there appeared an old peasant in a brown fur jacket, with his head cocked to one side, a frail and kindly figure. 'May I come into your house for a little?' asked K., 'I'm very tired.' He did not hear the old man's reply, but thankfully observed that a plank was pushed out towards him to rescue him from the snow, and in a few steps he was in the kitchen.

A large kitchen, dimly lit. Anyone coming in from outside could make out nothing at first. K. stumbled over a washing-tub, a woman's hand steadied him. The crying of children came loudly from one corner. From another steam was welling out and turning the dim light into darkness. K. stood as if in the clouds. 'He must be drunk,' said somebody. 'Who are you?' cried a hectoring voice, and then obviously to the old man: 'Why did you let him in? Are we to let in everybody that wanders about in the street?' 'I am the Count's Land Surveyor,' said K., trying to justify himself before this still invisible personage. 'Oh, it's the Land Surveyor,' said a woman's voice, and then came a complete silence. 'You know me, then?' asked K. 'Of course,' said the same voice curtly. The fact that he was known did not seem to be a recommendation.

At last the steam thinned a little, and K. was able gradually to make things out. It seemed to be a general washing-day. Near the door clothes were being washed. But the steam was coming from another corner, where in a wooden tub larger than any K. had ever seen, as wide as two beds, two men were bathing in steaming water. But still more astonishing, although one could not say what was so astonishing about it, was the scene in the right-hand corner. From a large opening, the only one in the back wall, a pale snowy light came in, apparently from the courtyard, and gave a gleam as of silk to the dress of a woman who was almost reclining in a high arm-chair. She was suckling an infant at her breast. Several children were playing around her, peasant children, as was obvious, but she seemed to be of another class, although of course illness and weariness give even peasants a look of refinement.

'Sit down!' said one of the men, who had a full beard and breathed heavily through his mouth which always hung open, pointing – it was a funny sight – with his wet hand over the edge of the tub towards a settle, and showering drops of warm water all over K.'s face as he did so. On the settle the old man who had admitted K. was already sitting, sunk in vacancy. K. was thankful to find a seat at last. Nobody paid any further attention to him. The woman at the washing-tub, young, plump and fair, sang in a low voice as she worked, the men stamped and rolled about in the bath, the children tried to get closer to them but were constantly driven back by mighty splashes of water which fell on K., too, and the woman in the arm-chair lay as if lifeless staring at the roof without even a glance towards the child at her bosom.

She made a beautiful, sad, fixed picture, and K. looked at her for what must have been a long time; then he must have fallen asleep, for when a loud voice roused him he found that his head was lying on the old man's shoulder. The men had finished with the tub – in which the children were now wallowing in charge of the fair-haired woman – and were standing fully dressed before K. It appeared that the hectoring one with the full beard was the less important of the two. The other, a still slow-thinking man who kept his head bent, was not taller than his companion and had a much smaller beard, but he was broader in the shoulders and had a broad face as well, and he it was who said: 'You can't stay here, sir. Excuse the discourtesy.' 'I don't want to stay,' said K., 'I only wanted to rest a little. I have rested, and now I shall go.' 'You're probably surprised at our lack of hospitality,' said the man, 'but hospitality is not our custom here, we have no use for visitors.' Somewhat refreshed by his sleep, his perceptions somewhat quickened, K. was pleased by the man's frankness. He felt less constrained, poked with his stick here and there, approached the woman in the arm-chair, and noted that he was physically the biggest man in the room.

'To be sure,' said K., 'what use would you have for visitors? But still you need one now and then, me, for example, the Land Surveyor.' 'I don't know about that,' replied the man slowly. 'If you've been asked to come you're probably needed, that's an exceptional case, but we small people stick to our tradition, and you can't blame us for that.' 'No, no,' said K., 'I am only grateful to you and everybody here.' And taking them all by surprise he made an adroit turn and stood before the reclining woman. Out of weary blue eyes she looked at him, a transparent silk kerchief hung down to the middle of her forehead, the infant was asleep on her bosom. 'Who are you?' asked K., and disdainfully – whether contemptuous of K. or her own answer was not clear – she replied: 'A girl from the Castle.'

It had only taken a second or so, but already the two men were at either side of K. and were pushing him towards the door, as if there were no other means of persuasion, silently, but putting out all their strength. Something in this procedure delighted the old man, and he clapped his hands. The woman at the bath-tub laughed too, and the children suddenly shouted like mad.

K. was soon out in the street, and from the threshold the two men surveyed him. Snow was again falling, yet the sky seemed a little brighter. The bearded man cried impatiently: 'Where do you want to go? This is the way to the Castle, and that to the village.' K. made no reply to him, but turned to the other, who in spite of his shyness seemed to him the more amiable of the two, and said: 'Who are you? Whom have I to thank for sheltering me?' 'I am the tanner Lasemann,' was the answer, 'but you owe thanks to nobody.' 'All right,' said K., 'perhaps we'll meet again.' 'I don't suppose so,' said the man. At that moment the other cried, with wave of his hand: 'Good morning, Arthur; good morning, Jeremiah!' K. turned round; so there were really people to be seen in the village streets! From the direction of the Castle came two young men of medium height, both very slim, in tight-fitting clothes, and like each other in their features. Although their skin was a dusky brown the blackness of their little pointed beards was actually striking by contrast. Considering the state of the road, they were walking at a great pace, their slim legs keeping time. 'Where are you off to?' shouted the bearded man. One had to shout to them, they were going so fast and they would not stop. 'On business,' they shouted back, laughing. 'Where?' 'At the inn.' 'I'm going there too,' yelled K. suddenly, louder than all the rest; he felt a strong desire to accompany them, not that he expected much from their acquaintance, but they were obviously good and jolly companions. They heard him, but only nodded, and were already out of sight.

K. was still standing in the snow, and was little inclined to extricate his feet only for the sake of plunging them in again; the tanner and his comrade, satisfied with having finally got rid of him, edged slowly into the house through the door which was now barely ajar, casting backward glances at K., and he was left alone in the falling snow. 'A fine setting for a fit of despair,' it occurred to him, 'if I were only standing here by accident instead of design.'

Just then in the hut on his left hand a tiny window was opened, which had seemed quite blue when shut, perhaps from the reflection of the snow, and was so tiny that when opened it did not permit the whole face of the person behind it to be seen, but only the eyes, old brown eyes. 'There he is,' K. heard a woman's trembling voice say. 'It's the Land Surveyor,' answered a man's voice. Then the man came to the window and asked, not unamiably, but still as if he were anxious to have no complications in front of his house: 'Are you waiting for somebody?' 'For a sledge, to pick me up,' said K. 'No sledges will pass here,' said the man, 'there's no traffic here.' 'But it's the road leading to the Castle,' objected K. 'All the same, all the same,' said the man with a certain finality, 'there's no traffic here.' Then they were both silent. But the man was obviously thinking of something, for he kept the window open. 'It's a bad road,' said K., to help him out. The only answer he got, however, was: 'Oh yes.' But after a little the man volunteered: 'If you like, I'll take you in my sledge.' 'Please do,' said K. delighted, 'what is your charge?' 'Nothing,' said the man. K. was very surprised. 'Well, you're the Land Surveyor,' explained the man, 'and you belong to the Castle. Where do you want to be taken?' 'To the Castle,' returned K. quickly. 'I won't take you there,' said the man without hesitation. 'But I belong to the Castle,' said K., repeating the other's very words. 'Maybe,' said the man shortly. 'Oh, well, take me to the inn,' said K. 'All right,' said the man, 'I'll be out with the sledge in a moment.' His whole behaviour had the appearance of springing not from any special desire to be friendly but rather from a kind of selfish, worried, and almost pedantic insistence on shifting K. away from the front of the house.

The gate of the courtyard opened, and a small light sledge, quite flat, without a seat of any kind, appeared, drawn by a feeble little horse, and behind it limped the man, a weakly stooped figure with a gaunt red snuffling face that looked peculiarly small beneath a tightly swathed woollen scarf. He was obviously ailing, and yet only to transport K. he had dragged himself out. K. ventured to mention it, but the man waved him aside. All that K. elicited was that he was a coachman called Gerstäcker, and that he had taken this uncomfortable sledge because it was standing ready, and to get out one of the others would have wasted too much time. 'Sit down,' he said, pointing to the sledge. 'I'll sit beside you,' said K. 'I'm going to walk,' said Gerstäcker. 'But why?' asked K. 'I'm going to walk,' repeated Gerstäcker, and was seized with a fit of coughing which shook him so severely that he had to brace his legs in the snow and hold on to the rim of the sledge. K. said no more, but sat down on the sledge, the man's cough slowly abated, and they drove off.

The Castle above them, which K. had hoped to reach that very day, was already beginning to grow dark, and retreated again into the distance. But as if to give him a parting sign till their next encounter a bell began to ring merrily up there, a bell which for at least a second made his heart palpitate for its tone was menacing, too, as if it threatened him with the fulfilment of his vague desire. This great bell soon died away, however, and its place was taken by a feeble monotonous little tinkle which might have come from the Castle, but might have been somewhere in the village. It certainly harmonised better with the slow-going journey, with the wretched-looking yet inexorable driver.

'I say,' cried K. suddenly – they were already near the church, the inn was not far off, and K. felt he could risk something – 'I'm surprised that you have the nerve to drive me round on your own responsibility; are you allowed to do that?' Gerstäcker paid no attention, but went on walking quietly beside the little horse. 'Hi!' cried K., scraping some snow from the sledge and flinging a snowball which hit Gerstäcker full in the ear. That made him stop and turn round; but when K. saw him at such close quarters – the sledge had slid forward a little – this stooping and somehow ill-used figure with the thin red tired face and cheeks that were different – one being flat and the other fallen in – standing listening with his mouth open, displaying only a few isolated teeth, he found that what he had just said out of malice had to be repeated out of pity, that is, whether Gerstäcker was likely to be penalised for driving him about. 'What do you mean?' asked Gerstäcker incomprehendingly, but without waiting for an answer he spoke to the horse and they moved on again.

II

WHEN by a turn in the road K. recognised that they were near the inn, he was greatly surprised to see that darkness had already set in. Had he been gone for such a long time? Surely not for more than an hour or two, by his reckoning.

And it had been morning when he left. And he had not felt any need of food. And just a short time ago it had been uniform daylight, and now the darkness of night was upon them. 'Short days, short days,' he said to himself, slipped off the sledge, and went towards the inn.

At the top of the little flight of steps leading into the house stood the landlord, a welcome figure, holding up a lighted lantern. Remembering his conductor for a fleeting moment K. stood still, there was a cough in the darkness behind him, that was he. Well, he would see him again soon. Not until he was level with the landlord, who greeted him humbly, did he notice two men, one on either side of the doorway. He took the lantern from his host's hand and turned the light upon them; it was the men he had already met, who were called Arthur and Jeremiah. They now saluted him. That reminded him of his soldiering days, happy days for him, and he laughed. 'Who are you?' he asked, looking from one to the other. 'Your assistants,' they answered. 'It's your assistants,' corroborated the landlord in a low voice. 'What?' said K., 'are you my old assistants whom I told to follow me and whom I am expecting?' They answered in the affirmative. 'That's good,' observed K. after a short pause. 'I'm glad you've come.' 'Well,' he said, after another pause, 'you've come very late, you're very slack.' 'It was a long way to come,' said one of them. 'A long way?' repeated K., 'but I met you just now coming from the Castle.' 'Yes,' said they without further explanation. 'Where is the apparatus?' asked K. 'We haven't any,' said they. 'The apparatus I gave you?' said K. 'We haven't any,' they reiterated. 'Oh, you are fine fellows!' said K., 'do you know anything about surveying?' 'No,' said they. 'But if you are my old assistants you must know something about it,' said K. They made no reply. 'Well, come in,' said K., pushing them before him into the house.

They sat down then all three together over their beer at a small table, saying little, K. in the middle with an assistant on each side. As on the other evening, there was only one other table occupied by a few peasants. 'You're a difficult problem,' said K., comparing them, as he had already done several times. 'How am I to know one of you from the other? The only difference between you is your names, otherwise you're as like as . . .' He stopped, and then went on involuntarily, 'You're as like as two snakes.' They smiled. 'People usually manage to distinguish us quite well,' they said in self-justification. 'I am sure they do,' said K., 'I was a witness of that myself, but I can only see with my own eyes, and with them I can't distinguish you. So I shall treat you as if you were one man and call you both Arthur, that's one of your names, yours, isn't it?' he asked one of them. 'No,' said the man, 'I'm Jeremiah.' 'It doesn't matter,' said K. 'I'll call you both Arthur. If I tell Arthur to go anywhere you must both go. If I give Arthur something to do you must both do it, that has the great disadvantage for me of preventing me from employing you on separate jobs, but the advantage that you will both be equally responsible for anything I tell you to do. How you divide the work between you doesn't matter to me, only you're not to excuse yourselves by blaming each other, for me you're only one man.' They considered this, and said: 'We shouldn't like that at all.' 'I don't suppose so,' said K.; 'of course you won't like it, but that's how it has to be.' For some little time one of the peasants had been sneaking round the table and K. had noticed him; now the fellow took courage and went up to one of the assistants to whisper something. 'Excuse me,' said K., bringing his hand down on the table and rising to his feet, 'these are my assistants and we're discussing private business. Nobody is entitled to disturb us.' 'Sorry, sir, sorry,' muttered the peasant anxiously, retreating backwards towards his friends. 'And this is my most important charge to you,' said K., sitting down again. 'You're not to speak to anyone without my permission. I am a stranger here, and if you are my old assistants you are strangers too. We three strangers must stand by each other therefore, give me your hands on that.' All too eagerly they stretched out their hands to K. 'Never mind the trimming,' said he, 'but remember that my command holds good. I shall go to bed now, and I recommend you to do the same. To-day we have missed a day's work, and to-morrow we must begin very early. You must get hold of a sleigh for taking me to the Castle and have it ready outside the house at six o'clock.' 'Very well,' said one. But the other interrupted him. 'You say "very well", and yet you know it can't be done.' 'Silence,' said K. 'You're trying already to dissociate yourselves from each other.' But then the first man broke in: 'He's right, it can't be done, no stranger can get into the Castle without a permit.' 'Where does one apply for a permit?' 'I don't know, perhaps to the Castellan.' 'Then we'll apply by telephone, go and telephone to the Castellan at once, both of you.' They rushed to the instrument, asked for the connection – how eager they were about it! in externals they were absurdly docile – and enquired if K. could come with them next morning into the Castle. The 'No' of the answer was audible even to K. at his table. But the answer went on and was still more explicit, it ran as follows: 'Neither to-morrow nor at any other time.' 'I shall telephone myself,' said K., and got up. While K. and his assistants hitherto had passed nearly unremarked except for the incident with the one peasant, his last statement aroused general attention. They all got up when K. did, and although the landlord tried to drive them away, crowded round him in a close semicircle at the telephone. The general opinion among them was that K. would get no answer at all. K. had to beg them to be quiet, saying he did not want to hear their opinion.

The receiver gave out a buzz of a kind that K. had never before heard on a telephone. It was like the hum of countless children's voices – but yet not a hum, the echo rather of voices singing at an infinite distance – blended by sheer impossibility into one high but resonant sound which vibrated on the ear as if it were trying to penetrate beyond mere hearing. K. listened without attempting to telephone, leaning his left arm on the telephone shelf.

He did not know how long he had stood there, but he stood until the landlord pulled at his coat saying that a messenger had come to speak with him. 'Go away!' yelled K. in an access of rage perhaps into the mouthpiece, for someone immediately answered from the other end. The following conversation ensued: 'Oswald speaking, who's there?' cried a severe arrogant voice with a small defect in its speech, as seemed to K., which its owner tried to cover by an exaggerated severity. K. hesitated to announce himself, for he was at the mercy of the telephone, the other could shout him down or hang up the receiver, and that might mean the blocking of a not unimportant way of access. K.'s hesitation made the man impatient. 'Who's there?' he repeated, adding, 'I should be obliged if there was less telephoning from down there, only a minute ago somebody rang up.' K. ignored this remark, and announced with sudden decision: 'The Land Surveyor's assistant speaking.' 'What Land Surveyor? What assistant?' K. recollected yesterday's telephone conversation, and said briefly, 'Ask Fritz.' This succeeded, to his own astonishment. But even more than at his success he was astonished at the organisation of the Castle service. The answer came: 'Oh, yes. That everlasting Land Surveyor. Quite so. What about it? What assistant?' 'Joseph,' said K. He was a little put out by the murmuring of the peasants behind his back, obviously they disapproved of his ruse. He had no time to bother about them, however, for the conversation absorbed all his attention. 'Joseph?' came the question. 'But the assistants are called . . .' there was a short pause, evidently to enquire the names from somebody else, 'Arthur and Jeremiah.' 'These are the new assistants,' said K. 'No, they are the old ones.' 'They are the new ones, I am the old assistant; I came to-day after the Land Surveyor.' 'No,' was shouted back. 'Then who am I?' asked K. as blandly as before.

And after a pause the same voice with the same defect answered him, yet with a deeper and more authoritative tone: 'You are the old assistant.'

K. was listening to the new note, and almost missed the question: 'What is it you want?' He felt like laying down the receiver. He had ceased to expect anything from this conversation. But being pressed, he replied quickly: 'When can my master come to the Castle?' 'Never,' was the answer. 'Very well,' said K., and hung the receiver up.

Behind him the peasants had crowded quite close. His assistants, with many side glances in his direction, were trying to keep them back. But they seemed not to take the matter very seriously, and in any case the peasants, satisfied with the result of the conversation, were beginning to give ground. A man came cleaving his way with rapid steps through the group, bowed before K. and handed him a letter. K. took it, but looked at the man, who for the moment seemed to him the more important. There was a great resemblance between this new-comer and the assistants, he was slim like them and clad in the same tight-fitting garments, had the same suppleness and agility, and yet he was quite different. How much K. would have preferred him as an assistant! He reminded K. a little of the girl with the infant whom he had seen at the tanner's. He was clothed nearly all in white, not in silk, of course; he was in winter clothes like all the others, but the material he was wearing had the softness and dignity of silk. His face was clear and frank, his eyes larger than ordinary. His smile was unusually joyous; he drew his hand over his face as if to conceal the smile, but in vain. 'Who are you?' asked K. 'My name is Barnabas,' said he, 'I am a messenger.' His lips were strong and yet gentle as he spoke. 'Do you approve of this kind of thing?' asked K., pointing to the peasants for whom he was still an object of curiosity, and who stood gaping at him with their open mouths, coarse lips, and literally tortured faces – their heads looked as if they had been beaten flat on top and their features as if the pain of the beating had twisted them to the present shape – and yet they were not exactly gaping at him, for their eyes often flitted away and studied some indifferent object in the room before fixing on him again, and then K. pointed also to his assistants who stood linked together, cheek against cheek, and smiling, but whether submissively or mockingly could not be determined. All these he pointed out as if presenting a train of followers forced upon him by circumstances, and as if he expected Barnabas – that indicated intimacy, it occurred to K. – always to discriminate between him and them. But Barnabas – quite innocently, it was clear – ignored the question, letting it pass as a well-bred servant ignores some remark of his master only apparently addressed to him, and merely surveyed the room in obedience to the question, greeting by a pressure of the hand various acquaintances among the peasants and exchanging a few words with the assistants, all with a free independence which set him apart from the others. Rebuffed but not mortified, K. returned to the letter in his hand and opened it. Its contents were as follows: 'My dear Sir, As you know, you have been engaged for the Count's service. Your immediate superior is the Superintendent of the village, who will give you all particulars about your work and the terms of your employment, and to whom you are responsible. I myself, however, will try not to lose sight of you. Barnabas, the bearer of this letter, will report himself to you from time to time to learn your wishes and communicate them to me. You will find me always ready to oblige you, in so far as that is possible. I desire my workers to be contented.' The signature was illegible, but stamped beside it was 'Chief of Department X.' 'Wait a little!' said K. to Barnabas, who bowed before him, then he commanded the landlord to show him to his room, for he wanted to be alone with the letter for a while. At the same time he reflected that Barnabas, although so attractive, was still only a messenger, and ordered a mug of beer for him. He looked to see how Barnabas would take it, but Barnabas was obviously quite pleased and began to drink the beer at once. Then K. went off with the landlord. The house was so small that nothing was available for K. but a little attic room, and even that had caused some difficulty, for two maids who had hitherto slept in it had had to be quartered elsewhere. Nothing indeed had been done but to clear the maids out, the room was otherwise quite unprepared, no sheets on the single bed, only some pillows and a horse-blanket still in the same rumpled state as in the morning. A few sacred pictures and photographs of soldiers were on the walls, the room had not even been aired; obviously they hoped that the new guest would not stay long, and were doing nothing to encourage him. K. felt no resentment, however, wrapped himself in the blanket, sat down at the table, and began to read the letter again by the light of a candle.

It was not a consistent letter; in part it dealt with him as with a free man whose independence was recognised, the mode of address for example, and the reference to his wishes. But there were other places in which he was directly or indirectly treated as a minor employee, hardly visible to the Heads of Departments; the writer would try to make an effort 'not to lose sight' of him, his superior was only the village Superintendent to whom he was actually responsible, probably his sole colleague would be the village policeman. These were inconsistencies, no doubt about it. They were so obvious that they had to be faced. It hardly occurred to K. that they might be due to indecision; that seemed a mad idea in connection with such an organisation. He was much more inclined to read into them a frankly offered choice, which left it to him to make what he liked out of the letter, whether he preferred to become a village worker with a distinctive but merely apparent connection with the Castle, or an ostensible village worker whose real occupation was determined through the medium of Barnabas. K. did not hesitate in his choice, and would not have hesitated even had he lacked the experience which had befallen him since his arrival. Only as a worker in the village, removed as far as possible from the sphere of the Castle, could he hope to achieve anything in the Castle itself; the village folk, who were now so suspicious of him, would begin to talk to him once he was their fellow-citizen, if not exactly their friend; and if he were to become indistinguishable from Gerstäcker or Lasemann – and that must happen as soon as possible, everything depended on that – then all kinds of paths would be thrown open to him, which would remain not only for ever closed to him but quite invisible were he to depend merely on the favour of the gentlemen in the Castle. There was of course a danger, and that was sufficiently emphasised in the letter, even elaborated with a certain satisfaction, as if it were unavoidable. That was sinking to the workman's level – service, superior work, terms of employment, responsible workers – the letter fairly reeked of it, and even though more personal messages were included they were written from the standpoint of an employer. If K. were willing to become a workman he could do so, but he would have to do it in grim earnest, without any other prospect. K. knew that he had no real compulsory discipline to fear, he was not afraid of that, and in this case least of all, but the pressure of a discouraging environment, of a growing resignation to disappointment, the pressure of the imperceptible influences of every moment, these things he did fear, but that was a danger he would have to guard against. Nor did the letter pass over the fact that if it should come to a struggle K. had had the hardihood to make the first advances; it was very subtly indicated and only to be sensed by an uneasy conscience – an uneasy conscience, not a bad one – it lay in the three words 'as you know,' referring to his engagement in the Count's service. K. had reported his arrival, and only after that, as the letter pointed out, had he known that he was engaged.

K. took down a picture from the wall and stuck the letter on the nail, this was the room he was to live in and the letter should hang there.

Then he went down to the inn parlour. Barnabas was sitting at a table with the assistants. 'Oh, there you are,' said K. without any reason, only because he was glad to see Barnabas, who jumped to his feet at once. Hardly had K. shown his face when the peasants got up and gathered round him – it had become a habit of theirs to follow him around. 'What are you always following me about for?' cried K. They were not offended, and slowly drifted back to their seats again. One of them in passing said casually in apology, with an enigmatic smile which was reflected on several of the others' faces: 'There's always something new to listen to,' and he licked his lips as if news were meat and drink to him. K. said nothing conciliatory, it was good for them to have a little respect for him, but hardly had he reached Barnabas when he felt a peasant breathing down the back of his neck. He had only come, he said, for the salt-cellar, but K. stamped his foot with rage and the peasant scuttled away without the salt-cellar. It was really easy to get at K., all one had to do was to egg on the peasants against him, their persistent interference seemed much more objectionable to him than the reserve of the others, nor were they free from reserve either, for if he had sat down at their table they would not have stayed. Only the presence of Barnabas restrained him from making a scene. But he turned round to scowl at them, and found that they, too, were all looking at him. When he saw them sitting like that, however, each man in his own place, not speaking to one another and without any apparent mutual understanding, united only by the fact that they were all gazing at him, he concluded that it was not out of malice that they pursued him, perhaps they really wanted something from him and were only incapable of expressing it, if not that, it might be pure childishness, which seemed to be in fashion at the inn; was not the landlord himself childish, standing there stock-still gazing at K. with a glass of beer in his hand which he should have been carrying to a customer, and oblivious of his wife, who was leaning out of the kitchen hatch calling to him?

With a quieter mind K. turned to Barnabas; he would have liked to dismiss his assistants, but could not think of an excuse. Besides, they were brooding peacefully over their beer. 'The letter,' began K., 'I have read it. Do you know the contents?' 'No,' said Barnabas, whose look seemed to imply more than his words. Perhaps K. was as mistaken in Barnabas's goodness as in the malice of the peasants, but his presence remained a comfort. 'You are mentioned in the letter, too, you are supposed to carry messages now and then from me to the Chief, that's why I thought you might know the contents.' 'I was only told,' said Barnabas, 'to give you the letter, to wait until you had read it, and then to bring back a verbal or written answer if you thought it needful.' 'Very well,' said K., 'there's no need to write anything; convey to the Chief – by the way, what's his name? I couldn't read his signature.' 'Klamm,' said Barnabas. 'Well, convey to Herr Klamm my thanks for his recognition and for his great kindness, which I appreciate, being as I am one who has not yet proved his worth here. I shall follow his instructions faithfully. I have no particular requests to make for to-day.' Barnabas, who had listened with close attention, asked to be allowed to recapitulate the message. K. assented, Barnabas repeated it word for word. Then he rose to take his leave.

K. had been studying his face the whole time, and now he gave it a last survey. Barnabas was about the same height as K., but his eyes seemed to look down on K., yet that was almost in a kind of humility, it was impossible to think that this man could put anyone to shame. Of course he was only a messenger, and did not know the contents of the letters he carried, but the expression in his eyes, his smile, his bearing, seemed also to convey a message, however little he might know about it. And K. shook him by the hand, which seemed obviously to surprise him, for he had been going to content himself with a bow.

As soon as he had gone – before opening the door he had leaned his shoulder against it for a moment and embraced the room generally in a final glance – K. said to the assistants: 'I'll bring down the plans from my room, and then we'll discuss what work is to be done first.' They wanted to accompany him. 'Stay here,' said K. Still they tried to accompany him. K. had to repeat his command more authoritatively. Barnabas was no longer in the hall. But he had only just gone out. Yet in front of the house – fresh snow was falling – K. could not see him either. He called out: 'Barnabas!' No answer. Could he still be in the house? Nothing else seemed possible. None the less K. yelled the name with the full force of his lungs. It thundered through the night. And from the distance came a faint response, so far away was Barnabas already. K. called him back, and at the same time went to meet him; the spot where they encountered each other was no longer visible from the inn.

'Barnabas,' said K., and could not keep his voice from trembling, 'I have something else to say to you. And that reminds me that it's a bad arrangement to leave me dependent on your chance comings for sending a message to the Castle. If I hadn't happened to catch you just now – how you fly along, I thought you were still in the house – who knows how long I might have had to wait for your next appearance.' 'You can ask the Chief,' said Barnabas, 'to send me at definite times appointed by yourself.' 'Even that would not suffice,' said K., 'I might have nothing to say for a year at a time, but something of urgent importance might occur to me a quarter of an hour after you had gone.'

'Well,' said Barnabas, 'shall I report to the Chief that between him and you some other means of communication should be established instead of me?' 'No, no,' said K., 'not at all, I only mention the matter in passing, for this time I have been lucky enough to catch you.' 'Shall we go back to the inn,' said Barnabas, 'so that you can give me the new message there?' He had already taken a step in the direction of the inn. 'Barnabas,' said K., 'it isn't necessary, I'll go a part of the way with you.' 'Why don't you want to go to the inn?' asked Barnabas. 'The people there annoy me,' said K.;

'you saw for yourself how persistent the peasants are.' 'We could go into your room,' said Barnabas. 'It's the maids' room,' said K., 'dirty and stuffy – it's to avoid staying there that I want to accompany you for a little, only,' he added, in order finally to overcome Barnabas's reluctance, 'you must let me take your arm, for you are surer of foot than I am.' And K. took his arm. It was quite dark, K. could not see Barnabas's face, his figure was only vaguely discernible, he had had to grope for his arm a minute or two.

Barnabas yielded and they moved away from the inn. K. realised, indeed, that his utmost efforts could not enable him to keep pace with Barnabas, that he was a drag on him, and that even in ordinary circumstances this trivial accident might be enough to ruin everything, not to speak of side-streets like the one in which he had got stuck that morning, out of which he could never struggle unless Barnabas were to carry him. But he banished all such anxieties, and was comforted by Barnabas's silence; for if they went on in silence then Barnabas, too, must feel that their excursion together was the sole reason for their association.

They went on, but K. did not know whither, he could discern nothing, not even whether they had already passed the church or not. The effort which it cost him merely to keep going made him lose control of his thoughts. Instead of remaining fixed on their goal they strayed. Memories of his home kept recurring and filled his mind. There, too, a church stood in the market-place, partly surrounded by an old graveyard which was again surrounded by a high wall. Very few boys had managed to climb that wall, and for some time K., too, had failed. It was not curiosity which had urged them on. The graveyard had been no mystery to them. They had often entered it through a small wicket-gate, it was only the smooth high wall that they had wanted to conquer. But one morning – the empty, quiet market-place had been flooded with sunshine, when had K. ever seen it like that either before or since? – he had succeeded in climbing it with astonishing ease; at a place where he had already slipped down many a time he had clambered with a small flag between his teeth right to the top at the first attempt. Stones were still rattling down under his feet, but he was at the top. He stuck the flag in, it flew in the wind, he looked down and round about him, over his shoulder, too, at the crosses mouldering in the ground, nobody was greater than he at that place and that moment. By chance the teacher had come past and with a stern face had made K. descend. In jumping down he had hurt his knee and had found some difficulty in getting home, but still he had been on the top of the wall. The sense of that triumph had seemed to him then a victory for life, which was not altogether foolish, for now so many years later on the arm of Barnabas in the snowy night the memory of it came to succour him.

He took a firmer hold, Barnabas was almost dragging him along, the silence was unbroken. Of the road they were following all that K. knew was that to judge from its surface they had not yet turned aside into a by-street. He vowed to himself that, however difficult the way and however doubtful even the prospect of his being able to get back, he would not cease from going on. He would surely have strength enough to let himself be dragged. And the road must come to an end some time. By day the Castle had looked within easy reach, and, of course, the messenger would take the shortest cut.

At that moment Barnabas stopped. Where were they? Was this the end? Would Barnabas try to leave him? He wouldn't succeed. K. clutched his arm so firmly that it almost made his hand ache. Or had the incredible happened, and were they already in the Castle or at its gates? But they had not done any climbing so far as K. could tell. Or had Barnabas taken him up by an imperceptibly mounting road? 'Where are we?' said K. in a low voice, more to himself than to Barnabas. 'At home,' said Barnabas in the same tone. 'At home?' 'Be careful now, sir, or you'll slip.

We go down here.' 'Down?' 'Only a step or two,' added Barnabas, and was already knocking at a door.

A girl opened it, and they were on the threshold of a large room almost in darkness, for there was no light save for a tiny oil lamp hanging over a table in the background. 'Who is with you, Barnabas?' asked the girl. 'The Land Surveyor,' said he. 'The Land Surveyor,' repeated the girl in a louder voice, turning towards the table. Two old people there rose to their feet, a man and a woman, as well as another girl. They greeted K. Barnabas introduced the whole family, his parents and his sisters Olga and Amalia. K. scarcely glanced at them and let them take his wet coat off to dry at the stove.

So it was only Barnabas who was at home, not he himself. But why had they come here? K. drew Barnabas aside and asked: 'Why have you come here? Or do you live in the Castle precincts?' 'The Castle precincts?' repeated Barnabas, as if he did not understand. 'Barnabas,' said K., 'you left the inn to go to the Castle.' 'No,' said Barnabas, 'I left it to come home, I don't go to the Castle till the early morning, I never sleep there.' 'Oh,' said K., 'so you weren't going to the Castle, but only here' – the man's smile seemed less brilliant, and his person more insignificant – 'Why didn't you say so?' 'You didn't ask me, sir,' said Barnabas, 'you only said you had a message to give me, but you wouldn't give it in the inn parlour, or in your room, so I thought you could speak to me quietly here in my parents' house. The others will all leave us if you wish – and, if you prefer, you could spend the night here. Haven't I done the right thing?' K. could not reply. It had been simply a misunderstanding, a common, vulgar misunderstanding, and K. had been completely taken in by it. He had been bewitched by Barnabas's close-fitting, silken-gleaming jacket, which, now that it was unbuttoned, displayed a coarse, dirty grey shirt patched all over, and beneath that the huge muscular chest of a labourer. His surroundings not only corroborated all this but even emphasised it, the old

gouty father who progressed more by the help of his groping hands than by the slow movements of his stiff legs, and
the mother with her hands folded on her bosom, who was
equally incapable of any but the smallest steps by reason of
her stoutness. Both of them, father and mother, had been
advancing from their corner towards K. ever since he had
come in, and were still a long way off. The yellow-haired
sisters, very like each other and very like Barnabas, but with
harder features than their brother, great strapping wenches,
hovered round their parents and waited for some word of
greeting from K. But he could not utter it. He had been
persuaded that in this village everybody meant something to
him, and indeed he was not mistaken, it was only for these
people here that he could feel not the slightest interest. If
he had been fit to struggle back to the inn alone he would
have left at once. The possibility of accompanying Barnabas
to the Castle early in the morning did not attract him. He
had hoped to penetrate into the Castle unremarked in the
night on the arm of Barnabas, but on the arm of the Barnabas he had imagined, a man who was more to him than
anyone else, the Barnabas he had conceived to be far above
his apparent rank and in the intimate confidence of the
Castle. With the son of such a family, however, a son who
integrally belonged to it, and who was already sitting at
table with the others, a man who was not even allowed to
sleep in the Castle, he could not possibly go to the Castle in
the broad light of day, it would be a ridiculous and hopeless
undertaking.

K. sat down on a window-seat where he determined to
pass the night without accepting any other favour. The
other people in the village, who turned him away or were
afraid of him, seemed much less dangerous, for all that they
did was to throw him back on his own resources, helping
him to concentrate his powers, but such ostensible helpers
as these who on the strength of a petty masquerade brought
him into their homes instead of into the Castle, deflected
him, whether intentionally or not, from his goal and only

helped to destroy him. An invitation to join the family at table he ignored completely, stubbornly sitting with bent head on his bench.

Then Olga, the gentler of the sisters, got up, not without a trace of maidenly embarrassment, came over to K. and asked him to join the family meal of bread and bacon, saying that she was going to fetch some beer. 'Where from?' asked K. 'From the inn,' she said. That was welcome news to K. He begged her instead of fetching beer to accompany him back to the inn, where he had important work waiting to be done. But the fact now emerged that she was not going so far as his inn, she was going to one much nearer, called the Herrenhof. None the less K. begged to be allowed to accompany her, thinking that there perhaps he might find a lodging for the night; however wretched it might be he would prefer it to the best bed these people could offer him. Olga did not reply at once, but glanced towards the table. Her brother stood up, nodded obligingly, and said: 'If the gentleman wishes.' This assent was almost enough to make K. withdraw his request, nothing could be of much value if Barnabas assented to it. But since they were already wondering whether K. would be admitted into that inn and doubting its possibility, he insisted emphatically upon going, without taking the trouble to give a colourable excuse for his eagerness; this family would have to accept him as he was, he had no feeling of shame where they were concerned. Yet he was somewhat disturbed by Amalia's direct and serious gaze, which was unflinching and perhaps a little stupid.

On their short walk to the inn – K. had taken Olga's arm and was leaning his whole weight on her as earlier on Barnabas, he could not get along otherwise – he learned that it was an inn exclusively reserved for gentlemen from the Castle, who took their meals there and sometimes slept there whenever they had business in the village. Olga spoke to K. in a low and confidential tone; to walk with her was pleasant, almost as pleasant as walking with her brother. K.

struggled against the feeling of comfort she gave him, but it persisted.

From outside the new inn looked very like the inn where K. was staying. All the houses in the village resembled one another more or less, but still a few small differences were immediately apparent here; the front steps had a balustrade, and a fine lantern was fixed over the doorway. Something fluttered over their heads as they entered, it was a flag with the Count's colours. In the hall they were at once met by the landlord, who was obviously on a tour of inspection; he glanced at K. in passing with small eyes that were either screwed up critically, or half-asleep, and said: 'The Land Surveyor mustn't go anywhere but into the bar.' 'Certainly,' said Olga, who took K.'s part at once, 'he's only escorting me.' But K. ungratefully let go her arm and drew the landlord aside. Olga meanwhile waited patiently at the end of the hall. 'I should like to spend the night here,' said K. 'I'm afraid that's impossible,' said the landlord. 'You don't seem to be aware that this house is reserved exclusively for gentlemen from the Castle.' 'Well, that may be the rule,' said K., 'but it's surely possible to let me sleep in a corner somewhere.' 'I should be only too glad to oblige you,' said the landlord, 'but besides the strictness with which the rule is enforced – and you speak about it as only a stranger could – it's quite out of the question for another reason; the Castle gentlemen are so sensitive that I'm convinced they couldn't bear the sight of a stranger, at least unless they were prepared for it; and if I were to let you sleep here, and by some chance or other – and chances are always on the side of the gentlemen – you were discovered, not only would it mean my ruin but yours too. That sounds ridiculous, but it's true.' This tall and closely-buttoned man who stood with his legs crossed, one hand braced against the wall and the other on his hip, bending down a little towards K. and speaking confidentially to him, seemed to have hardly anything in common with the village, even although his dark clothes looked like a peasant's finery. 'I believe you absolutely,' said K., 'and I didn't mean to belittle the rule, although I expressed myself badly. Only there's something I'd like to point out, I have some influence in the Castle, and shall have still more, and that secures you against any danger arising out of my stay here overnight, and is a guarantee that I am able fully to recompense any small favour you may do me.' 'Oh, I know,' said the landlord, and repeated again, 'I know all that.' Now was the time for K. to state his wishes more clearly, but this reply of the landlord's disconcerted him, and so he merely asked, 'Are there many of the Castle gentlemen staying in the house to-night?' 'As far as that goes, to-night is favourable,' returned the landlord, as if in encouragement, 'there's only one gentleman.' Still K. felt incapable of urging the matter, but being in hopes that he was as good as accepted, he contented himself by asking the name of the gentleman. 'Klamm,' said the landlord casually, turning meanwhile to his wife who came rustling towards them in a remarkably shabby, old-fashioned gown overloaded with pleats and frills, but of a fine city cut. She came to summon the landlord, for the Chief wanted something or other. Before the landlord complied, however, he turned once more to K., as if it lay with K. to make the decision about staying all night. But K. could not utter a word, overwhelmed as he was by the discovery that it was his patron who was in the house. Without being able to explain it completely to himself he did not feel the same freedom of action in relation to Klamm as he did to the rest of the Castle, and the idea of being caught in the inn by Klamm, although it did not terrify him as it did the landlord, gave him a twinge of uneasiness, much as if he were thoughtlessly to hurt the feelings of someone to whom he was bound by gratitude; at the same time, however, it vexed him to recognise already in these qualms the obvious effects of that degradation to an inferior status which he had feared, and to realise that although they were so obvious he was not even in a position to counteract them. So he stood there biting his lips and said nothing. Once more the landlord looked back at him before disappearing through a doorway, and K. returned the look without moving from the spot, until Olga came up and drew him away. 'What did you want with the landlord?' she asked. 'I wanted a bed for the night,' said K. 'But you're staying with us!' said Olga in surprise. 'Of course,' said K., leaving her to make what she liked of it.

III

IN the bar, which was a large room with a vacant space in the middle, there were several peasants sitting by the wall on the tops of some casks, but they looked different from those in K.'s inn. They were more neatly and uniformly dressed in coarse yellowish-grey cloth, with loose jackets and tightly-fitting trousers. They were smallish men with at first sight a strong mutual resemblance, having flat bony faces, but rounded cheeks. They were all quiet, and sat with hardly a movement, except that they followed the new-comers with their eyes, but they did even that slowly and indifferently. Yet because of their numbers and their quiet-ness they had a certain effect on K. He took Olga's arm again as if to explain his presence there. A man rose up from one corner, an acquaintance of Olga's, and made to-wards her, but K. wheeled her round by the arm in another direction. His action was perceptible to nobody but Olga, and she tolerated it with a smiling side-glance.

The beer was drawn off by a young girl called Frieda. An unobtrusive little girl with fair hair, sad eyes, and hollow cheeks, with a striking look of conscious superiority. As soon as her eye met K.'s it seemed to him that her look decided something concerning himself, something which he had not known to exist, but which her look assured him did exist. He kept on studying her from the side, even while she was speaking to Olga. Olga and Frieda were apparently not intimate, they exchanged only a few cold words. K. wanted to hear more, and so interposed with a question on his own account: 'Do you know Herr Klamm?' Olga laughed out loud. 'What are you laughing at?' asked K. irritably. 'I'm not laughing,' she protested, but went on laughing. 'Olga is a childish creature,' said K. bending far over the counter in order to attract Frieda's gaze again. But she kept her eyes lowered and laughed shyly. 'Would you like to see Herr Klamm?' K. begged for a sight of him. She pointed to a door just on her left. 'There's a little peephole there, you can look through.' 'What about the others?' asked K. She curled her underlip and pulled K. to the door with a hand that was unusually soft. The little hole had obviously been bored for spying through, and commanded almost the whole of the neighbouring room. At a desk in the middle of the room in a comfortable arm-chair sat Herr Klamm, his face brilliantly lit up by an incandescent lamp which hung low before him. A middle-sized, plump, and ponderous man. His face was still smooth, but his cheeks were already somewhat flabby with age. His black moustache had long points, his eyes were hidden behind glittering pince-nez that sat awry. If he had been planted squarely before his desk K. would only have seen his profile, but since he was turned directly towards K. his whole face was visible. His left elbow lay on the desk, his right hand, in which was a Virginia cigar, rested on his knee. A beer-glass was standing on the desk, but there was a rim round the desk which prevented K. from seeing whether any papers were lying on it, he had the idea, however, that there were none. To make it certain he asked Frieda to look through the hole and tell him if there were any. But since she had been in that room a short time ago, she was able to inform him without further ado that the desk was empty. K. asked Frieda if his time was up, but she told him to go on looking as long as he liked. K. was now alone with Frieda. Olga, as a hasty glance assured him, had found her way to her acquaintance, and was sitting high on a cask swinging her legs. 'Frieda,' said K. in a whisper, 'do you know Herr Klamm well?' 'Oh, yes,' she said, 'very well.' She leaned over to K. and he became aware that she was coquettishly fingering the low-cut cream-coloured blouse which sat oddly on her poor thin body. Then she said: 'Didn't you notice how Olga laughed?' 'Yes, the rude creature,' said K. 'Well,' she said extenuatingly, 'there was a reason for laughing. You asked if I knew Klamm, and you see I' – here she involuntarily lifted her chin a little, and again her triumphant glance, which had no connection whatever with what she was saying, swept over K. – 'I am his mistress.' 'Klamm's mistress,' said K. She nodded. 'Then,' said K. smiling, to prevent the atmosphere from being too charged with seriousness, 'you are for me a highly respectable person.' 'Not only for you,' said Frieda amiably, but without returning his smile. K. had a weapon for bringing down her pride, and he tried it: 'Have you ever been in the Castle?' But it missed the mark, for she answered: 'No, but isn't it enough for me to be here in the bar?' Her vanity was obviously boundless, and she was trying, it seemed, to get K. in particular to minister to it. 'Of course,' said K., 'here in the bar you're taking the landlord's place.' 'That's so,' she assented, 'and I began as a byre-maid at the inn by the bridge.' 'With those delicate hands,' said K. half-questioningly, without knowing himself whether he was only flattering her or was compelled by something in her. Her hands were certainly small and delicate, but they could quite as well have been called weak and characterless. 'Nobody bothered about them then,' she said, 'and even now . . .' K. looked at her enquiringly. She shook her head and would say no more. 'You have your secrets, naturally,' said K., 'and you're not likely to give them away to somebody you've known for only half an hour, and who hasn't had the chance yet to tell you anything about himself.' This remark proved to be ill-chosen, for it seemed to arouse Frieda as from a trance that was favourable to him. Out of the leather bag hanging at her girdle she took a small piece of wood, stopped up the peephole with it, and said to

K. with an obvious attempt to conceal the change in her attitude; 'Oh, I know all about you, you're the Land Surveyor,' and then adding: 'but now I must go back to my work,' she returned to her place behind the bar counter, while a man here and there came up to get his empty glass refilled. K. wanted to speak to her again, so he took an empty glass from a stand and went up to her, saying: 'One thing more, Fräulein Frieda, it's an extraordinary feat and a sign of great strength of mind to have worked your way up from byre-maid to this position in the bar, but can it be the end of all ambition for a person like you? An absurd idea. Your eyes – don't laugh at me, Fräulein Frieda – speak to me far more of conquests still to come than of conquests past. But the opposition one meets in the world is great, and becomes greater the higher one aims, and it's no disgrace to accept the help of a man who's fighting his way up too, even though he's a small and uninfluential man. Perhaps we could have a quiet talk together sometime, without so many onlookers?' 'I don't know what you're after,' she said, and in her tone this time there seemed to be, against her will, an echo rather of countless disappointments than of past triumphs. 'Do you want to take me away from Klamm perhaps? O heavens!' and she clapped her hands. 'You've seen through me,' said K., as if wearied by so much mistrust, 'that's exactly my real secret intention. You ought to leave Klamm and become my sweetheart. And now I can go. Olga!' he cried, 'we're going home.' Obediently Olga slid down from her cask but did not succeed immediately in breaking through her ring of friends. Then Frieda said in a low voice with a hectoring look at K.: 'When can I talk to you?' 'Can I spend the night here?' asked K. 'Yes,' said Frieda. 'Can I stay now?' 'Go out first with Olga, so that I can clear out all the others. Then you can come back in a little.' 'Right,' said K., and he waited impatiently for Olga. But the peasants would not let her go; they had made up a dance in which she was the central figure, they circled round her yelling all together and every now and then one of them left the ring, seized Olga firmly round the waist and whirled her round and round; the pace grew faster and faster, the yells more hungry, more raucous, until they were insensibly blended into one continuous howl. Olga, who had begun laughingly by trying to break out of the ring, was now merely reeling with flying hair from one man to the other. 'That's the kind of people I'm saddled with,' said Frieda, biting her thin lips in scorn. 'Who are they?' asked K. 'Klamm's servants,' said Frieda, 'he keeps on bringing those people with him, and they upset me. I can hardly tell what I've been saying to you, but please forgive me if I've offended you, it's these people who are to blame, they're the most contemptible and objectionable creatures I know, and I have to fill their glasses up with beer for them. How often I've implored Klamm to leave them behind him, for though I have to put up with the other gentlemen's servants, he could surely have some consideration for me; but it's all no use, an hour before his arrival they always come bursting in like cattle into their stalls. But now they've really got to get into the stalls, where they belong. If you weren't here I'd fling open this door and Klamm would be forced to drive them out himself.' 'Can't he hear them, then?' asked K. 'No,' said Frieda, 'he's asleep.' 'Asleep?' cried K. 'But when I peeped in he was awake and sitting at the desk.' 'He always sits like that,' said Frieda, 'he was sleeping when you saw him. Would I have let you look in if he hadn't been asleep? That's how he sleeps, the gentlemen do sleep a great deal, it's hard to understand. Anyhow, if he didn't sleep so much, he wouldn't be able to put up with his servants. But now I'll have to turn them out myself.' She took a whip from a corner and sprang among the dancers with a single bound, a little uncertainly, as a young lamb might spring. At first they faced her as if she were merely a new partner, and actually for a moment Frieda seemed inclined to let the whip fall, but she soon raised it again, crying: 'In the name of Klamm into the stall with you, into the stall, all of you!' When they saw that she was in earnest they began to press towards the back wall in a kind of panic incomprehensible to K., and under the impact of the first few a door shot open, letting in a current of night air through which they all vanished with Frieda behind them openly driving them across the courtyard into the stalls.

In the sudden silence which ensued K. heard steps in the vestibule. With some idea of securing his position he dodged behind the bar counter, which afforded the only possible cover in the room. He had an admitted right to be in the bar, but since he meant to spend the night there he had to avoid being seen. So when the door was actually opened he slid under the counter. To be discovered there of course would have its dangers too, yet he could explain plausibly enough that he had only taken refuge from the wild licence of the peasants. It was the landlord who came in. 'Frieda!' he called, and walked up and down the room several times.

Fortunately Frieda soon came back, she did not mention K., she only complained about the peasants, and in the course of looking round for K. went behind the counter, so that he was able to touch her foot. From that moment he felt safe. Since Frieda made no reference to K., however, the landlord was compelled to do it. 'And where is the Land Surveyor?' he asked. He was probably courteous by nature, refined by constant and relatively free intercourse with men who were much his superior, but there was remarkable consideration in his tone to Frieda, which was all the more striking because in his conversation he did not cease to be an employer addressing a servant, and a saucy servant at that. 'The Land Surveyor – I forgot all about him,' said Frieda, setting her small foot on K.'s chest. 'He must have gone out long ago.' 'But I haven't seen him,' said the landlord, 'and I was in the hall nearly the whole time.' 'Well, he isn't in here,' said Frieda coolly. 'Perhaps he's hidden somewhere,' went on the landlord. 'From the impression I had of him he's capable of a good deal.' 'He would hardly have the cheek to do that,' said Frieda, pressing her foot down on K. There was a certain mirth and freedom about her which K. had not previously remarked, and quite unexpectedly it took the upper hand, for suddenly laughing she bent down to K. with the words: 'Perhaps he's hidden underneath here,' kissed him lightly and sprang up again saying with a troubled air: 'No, he's not there.' Then the landlord, too, surprised K. when he said: 'It bothers me not to know for certain that he's gone. Not only because of Herr Klamm, but because of the rule of the house. And the rule applies to you, Fräulein Frieda, just as much as to me. Well, if you answer for the bar, I'll go through the rest of the rooms. Good night! Sleep well!' He could hardly have left the room before Frieda had turned out the electric light and was under the counter beside K. 'My darling! My darling!' she whispered, but she did not touch him. As if swooning with love she lay on her back and stretched out her arms; time must have seemed endless to her in the prospect of her happiness, and she sighed rather than sang some little song or other. Then as K. still lay absorbed in thought, she started up and began to tug at him like a child: 'Come on, it's too close down here,' and they embraced each other, her little body burned in K.'s hands, in a state of unconsciousness which K. tried again and again but in vain to master as they rolled a little way, landing with a thud on Klamm's door, where they lay among the small puddles of beer and other refuse gathered on the floor. There, hours went past, hours in which they breathed as one, in which their hearts beat as one, hours in which K. was haunted by the feeling that he was losing himself or wandering into a strange country, farther than ever man had wandered before, a country so strange that not even the air had anything in common with his native air, where one might die of strangeness, and yet whose enchantment was such that one could only go on and lose oneself further. So it came to him not as a shock but as a faint glimmer of comfort when from Klamm's room a deep, authoritative impersonal voice called for Frieda. 'Frieda,' whispered K. in Frieda's ear, passing on the summons. With a mechanical instinct of obedience Frieda made as if to spring to her feet, then she remembered where she was, stretched herself, laughing quietly, and said: 'I'm not going, I'm never going to him again.' K. wanted to object, to urge her to go to Klamm, and began to fasten up her disordered blouse, but he could not bring himself to speak, he was too happy to have Frieda in his arms, too troubled also in his happiness, for it seemed to him that in letting Frieda go he would lose all he had. And as if his support had strengthened her Frieda clenched her fist and beat upon the door, crying: 'I'm with the Land Surveyor!' That silenced Klamm at any rate, but K. started up, and on his knees beside Frieda gazed round him in the uncertain light of dawn. What had happened? Where were his hopes? What could he expect from Frieda now that she had betrayed everything? Instead of feeling his way with the prudence befitting the greatness of his enemy and of his ambition, he had spent a whole night wallowing in puddles of beer, the smell of which was nearly over-powering. 'What have you done?' he said as if to himself. 'We are both ruined.' 'No,' said Frieda, 'it's only me that's ruined, but then I've won you. Don't worry. But just look how these two are laughing.' 'Who?' asked K., and turned round. There on the bar counter sat his two assistants, a little heavy-eyed for lack of sleep, but cheerful. It was a cheerfulness arising from a sense of duty well done. 'What are you doing here?' cried K. as if they were to blame for everything. 'We had to search for you,' explained the assistants, 'since you didn't come back to the inn; we looked for you at Barnabas's and finally found you here. We have been sitting here all night. Ours is no easy job.' 'It's in the day-time I need you,' said K., 'not in the night. Clear out.' 'But it's day-time now,' said they without moving. It was really day, the doors into the courtyard were opened, the peasants came streaming in and with them Olga, whom K. had completely forgotten.

Although her hair and clothes were in disorder Olga was as alert as on the previous evening, and her eyes flew to K. before she was well over the threshold. 'Why did you not come home with me?' she asked, almost weeping. 'All for a creature like that!' she said then, and repeated the remark several times. Frieda, who had vanished for a moment, came back with a small bundle of clothing, and Olga moved sadly to one side. 'Now we can be off,' said Frieda, it was obvious she meant that they should go back to the inn by the bridge. K. walked with Frieda, and behind them the assistants; that was the little procession. The peasants displayed a great contempt for Frieda, which was understandable, for she had lorded it over them hitherto; one of them even took a stick and held it as if to prevent her from going out until she had jumped over it, but a look from her sufficed to quell him. When they were out in the snow K. breathed a little more freely. It was such a relief to be in the open air that the journey seemed less laborious; if he had been alone he would have got on still better. When he reached the inn he went straight to his room and lay down on the bed. Frieda prepared a couch for herself on the floor beside him. The assistants had pushed their way in too, and on being driven out came back through the window. K. was too weary to drive them out again. The landlady came up specially to welcome Frieda, who hailed her as 'mother'; their meeting was inexplicably affectionate, with kisses and long embracings. There was little peace and quietness to be had in the room, for the maids too came clumping in with their heavy boots, bringing or seeking various articles, and whenever they wanted anything from the miscellaneous assortment on the bed they simply pulled it out from under K. They greeted Frieda as one of themselves. In spite of all this coming and going K. stayed in bed the whole day through, and the whole night. Frieda performed little offices for him. When he got up at last on the following morning he was much refreshed, and it was the fourth day since his arrival in the village.

IV

HE would have liked an intimate talk with Frieda, but the assistants hindered this simply by their importunate presence, and Frieda, too, laughed and joked with them from time to time. Otherwise they were not at all exacting, they had simply settled down in a corner on two old skirts spread out on the floor. They made it a point of honour, as they repeatedly assured Frieda, not to disturb the Land Surveyor and to take up as little room as possible, and in pursuit of this intention, although with a good deal of whispering and giggling, they kept on trying to squeeze themselves into a smaller compass, crouching together in the corner so that in the dim light they looked like one large bundle. From his experience of them by daylight, however, K. was all too conscious that they were acute observers and never took their eyes off him, whether they were fooling like children and using their hands as spyglasses, or merely glancing at him while apparently completely absorbed in grooming their beards, on which they spent much thought and which they were for ever comparing in length and thickness, calling on Frieda to decide between them. From his bed K. often watched the antics of all three with the completest indifference.

When he felt himself well enough to leave his bed, they all ran to serve him. He was not yet strong enough to ward off their services, and noted that that brought him into a state of dependence on them which might have evil consequences, but he could not help it. Nor was it really unpleasant to drink at the table the good coffee which Frieda had brought, to warm himself at the stove which Frieda had lit, and to have the assistants racing ten times up and down the stairs in their awkwardness and zeal to fetch him soap and water, comb and looking-glass, and eventually even a small glass of rum because he had hinted in a low voice at his desire for one.

Among all this giving of orders and being waited on, K. said, more out of good humour than any hope of being obeyed: 'Go away now, you two, I need nothing more for the present, and I want to speak to Fräulein Frieda by herself.' And when he saw no direct opposition on their faces he added, by way of excusing them: 'We three shall go to the village Superintendent afterwards, so wait downstairs in the bar for me.' Strangely enough they obeyed him, only turning to say before going: 'We could wait here.' But K. answered: 'I know, but I don't want you to wait here.'

It annoyed him, however, and yet in a sense pleased him when Frieda, who had settled on his knee as soon as the assistants were gone, said: 'What's your objection to the assistants, darling? We don't need to have any mysteries before them. They are true friends.' 'Oh, true friends,' said K., 'they keep spying on me the whole time, it's nonsensical but abominable.' 'I believe I know what you mean,' she said, and she clung to his neck and tried to say something else but could not go on speaking, and since their chair was close to it they reeled over and fell on the bed. There they lay, but not in the forgetfulness of the previous night. She was seeking and he was seeking, they raged and contorted their faces and bored their heads into each other's bosoms in the urgency of seeking something, and their embraces and their tossing limbs did not avail to make them forget, but only reminded them of what they sought; like dogs desperately tearing up the ground they tore at each other's bodies, and often, helplessly baffled, in a final effort to attain happiness they nuzzled and tongued each other's face. Sheer weariness stilled them at last and brought them gratitude to each other. Then the maids came in. 'Look how they're lying there,' said one, and sympathetically cast a coverlet over them.

When somewhat later K. freed himself from the coverlet and looked round, the two assistants – and he was not surprised at that – were again in their corner, and with a finger jerked towards K. nudged each other to a formal salute, but besides them the landlady was sitting near the bed knitting away at a stocking, an infinitesimal piece of work hardly suited to her enormous bulk which almost darkened the room. 'I've been here a long time,' she said, lifting up her broad and much furrowed face which was, however, still rounded and might once have been beautiful. The words sounded like a reproach, an ill-timed reproach, for K. had not desired her to come. So he merely acknowledged them by a nod, and sat up. Frieda also got up, but left K. to lean over the landlady's chair. 'If you want to speak to me,' said K. in bewilderment, 'couldn't you put it off until after I come back from visiting the Superintendent? I have important business with him.' 'This is important, believe me, sir,' said the landlady, 'your other business is probably only a question of work, but this concerns a living person, Frieda, my dear maid.' 'Oh, if that's it,' said K., 'then of course you're right, but I don't see why we can't be left to settle our own affairs.' 'Because I love her and care for her,' said the landlady, drawing Frieda's head towards her, for Frieda as she stood only reached up to the landlady's shoulder. 'Since Frieda puts such confidence in you,' cried K., 'I must do the same, and since not long ago Frieda called my assistants true friends we are all friends together. So I can tell you that what I would like best would be for Frieda and myself to get married, the sooner the better. I know, oh, I know that I'll never be able to make up to Frieda for all she has lost for my sake, her position in the Herrenhof and her friendship with Klamm.' Frieda lifted up her face, her eyes were full of tears and had not a trace of triumph. 'Why? Why am I chosen out from other people?' 'What?' asked K. and the landlady simultaneously. 'She's upset, poor child,' said the landlady, 'upset by the conjunction of too much happiness and unhappiness.' And as if in confirmation of those words Frieda now flung herself upon K., kissing him wildly as if there were nobody else

48

in the room, and then weeping, but still clinging to him, fell on her knees before him. While he caressed Frieda's hair with both hands K. asked the landlady: 'You seem to have no objection?' 'You are a man of honour,' said the landlady, who also had tears in her eyes. She looked a little worn and breathed with difficulty, but she found strength enough to say: 'There's only the question now of what guarantees you are to give Frieda, for great as is my respect for you, you're a stranger here; there's nobody here who can speak for you, your family circumstances aren't known here, so some guarantee is necessary. You must see that, my dear sir, and indeed you touched on it yourself when you mentioned how much Frieda must lose through her association with you.' 'Of course, guarantees, most certainly,' said K., 'but they'll be best given before the notary, and at the same time other officials of the Count's will perhaps be concerned. Besides, before I'm married there's something I must do. I must have a talk with Klamm.' 'That's impossible,' said Frieda, raising herself a little and pressing close to K., 'what an idea!' 'But it must be done,' said K., 'if it's impossible for me to manage it, you must.' 'I can't, K.; I can't,' said Frieda. 'Klamm will never talk to you. How can you even think of such a thing!' 'And won't he talk to you?' asked K. 'Not to me either,' said Frieda, 'neither to you nor to me, it's simply impossible.' She turned to the landlady with outstretched arms: 'You see what he's asking for!' 'You're a strange person,' said the landlady, and she was an awe-inspiring figure now that she sat more upright, her legs spread out and her enormous knees projecting under her thin skirt, 'you ask for the impossible.' 'Why is it impossible?' said K. 'That's what I'm going to tell you,' said the landlady in a tone which sounded as if her explanation were less a final concession to friendship than the first item in a score of penalties she was enumerating, 'that's what I shall be glad to let you know. Although I don't belong to the Castle, and am only a woman, only a landlady here in an inn of the lowest kind – it's not of the very lowest but not

49

far from it – and on that account you may not perhaps set much store by my explanation, still I've kept my eyes open all my life and met many kinds of people and taken the whole burden of the inn on my own shoulders, for Martin is no landlord although he's a good man, and responsibility is a thing he'll never understand. It's only his carelessness, for instance, that you've got to thank – for I was tired to death on that evening – for being here in the village at all, for sitting here on this bed in peace and comfort.' 'What?' said K., waking from a kind of absent-minded distraction, pricked more by curiosity than by anger. 'It's only his care-lessness you've got to thank for it,' cried the landlady again, pointing with her forefinger at K. Frieda tried to silence her. 'I can't help it,' said the landlady with a swift turn of her whole body. 'The Land Surveyor asked me a question and I must answer it. There's no other way of making him understand what we take for granted, that Herr Klamm will never speak to him – will never speak, did I say? – can never speak to him. Just listen to me, sir. Herr Klamm is a gentleman from the Castle, and that in itself, without con-sidering Klamm's position there at all, means that he is of very high rank. But what are you, for whose marriage we are humbly considering here ways and means of getting permission? You are not from the Castle, you are not from the village, you aren't anything. Or rather, unfortunately, you are something, a stranger, a man who isn't wanted and is in everybody's way, a man who's always causing trouble, a man who takes up the maids' room, a man whose inten-tions are obscure, a man who has ruined our dear little Frieda and whom we must unfortunately accept as her hus-band. I don't hold all that up against you. You are what you are, and I have seen enough in my lifetime to be able to face facts. But now consider what it is you ask. A man like Klamm is to talk with you. It vexed me to hear that Frieda let you look through the peephole, when she did that she was already corrupted by you. But just tell me, how did you have the face to look at Klamm? You needn't answer, I know you think you were quite equal to the occasion. You're not even capable of seeing Klamm as he really is, that's not merely an exaggeration, for I myself am not capable of it either. Klamm is to talk to you, and yet Klamm doesn't talk even to people from the village, never yet has he spoken a word himself to anyone in the village. It was Frieda's great distinction, a distinction I'll be proud of to my dying day, that he used at least to call out her name, and that she could speak to him whenever she liked and was permitted the freedom of the peephole, but even to her he never talked. And the fact that he called her name didn't mean of necessity what one might think, he simply mentioned the name Frieda – who can tell what he was thinking of? – and that Frieda naturally came to him at once was her affair, and that she was admitted without let or hindrance was an act of grace on Klamm's part, but that he deliberately summoned her is more than one can maintain. Of course that's all over now for good. Klamm may perhaps call 'Frieda' as before, that's possible, but she'll never again be admitted to his presence, a girl who has thrown herself away upon you. And there's just one thing, one thing my poor head can't understand, that a girl who had the honour of being known as Klamm's mistress – a wild exaggeration in my opinion – should have allowed you even to lay a finger on her.'

'Most certainly, that's remarkable,' said K., drawing Frieda to his bosom – she submitted at once although with bent head – 'but in my opinion that only proves the possibility of your being mistaken in some respects. You're quite right, for instance, in saying that I'm a mere nothing compared with Klamm, and even though I insist on speaking to Klamm in spite of that, and am not dissuaded even by your arguments, that does not mean at all that I'm able to face Klamm without a door between us, or that I mayn't run from the room at the very sight of him. But such a conjecture, even though well founded, is no valid reason in my eyes for refraining from the attempt. If I only succeed in holding my ground there's no need for him to speak to me at all, it will be sufficient for me to see what effect my words have on him, and if they have no effect or if he simply ignores them, I shall at any rate have the satisfaction of having spoken my mind freely to a great man. But you, with your wide knowledge of men and affairs, and Frieda, who was only yesterday Klamm's mistress – I see no reason for questioning that title – could certainly procure me an interview with Klamm quite easily; if it could be done in no other way I could surely see him in the Herrenhof, perhaps he's still there.'

'It's impossible,' said the landlady, 'and I can see that you're incapable of understanding why. But just tell me what you want to speak to Klamm about?'

'About Frieda, of course,' said K.

'About Frieda?' repeated the landlady incomprehendingly, and turned to Frieda. 'Do you hear that, Frieda, it's about you that he, he, wants to speak to Klamm, to Klamm!'

'Oh,' said K., 'you're a clever and admirable woman, and yet every trifle upsets you. Well, there it is, I want to speak to him about Frieda; that's not monstrous, it's only natural. And you're quite wrong, too, in supposing that from the moment of my appearance Frieda has ceased to be of any importance to Klamm. You underestimate him if you suppose that. I'm well aware that it's impertinence in me to lay down the law to you in this matter, but I must do it. I can't be the cause of any alteration in Klamm's relation to Frieda. Either there was no essential relationship between them – and that's what it amounts to if people deny that he was her honoured lover – in which case there is still no relationship between them, or else there was a relationship, and then how could I, a cipher in Klamm's eyes, as you rightly point out, how could I make any difference to it? One flies to such suppositions in the first moment of alarm, but the smallest reflection must correct one's bias. Anyhow, let us hear what Frieda herself thinks about it.'

With a far-away look in her eyes and her cheek on K.'s breast, Frieda said: 'It's certain, as mother says, that Klamm will have nothing more to do with me. But I agree that it's not because of you, darling, nothing of that kind could upset him. I think on the other hand that it was entirely his work that we found each other under the bar counter, we should bless that hour and not curse it.'

'If that is so,' said K. slowly, for Frieda's words were sweet, and he shut his eyes a moment or two to let their sweetness penetrate him, 'if that is so, there is less ground than ever to flinch from an interview with Klamm.'

'Upon my word,' said the landlady, with her nose in the air, 'you put me in mind of my own husband, you're just as childish and obstinate as he is. You've been only a few days in the village and already you think you know everything better than people who have spent their lives here, better than an old woman like me, and better than Frieda who has seen and heard so much in the Herrenhof. I don't deny that it's possible once in a while to achieve something in the teeth of every rule and tradition. I've never experienced anything of that kind myself, but I believe there are precedents for it. That may well be, but it certainly doesn't happen in the way you're trying to do it, simply by saying "no, no," and sticking to your own opinions and flouting the most well-meant advice. Do you think it's you I'm anxious about? Did I bother about you in the least so long as you were by yourself? Even though it would have been a good thing and saved a lot of trouble? The only thing I ever said to my husband about you was: "Keep your distance where he's concerned." And I should have done that myself to this very day if Frieda hadn't got mixed up with your affairs. It's her you have to thank – whether you like it or not – for my interest in you, even for my noticing your existence at all. And you can't simply shake me off, for I'm the only person who looks after little Frieda, and you're strictly answerable to me. Maybe Frieda is right, and all that has happened is Klamm's will, but I have nothing to do with

Klamm here and now. I shall never speak to him, he's quite beyond my reach. But you're sitting here, keeping my Frieda, and being kept yourself – I don't see why I shouldn't tell you – by me. Yes, by me, young man, for let me see you find a lodging anywhere in this village if I throw you out, even it were only in a dog-kennel.'

'Thank you,' said K., 'that's frank and I believe you absolutely. So my position is as uncertain as that, is it, and Frieda's position, too?'

'No!' interrupted the landlady furiously. 'Frieda's position in this respect has nothing at all to do with yours. Frieda belongs to my house, and nobody is entitled to call her position here uncertain.'

'All right, all right,' said K., 'I'll grant you that, too, especially since Frieda for some reason I'm not able to fathom seems to be too afraid of you to interrupt. Stick to me then for the present. My position is quite uncertain, you don't deny that, indeed you rather go out of your way to emphasise it. Like everything else you say, that has a fair proposition of truth in it, but it isn't absolutely true. For instance, I know where I could get a very good bed if I wanted it.'

'Where? Where?' cried Frieda and the landlady simultaneously and so eagerly that they might have had the same motive for asking.

'At Barnabas's,' said K.

'That scum!' cried the landlady. 'That rascally scum! At Barnabas's! Do you hear –' and she turned towards the corner, but the assistants had long quitted it and were now standing arm-in-arm behind her. And so now, as if she needed support, she seized one of them by the hand: 'Do you hear where the man goes hob-nobbing, with the family of Barnabas? Oh, certainly he'd get a bed there; I only wished he'd stay'd there overnight instead of in the Herrenhof. But where were you two?'

'Madam,' said K., before the assistants had time to answer, 'these are my assistants. But you're treating them as if they were your assistants and my keepers. In every other respect I'm willing at least to argue the point with you courteously, but not where my assistants are concerned, that's too obvious a matter. I request you therefore not to speak to my assistants, and if my request proves ineffective I shall forbid my assistants to answer you.'

'So I'm not allowed to speak to you,' said the landlady, and they laughed all three, the landlady scornfully, but with less anger than K. had expected, and the assistants in their usual manner, which meant both much and little and disclaimed all responsibility.

'Don't get angry,' said Frieda, 'you must try to understand why we're upset. I can put it in this way, it's all owing to Barnabas that we belong to each other now. When I saw you for the first time in the bar – when you came in arm-in-arm with Olga – well, I knew something about you, but I was quite indifferent to you. I was indifferent not only to you but to nearly everything, yes, nearly everything. For at that time I was discontented about lots of things, and often annoyed, but it was a queer discontent and a queer annoyance. For instance, if one of the customers in the bar insulted me – and they were always after me – you saw what kind of creatures they were, but there were many worse than that, Klamm's servants weren't the worst – well, if one of them insulted me, what did that matter to me? I regarded it as if it had happened years before, or as if it had happened to someone else, or as if I had only heard tell of it, or as if I had already forgotten about it. But I can't describe it, I can hardly imagine it now, so different has everything become since losing Klamm.'

And Frieda broke off short, letting her head drop sadly, folding her hands on her bosom.

'You see,' cried the landlady, and she spoke not as if in her own person but as if she had merely lent Frieda her voice; she moved nearer, too, and sat close beside Frieda, 'you see, sir, the results of your actions, and your assistants too, whom I am not allowed to speak to, can profit by looking on at them. You've snatched Frieda from the happiest state she had ever known, and you managed to do that largely because in her childish susceptibility she could not bear to see you arm-in-arm with Olga, and so apparently delivered hand and foot to the Barnabas family. She rescued you from that and sacrificed herself in doing so. And now that it's done, and Frieda has given up all she had for the pleasure of sitting on your knee, you come out with this fine trump card that once you had the chance of getting a bed from Barnabas. That's by way of showing me that you're independent of me. I assure you, if you had slept in that house you would be so independent of me that in the twinkling of an eye you would be put out of this one.'

'I don't know what sins the family of Barnabas have committed,' said K., carefully raising Frieda – who drooped as if lifeless – setting her slowly down on the bed and standing up himself, 'you may be right about them, but I know that I was right in asking you to leave Frieda and me to settle our own affairs. You talked then about your care and affection, yet I haven't seen much of that, but a great deal of hatred and scorn and forbidding me your house. If it was your intention to separate Frieda from me or me from Frieda it was quite a good move, but all the same I think it won't succeed, and if it does succeed – it's my turn now to issue vague threats – you'll repent it. As for the lodging you favour me with – you can only mean this abominable hole – it's not at all certain that you do it of your own free will, it's much more likely that the authorities insist upon it. I shall now inform them that I have been told to go – and if I am allotted other quarters you'll probably feel relieved, but not so much as I will myself. And now I'm going to discuss this and other business with the Superintendent, please be so good as to look after Frieda at least, whom you have reduced to a bad enough state with your so-called motherly counsel.'

Then he turned to the assistants. 'Come along,' he said, taking Klamm's letter from its nail and making for the door. The landlady looked at him in silence, and only when his hand was on the latch did she say: 'There's something else to take away with you, for whatever you say and however you insult an old woman like me, you're after all Frieda's future husband. That's my sole reason for telling you now that your ignorance of the local situation is so appalling that it makes my head go round to listen to you and compare your ideas and opinions with the real state of things. It's a kind of ignorance which can't be enlightened at one attempt, and perhaps never can be, but there's a lot you could learn if you would only believe me a little and keep your own ignorance constantly in mind. For instance, you would at once be less unjust to me, and you would begin to have an inkling of the shock it was to me – a shock from which I'm still suffering – when I realised that my dear little Frieda had, so to speak, deserted the eagle for the snake in the grass, only the real situation is much worse even than that, and I have to keep on trying to forget it so as to be able to speak civilly to you at all. Oh, now you're angry again! No, don't go away yet, listen to this one appeal; wherever you may be, never forget that you're the most ignorant person in the village, and be cautious; here in this house where Frieda's presence saves you from harm you can drivel on to your heart's content, for instance, here you can explain to us how you mean to get an interview with Klamm, but I entreat you, I entreat you, don't do it in earnest.'

She stood up, tottering a little with agitation, went over to K., took his hand and looked at him imploringly. 'Madam,' said K., 'I don't understand why you should stoop to entreat me about a thing like this. If as you say, it's impossible for me to speak to Klamm, I won't manage it in any case whether I'm entreated or not. But if it proves to be possible, why shouldn't I do it, especially as that would remove your main objection and so make your other premises questionable. Of course I'm ignorant, that's an unshaken truth and a sad truth for me, but it gives me all the advantage of ignorance, which is greater daring, and so I'm prepared to put up with my ignorance, evil consequences and all, for some time to come, so long as my strength holds out. But these consequences really affect nobody but myself, and that's why I simply can't understand your pleading. I'm certain you would always look after Frieda, and if I were to vanish from Frieda's ken you couldn't regard that as anything but good luck. So what are you afraid of? Surely you're not afraid – an ignorant man thinks everything possible' – here K. flung the door open – 'surely you're not afraid for Klamm?' The landlady gazed after him in silence as he ran down the staircase with the assistants following him.

V

To his own surprise K. had little difficulty in obtaining an interview with the Superintendent. He sought to explain this to himself by the fact that, going by his experience hitherto, official intercourse with the authorities for him was always very easy. This was caused on the one hand by the fact that the word had obviously gone out once and for all to treat his case with the external marks of indulgence, and on the other, by the admirable autonomy of the service, which one divined to be peculiarly effective precisely where it was not visibly present. At the mere thought of those facts, K. was often in danger of considering his situation hopeful; nevertheless, after such fits of easy confidence, he would hasten to tell himself that just there lay his danger.

Direct intercourse with the authorities was not particularly difficult then, for well organised as they might be, all they did was to guard the distant and invisible interests of distant and invisible masters, while K. fought for something vitally near to him, for himself, and moreover, at least at the very beginning, on his own initiative, for he was the attacker; and besides he fought not only for himself, but clearly for other powers as well which he did not know, but in which, without infringing the regulations of the authorities, he was permitted to believe. But now by the fact that they had at once amply met his wishes in all unimportant matters – and hitherto only unimportant matters had come up – they had robbed him of the possibility of light and easy victories, and with that of the satisfaction which must accompany them and the well-grounded confidence for further and greater struggles which must result from them. Instead, they let K. go anywhere he liked – of course only within the village – and thus pampered and enervated him, ruled out all possibility of conflict, and transposed him to an unofficial, totally unrecognised, troubled, and alien existence. In this life it might easily happen, if he were not always on his guard, that one day or other, in spite of the amiability of the authorities and the scrupulous fulfilment of all his exaggeratedly light duties, he might – deceived by the apparent favour shown him – conduct himself so imprudently that he might get a fall; and the authorities, still ever mild and friendly, and as it were against their will, but in the name of some public regulation unknown to him, might have to come and clear him out of the way. And what was it, this other life to which he was consigned? Never yet had K. seen vocation and life so interlaced as here, so interlaced that sometimes one might think that they had exchanged places. What importance, for example, had the power, merely formal up till now, which Klamm exercised over K.'s services, compared with the very real power which Klamm possessed in K.'s bedroom? So it came about that while a light and frivolous bearing, a certain deliberate carelessness was sufficient when one came in direct contact with the authorities, one needed in everything else the greatest caution, and had to look round on every side before one made a single step.

K. soon found his opinion of the authorities of the place confirmed when he went to see the Superintendent. The

Superintendent, a kindly, stout, clean-shaven man, was laid up; he was suffering from a severe attack of gout, and received K. in bed. 'So here is our Land Surveyor,' he said, and tried to sit up, failed in the attempt and flung himself back again on the cushions, pointing apologetically to his leg. In the faint light of the room, where the tiny windows were still further darkened by curtains, a noiseless, almost shadowing woman pushed forward a chair for K. and placed it beside the bed. 'Take a seat, Land Surveyor, take a seat,' said the Superintendent, 'and let me know your wishes.' K. read out Klamm's letter and adjoined a few remarks to it. Again he had this sense of extraordinary ease in intercourse with the authorities. They seemed literally to bear every burden, one could lay everything on their shoulders and remain free and untouched oneself. As if he, too, felt this in his way, the Superintendent made a movement of discomfort on the bed. At length he said: 'I know about the whole business as, indeed, you have remarked. The reason why I've done nothing is, firstly, that I've been unwell, and secondly, that you've been so long in coming; I thought finally that you had given up the business. But now that you've been so kind as to look me up, really I must tell you the plain unvarnished truth of the matter. You've been taken on as Land Surveyor, as you say, but, unfortunately, we have no need of a Land Surveyor. There wouldn't be the least use for one here. The frontiers of our little state are marked out and all officially recorded. So what should we do with a Land Surveyor?' Though he had not given the matter a moment's thought before, K. was convinced now at the bottom of his heart that he had expected some such response as this. Exactly for that reason he was able to reply immediately: 'This is a great surprise for me. It throws all my calculations out. I can only hope that there's some misunderstanding.' 'No, unfortunately,' said the Superintendent, 'it's as I've said.' 'But how is that possible?' cried K. 'Surely I haven't made this endless journey just to be sent back again.' 'That's another question,' replied the

Superintendent, 'which isn't for me to decide, but how this misunderstanding became possible, I can certainly explain that. In such a large governmental office as the Count's, it may occasionally happen that one department ordains this, another that; neither knows of the other, and though the supreme control is absolutely efficient, it comes by its nature too late, and so every now and then a trifling miscalculation arises. Of course that applies only to the pettiest little affairs, as for example your case. In great matters I've never known of any error yet, but even little affairs are often painful enough. Now as for your case, I'll be open with you about its history, and make no official mystery of it – I'm not enough of the official for that, I'm a farmer and always will remain one. A long time ago – I had only been Superintendent for a few months – there came an order, I can't remember from what department, in which in the usual categorical way of the gentlemen up there, it was made known that a Land Surveyor was to be called in, and the municipality were instructed to hold themselves ready for the plans and measurements necessary for his work. This order obviously couldn't have concerned you, for it was many years ago, and I shouldn't have remembered it if I weren't ill just now and with ample time in bed to think of the most absurd things – Mizzi,' he said, suddenly inter-rupting his narrative, to the woman who was still flitting about the room in incomprehensible activity, 'please have a look in the cabinet, perhaps you'll find the order.' 'You see, it belongs to my first months here,' he explained to K., 'at that time I still filed everything away.' The woman opened the cabinet at once. K. and the Superintendent looked on. The cabinet was crammed full of papers. When it was opened two large packages of papers rolled out, tied in round bundles, as one usually binds firewood; the woman sprang back in alarm. 'It must be down below, at the bot-tom,' said the Superintendent, directing operations from the bed. Gathering the papers in both arms the woman obe-diently threw them all out of the cabinet so as to read those at the bottom. The papers now covered half the floor. 'A great deal of work is got through here,' said the Superintendent nodding his head, 'and that's only a small fraction of it. I've put away the most important pile in the shed, but the great mass of it has simply gone astray. Who could keep it all together? But there's piles and piles more in the shed.' 'Will you be able to find the order?' he said, turning again to his wife; 'you must look for a document with the word Land Surveyor underlined in blue pencil.' 'It's too dark,' said the woman, 'I'll fetch a candle,' and she stamped through the papers to the door. 'My wife is a great help to me,' said the Superintendent, 'in these difficult official affairs, and yet we can never quite keep up with them. True, I have another assistant for the writing that has to be done, the teacher; but all the same it's impossible to get things shipshape, there's always a lot of business that has to be left lying, it has been put away in that chest there,' and he pointed to another cabinet. 'And just now, when I'm laid up, it has got the upper hand,' he said, and lay back with a weary yet proud air. 'Couldn't I,' asked K., seeing that the woman had now returned with the candle and was kneeling before the chest looking for the paper, 'couldn't I help your wife to look for it?' The Superintendent smilingly shook his head: 'As I said before, I don't want to make any parade of official secrecy before you, but to let you look through these papers yourself – no, I can't go so far as that.' Now stillness fell in the room, only the rustling of the papers was to be heard; it looked, indeed, for a few minutes, as if the Superintendent were dozing. A faint rapping on the door made K. turn round. It was of course the assistants. All the same they showed already some of the effects of their training, they did not rush at once into the room, but whispered at first through the door which was slightly ajar: 'It's cold out here.' 'Who's that?' asked the Superintendent, starting up. 'It's only my assistants,' replied K. 'I don't know where to ask them to wait for me, it's too cold outside and here they would be in the way.' 'They won't disturb me,' said the

Superintendent indulgently. 'Ask them to come in. Besides I know them. Old acquaintances.' 'But they're in *my* way,' K. replied bluntly, letting his gaze wander from the assistants to the Superintendent and back again, and finding on the faces of all three the same smile. 'But seeing you're here as it is,' he went on experimentally, 'stay and help the Superintendent's lady there to look for a document with the word Land Surveyor underlined in blue pencil.' The Superintendent raised no objection. What had not been permitted to K. was allowed to the assistants; they threw themselves at once on the papers, but they did not so much seek for anything as rummage about in the heap, and while one was spelling out a document the other would immediately snatch it out of his hand. The woman meanwhile knelt before the empty chest, she seemed to have completely given up looking, in any case the candle was standing quite far away from her.

'The assistants,' said the Superintendent with a self-complacent smile, which seemed to indicate that he had the lead, though nobody was in a position even to assume this, 'they're in your way then? Yet they're your own assistants.' 'No,' replied K. coolly, 'they only ran into me here.' 'Ran into you,' said he; 'you mean, of course, were assigned to you.' 'All right then, were assigned to me,' said K., 'but they might as well have fallen from the sky, for all the thought that was spent in choosing them.' 'Nothing here is done without taking thought,' said the Superintendent, actually forgetting the pain in his foot and sitting up. 'Nothing!' said K., 'and what about my being summoned here then?' 'Even your being summoned was carefully considered,' said the Superintendent; 'it was only certain auxiliary circumstances that entered and confused the matter, I'll prove it to you from the official papers.' 'The papers will not be found,' said K. 'Not be found?' said the Superintendent. 'Mizzi, please hurry up a bit! Still I can tell you the story even without the papers. We replied with thanks to the order that I've mentioned already, saying that we didn't need a Land Surveyor. But this reply doesn't appear to have reached the original department – I'll call it A – but by mistake went to another department, B. So Department A remained without an answer, but unfortunately our full reply didn't reach B either; whether it was that the order itself was not enclosed by us, or whether it got lost on the way – it was certainly not lost in my department, that I can vouch for – in any case all that arrived at Department B was the covering letter, in which was merely noted that the enclosed order, unfortunately an impracticable one, was concerned with the engagement of a Land Surveyor. Meanwhile Department A was waiting for our answer, they had, of course, made a memorandum of the case, but as excusably enough often happens and is bound to happen even under the most efficient handling, our correspondent trusted to the fact that we would answer him, after which he would either summon the Land Surveyor, or else if need be write us further about the matter. As a result he never thought of referring to his memorandum and the whole thing fell into oblivion. But in Department B the covering letter came into the hands of a correspondent, famed for his conscientiousness, Sordini by name, an Italian; it is incomprehensible even to me, though I am one of the initiated, why a man of his capacities is left in an almost subordinate position. This Sordini naturally sent back the unaccompanied covering letter for completion. Now months, if not years, had passed by this time since that first communication from Department A, which is understandable enough, for when – which is the rule – a document goes the proper route, it reaches the department at the outside in a day and is settled that day, but when it once in a while loses its way then in an organisation so efficient as ours its proper destination must be sought for literally with desperation, otherwise it mightn't be found; and then, well then the search may last really for a long time. Accordingly, when we got Sordini's note we had only a vague memory of the affair, there were only two of us to do the work at that time. Mizzi and myself, the teacher hadn't yet been assigned to us, we only kept copies in the most important instances, so we could only reply in the most vague terms that we knew nothing of this engagement of a Land Surveyor and that as far as we knew there was no need for one.

'But,' here the Superintendent interrupted himself as if, carried on by his tale, he had gone too far, or as if at least it were possible that he had gone too far, 'doesn't the story bore you?'

'No,' said K., 'it amuses me.'

Thereupon the Superintendent said: 'I'm not telling it to amuse you.'

'It only amuses me,' said K., 'because it gives me an insight into the ludicrous bungling which in certain circumstances may decide the life of a human being.'

'You haven't been given any insight into that yet,' replied the Superintendent gravely, 'and I can go on with my story. Naturally Sordini was not satisfied with our reply. I admire the man, although he is a plague to me. He literally distrusts everyone; even if, for instance, he has come to know somebody, through countless circumstances, as the most reliable man in the world, he distrusts him as soon as fresh circumstances arise, as if he didn't want to know him, or rather as if he wanted to know that he was a scoundrel. I consider that right and proper, an official must behave like that; unfortunately with my nature I can't follow out this principle; you see yourself how frank I am with you, a stranger, about those things, I can't act in any other way. But Sordini, on the contrary, was seized by suspicion when he read our reply. Now a large correspondence began to grow. Sordini enquired how I had suddenly recalled that a Land Surveyor shouldn't be summoned. I replied, drawing on Mizzi's splendid memory, that the first suggestion had come from the chancellory itself (but that it had come from a different department we had of course forgotten long before this). Sordini countered: 'Why had I only mentioned this official order now?' I replied: 'Because I had just remembered it.' Sordini: 'That was very extraordinary.' Myself: 'It was not in the least extraordinary in such a long-drawn-out business.' Sordini: 'Yes, it was extraordinary, for the order that I remembered didn't exist.' Myself: 'Of course it didn't exist, for the whole document had gone a-missing.' Sordini: 'But there must be a memorandum extant relating to this first communication, and there wasn't one extant.' That drew me up, for that an error should happen in Sordini's department I neither dared to maintain nor to believe. Perhaps, my dear Land Surveyor, you'll make the reproach against Sordini in your mind, that in consideration of my assertion he should have been moved at least to make enquiries in the other departments about the affair. But that is just what would have been wrong; I don't want any blame to attach to this man, no, not even in your thoughts. It's a working principle of the Head Bureau that the very possibility of error must be ruled out of account. This ground principle is justified by the consummate organisation of the whole authority, and it is necessary if the maximum speed in transacting business is to be attained. So it wasn't within Sordini's power to make enquiries in other departments, besides they simply wouldn't have answered, because they would have guessed at once that it was a case of hunting out a possible error.'

'Allow me, Superintendent, to interrupt you with a question,' said K. 'Did you not mention once before a Control Authority? From your description the whole economy is one that would rouse one's apprehension if one could imagine the control failing.'

'You're very strict,' said the Superintendent, 'but multiply your strictness a thousand times and it would still be nothing compared with the strictness which the Authority imposes on itself. Only a total stranger could ask a question like yours. Is there a Control Authority? There are only control authorities. Frankly it isn't their function to hunt out errors in the vulgar sense, for errors don't happen, and even when once in a while an error does happen, as in your case, who can say finally that it's an error?'

'This is news indeed!' cried K.

'It's very old news to me,' said the Superintendent. 'Not unlike yourself I'm convinced that an error has occurred, and as a result Sordini is quite ill with despair, and the first Control Officials, whom we have to thank for discovering the source of error, recognise that there is an error. But who can guarantee that the second Control Officials will decide in the same way and the third lot and all the others?'

'That may be,' said K. 'I would much rather not mix in these speculations yet, besides this is the first mention I've heard of those Control Officials and naturally I can't understand them yet. But I fancy that two things must be distinguished here: firstly, what is transacted in the offices and can be construed again officially this way or that, and secondly, my own actual person, me myself, situated outside of the offices and threatened by their encroachments, which are so meaningless that I can't even yet believe in the seriousness of the danger. The first evidently is covered by what you, Superintendent, tell me in such extraordinary and disconcerting detail; all the same I would like to hear a word now about myself.'

'I'm coming to that too,' said the Superintendent, 'but you couldn't understand it without my giving a few more preliminary details. My mentioning the Control Officials just now was premature. So I must turn back to the discrepancies with Sordini. As I said, my defence gradually weakened. But whenever Sordini has in his hands even the slightest hold against anyone, he has as good as won, for then his vigilance, energy, and alertness are actually increased and it's a terrible moment for the victim, and a glorious one for the victim's enemies. It's only because in other circumstances I have experienced this last feeling that I'm able to speak of him as I do. All the same I have never managed yet to come within sight of him. He can't get down here, he's so overwhelmed with work; from the descriptions I've heard of his room every wall is covered with columns of documents tied together, piled on top of one another; those are only the documents that Sordini is working on at the time, and as bundles of papers are continually being taken away and brought in, and all in great haste, those columns are always falling on the floor, and it's just those perpetual crashes, following fast on one another, that have come to distinguish Sordini's workroom. Yes, Sordini is a worker and he gives the same scrupulous care to the smallest case as to the greatest.'

'Superintendent,' said K., 'you always call my case one of the smallest, and yet it has given hosts of officials a great deal of trouble, and if, perhaps, it was unimportant at the start, yet through the diligence of officials of Sordini's type it has grown into a great affair. Very much against my will, unfortunately, for my ambition doesn't run to seeing columns of documents, all about me, rising and crashing together, but to working quietly at my drawing-board as a humble Land Surveyor.'

'No,' said the Superintendent, 'it's not at all a great affair, in that respect you've no ground for complaint – it's one of the least important among the least important. The importance of a case is not determined by the amount of work it involves, you're far from understanding the authorities if you believe that. But even if it's a question of the amount of work, your case would remain one of the slightest; ordinary cases, those without any so-called errors I mean, provide far more work and far more profitable work as well. Besides you know absolutely nothing yet of the actual work which was caused by your case. I'll tell you about that now. Well, presently Sordini left me out of count, but the clerks arrived, and every day a formal enquiry involving the most prominent members of the community was held in the Herrenhof. The majority stuck by me, only a few held back – the question of a Land Surveyor appeals to peasants – they scented secret plots and injustices and what not, found a leader, no less, and Sordini was forced by their assertions to the conviction that if I had brought the question forward in the Town Council, every voice wouldn't have been against the summoning of a Land Surveyor. So a commonplace – namely, that a Land Surveyor wasn't needed – was turned after all into a doubtful matter at least. A man called Brunswick distinguished himself especially, you don't know him, of course; probably he's not a bad man, only stupid and fanciful, he's a son-in-law of Lasemann's.'

'Of the Master Tanner?' asked K., and he described the full-bearded man whom he had seen at Lasemann's.

'Yes, that's the man,' said the Superintendent.

'I know his wife, too,' said K., a little at random.

'That's possible,' replied the Superintendent briefly.

'She's beautiful,' said K., 'but rather pale and sickly. She comes, of course, from the Castle?' It was half a question.

The Superintendent looked at the clock, poured some medicine into a spoon, and gulped at it hastily.

'You only know the official side of the Castle?' asked K. bluntly.

'That's so,' replied the Superintendent, with an ironical and yet grateful smile, 'and it's the most important. And as for Brunswick; if we could exclude him from the Council we would almost all be glad, and Lasemann not least. But at that time Brunswick gained some influence, he's not an orator of course, but a shouter; but even that can do a lot. And so it came about that I was forced to lay the matter before the Town Council; however, it was Brunswick's only immediate triumph, for of course the Town Council refused by a large majority to hear anything about a Land Surveyor. That, too, was a long time ago, but the whole time since the matter has never been allowed to rest, partly owing to Sordini's conscientiousness, who by the most painful sifting of data sought to fathom the motives of the majority no less than the opposition, partly owing to Brunswick's stupidity and ambition, who had several personal acquaintances among the authorities whom he set working with fresh inventions of his fancy. Sordini, at any rate, didn't let himself be deceived by Brunswick – how could Brunswick deceive Sordini? – but simply to prevent himself from being deceived a new sifting of data was necessary, and long before it was ended Brunswick had already thought out something new; he's very, very versatile, no doubt of it, that goes with his stupidity. And now I come to a peculiar characteristic of our administrative apparatus. Along with its precision it's extremely sensitive as well. When an affair has been weighed for a very long time, it may happen, even before the matter has been fully considered, that suddenly in a flash the decision comes in some unforeseen place that, moreover, can't be found any longer later on, a decision that settles the matter, if in most cases justly, yet all the same arbitrarily. It's as if the administrative apparatus were unable any longer to bear the tension, the year-long irritation caused by the same affair – probably trivial in itself – and had hit upon the decision by itself, without the assistance of the officials. Of course a miracle didn't happen and certainly it was some clerk who hit upon the solution or the unwritten decision, but in any case it couldn't be discovered by us, at least by us here, or even by the Head Bureau, which clerk had decided in this case and on what grounds. The Control Officials only discovered that much later, but we will never learn it; besides by this time it would scarcely interest anybody. Now, as I said, it's just these decisions that are generally excellent. The only annoying thing about them – it's usually the case with such things – is that one learns too late about them and so in the meantime keeps on still passionately canvassing things that were decided long ago. I don't know whether in your case a decision of this kind happened – some people say yes, others no – but if it had happened then the summons would have been sent to you and you would have made the long journey to this place, much time would have passed, and in the meanwhile Sordini would have been working away here all the time on the same case until he was exhausted, Brunswick would have been intriguing, and I would have been plagued by both of them. I only indicate this possibility, but I know the following for a fact: a Control Official discovered meanwhile that a query had gone out from the Department A to the Town Council many years before regarding a Land Surveyor, without having received a reply up till then. A new enquiry was sent to me, and now the whole business was really cleared up. Department A was satisfied with my answer that a Land Surveyor was not needed, and Sordini was forced to recognise that he had not been equal to this case and, innocently it is true, had got through so much nerve-racking work for nothing. If new work hadn't come rushing in as ever from every side, and if your case hadn't been a very unimportant case – one might almost say the least important among the unimportant – we might all of us have breathed freely again, I fancy even Sordini himself; Brunswick was the only one that grumbled, but that was only ridiculous. And now imagine to yourself, Land Surveyor, my dismay when after the fortunate end of the whole business – and since then, too, a great deal of time had passed by – suddenly you appear and it begins to look as if the whole thing must begin all over again. You'll understand of course that I'm firmly resolved, so far as I'm concerned, not to let that happen in any case?'

'Certainly,' said K., 'but I understand better still that a terrible abuse of my case, and probably of the law, is being carried on. As for me, I shall know how to protect myself against it.'

'How will you do it?' asked the Superintendent.

'I'm not at liberty to reveal that,' said K.

'I don't want to press myself upon you,' said the Superintendent, 'only I would like you to reflect that in me you have – I won't say a friend, for we're complete strangers of course – but to some extent a business friend. The only thing I will not agree to is that you should be taken on as Land Surveyor, but in other matters you can draw on me with confidence, frankly to the extent of my power, which isn't great.'

'You always talk of the one thing,' said K., 'that I shan't be taken on as Land Surveyor, but I'm Land Surveyor already, here is Klamm's letter.'

'Klamm's letter,' said the Superintendent. 'That's valuable and worthy of respect on account of Klamm's signature which seems to be genuine, but all the same – yet I won't dare to advance it on my own unsupported word. Mizzi,' he called, and then: 'But what are you doing?'

Mizzi and the assistants, left so long unnoticed, had clearly not found the paper they were looking for, and had then tried to shut everything up again in the cabinet, but on account of the confusion and super-abundance of papers had not succeeded. Then the assistants had hit upon the idea which they were carrying out now. They had laid the cabinet on its back on the floor, crammed all the documents in, then along with Mizzi had knelt on the cabinet door and were trying now in this way to get it shut.

'So the paper hasn't been found,' said the Superintendent. 'A pity, but you know the story already; really we don't need the paper now, besides it will certainly be found sometime yet; probably it's at the teacher's place, there's a great pile of papers there too. But come over here now with the candle, Mizzi, and read this letter for me.'

Mizzi went over and now looked still more grey and insignificant as she sat on the edge of the bed and leaned against the strong, vigorous man, who put his arm round her. In the candlelight only her pinched face was cast into relief, its simple and austere lines softened by nothing but age. Hardly had she glanced at the letter when she clasped her hands lightly and said: 'From Klamm.' Then they read the letter together, whispered for a moment, and at last, just as the assistants gave a 'Hurrah!' for they had finally got the cabinet door shut – which earned them a look of silent gratitude from Mizzi – the Superintendent said:

'Mizzi is quite of my opinion and now I am at liberty to express it. This letter is in no sense an official letter, but only a private letter. That can be clearly seen in the very mode of address: "My dear Sir." Moreover, there isn't a single word in it showing that you've been taken on as Land Surveyor; on the contrary it's all about state service in general, and even that is not absolutely guaranteed, as you know, that is, the task of proving that you are taken on is laid on you. Finally, you are officially and expressly referred to me, the Superintendent, as your immediate superior, for more detailed information, which, indeed, has in great part been given already. To anyone who knows how to read official communications, and consequently knows still better how to read unofficial letters, all this is only too clear. That you, a stranger, don't know it doesn't surprise me. In general the letter means nothing more than that Klamm intends to take a personal interest in you if you should be taken into the state service.'

'Superintendent,' said K., 'you interpret the letter so well that nothing remains of it but a signature on a blank sheet of paper. Don't you see that in doing this you depreciate Klamm's name, which you pretend to respect?'

'You misunderstand me,' said the Superintendent, 'I don't misconstrue the meaning of the letter, my reading of it doesn't disparage it, on the contrary. A private letter from Klamm has naturally far more significance than an official letter, but it hasn't precisely the kind of significance that you attach to it.'

'Do you know Schwarzer?' asked K.

'No,' replied the Superintendent. 'Perhaps you know him, Mizzi? You don't know him either? No, we don't know him.'

'That's strange,' said K., 'he's a son of one of the under-castellans.'

'My dear Land Surveyor,' replied the Superintendent, 'how on earth should I know all the sons of all the under-castellans?'

'Right,' said K., 'then you'll just have to take my word that he is one. I had a sharp encounter with this Schwarzer on the very day of my arrival. Afterwards he made a telephone enquiry of an under-castellan called Fritz and received the information that I was engaged as Land Surveyor. How do you explain that, Superintendent?'

'Very simply,' replied the Superintendent. 'You haven't once up till now come into real contact with our authorities. All those contacts of yours have been illusory, but owing to your ignorance of the circumstances you take them to be real. And as for the telephone. As you see, in my place, though I've certainly enough to do with the authorities, there's no telephone. In inns and suchlike places it may be of real use, as much use say as a penny-in-the-slot musical instrument, but it's nothing more than that. Have you ever telephoned here? Yes? Well, then perhaps you'll understand what I say. In the Castle the telephone works beautifully of course, I've been told it's going there all the time, that naturally speeds up the work a great deal. We can hear this continual telephoning in our telephones down here as a humming and singing, you must have heard it too. Now this humming and singing transmitted by our telephones is the only real and reliable thing you'll hear, everything else is deceptive. There's no fixed connection with the Castle, no central exchange which transmits our calls further. When anybody calls up the Castle from here the instruments in all the subordinate departments ring, or rather they would all ring if practically all the departments – I know it for a certainty – didn't leave their receivers off. Now and then, however, a fatigued official may feel the need of a little distraction, especially in the evenings and at night and may hang the receiver on. Then we get an answer, but an answer of course that's merely a practical joke. And that's very understandable too. For who would take the responsibility of interrupting, in the middle of the night, the extremely important work up there that goes on furiously the whole time, with a message about his own

74

little private troubles? I can't comprehend how even a stranger can imagine that when he calls up Sordini, for example, it's really Sordini that answers. Far more probably it's a little copying clerk from an entirely different department. On the other hand, it may certainly happen once in a blue moon that when one calls up the little copying clerk Sordini will answer himself. Then finally the best thing is to fly from the telephone before the first sound comes through.'

'I didn't know it was like that, certainly,' said K. 'I couldn't know of all these peculiarities, but I didn't put much confidence in those telephone conversations and I was always aware that the only things of real importance were those that happened in the Castle itself.'

'No,' said the Superintendent, holding firmly on to the word, 'these telephone replies certainly have a meaning, why shouldn't they? How could a message given by an official from the Castle be unimportant? As I remarked before apropos Klamm's letter. All these utterances have no official significance; when you attach official significance to them you go astray. On the other hand, their private significance in a friendly or hostile sense is very great, generally greater than an official communication could ever be.'

'Good,' said K. 'Granted that all this is so, I should have lots of good friends in the Castle: looked at rightly the sudden inspiration of that department all these years ago – saying that a Land Surveyor should be asked to come – was an act of friendship towards myself; but then in the sequel one act was followed by another, until at last, on an evil day, I was enticed here and then threatened with being thrown out again.'

'There's a certain amount of truth in your view of the case,' said the Superintendent; 'you're right in thinking that the pronouncements of the Castle are not to be taken literally. But caution is always necessary, not only here, and always the more necessary the more important the pronouncement in question happens to be. But when you went on to talk about being enticed, I ceased to fathom you. If you had followed my explanation more carefully, then you must have seen that the question of your being summoned here is far too difficult to be settled here and now in the course of a short conversation.'

'So the only remaining conclusion,' said K., 'is that everything is very uncertain and insoluble, including my being thrown out.'

'Who would take the risk of throwing you out, Land Surveyor?' asked the Superintendent. 'The very uncertainty about your summons guarantees you the most courteous treatment, only you're too sensitive by all appearances. Nobody keeps you here, but that surely doesn't amount to throwing you out.'

'Oh, Superintendent,' said K., 'now again you're taking far too simple a view of the case. I'll enumerate for your benefit a few of the things that keep me here: the sacrifice I made in leaving my home, the long and difficult journey, the well-grounded hopes I built on my engagement here, my complete lack of means, the impossibility after this of finding some other suitable job at home, and last but not least my fiancée, who lives here.'

'Oh, Frieda!' said the Superintendent without showing any surprise. 'I know. But Frieda would follow you anywhere. As for the rest of what you said, some consideration will be necessary and I'll communicate with the Castle about it. If a decision should be come to, or if it should be necessary first to interrogate you again, I'll send for you. Is that agreeable to you?'

'No, absolutely,' said K. 'I don't want any act of favour from the Castle, but my rights.'

'Mizzi,' the Superintendent said to his wife, who still sat pressed against him, and lost in a day-dream was playing with Klamm's letter, which she had folded into the shape of a little boat – K. snatched it from her in alarm. 'Mizzi, my foot is beginning to throb again, we must renew the compress.'

K. got up. 'Then I'll take my leave,' he said. 'Hm,' said Mizzi, who was already preparing a poultice, 'the last one was drawing too strongly.' K. turned away. At his last words the assistants with their usual misplaced zeal to be useful had thrown open both wings of the door. To protect the sickroom from the strong draught of cold air which was rushing in, K. had to be content with making the Superintendent a hasty bow. Then, pushing the assistants in front of him, he rushed out of the room and quickly closed the door.

VI

BEFORE the inn the landlord was waiting for him. Without being questioned he would not have ventured to address him, accordingly K. asked what he wanted. 'Have you found new lodgings yet?' asked the landlord, looking at the ground. 'You were told to ask by your wife?' replied K., 'you're very much under her influence?' 'No,' said the landlord, 'I didn't ask because of my wife. But she's very bothered and unhappy on your account, can't work, lies in bed and sighs and complains all the time.' 'Shall I go and see her?' asked K. 'I wish you would,' said the landlord. 'I've been to the Superintendent's already to fetch you. I listened at the door but you were talking. I didn't want to disturb you, besides I was anxious about my wife and ran back again; but she wouldn't see me, so there was nothing for it but to wait for you.' 'Then let's go at once,' said K., 'I'll soon reassure her.' 'If you could only manage it,' said the landlord.

They went through the bright kitchen where three or four maids, engaged all in different corners at the work they were happening to be doing, visibly stiffened on seeing K. From the kitchen the sighing of the landlady could already be heard. She lay in a windowless annex separated from the kitchen by thin lath boarding. There was room in it only for a huge family bed and a chest. The bed was so placed that from it one could overlook the whole kitchen and superintend the work. From the kitchen, on the other hand, hardly anything could be seen in the annex. There it was quite dark: only the faint gleam of the purple bed-coverlet could be distinguished. Not until one entered and one's eyes became used to the darkness did one detach particular objects.

'You've come at last,' said the landlady feebly. She was lying stretched out on her back, she breathed with visible difficulty, she had thrown back the feather quilt. In bed she looked much younger than in her clothes, but a nightcap of delicate lacework which she wore, although it was too small and nodded on her head, made her sunk face look pitiable. 'Why should I have come?' asked K. mildly. 'You didn't send for me.' 'You shouldn't have kept me waiting so long,' said the landlady with the capriciousness of an invalid. 'Sit down,' she went on, pointing to the bed, 'and you others go away.' Meantime the maids as well as the assistants had crowded in. 'I'll go too, Gardana,' said the landlord. This was the first time that K. had heard her name. 'Of course,' she replied slowly, and as if she were occupied with other thoughts she added absently: 'Why should you remain any more than the others?' But when they had all retreated to the kitchen – even the assistants this time went at once, besides, a maid was behind them – Gardana was alert enough to grasp that everything she said could be heard in there, for the annex lacked a door, and so she commanded everyone to leave the kitchen as well. It was immediately done.

'Land Surveyor,' said Gardana, 'there's a wrap hanging over there beside the chest, will you please reach me it? I'll lay it over me. I can't bear the feather quilt, my breathing is so bad.' And as K. handed her the wrap, she went on: 'Look, this is a beautiful wrap, isn't it?' To K. it seemed to be an ordinary woollen wrap; he felt it with his fingers again merely out of politeness, but did not reply. 'Yes, it's a beautiful wrap,' said Gardana covering herself up. Now she lay back comfortably, all her pain seemed to have gone, she actually had enough strength to think of the state of her hair which had been disordered by her lying position; she raised herself up for a moment and rearranged her coiffeur a little round the nightcap. Her hair was abundant.

K. became impatient, and began: 'You asked me, madam, whether I had found other lodgings yet.' 'I asked you?' said the landlady, 'no, you're mistaken.' 'Your husband asked me a few minutes ago.' 'That may well be,' said the landlady; 'I'm at variance with him. When I didn't want you here, he kept you here, now that I'm glad to have you here, he wants to drive you away. He's always like that.' 'Have you changed your opinion of me so greatly, then?' asked K. 'In a couple of hours?' 'I haven't changed my opinion,' said the landlady more freely again; 'give me your hand. There, and now promise to be quite frank with me and I'll be the same with you.' 'Right,' said K., 'but who's to begin first?' 'I shall,' said the landlady. She did not give so much the impression of one who wanted to meet K. half-way, as of one who was eager to have the first word.

She drew a photograph from under the pillow and held it out to K. 'Look at that portrait,' she said eagerly. To see it better K. stepped into the kitchen, but even there it was not easy to distinguish anything on the photograph, for it was faded with age, cracked in several places, crumpled, and dirty. 'It isn't in very good condition,' said K. 'Unluckily no,' said the landlady, 'when one carries a thing about with one for years it's bound to be the case. But if you look at it carefully, you'll be able to make everything out, you'll see. But I can help you; tell me what you see, I like to hear anyone talk about the portrait. Well, then?' 'A young man,' said K. 'Right,' said the landlady, 'and what is he doing?' 'It seems to me he's lying on a board stretching himself and yawning.' The landlady laughed. 'Quite wrong,' she said. 'But here's the board and here he is lying on it,' persisted K. on his side. 'But look more carefully,' said the landlady in annoyance, 'is he really lying down?' 'No,' said K. now, 'he's floating, and now I can see it, it's not a board at all, but probably a rope, and the young man is taking a high leap.' 'You see!' replied the landlady triumphantly, 'he's leaping, that's how the official messengers practise. I knew quite well that you would make it out. Can you make out his face, too?' 'I can only make out his face very dimly,' said K., 'he's obviously making a great effort, his mouth is open, his eyes tightly shut and his hair fluttering.' 'Well done,' said the landlady appreciatively, 'nobody who never saw him could have made out more than that. But he was a beautiful young man. I only saw him once for a second and I'll never forget him.' 'Who was he then?' asked K. 'He was the messenger that Klamm sent to call me to him the first time.'

K. could not hear properly, his attention was distracted by the rattling of glass. He immediately discovered the cause of the disturbance. The assistants were standing outside in the yard hopping from one foot to the other in the snow, behaving as if they were glad to see him again; in their joy they pointed each other out to him and kept tapping all the time on the kitchen window. At a threatening gesture from K. they stopped at once, tried to pull one another away, but the one would slip immediately from the grasp of the other and soon they were both back at the window again. K. hurried into the annex where the assistants could not see him from outside and he would not have to see them. But the soft and as it were beseeching tapping on the window-pane followed him there too for a long time.

'The assistants again,' he said apologetically to the landlady and pointed outside. But she paid no attention to him; she had taken the portrait from him, looked at it, smoothed it out, and pushed it again under her pillow. Her movements had become slower, but not with weariness, but with the burden of memory. She had wanted to tell K. the story of her life and had forgotten about him in thinking of the story itself. She was playing with the fringe of her wrap. A little time went by before she looked up, passed her hand over her eyes, and said: 'This wrap was given me by Klamm. And the nightcap, too. The portrait, the wrap, and the nightcap, these are the only three things of his I have as keepsakes. I'm not young like Frieda, I'm not so ambitious as she is, nor so sensitive either, she's very sensitive to put it bluntly, I know how to accommodate myself to life, but one thing I must admit, I couldn't have held out so long here without these three keepsakes. Perhaps these three things seem very trifling to you, but let me tell you, Frieda, who has had relations with Klamm for a long time, doesn't possess a single keepsake from him. I have asked her, she's too fanciful, and too difficult to please besides; I, on the other hand, though I was only three times with Klamm – after that he never asked me to come again, I don't know why – I managed to bring three presents back with me all the same, having a premonition that my time would be short. Of course one must make a point of it. Klamm gives nothing of himself, but if one sees something one likes lying about there, one can get it out of him.'

K. felt uncomfortable listening to these tales, much as they interested him. 'How long ago was all that, then?' he asked with a sigh.

'Over twenty years ago,' replied the landlady, 'considerably over twenty years.'

'So one remains faithful to Klamm as long as that,' said K. 'But are you aware, madam, that these stories give me grave alarm when I think of my future married life?'

The landlady seemed to consider this intrusion of his own affairs unseasonable and gave him an angry sidelook.

'Don't be angry, madam,' said K. 'I've nothing at all to say against Klamm. All the same, by force of circumstances I have come in a sense in contact with Klamm; that can't be gainsaid even by his greatest admirer. Well, then. As a result of that I am forced whenever Klamm is mentioned to think of myself as well, that can't be altered. Besides, madam,' here K. took hold of her reluctant hand, 'reflect how badly our last talk turned out and that this time we want to part in peace.'

'You're right,' said the landlady, bowing her head, 'but spare me. I'm not more touchy than other people; on the contrary, everyone has his sensitive spots, and I have only this one.'

'Unfortunately it happens to be mine too,' said K., 'but I promise to control myself. Now tell me, madam, how I am to put up with my married life in face of this terrible fidelity, granted that Frieda, too, resembles you in that?'

'Terrible fidelity!' repeated the landlady with a growl. 'Is it a question of fidelity? I'm faithful to my husband – but Klamm? Klamm once chose me as his mistress, can I ever lose that honour? And you ask how you are to put up with Frieda? Oh, Land Surveyor, who are you after all that you dare to ask such things?'

'Madam,' said K. warningly.

'I know,' said the landlady, controlling herself, 'but my husband never put such questions. I don't know which to call the unhappier, myself then or Frieda now. Frieda who saucily left Klamm, or myself whom he stopped asking to come. Yet it is probably Frieda, though she hasn't even yet guessed the full extent of her unhappiness, it seems. Still, my thoughts were more exclusively occupied by my unhappiness then, all the same, for I had always to be asking myself one question, and in reality haven't ceased to ask it to this day: Why did this happen? Three times Klamm sent for me, but he never sent a fourth time, no, never a fourth time! What else could I have thought of during those days? What else could I have talked about with my husband, whom I married shortly afterwards? During the day we had no time – we had taken over this inn in a wretched condition and had to struggle to make it respectable – but at night! For years all our nightly talks turned on Klamm and the reason for his changing his mind. And if my husband fell asleep during those talks I woke him and we went on again.'

'Now,' said K., 'if you'll permit me, I'm going to ask a very rude question.'

The landlady remained silent.

'Then I mustn't ask it,' said K. 'Well, that serves my purpose as well.'

'Yes,' replied the landlady, 'that serves your purpose as well, and just that serves it best. You misconstrue everything, even a person's silence. You can't do anything else. I allow you to ask your question.'

'If I misconstrue everything, perhaps I misconstrue my question as well, perhaps it's not so rude after all. I only want to know how you came to meet your husband and how this inn came into your hands.'

The landlady wrinkled her forehead, but said indifferently: 'That's a very simple story. My father was the blacksmith, and Hans, my husband, who was a groom at a big farmer's place, came often to see him. That was just after my last meeting with Klamm. I was very unhappy and really had no right to be so, for everything had gone as it should, and that I wasn't allowed any longer to see Klamm was Klamm's own decision. It was as it should be then, only the grounds for it were obscure. I was entitled to enquire into them, but I had no right to be unhappy; still I was, all the same, couldn't work, and sat in our front garden all day. There Hans saw me, often sat down beside me. I didn't complain to him, but he knew how things were, and as he was a good young man, he wept with me. The wife of the landlord at that time had died and he had consequently to give up business – besides he was already an old man. Well once as he passed our garden and saw us sitting there, he stopped, and without more ado offered us the inn to rent, didn't ask for any money in advance, for he trusted us, and set the rent at a very low figure. I didn't want to be a burden on my father, nothing else mattered to me, and so thinking of the inn and of my new work that might perhaps help me to forget a little, I gave Hans my hand. That's the whole story.'

There was silence for a little, then K. said: 'The behaviour of the landlord was generous, but rash, or had he particular grounds for trusting you both?'

'He knew Hans well,' said the landlady; 'he was Hans's uncle.'

'Well then,' said K., 'Hans's family must have been very anxious to be connected with you?'

'It may be so,' said the landlady, 'I don't know, I've never bothered about it.'

'But it must have been so all the same,' said K., 'seeing that the family was ready to make such a sacrifice and to give the inn into your hands absolutely without security.'

'It wasn't imprudent, as was proved later,' said the landlady. 'I threw myself into the work, I was strong, I was the blacksmith's daughter, I didn't need maid or servant. I was everywhere, in the taproom, in the kitchen, in the stables, in the yard. I cooked so well that I even enticed some of the Herrenhof's customers away. You've never been in the inn yet at lunch-time, you don't know our day customers; at that time there were more of them, many of them have stopped coming since. And the consequence was that we were able not merely to pay the rent regularly, but that after a few years we bought the whole place and to-day it's practically free of debt. The further consequence, I admit, was that I ruined my health, got heart disease, and am now an old woman. Probably you think that I'm much older than Hans, but the fact is that he's only two or three years younger than me and will never grow any older either, for at his work – smoking his pipe, listening to the customers, knocking out his pipe again, and fetching an occasional pot of beer – at that sort of work one doesn't grow old.'

'What you've done has been splendid,' said K. 'I don't doubt that for a moment, but we were speaking of the time before your marriage, and it must have been an extraordinary thing at that stage for Hans's family to press on the marriage – at a money sacrifice, or at least at such a great risk as the handing over of the inn must have been – and without trusting in anything but your powers of work, which besides nobody knew of then, and Hans's powers of work, which everybody must have known beforehand were nil.'

'Oh, well,' said the landlady wearily, 'I know what you're getting at and how wide you are of the mark. Klamm had absolutely nothing to do with the matter. Why should he have concerned himself about me, or better, how could he in any case have concerned himself about me? He knew nothing about me by that time. The fact that he had ceased to summon me was a sign that he had forgotten me. When he stops summoning people, he forgets them completely. I didn't want to talk of this before Frieda. And it's not mere forgetting, it's something more than that. For anybody one has forgotten can come back to one's memory again, of course. With Klamm that's impossible. Anybody that he stops summoning he has forgotten completely, not only as far as the past is concerned, but literally for the future as well. If I try very hard I can of course think myself into your ideas, valid, perhaps, in the very different land you come from. But it's next thing to madness to imagine that Klamm could have given me Hans as a husband simply that I might have no great difficulty in going to him if he should summon me sometime again. Where is the man who could hinder me from running to Klamm if Klamm lifted his little finger? Madness, absolute madness, one begins to feel confused oneself when one plays with such mad ideas.'

'No,' said K., 'I've no intention of getting confused; my thoughts hadn't gone so far as you imagined, though, to tell the truth, they were on that road. For the moment the only thing that surprises me is that Hans's relations expected so much from his marriage and that these expectations were actually fulfilled, at the sacrifice of your sound heart and your health, it is true. The idea that these facts were connected with Klamm occurred to me I admit, but not with the bluntness, or not till now with the bluntness that you give it – apparently with no object but to have a dig at me, because that gives you pleasure. Well, make the most of your pleasure! My idea, however, was this: first of all Klamm was obviously the occasion of your marriage. If it hadn't been for Klamm you wouldn't have been unhappy and wouldn't have been sitting doing nothing in the garden, if it hadn't been for Klamm Hans wouldn't have seen you sitting there, if it hadn't been that you were unhappy a shy man like Hans would never have ventured to speak, if it hadn't been for Klamm Hans would never have found you in tears, if it hadn't been for Klamm the good old uncle would never have seen you sitting there together peacefully, if it hadn't been for Klamm you wouldn't have been indifferent to what life still offered you, and therefore would never have married Hans. Now in all this there's enough of Klamm already, it seems to me. But that's not all. If you hadn't been trying to forget, you certainly wouldn't have overtaxed your strength so much and done so splendidly with the inn. So Klamm was there too. But apart from that Klamm is also the root cause of your illness, for before your marriage your heart was already worn out with your hopeless passion for him. The only question that remains now is, what made Hans's relatives so eager for the marriage? You yourself said just now that to be Klamm's mistress is a distinction that can't be lost, so it may have been that that attracted them. But besides that, I imagine, they had the hope that the lucky star that led you to Klamm – assuming that it was a lucky star, but you maintain that it was – was your star and so would remain constant to you and not leave you quite so quickly and suddenly as Klamm did.'

'Do you mean all this in earnest?' asked the landlady.

'Yes, in earnest,' replied K. immediately, 'only I consider Hans's relations were neither entirely right nor entirely wrong in their hopes, and I think, too, I can see the mistake that they made. In appearance, of course, everything seems to have succeeded. Hans is well provided for, he has a handsome wife, is looked up to, and the inn is free of debt. Yet in reality everything has not succeeded, he would certainly have been much happier with a simple girl who gave him her first love, and if he sometimes stands in the inn there as if lost, as you complain, and because he really feels as if he were lost – without being unhappy over it, I grant you, I know that much about him already – it's just as true that a handsome, intelligent young man like him would be happier with another wife, and by happier I mean more independent, industrious, manly. And you yourself certainly can't be happy, seeing you say you wouldn't be able to go on without these three keepsakes, and your heart is bad, too. Then were Hans's relatives mistaken in their hopes? I don't think so. The blessing was over you, but they didn't know how to bring it down.'

'Then what did they miss doing?' asked the landlady. She was lying outstretched on her back now gazing up at the ceiling.

'To ask Klamm,' said K.

'So we're back at your case again,' said the landlady.

'Or at yours,' said K. 'Our affairs run parallel.'

'What do you want from Klamm?' asked the landlady. She had sat up, had shaken out the pillows so as to lean her back against them, and looked K. full in the eyes. 'I've told you frankly about my experiences, from which you should have been able to learn something. Tell me now as frankly what you want to ask Klamm. I've had great trouble in persuading Frieda to go up to her room and stay there, I was afraid you wouldn't talk freely enough in her presence.'

'I have nothing to hide,' said K. 'But first of all I want to draw your attention to something. Klamm forgets immediately, you say. Now in the first place that seems very improbable to me, and secondly it is undemonstrable, obviously nothing more than legend, thought out moreover by the flapperish minds of those who have been in Klamm's favour. I'm surprised that you believe in such a banal invention.'

'It's no legend,' said the landlady, 'it's much rather the result of general experience.'

'I see, a thing then to be refuted by further experience,' said K. 'Besides there's another distinction still between your case and Frieda's. In Frieda's case it didn't happen that Klamm never summoned her again, on the contrary he summoned her but she didn't obey. It's even possible that he's still waiting for her.'

The landlady remained silent, and only looked K. up and down with a considering stare. At last she said: 'I'll try to listen quietly to what you have to say. Speak frankly and don't spare my feelings. I've only one request. Don't use Klamm's name. Call him "him" or something, but don't mention him by name.'

'Willingly,' replied K., 'but what I want from him is difficult to express. Firstly, I want to see him at close quarters; then I want to hear his voice; then I want to get from him what his attitude is to our marriage. What I shall ask from him after that depends on the outcome of our interview. Lots of things may come up in the course of talking, but still the most important thing for me is to be confronted with him. You see I haven't yet spoken with a real official. That seems to be more difficult to manage than I had thought. But now I'm put under the obligation of speaking to him as a private person, and that, in my opinion, is much easier to bring about. As an official I can only speak to him in his bureau in the Castle, which may be inaccessible, or – and that's questionable, too – in the Herrenhof. But as a private person I can speak to him anywhere, in a house, in the street, wherever I happen to meet him. If I should find the official in front of me, then I would be glad to accost him as well, but that's not my primary object.'

'Right,' said the landlady pressing her face into the pillows as if she were uttering something shameful, 'if by using my influence I can manage to get your request for an interview passed on to Klamm, promise me to do nothing on your own account until the reply comes back.'

'I can't promise that,' said K., 'glad as I would be to fulfil your wishes or your whims. The matter is urgent, you see, especially after the unfortunate outcome of my talk with the Superintendent.'

'That excuse falls to the ground,' said the landlady, 'the Superintendent is a person of no importance. Haven't you found that out? He couldn't remain another day in his post if it weren't for his wife, who runs everything.'

'Mizzi?' asked K. The landlady nodded. 'She was present,' said K. 'Did she express her opinion?' asked the landlady.

'No,' replied K., 'but I didn't get the impression that she could.'

'There,' said the landlady, 'you see how distorted your view of everything here is. In any case: the Superintendent's arrangements for you are of no importance, and I'll talk to his wife when I have time. And if I promise now in addition that Klamm's answer will come in a week at latest, you can't surely have any further grounds for not obliging me.'

'All that is not enough to influence me,' said K. 'My decision is made, and I would try to carry it out even if an unfavourable answer were to come. And seeing that this is my fixed intention, I can't very well ask for an interview beforehand. A thing that would remain a daring attempt, but still an attempt in good faith so long as I didn't ask for an interview, would turn into an open transgression of the law after receiving an unfavourable answer. That frankly would be far worse.'

'Worse?' said the landlady. 'It's a transgression of the law in any case. And now you can do what you like. Reach me over my skirt.'

Without paying any regard to K.'s presence she pulled on her skirt and hurried into the kitchen. For a long time already K. had been hearing noises in the dining-room. There was a tapping on the kitchen-hatch. The assistants had unfastened it and were shouting that they were hungry. Then other faces appeared at it. One could even hear a subdued song being chanted by several voices.

Undeniably K.'s conversation with the landlady had greatly delayed the cooking of the midday meal, it was not ready yet and the customers had assembled. Nevertheless nobody had dared to set foot in the kitchen after the landlady's order. But now when the observers at the hatch reported that the landlady was coming, the maids immediately ran back to the kitchen, and as K. entered the dining-room a surprisingly large company, more than twenty, men and women – all attired in provincial but not rustic clothes – streamed back from the hatch to the tables to make sure of their seats. Only at one little table in the corner was a married couple seated already with a few children. The man, a kindly, blue-eyed person with disordered grey hair and beard, stood bent over the children and with a knife beat time to their singing, which he perpetually strove to soften. Perhaps he was trying to make them forget their hunger by singing. The landlady threw a few indifferent words of apology to her customers, nobody complained of her conduct. She looked round for the landlord, who had fled from the difficulty of the situation, however, long ago. Then she went slowly into the kitchen; she did not take any more notice of K., who hurried to Frieda in her room.

VII

UPSTAIRS K. ran into the teacher. The room was improved almost beyond recognition so well had Frieda set to work. It was well aired, the stove amply stoked, the floor scrubbed, the bed put in order, the maids' filthy pile of things and even their photographs cleared away; the table, which had literally struck one in the eye before with its crust of accumulated dust, was covered with a white embroidered cloth. One was in a position to receive visitors now. K.'s small change of underclothes hanging before the fire – Frieda must have washed them early in the morning – did not spoil the impression much. Frieda and the teacher were sitting at the table, they rose at K.'s entrance. Frieda greeted K. with a kiss, the teacher bowed slightly. Distracted and still agitated by his talk with the landlady, K. began to apologise for not having been able yet to visit the teacher; it was as if he were assuming that the teacher had called on him finally because he was impatient at K.'s absence. On the other hand, the teacher in his precise way only seemed now gradually to remember that sometime or other there had been some mention between K. and himself of a visit. 'You must be, Land Surveyor,' he said slowly, 'the stranger I had a few words with the other day in the church square.' 'I am,' replied K. shortly; the behaviour which he had submitted to when he felt homeless he did not intend to put up with now here in his room. He turned to Frieda and consulted with her about an important visit which he had to pay at once and for which he would need his best clothes. Without further enquiry Frieda called over the assistants, who were already busy examining the new tablecloth, and commanded them to brush K.'s suit and shoes – which he had begun to take off – down in the yard. She herself took a shirt from the line and ran down to the kitchen to iron it.

Now K. was left alone with the teacher, who was seated silently again at the table; K. kept him waiting for a little longer, drew off his shirt and began to wash himself at the tap. Only then, with his back to the teacher, did he ask him the reason for his visit. 'I have come at the instance of the Parish Superintendent,' he said. K. made ready to listen. But as the noise of the water made it difficult to catch what K. said, the teacher had to come nearer and lean against the wall beside him. K. excused his washing and his hurry by the urgency of his coming appointment. The teacher swept aside his excuses, and said: 'You were discourteous to the Parish Superintendent, an old and experienced man who should be treated with respect.' 'Whether I was discourteous or not I can't say,' said K. while he dried himself, 'but that I had other things to think of than polite behaviour is true enough, for my existence is at stake, which is threatened by a scandalous official bureaucracy whose particular failings I needn't mention to you, seeing that you're an acting member of it yourself. Has the Parish Superintendent complained about me?' 'Where's the man that he would need to complain of?' asked the teacher. 'And even if there was anyone, do you think he would ever do it? I've only made out at his dictation a short protocol on your interview, and that has shown me clearly enough how kind the Superintendent was and what your answers were like.'

While K. was looking for his comb, which Frieda must have cleared away somewhere, he said: 'What? A protocol? Drawn up afterwards in my absence by someone who wasn't at the interview at all? That's not bad. And why on earth a protocol? Was it an official interview, then?' 'No,' replied the teacher, 'a semi-official one, the protocol too was only semi-official. It was merely drawn up because with us everything must be done in strict order. In any case it's finished now, and it doesn't better your credit.' K., who had at last found the comb, which had been tucked into the bed, said more calmly: 'Well then, it's finished. Have you come to tell me that?' 'No,' said the teacher, 'but I'm not a machine and I had to give you my opinion. My instructions are only another proof of the Superintendent's kindness; I want to emphasise that his kindness in this instance is incomprehensible to me, and that I only carry out his instructions because it's my duty and out of respect to the Superintendent.' Washed and combed, K. now sat down at the table to wait for his shirt and clothes; he was not very curious to know the message that the teacher had brought, he was influenced besides by the landlady's low opinion of the Superintendent. 'It must be after twelve already, surely?' he said, thinking of the distance he had to walk; then he remembered himself, and said: 'You want to give me some message from the Superintendent.' 'Well, yes,' said the teacher, shrugging his shoulders as if he were discarding all responsibility. 'The Superintendent is afraid that, if the decision in your case takes too long, you might do something rash on your own account. For my own part I don't know why he should fear that – my own opinion is that you should just be allowed to do what you like. We aren't your guardian angels and we're not obliged to run after you in all your doings. Well and good. The Superintendent, however, is of a different opinion. He can't of course hasten the decision itself, which is a matter for the authorities. But in his own sphere of jurisdiction he wants to provide a temporary and truly generous settlement; it simply lies with you to accept it. He offers you provisionally the post of school janitor.' At first K. thought very little of the offer made him, but the fact that an offer had been made seemed to him not without significance. It seemed to point to the fact that in the Superintendent's opinion he was in a position to look after himself, to carry out projects against which the Town Council itself was preparing certain counter measures. And how seriously they were taking the matter! The teacher, who had already been waiting for a while, and who before that, moreover, had made out the protocol, must of course have been told to run here by the Superintendent. When the teacher saw that he had made K. reflect at last, he went on: 'I put my objections. I pointed out that up till now a janitor hadn't been found necessary; the churchwarden's wife cleared up the place from time to time, and Fräulein Gisa, the second teacher, overlooked the matter. I had trouble enough with the children, I didn't want to be bothered by a janitor as well. The Superintendent pointed out that all the same the school was very dirty. I replied, keeping to the truth, that it wasn't so very bad. And, I went on, would it be any better if we took on this man as janitor? Most certainly not. Apart from the fact that he didn't know the work, there were only two big classrooms in the school, and no additional room; so the janitor and his family would have to live, sleep, perhaps even cook in one of the classrooms, which could hardly make for greater cleanliness. But the Superintendent laid stress on the fact that this post would keep you out of difficulties, and that consequently you would do your utmost to fill it creditably; he suggested further, that along with you we would obtain the services of your wife and your assistants, so that the school should be kept in first-rate order, and not only it, but the school-garden as well. I easily proved that this would not hold water. At last the Superintendent couldn't bring forward a single argument in your favour; he laughed and merely said that you were a Land Surveyor after all and so should be able to lay out the vegetable beds beautifully. Well, against a joke there's no argument, and so I came to you with the proposal.' 'You've taken your trouble for nothing, teacher,' said K. 'I have no intention of accepting the post.' 'Splendid!' said the teacher. 'Splendid! You decline quite unconditionally,' and he took his hat, bowed, and went.

Immediately afterwards Frieda came rushing up the stairs with an excited face, the shirt still unironed in her hand; she did not reply to K.'s enquiries. To distract her he told her about the teacher and the offer; she had hardly heard it when she flung the shirt on the bed and ran out again. She soon came back, but with the teacher, who looked annoyed and entered without any greeting. Frieda begged him to have a little patience – obviously she had done that already several times on the way up – then drew K. through a side door of which he had never suspected the existence, on to the neighbouring loft, and then at last, out of breath with excitement, told what had happened to her. Enraged that Frieda had humbled herself by making an avowal to K., and – what was still worse – had yielded to him merely to secure him an interview with Klamm, and after all had gained nothing but, so she alleged, cold and moreover insincere professions, the landlady was resolved to keep K. no longer in her house; if he had connections with the Castle, then he should take advantage of them at once, for he must leave the house that very day, that very minute, and she would only take him back again at the express order

94

and command of the authorities; but she hoped it would not come to that, for she too had connections with the Castle and would know how to make use of them. Besides he was only in the inn because of the landlord's negligence, and moreover he was not in a state of destitution, for this very morning he had boasted of a roof which was always free to him for the night. Frieda of course was to remain; if Frieda wanted to go with K. she, the landlady, would be very sorry; down in the kitchen she had sunk into a chair by the fire and cried at the mere thought of it. The poor, sick woman; but how could she behave otherwise, now that, in her imagination at any rate, it was a matter involving the honour of Klamm's keepsakes? That was how matters stood with the landlady. Frieda of course would follow him, K., wherever he wanted to go. Yet the position of both of them was very bad in any case, just for that reason she had greeted the teacher's offer with such joy; even if it was not a suitable post for K., yet it was – that was expressly insisted on – only a temporary post; one would gain a little time and would easily find other chances, even if the final decision should turn out to be unfavourable. 'If it comes to the worst,' cried Frieda at last, falling on K.'s neck, 'we'll go away, what is there in the village to keep us? But for the time being, darling, we'll accept the offer, won't we? I've fetched the teacher back again, you've only to say to him "Done," that's all, and we'll move over to the school.'

'It's a great nuisance,' said K. without quite meaning it, for he was not much concerned about his lodgings, and in his underclothes he was shivering up here in the loft, which without wall or window on two sides was swept by a cold draught, 'you've arranged the room so comfortably and now we must leave it. I would take up the post very, very unwillingly; the few snubs I've already had from the teacher have been painful enough, and now he's to become my superior, no less. If we could only stay here a little while longer, perhaps my position might change for the better this very afternoon. If you would only remain here at least, we could wait on for a little and give the teacher a non-committal answer. As for me, if it came to the worst, I could really always find a lodging for the night with Bar –' Frieda stopped him by putting her hand over his mouth. 'No, not that,' she said beseechingly, 'please never mention that again. In everything else I'll obey you. If you like I'll stay on here by myself, sad as it will be for me. If you like, we'll refuse the offer, wrong as that would seem to me. For look here, if you find another possibility, even this after-noon, why, it's obvious that we would throw up the post in the school at once; nobody would object. And as for your humiliation in front of the teacher, let me see to it that there will be none; I'll speak to him myself, you'll only have to be there and needn't say anything, and later, too, it will be just the same, you'll never be made to speak to him if you don't want to, I – I alone – will be his subordinate in reality, and I won't be even that, for I know his weak points. So you see nothing will be lost if we take on the post, and a great deal if we refuse it; above all, if you don't wring something out of the Castle this very day, you'll never manage to find, even for yourself, anywhere at all in the village to spend the night in, anywhere, that is, of which I needn't be ashamed as your future wife. And if you don't manage to find a roof for the night, do you really expect me to sleep here in my warm room, while I know that you are wandering about out there in the dark and cold?' K., who had been trying to warm himself all this time by clapping his chest with his arms like a carter, said: 'Then there's nothing left but to accept; come along!'

When they returned to the room he went straight over to the fire; he paid no attention to the teacher; the latter, sit-ting at the table, drew out his watch and said: 'It's getting late.' 'I know, but we're completely agreed at last,' said Frieda, 'we accept the post.' 'Good,' said the teacher, 'but the post is offered to the Land Surveyor; he must say the word himself.' Frieda came to K.'s help. 'Really,' she said, 'he accepts the post. Don't you, K.?' So K. could confine his declaration to a simple 'Yes,' which was not even directed to the teacher but to Frieda. 'Then,' said the teacher, 'the only thing that remains for me is to acquaint you with your duties, so that in that respect we can understand each other once and for all. You have, Land Surveyor, to clean and heat both classrooms daily, to make any small repairs in the house, further, to look after the class and gymnastic apparatus personally, to keep the garden path free of snow, run messages for me and the lady teacher, and look after all the work in the garden in the warmer seasons of the year. In return for that you have the right to live in whichever one of the classrooms you like; but, when both rooms are not being used at the same time for teaching, and you are in the room that is needed, you must of course move to the other room. You mustn't do any cooking in the school; in return you and your dependants will be given your meals here in the inn at the cost of the Town Council. That you must behave in a manner consonant with the dignity of the school, and in particular that the children during school hours must never be allowed to witness any unedifying matrimonial scenes, I mention only in passing, for as an educated man you must of course know that. In connection with that I want to say further that we must insist on your relations with Fräulein Frieda being legitimised at the earliest possible moment. About all this and a few other trifling matters, an agreement will be made out, which as soon as you move over to the school must be signed by you.' To K. all this seemed of no importance, as if it did not concern him or at any rate did not bind him, but the self-importance of the teacher irritated him, and he said carelessly: 'I know, they're the usual duties.' To wipe away the impression created by this remark Frieda enquired about the salary. 'Whether there will be any salary,' said the teacher, 'will only be considered after a month's trial service.' 'But that is hard on us,' said Frieda. 'We'll have to marry on practically nothing, and have nothing to set up house on. Couldn't you make a representation to the Town

97

Council, sir, to give us a small salary at the start? Couldn't you advise that?' 'No,' replied the teacher, who continued to direct his words to K. 'Representations to the Town Council will only be made if I give the word, and I shan't give it. The post has only been given to you as a personal favour, and one can't stretch a favour too far, if one has any consciousness of one's obvious responsibilities.' Now K. intervened at last, almost against his will. 'As for the favour, teacher,' he said, 'it seems to me that you're mistaken. The favour is perhaps rather on my side.' 'No,' replied the teacher, smiling now that he had compelled K. to speak at last. 'I'm completely grounded on that point. Our need for a janitor is just about as urgent as our need for a Land Surveyor. Janitor, Land Surveyor, in both cases it's a burden on our shoulders. I'll still have a lot of trouble thinking out how I'm to justify the post to the Town Council. The best thing and the most honest thing would be to throw the proposal on the table and not justify anything.' 'That's just what I meant,' replied K., 'you must take me on against your will. Although it causes you grave perturbation, you must take me on. But when one is compelled to take someone else on, and this someone else allows himself to be taken on, then he is the one who grants the favour.' 'Strange!' said the teacher. 'What is it that compels us to take you on? The only thing that compels us is the Superintendent's kind heart, his too kind heart. I see, Land Surveyor, that you'll have to rid yourself of a great many illusions, before you can become a serviceable janitor. And remarks such as these hardly produce the right atmosphere for the granting of an eventual salary. I notice, too, with regret that your attitude will give me a great deal of trouble yet; all this time – I've seen it with my own eyes and yet can scarcely believe it – you've been talking to me in your shirt and drawers.' 'Quite so,' exclaimed K. with a laugh, and he clapped his hands. 'These terrible assistants, where have they been all this time?' Frieda hurried to the door; the teacher, who noticed that K. was no longer to be drawn into conversation, asked her when she would move into the school. 'To-day,' said Frieda. 'Then tomorrow I'll come to inspect matters,' said the teacher, waved a good-bye and made to go out through the door, which Frieda had opened for herself, but ran into the maids, who already were arriving with their things to take possession of the room again; and he, who made way for nobody, had to slip between them: Frieda followed him. 'You're surely in a hurry,' said K., who this time was very pleased with the maids; 'had you to push your way in while we're still here?' They did not answer, only twisted their bundles in embarrassment, from which K. saw the well-known filthy rags projecting. 'So you've never washed your things yet,' said K. It was not said maliciously, but actually with a certain indulgence. They noticed it, opened their hard mouths in concert, showed their beautiful animal-like teeth and laughed noiselessly. 'Come along,' said K., 'put your things down, it's your room after all.' As they still hesitated, however – the room must have seemed to them all too well transformed – K. took one of them by the arm to lead her forward. But he let her go at once, so astonished was the gaze of both, which, after a brief glance between them, was now turned unflinchingly on K. 'But now you've stared at me long enough,' he said, repelling a vague, unpleasant sensation, and he took up his clothes and boots, which Frieda, timidly followed by the assistants, had just brought, and drew them on. The patience which Frieda had with the assistants, always incomprehensible to him, now struck him again. After a long search she had found them below peacefully eating their lunch, the untouched clothes which they should have been brushing in the yard crumpled in their laps; then she had had to brush everything herself, and yet she, who knew how to keep the common people in their places, had not even scolded them, and instead spoke in their presence of their grave negligence as if it were a trifling peccadillo, and even slapped one of them lightly, almost caressingly, on the cheek. Presently K. would have to talk to her about this.

But now it was high time to be gone. 'The assistants will stay here to help you with the removing,' he said. They were not in the least pleased with this arrangement; happy and full, they would have been glad of a little exercise. Only when Frieda said, 'Certainly, you stay here,' did they yield. 'Do you know where I'm going?' asked K. 'Yes,' replied Frieda. 'And you don't want to hold me back any longer?' asked K. 'You'll find obstacles enough,' she replied, 'what does anything I say matter in comparison!' She kissed K. good-bye, and as he had had nothing at lunch-time, gave him a little packet of bread and sausage which she had brought for him from downstairs, reminded him that he must not return here again but to the school, and accompanied him, with her hand on his shoulder, to the door.

VIII

AT first K. was glad to have escaped from the crush of the maids and the assistants in the warm room. It was freezing a little, the snow was firmer, the going easier. But already darkness was actually beginning to fall, and he hastened his steps.

The Castle, whose contours were already beginning to dissolve, lay silent as ever; never yet had K. seen there the slightest sign of life – perhaps it was quite impossible to recognise anything at that distance, and yet the eye demanded it and could not endure that stillness. When K. looked at the Castle, often it seemed to him as if he were observing someone who sat quietly there in front of him gazing, not lost in thought and so oblivious of everything, but free and untroubled, as if he were alone with nobody to observe him, and yet must notice that he was observed, and all the same remained with his calm not even slightly disturbed; and really – one did not know whether it was cause or effect – the gaze of the observer could not remain concentrated there, but slid away. This impression to-day was strengthened still further by the early dusk; the longer he looked, the less he could make out and the deeper everything was lost in the twilight.

Just as K. reached the Herrenhof, which was still unlighted, a window was opened in the first storey, and a stout, smooth-shaven young man in a fur coat leaned out and then remained at the window. He did not seem to make the slightest response to K.'s greeting. Neither in the hall nor in the taproom did K. meet anybody; the smell of stale beer was still worse than last time; such a state of things was never allowed even in the inn by the bridge. K. went straight over to the door through which he had observed Klamm, and lifted the latch cautiously, but the door was barred; then he felt for the place where the peephole was, but the pin apparently was fitted so well that he could not find the place, so he struck a match. He was startled by a cry. In the corner between the door and the till, near the fire, a young girl was crouching and staring at him in the flare of the match, with partially opened sleep-drunken eyes. She was evidently Frieda's successor. She soon collected herself and switched on the electric light; her expression was cross, then she recognised K. 'Ah, the Land Surveyor,' she said smiling, held out her hand and introduced herself. 'My name is Pepi.' She was small, red-cheeked, plump; her opulent reddish golden hair was twisted into a strong plait, yet some of it escaped and curled round her temples; she was wearing a dress of grey shimmering material, falling in straight lines, which did not suit her in the least; at the foot it was drawn together by a childishly clumsy silken band with tassels falling from it, which impeded her movements. She enquired after Frieda and asked whether she would come back soon. It was a question which verged on insolence. 'As soon as Frieda went away,' she said next, 'I was called here urgently because they couldn't find anybody suitable at the moment; I've been a chambermaid till now, but this isn't a change for the better. There's lots of evening and night work in this job, it's very tiring, I don't think I'll be able to stand it. I'm not surprised that Frieda threw it up.' 'Frieda was very happy here,' said K., to make her aware definitely of the difference between Frieda and herself, which she did not seem to appreciate. 'Don't you believe her,' said Pepi. 'Frieda can keep a straight face better than other people can. She doesn't admit what she doesn't want to admit, and so nobody noticed that she had anything to admit. I've been in service here with her several years already. We've slept together all that time in the same bed, yet I'm not intimate with her, and by now I'm quite out of her thoughts, that's certain. Perhaps her only friend is the old landlady of the Bridge Inn, and that tells a story too.' 'Frieda is my fiancée,' said K., searching at the same time for the peephole in the door. 'I know,' said Pepi, 'that's just the reason why I've told you. Otherwise it wouldn't have any interest for you.'

'I understand,' said K. 'You mean that I should be proud to have won such a reticent girl?' 'That's so,' said she, laughing triumphantly, as if she had established a secret understanding with K. regarding Frieda.

But it was not her actual words that troubled K. and deflected him for a little from his search, but rather her appearance and her presence in this place. Certainly she was much younger than Frieda, almost a child still, and her clothes were ludicrous; she had obviously dressed in accordance with the exaggerated notions which she had of the importance of a barmaid's position. And these notions were right enough in their way in her, for this position of which she was still incapable had come to her unearned and unexpectedly, and only for the time being; not even the leather reticule which Frieda always wore on her belt had been entrusted to her. And her ostensible dissatisfaction with the position was nothing but showing off. And yet, in spite of her childish mind, she too, apparently, had connections with the Castle; if she was not lying, she had been a chambermaid; without being aware of what she possessed she slept through the days here, and though if he took this tiny, plump, slightly round-backed creature in his arms he could not extort from her what she possessed, yet that could bring him in contact with it and inspirit him for his difficult task. Then could her case now be much the same as Frieda's? Oh, no, it was different. One had only to think of Frieda's look to know that. K. would never have touched Pepi. All the same he had to lower his eyes for a little now, so greedily was he staring at her.

'It's against orders for the light to be on,' said Pepi, switching it off again. 'I only turned it on because you gave me such a fright. What do you want here really? Did Frieda forget anything?' 'Yes,' said K., pointing to the door, 'a table-cover, a white embroidered table-cover, here in the next room.' 'Yes, her table-cover,' said Pepi. 'I remember it, a pretty piece of work. I helped with it myself, but it can hardly be in that room.' 'Frieda thinks it is. Who lives in it, then?' asked K. 'Nobody,' said Pepi, 'it's the gentlemen's room; the gentlemen eat and drink there; that is, it's reserved for that, but most of them remain upstairs in their rooms.' 'If I knew,' said K., 'that nobody was in there just now, I would like very much to go in and have a look for the table-cover. But one can't be certain; Klamm, for instance, is often in the habit of sitting there.' 'Klamm is certainly not there now,' said Pepi. 'He's making ready to leave this minute, the sledge is waiting for him in the yard.'

Without a word of explanation K. left the taproom at once; when he reached the hall he returned, instead of to the door, to the interior of the house, and in a few steps reached the courtyard. How still and lovely it was here! A four-square yard, bordered on three sides by the house buildings, and towards the street – a sidestreet which K. did not know – by a high white wall with a huge, heavy gate, open now. Here where the court was, the house seemed stiller than at the front; at any rate the whole first storey jutted out and had a more impressive appearance, for it was encircled by a wooden gallery closed in except for one tiny slit for looking through. At the opposite side from K. and on the ground floor, but in the corner where the opposite wing of the house joined the main building, there was an entrance to the house, open, and without a door. Before it was standing a dark, closed sledge to which a pair of horses was yoked. Except for the coachman, whom at that distance and in the falling twilight K. guessed at rather than recognised, nobody was to be seen.

Looking about him cautiously, his hands in his pockets, K. slowly coasted round two sides of the yard until he reached the sledge. The coachman – one of the peasants who had been the other night in the taproom – smart in his fur coat, watched K. approaching non-committally, much as one follows the movements of a cat. Even when K. was standing beside him and had greeted him, and the horses were becoming a little restive at seeing a man looming out of the dusk, he remained completely detached. That exactly suited K.'s purpose. Leaning against the wall of the house he took out his lunch, thought gratefully of Frieda and her solicitous provision for him, and meanwhile peered into the house. A very angular and broken stair led downwards and was crossed down below by a low but apparently deep passage; everything was clean and whitewashed, sharply and distinctly defined.

The wait lasted longer than K. had expected. Long ago he had finished his meal, he was getting chilled, the twilight had changed into complete darkness, and still Klamm had not arrived. 'It might be a long time yet,' said a rough voice suddenly, so near to him that K. started. It was the coachman, who, as if wakening up, stretched himself and yawned loudly. 'What might be a long time yet?' asked K., not ungrateful at being disturbed, for the perpetual silence and tension had already become a burden. 'Before you go away,' said the coachman. K. did not understand him, but did not ask further; he thought that would be the best means of making the insolent fellow speak. Not to answer here in this darkness was almost a challenge. And actually the coachman asked, after a pause: 'Would you like some brandy?' 'Yes,' said K. without thinking, tempted only too keenly by the offer, for he was freezing. 'Then open the door of the sledge,' said the coachman; 'in the side pocket there are some flasks, take one and have a drink and then hand it up to me. With this fur coat it's difficult for me to get down.' K. was annoyed at being ordered about, but seeing that he had struck up with the coachman he obeyed, even at the possible risk of being surprised by Klamm in the sledge. He opened the wide door and could without more ado have drawn a flask out of the side pocket which was fastened to the inside of the door; but now that it was open he felt an impulse which he could not withstand to go inside the sledge; all he wanted was to sit there for a minute. He slipped inside. The warmth within the sledge was extraordinary, and it remained although the door, which K. did not dare to close, was wide open. One could not tell whether it was a seat one was sitting on, so completely was one surrounded by blankets, cushions, and furs; one could turn and stretch on every side, and always one sank into softness and warmth. His arms spread out, his head supported on pillows which always seemed to be there, K. gazed out of the sledge into the dark house. Why was Klamm such a long time in coming? As if stupefied by the warmth after his long wait in the snow, K. began to wish that Klamm would come soon. The thought that he would much rather not be seen by Klamm in his present position touched him only vaguely as a faint disturbance of his comfort. He was supported in this obliviousness by the behaviour of the coachman, who certainly knew that he was in the sledge and yet let him stay there without once demanding the brandy. That was very considerate, but still K. wanted to oblige him. Slowly, without altering his position, he reached out his hand to the side-pocket. But not the one in the open door, but the one behind him in the closed door; after all, it didn't matter, there were flasks in that one too. He pulled one out, unscrewed the stopper, and smelt; involuntarily he smiled, the perfume was so sweet, so caressing, like praise and good words from someone whom one likes very much, yet one does not know clearly what they are for and has no desire to know, and is simply happy in the knowledge that it is one's friend who is saying them. 'Can this be brandy?' K. asked himself doubtfully and took a taste out of curiosity. Yes, strangely enough it was brandy, and burned and warmed him. How wonderfully it was transformed in drinking out of something which seemed hardly more than a sweet perfume into a drink fit for a coachman! 'Can it be?' K. asked himself as if self-reproachfully, and took another sip.

Then – as K. was just in the middle of a long swig – everything became bright, the electric lights blazed inside on the stairs, in the passages, in the entrance hall, outside above the door. Steps could be heard coming down the stairs, the flask fell from K.'s hand, the brandy was spilt over a rug, K. sprang out of the sledge, he had just time to slam the door to, which made a loud noise, when a gentleman came slowly out of the house. The only consolation that remained was that it was not Klamm, or was not that rather a pity? It was the gentleman whom K. had already seen at the window on the first floor. A young man, very good-looking, pink and white, but very serious. K., too, looked at him gravely, but his gravity was on his own account. Really he would have done better to have sent his assistants here, they couldn't have behaved more foolishly than he had done. The gentleman still regarded him in silence, as if he had not enough breath in his overcharged bosom for what has to be said. 'This is unheard of,' he said at last, pushing his hat a little back on his forehead. What next? The gentleman knew nothing apparently of K.'s stay in the sledge, and yet found something that was unheard of? Perhaps that K. had pushed his way in as far as the courtyard? 'How do you come to be here?' the gentleman asked next, more softly now, breathing freely again, resigning himself to the inevitable. What questions to ask! And what could one answer? Was K. to admit simply and flatly to this man that his attempt, begun with so many hopes, had failed? Instead of replying, K. turned to the sledge, opened the door and retrieved his cap, which he had forgotten there. He noticed with discomfort that the brandy was dripping from the footboard.

Then he turned again to the gentleman, to show him that he had been in the sledge gave him no more compunction now, besides that wasn't the worst of it; when he was questioned, but only then, he would divulge the fact that the coachman himself had at least asked him to open the door of the sledge. But the real calamity was that the gentleman had surprised him, that there had not been enough time left to hide from him so as afterwards to wait in peace for Klamm, or rather that he had not had enough presence of mind to remain in the sledge, close the door and wait there among the rugs for Klamm, or at least to stay there as long as this man was about. True, he couldn't know of course whether it might not be Klamm himself who was coming, in which case it would naturally have been much better to accost him outside the sledge. Yes, there had been many things here for thought, but now there was none, for this was the end.

'Come with me,' said the gentleman, not really as a command, for the command lay not in the words, but in a slight, studiedly indifferent gesture of the hand which accompanied them. 'I'm waiting here for somebody,' said K., no longer in the hope of any success, but simply on principle. 'Come,' said the gentleman once more quite imperturbably, as if he wanted to show that he had never doubted that K. was waiting for somebody. 'But then I would miss the person I'm waiting for,' said K. with an emphatic nod of his head. In spite of everything that had happened he had the feeling that what he had achieved thus far was something gained, which it was true he only held now in seeming, but which he must not relinquish all the same merely on account of a polite command. 'You'll miss him in any case, whether you go or stay,' said the gentleman, expressing himself bluntly, but showing an unexpected consideration for K.'s line of thought. 'Then I would rather wait for him and miss him,' said K. defiantly; he would certainly not be driven away from here by the mere talk of this young man. Thereupon with his head thrown back and a supercilious look on his face the gentleman closed his eyes for a few minutes, as if he wanted to turn from K.'s senseless stupidity to his own sound reason again, ran the tip of his tongue round his slightly parted lips, and said at last to the coachman: 'Unyoke the horses.'

Obedient to the gentleman, but with a furious side-glance at K., the coachman had now to get down in spite of his fur coat, and began very hesitatingly – as if he did not so much expect a counter-order from the gentleman as a sensible remark from K. – to back the horses and the sledge closer to the side wing, in which apparently, behind a big door, was the shed where the vehicles were kept. K. saw himself deserted, the sledge was disappearing in one direction, in the other, by the way he had come himself, the gentleman was receding, both it was true very slowly, as if they wanted to show K. that it was still in his power to call them back.

Perhaps he had this power, but it would have availed him nothing; to call the sledge back would be to drive himself away. So he remained standing as one who held the field, but it was a victory which gave him no joy. Alternately he looked at the backs of the gentleman and the coachman. The gentleman had already reached the door through which K. had first come into the courtyard; yet once more he looked back, K. fancied he saw him shaking his head over such obstinacy, then with a short, decisive, final movement he turned away and stepped into the hall, where he immediately vanished. The coachman remained for a while still in the courtyard, he had a great deal of work with the sledge, he had to open the heavy door of the shed, back the sledge into its place, unyoke the horses, lead them to their stalls; all this he did gravely, with concentration, evidently without any hope of starting soon again, and this silent absorption which did not spare a single side-glance for K. seemed to the latter a far heavier reproach than the behaviour of the gentleman. And when now, after finishing his work in the shed, the coachman went across the courtyard in his slow, rolling walk, closed the huge gate and then returned, all very slowly, while he literally looked at nothing but his own footprints in the snow – and finally shut himself into the shed; and now as all the electric lights went out too – for whom should they remain on? – and only up above the slit in the wooden gallery still remained bright, holding one's wandering gaze for a little, it seemed to K. as if at last those people had broken off all relations with him, and as if now in reality he were freer than he had ever been, and at liberty to wait here in this place usually forbidden to him as long as he desired, and had won a freedom such as hardly anybody else had ever succeeded in winning, and as if nobody could dare to touch him or drive him away, or even speak to him; but – this conviction was at least equally strong – as if at the same time there was nothing more senseless, nothing more hopeless, than this freedom, this waiting, this inviolability.

IX

AND he tore himself free and went back into the house – this time not along the wall but straight through the snow – and met the landlord in the hall, who greeted him in silence and pointed towards the door of the taproom. K. followed the hint, for he was shivering and wanted to see human faces; but he was greatly disappointed when he saw there, sitting at a little table – which must have been specially set out, for usually the customers put up with upturned barrels – the young gentleman, and standing before him – an unwelcome sight for K. – the landlady from the Bridge Inn. Pepi, proud, her head thrown back and a fixed smile on her face, conscious of her incontestable dignity, her plait nodding with every movement, hurried to and fro, fetching beer and then pen and ink, for the gentleman had already spread out papers in front of him, was comparing dates which he looked up now in this paper, then again in a paper at the other end of the table, and was preparing to write. From her full height the landlady silently overlooked the gentleman and the papers, her lips pursed a little as if musing; it was as if she had already said everything necessary and it had been well received. 'The Land Surveyor at last,' said the gentleman at K.'s entrance, looking up briefly, then burying himself again in his papers. The landlady, too, only gave K. an indifferent and not in the least surprised glance. But Pepi actually seemed to notice K. for the first time when he went up to the bar and ordered a brandy.

K. leaned there, his hands pressed to his eyes, oblivious of everything. Then he took a sip of the brandy and pushed it back, saying it was undrinkable. 'All the gentlemen drink it,' replied Pepi curtly, poured out the remainder, washed the glass and set it on the rack. 'The gentlemen have better stuff as well,' said K. 'It's possible,' replied Pepi, 'but I haven't,' and with that she was finished with K. and once more at the gentleman's service, who, however, was in need of nothing, and behind whom she only kept walking to and fro in circles, making respectful attempts to catch a glimpse of the papers over his shoulder; but that was only her senseless curiosity and self-importance, which the landlady, too, reprehended with knitted brows.

Then suddenly the landlady's attention was distracted, she stared, listening intently, into vacancy. K. turned round, he could not hear anything in particular, nor did the others seem to hear anything; but the landlady ran on tiptoe and taking large steps to the door which led to the courtyard, peered through the keyhole, turned then to the others with wide, staring eyes and flushed cheeks, signed to them with her finger to come near, and now they peered through the keyhole by turns; the landlady had, of course,

the lion's share, but Pepi, too, was considered; the gentleman was on the whole the most indifferent of the three.
Pepi and the gentleman came away soon, but the landlady
kept on peering anxiously, bent double, almost kneeling;
one had almost the feeling that she was only imploring the
keyhole now to let her through, for there had certainly been
nothing more to see for a long time. When at last she got
up, passed her hand over her face, arranged her hair, took a
deep breath, and now at last seemed to be trying with
reluctance to accustom her eyes again to the room and the
people in it, K. said, not so much to get his suspicions
confirmed, as to forestall the announcement, so open to
attack did he feel now: 'Has Klamm gone already then?'
The landlady walked past him in silence, but the gentleman
answered from his table: 'Yes, of course. As soon as you
gave up your sentry go, Klamm was able to leave. But it's
strange how sensitive he is. Did you notice, landlady, how
uneasily Klamm looked round him?' The landlady did not
appear to have noticed it, but the gentleman went on: 'Well,
fortunately there was nothing more to be seen, the coachman had effaced even the footprints in the snow.' 'The
landlady didn't notice anything,' said K., but he said it
without conviction, merely provoked by the gentleman's
assertion, which was uttered in such a final and unanswer-
able tone. 'Perhaps I wasn't at the keyhole just then,' said
the landlady presently, to back up the gentleman, but then
she felt compelled to give Klamm his due as well, and
added: 'All the same, I can't believe in this terrible sensitiveness of Klamm. We are anxious about him and try to
guard him, and so go on to infer that he's terribly sensitive.
That's as it should be and it's certainly Klamm's will. But
how it is in reality we don't know. Certainly, Klamm will
never speak to anybody that he doesn't want to speak to, no
matter how much trouble this anybody may take, and no
matter how insufferably forward he may be; but that fact
alone, that Klamm will never speak to him, never allow him
to come into his presence, is enough in itself: why after all

should it follow that he isn't able to endure seeing this anybody? At any rate, it can't be proved, seeing that it will never come to the test.' The gentleman nodded eagerly. 'That is essentially my opinion too, of course,' he said, 'if I expressed myself a little differently, it was to make myself comprehensible to the Land Surveyor. All the same it's a fact that when Klamm stepped out of the doorway he looked round him several times.' 'Perhaps he was looking for me,' said K. 'Possibly,' said the gentleman. 'I hadn't thought of that.' They all laughed, Pepi, who hardly understood anything that was being said, loudest of all.

'Seeing we're all so happy here now,' the gentleman went on, 'I want to beg you very seriously, Land Surveyor, to enable me to complete my papers by answering a few questions.' 'There's a great deal of writing there,' said K. glancing at the papers from where he was standing. 'Yes, a wretched bore,' said the gentleman laughing again, 'but perhaps you don't know yet who I am. I'm Momus, Klamm's village secretary.' At these words seriousness descended on the room; although the landlady and Pepi knew quite well who the gentleman was, yet they seemed staggered by the utterance of his name and rank. And even the gentleman himself, as if he had said more than his judgment sanctioned, and as if he were resolved to escape at least from any after-effects of the solemn import implicit in his own words, buried himself in his papers and began to write, so that nothing was heard in the room but the scratching of his pen. 'What is that: village secretary?' asked K. after a pause. The landlady answered for Momus, who now that he had introduced himself did not regard it seemly to give such explanations himself: 'Herr Momus is Klamm's secretary in the same sense as any of Klamm's secretaries, but his official province, and if I'm not mistaken, his official standing' – still writing Momus shook his head decidedly and the landlady amended her phrase – 'well then, his official province, but not his official standing, is confined to the village. Herr Momus despatches any clerical work of Klamm's which may become necessary in the village and as Klamm's deputy receives any petitions to Klamm which may be sent by the village.' As, still quite unimpressed by these facts, K. looked at the landlady with vacant eyes, she added in a half-embarrassed tone: 'That's how it's arranged; all the gentlemen in the Castle have their village secretaries.' Momus, who had been listening far more attentively than K., supplied the landlady with a supplementary fact: 'Most of the village secretaries work only for one gentleman, but I work for two, for Klamm and for Vallabene.' 'Yes,' went on the landlady, remembering now on her side too, and turning to K., 'Herr Momus works for two gentlemen, for Klamm and for Vallabene, and so is twice a village secretary.' 'Actually twice,' said K., nodding to Momus – who now, leaning slightly forward, looked him full in the face – as one nods to a child whom one has just heard being praised. If there was a certain contempt in the gesture, then it was either unobserved or else actually expected. Precisely to K., it seemed, who was not considered worthy even to be seen in passing by Klamm, these people had described in detail the services of a man out of Klamm's circle with the unconcealed intention of evoking K.'s recognition and admiration. And yet K. had no proper appreciation of it; he, who with all his powers strove to get a glimpse of Klamm, valued very little, for example, the post of a Momus who was permitted to live in Klamm's eye; for it was not Klamm's environment in itself that seemed to him worth striving for, but rather that he, K., he only and no one else, should attain to Klamm, and should attain to him not to rest with him, but to go on beyond him, farther yet, into the Castle.

And he looked at his watch and said: 'But now I must be going home.' Immediately the position changed in Momus's favour. 'Yes, of course,' the latter replied, 'the school work calls. But you must favour me with just a moment of your time. Only a few short questions.' 'I don't feel in the mood for it,' said K. and turned towards the door. Momus brought down a document on the table and stood up; 'In the name of Klamm I command you to answer my questions.' 'In the name of Klamm!' repeated K., 'does he trouble himself about my affairs, then?' 'As to that,' replied Momus, 'I have no information and you certainly have still less; we can safely leave that to him. All the same I command you by virtue of my function granted by Klamm to stay here and to answer.' 'Land Surveyor,' broke in the landlady. 'I refuse to advise you any further, my advice till now, the most well-meaning that you could have got, has been cast back at me in the most unheard-of manner; and I have come here to Herr Momus – I have nothing to hide – simply to give the office an adequate idea of your behaviour and your intentions and to protect myself for all time from having you quartered on me again; that's how we stand towards each other and that's how we'll always stand, and if I speak my mind accordingly now, I don't do it, I can tell you, to help you, but to ease a little the hard job which Herr Momus is bound to have in dealing with a man like you. All the same, just because of my absolute frankness – and I couldn't deal otherwise than frankly with you even if I were to try – you can extract some advantage for yourself out of what I say, if you only take the trouble. In the present case I want to draw your attention to this, that the only road that can lead you to Klamm is through this protocol here of Herr Momus. But I don't want to exaggerate, perhaps that road won't get you as far as Klamm, perhaps it will stop long before it reaches him; the judgment of Herr Momus will decide that. But in any case that's the only road that will take you in the direction of Klamm. And do you intend to reject that road, for nothing but pride?' 'Oh, madam,' said K., 'that's neither the only road to Klamm, nor is it any better than the others. But you, Mr. Secretary, decide this question, whether what I may say here can get as far as Klamm or not.' 'Of course it can,' said Momus, lowering his eyes proudly and gazing at nothing, 'otherwise why should I be secretary here?' 'Now you see, madam,' said K., 'I don't need a road to Klamm, but only to Mr. Secretary.' 'I wanted to throw open this road for you,' said the landlady, 'didn't I offer this morning to send your request to Klamm? That might have been done through Herr Momus. But you refused, and yet from now on no other way will remain for you but this one. But frankly, after your attempt on Klamm's privacy, with much less prospect of success. All the same this last, tiny, vanishing, yes, actually invisible hope, is your only one.' 'How is it, madam,' said K., 'that originally you tried so hard to keep me from seeing Klamm, and yet now take my wish to see him quite seriously, and seem to consider me lost largely on account of the miscarrying of my plan? If at one time you can advise me sincerely from your heart against trying to see Klamm at all, how can you possibly drive me on the road to Klamm now, apparently just as sincerely, even though it's admitted that the road may not reach as far as him?' 'Am I driving you on?' asked the landlady. 'Do you call it driving you on when I tell you that your attempt is hopeless? It would really be the limit of audacity if you tried in that way to push the responsibility on to me. Perhaps it's Herr Momus's presence that encourages you to do it. No, Land Surveyor, I'm not trying to drive you on to anything. I can admit only one mistake, that I overestimated you a little when I first saw you. Your immediate victory over Frieda frightened me, I didn't know what you might still be capable of. I wanted to prevent further damage, and thought that the only means of achieving that was to shake your resolution by prayers and threats. Since then I have learned to look on the whole thing more calmly. You can do what you like. Your actions may no doubt leave deep footprints in the snow out there in the courtyard, but they'll do nothing more.' 'The contradiction doesn't seem to me to be quite cleared up,' said K., 'but I'm content with having drawn attention to it. But now I beg you, Mr. Secretary, to tell me whether the landlady's opinion is correct, that is, that the protocol which you want to take down from my answers can have the result of gaining me admission to Klamm. If that's the case, I'm ready to answer all your questions at once. In that direction I'm ready, indeed, for anything.' 'No,' replied Momus, 'that doesn't follow at all. It's simply a matter of keeping an adequate record of this afternoon's happenings for Klamm's village register. The record is already complete, there are only two or three omissions which you must fill in for the sake of order; there's no other object in view and no other object can be achieved.' K. gazed at the landlady in silence. 'Why are you looking at me?' asked she, 'did I say anything else? He's always like that, Mr. Secretary, he's always like that. Falsifies the information one gives him, and then maintains that he received false information. I've told him from the first and I tell him again to-day that he hasn't the faintest prospect of being received by Klamm; well, if there's no prospect in any case he won't alter that fact by means of this protocol. Could anything be clearer? I said further that this protocol is the only real official connection that he can have with Klamm. That too is surely clear and incontestable enough. But if in spite of that he won't believe me, and keeps on hoping – I don't know why or with what idea – that he'll be able to reach Klamm, then so long as he remains in that frame of mind, the only thing that can help him is this one real official connection he has with Klamm, in other words, this protocol. That's all I have said, and whoever maintains the contrary twists my words maliciously.' 'If that is so, madam,' said K., 'then I beg your pardon, and I've misunderstood you; for I thought – erroneously, as it turns out now – that I could take out of your former words that there was still some very tiny hope for me.' 'Certainly,' replied the landlady, 'that's my meaning exactly. You're twisting my words again, only this time in the opposite way. In my opinion there is such a hope for you, and founded actually on this protocol and nothing else. But it's not of such a nature that you can simply fall on Herr Momus with the question: "Will I be allowed to see Klamm if I answer your questions?" When a child asks questions like that people laugh, when a grown man does it it is an insult to all authority; Herr Momus graciously concealed this under the politeness of his reply. But the hope that I mean consists simply in this, that through the protocol you have a sort of connection, a sort of connection perhaps with Klamm. Isn't that enough? If anyone enquired for any service which might earn you the privilege of such a hope, could you bring forward the slightest one? For the last time, that's the best that can be said about this hope of yours, and certainly Herr Momus in his official capacity could never give even the slightest hint of it. For him it's a matter, as he says, merely of keeping a record of this afternoon's happenings, for the sake of order; more than that he won't say, even if you ask him this minute his opinion of what I've said.' 'Will Klamm, then, Mr. Secretary,' asked K., 'read the protocol?' 'No,' replied Momus, 'why should he? Klamm can't read every protocol, in fact he reads none. "Keep away from me with your protocols!" he usually says.' 'Land Surveyor,' groaned the landlady, 'you exhaust me with such questions. Do you think it's necessary, or even simply desirable, that Klamm should read this protocol and become acquainted word for word with the trivialities of your life? Shouldn't you rather pray humbly that the protocol should be concealed from Klamm – a prayer, however, that would be just as unreasonable as the other, for who can hide anything from Klamm even though he has given many signs of his sympathetic nature? And is it even necessary for what you call your hope? Haven't you admitted yourself that you would be content if you only got the chance of speaking to Klamm, even if he never looked at you and never listened to you? And won't you achieve that at least through the protocol, perhaps much more?' 'Much more?' asked K. 'In what way?' 'If you wouldn't always talk about things like a child, as if they were for eating! Who on earth can give any answer to such questions? The protocol will be put in Klamm's village register, you have heard that already, more than that can't be

said with certainty. But do you know yet the full importance of the protocol, and of Herr Momus, and of the village
register? Do you know what it means to be examined by
Herr Momus? Perhaps – to all appearances at least – he
doesn't know it himself. He sits quietly there and does his
duty, for the sake of order, as he says. But consider that
Klamm appointed him, that he acts in Klamm's name, that
what he does, even if it never reaches Klamm, has yet
Klamm's assent in advance. And how can anything have
Klamm's assent that isn't filled by his spirit? Far be it from
me to offer Herr Momus crude flattery – besides he would
absolutely forbid it himself – but I'm speaking of him not as
an independent person, but as he is when he has Klamm's
assent, as at present; then he's an instrument in the hand of
Klamm, and woe to anybody who doesn't obey him.'

The landlady's threats did not daunt K.; of the hopes
with which she tried to catch him he was weary. Klamm
was far away. Once the landlady had compared Klamm to
an eagle, and that had seemed absurd in K.'s eyes, but it did
not seem absurd now; he thought of Klamm's remoteness,
of his impregnable dwelling, of his silence, broken perhaps
only by cries such as K. had never yet heard, of his down-
ward-pressing gaze, which could never be proved or disproved, of his wheelings which could never be disturbed by
anything that K. did down below, which far above he followed at the behest of incomprehensible laws and which
only for instants were visible – all these things Klamm and
the eagle had in common. But assuredly these had nothing
to do with the protocol, over which just now Momus was
crumbling a roll dusted with salt, which he was eating with
beer to help it out, in the process all the papers becoming
covered with salt and caraway seeds.

'Good night,' said K. 'I've an objection to any kind of
examination,' and now he went at last to the door. 'He's
going after all,' said Momus almost anxiously to the landlady. 'He won't dare,' said she; K. heard nothing more, he
was already in the hall. It was cold and a strong wind was

blowing. From a door on the opposite side came the landlord, he seemed to have been keeping the hall under observation from behind a peephole. He had to hold the tail of
his coat round his knees, the wind tore so strongly at him in
the hall. 'You're going already, Land Surveyor?' he asked.
'You're surprised at that?' asked K. 'I am,' said the landlord, 'haven't you been examined then?' 'No,' replied K. 'I
didn't let myself be examined.' 'Why not?' asked the landlord. 'I don't know,' said K., 'why I should let myself be
examined, why I should give in to a joke or an official
whim. Perhaps some other time I might have taken it on
my side too as a joke or as a whim, but not to-day.' 'Why
certainly, certainly,' said the landlord, but he agreed only
out of politeness, not from conviction. 'I must let the servants into the taproom now,' he said presently, 'it's long
past their time. Only I didn't want to disturb the examination.' 'Did you consider it as important as all that?' asked
K. 'Well, yes,' replied the landlord. 'I shouldn't have
refused,' said K. 'No,' replied the landlord, 'you shouldn't
have done that.' Seeing that K. was silent, he added,
whether to comfort K. or to get away sooner: 'Well, well,
the sky won't rain sulphur for all that.' 'No,' replied K.,
'the weather signs don't look like it.' And they parted
laughing.

X

K. STEPPED out into the windswept street and peered into
the darkness. Wild, wild weather. As if there were some
connection between the two he reflected again how the
landlady had striven to make him accede to the protocol,
and how he had stood out. The landlady's attempt had of
course not been a straightforward one, surreptitiously she
had tried to put him against the protocol at the same time;
in reality he could not tell whether he had stood out or

given in. An intriguing nature, acting blindly, it seemed, like the wind, according to strange and remote behests which one could never guess at.

He had only taken a few steps along the main street when he saw two swaying lights in the distance; these signs of life gladdened him and he hastened towards them, while they, too, made in his direction. He could not tell why he was so disappointed when he recognised the assistants. Still, they were coming to meet him, evidently sent by Frieda, and the lanterns which delivered him from the darkness roaring round him were his own; nevertheless he was disappointed, he had expected something else, not those old acquaintances who were such a burden to him. But the assistants were not alone; out of the darkness between them Barnabas stepped out. 'Barnabas!' cried K. and he held out his hand, 'have you come to see me?' The surprise at meeting him again drowned at first all the annoyance which he had once felt at Barnabas. 'To see you,' replied Barnabas unalterably friendly as before, 'with a letter from Klamm.' 'A letter from Klamm!' cried K. throwing back his head. 'Lights here!' he called to the assistants, who now pressed close to him on both sides holding up their lanterns. K. had to fold the large sheet in small compass to protect it from the wind while reading it. Then he read: 'To the Land Surveyor at the Bridge Inn. The surveying work which you have carried out thus far has been appreciated by me. The work of the assistants, too, deserves praise. You know how to keep them at their jobs. Do not slacken in your efforts! Carry your work on to a fortunate conclusion. Any interruption would displease me. For the rest be easy in your mind; the question of salary will presently be decided. I shall not forget you.' K. only looked up from the letter when the assistants, who read far more slowly than he, gave three loud cheers at the good news and waved their lanterns. 'Be quiet,' he said, and to Barnabas: 'There's been a misunderstanding.' Barnabas did not seem to comprehend. 'There's been a misunderstanding,' K. repeated, and the weariness he had felt in the afternoon came over him again, the road to the schoolhouse seemed very long, and behind Barnabas he could see his whole family, and the assistants were still jostling him so closely that he had to drive them away with his elbows; how could Frieda have sent them to meet him when he had commanded that they should stay with her? He could quite well have found his own way home, and better alone, indeed, than in this company. And to make matters worse one of them had wound a scarf round his neck whose free ends flapped in the wind and had several times been flung against K.'s face; it is true, the other assistant had always disengaged the wrap at once with his long, pointed, perpetually mobile fingers, but that had not made things any better. Both of them seemed to have considered it an actual pleasure to walk here and back, and the wind and the wildness of the night threw them into raptures. 'Get out!' shouted K., 'seeing that you've come to meet me, why haven't you brought my stick? What have I now to drive you home with?' They crouched behind Barnabas, but they were not too frightened to set their lanterns on their protector's shoulders, right and left; however, he shook them off at once. 'Barnabas,' said K., and he felt a weight on his heart when he saw that Barnabas obviously did not understand him, that though his tunic shone beautifully when fortune was there, when things became serious no help was to be found in him, but only dumb opposition, opposition against which one could not fight, for Barnabas himself was helpless, he could only smile, but that was of just as little help as the stars up there against this tempest down below. 'Look what Klamm has written!' said K., holding the letter before his face. 'He has been wrongly informed. I haven't done any surveying at all, and you see yourself how much the assistants are worth. And obviously, too, I can't interrupt work which I've never begun; I can't even excite the gentleman's displeasure, so how can I have earned his appreciation? As for being easy in my mind, I can never be that.' 'I'll see to it,' said Barnabas, who all the time had been gazing past the letter, which he could not have read in any case, for he was holding it too close to his face. 'Oh,' said K., 'you promise me that you'll see to it, but can I really believe you? I'm in need of a trustworthy messenger, now more than ever.' K. bit his lips with impatience. 'Sir,' replied Barnabas, with a gentle inclination of the head – K. almost allowed himself to be seduced by it again into believing Barnabas – 'I'll certainly see to it, and I'll certainly see to the message you gave me last time as well.' 'What!' cried K., 'haven't you seen to that yet then? Weren't you at the Castle next day?' 'No,' replied Barnabas, 'my father is old, you've seen him yourself, and there happened to be a great deal of work just then, I had to help him, but now I'll be going to the Castle again soon.' 'But what are you thinking of, you incomprehensible fellow?' cried K., beating his brow with his fist, 'don't Klamm's affairs come before everything else, then? You're in an important position, you're a messenger, and yet you fail me in this wretched manner! What does your father's work matter? Klamm is waiting for this information, and instead of breaking your neck hurrying with it to him, you prefer to clean the stable!' 'My father is a cobbler,' replied Barnabas calmly, 'he had orders from Brunswick, and I'm my father's assistant.' 'Cobbler-orders-Brunswick!' cried K. bitingly, as if he wanted to abolish the words for ever. 'And who can need boots here in these eternally empty streets? And what is all this cobbling to me? I entrusted you with a letter, not so that you might mislay it and crumple it on your bench, but that you might carry it at once to Klamm!' K. became a little more composed now as he remembered that after all Klamm had apparently been all this time in the Herrenhof and not in the Castle at all; but Barnabas exasperated him again when, to prove that he had not forgotten K.'s first message he now began to recite it. 'Enough! I don't want to hear any more,' he said. 'Don't be angry with me, sir,' said Barnabas, and as if unconsciously wishing to show disapproval of K. he withdrew his gaze from him and lowered his eyes, but probably he was only dejected by K.'s out-burst. 'I'm not angry with you,' said K., and his exasper-ation turned now against himself. 'Not with you, but it's a bad lookout for me only to have a messenger like you for important affairs.' 'Look here,' said Barnabas, and it was as if, to vindicate his honour as a messenger, he was saying more than he should, 'Klamm is really not waiting for your message, he's actually cross when I arrive. "Another new message," he said once, and generally he gets up when he sees me coming in the distance and goes into the next room and doesn't receive me. Besides, it isn't laid down that I should go at once with every message; if it were laid down of course I would go at once; but it isn't laid down, and if I never went at all, nothing could be said to me. When I take a message it's of my own free will.' 'Well and good,' replied K., staring at Barnabas and intentionally ignoring the assistants, who kept on slowly raising their heads by turns behind Barnabas's shoulder as from a trap-door, and hastily disappearing again with a soft whistle in imitation of the whistling of the wind, as if they were terrified at K.; they enjoyed themselves like this for a long time. 'What it's like with Klamm I don't know, but that you can understand everything there properly I very much doubt, and even if you did, we couldn't better things there. But you can carry a message and that's all I ask you. A quite short message. Can you carry it for me to-morrow and bring me the answer to-morrow, or at least tell me how you were received? Can you do that and will you do that? It would be of great ser-vice to me. And perhaps I'll have a chance yet of rewarding you properly, or have you any wish now, perhaps, that I can fulfil?' 'Certainly I'll carry out your orders,' said Barnabas. 'And will you do your utmost to carry them out as well as you can, to give the message to Klamm himself, to get a reply from Klamm himself, and immediately, all this imme-diately, to-morrow, in the morning, will you do that?' 'I'll do my best,' replied Barnabas, 'but I always do that.' 'We won't argue any more about it now,' said K. 'This is the message: "The Land Surveyor begs the Director to grant him a personal interview; he accepts in advance any conditions which may be attached to the permission to do this. He is driven to make this request because until now every intermediary has completely failed; in proof of this he advances the fact that till now he has not carried out any surveying at all, and according to the information given him by the village Superintendent will never carry out such work; consequently it is with humiliation and despair that he has read the last letter of the Director; only a personal interview with the Director can be of any help here. The Land Surveyor knows how extraordinary his request is, but he will exert himself to make his disturbance of the Director as little felt as possible; he submits himself to any and every limitation of time, also any stipulation which may be considered necessary as to the number of words which may be allowed him during the interview, even with ten words he believes he will be able to manage. In profound respect and extreme impatience he awaits your decision." K. had forgotten himself while he was speaking, it was as if he were standing before Klamm's door talking to the porter. 'It has grown much longer than I had thought,' he said, 'but you must learn it by heart, I don't want to write a letter, it would only go the same endless way as the other papers.' So for Barnabas's guidance, K. scribbled it on a scrap of paper on the back of one of the assistants, while the other assistant held up the lantern; but already K. could take it down from Barnabas's dictation, for he had retained it all and spoke it out correctly without being put off by the misleading interpolations of the assistants. 'You've an extraordinary memory,' said K., giving him the paper, 'but now show yourself extraordinary in the other thing as well. And any requests? Have you none? It would reassure me a little – I say it frankly – regarding the fate of my message, if you had any.' At first Barnabas remained silent, then he said: 'My sisters send you their greetings.' 'Your sisters,' replied K. 'Oh, yes, the big strong girls.' 'Both send you their greetings, but

Amalia in particular,' said Barnabas, 'besides it was she who brought me this letter for you to-day from the Castle.' Struck by this piece of information, K. asked: 'Couldn't she take my message to the Castle as well? Or couldn't you both go and each of you try your luck?' 'Amalia isn't allowed into the Chancellory,' said Barnabas, 'otherwise she would be very glad to do it.' 'I'll come and see you perhaps to-morrow,' said K., 'only you come to me first with the answer. I'll wait for you in the school. Give my greetings to your sisters, too.' K.'s promise seemed to make Barnabas very happy, and after they had shaken hands he could not help touching K. lightly on the shoulder. As if everything were once more as it had been when Barnabas first walked into the inn among the peasants in all his glory, K. felt this touch on his shoulder as a distinction, though he smiled at it. In a better mood now, he let the assistants do as they pleased on the way home.

XI

HE reached the school chilled through and through, it was quite dark, the candles in the lanterns had burned down; led by the assistants, who already knew their way here, he felt his road into one of the classrooms. 'Your first praiseworthy service,' he said, remembering Klamm's letter. Still half-asleep Frieda cried out from a corner: 'Let K. sleep! Don't disturb him!' so entirely did K. occupy her thoughts, even though she had been so overcome with sleep that she had not been able to wait up for him. Now a light was got, but the lamp could not be turned up very far, for there was only a little paraffin left. The new household was still without many necessaries. The room had been heated, it was true, but it was a large one, sometimes used as the gymnasium – the gymnastic apparatus was standing about and hanging from the ceiling – and it had already used up all the supply of wood – had been very warm and cosy too, as K. was assured, but unfortunately had grown quite cold again. There was, however, a large supply of wood in a shed, but the shed was locked and the teacher had the key; he only allowed this wood to be used for heating the school during teaching hours. The room could have been endured if there had been beds where one might have taken refuge. But in that line there was nothing but one sack stuffed with straw, covered with praiseworthy tidiness by a woollen rug of Frieda's, but with no feather-bed and only two rough, stiff blankets, which hardly served to keep one warm. And it was precisely at this wretched sack of straw that the assistants were staring greedily, but of course without any hope of ever being allowed to lie on it. Frieda looked anxiously at K.; that she knew how to make a room, even the most wretched, habitable, she had proved in the Bridge Inn, but here she had not been able to make any headway, quite without means as she was. 'Our only ornaments are the gymnastic contraptions,' said she, trying to smile through her tears. But for the chief deficiencies, the lack of sleeping accommodation and fuel, she promised absolutely to find help the very next day, and begged K. only to be patient till then. From no word, no hint, no sign could one have concluded that she harboured even the slightest trace of bitterness against K. in her heart, although, as he had to admit himself, he had torn her away first from the Herrenhof and now from the Bridge Inn as well. So in return K. did his best to find everything tolerable, which was not difficult for him, indeed, because in thought he was still with Barnabas repeating his message word for word, not however as he had given it to Barnabas, but as he thought it would sound before Klamm. After all, however, he was very sincerely glad of the coffee which Frieda had boiled for him on a spirit burner, and leaning against the almost cold stove followed the nimble, practised movements with which she spread the indispensable white table-cover on the teacher's table, brought out a flowered cup, then some bread and sausage, and actually a box of sardines. Now everything was ready; Frieda, too, had not eaten yet, but had waited for K. Two chairs were available, there K. and Frieda sat down to their table, the assistants at their feet on the dais, but they could never stay quiet, even while eating they made a disturbance. Although they had received an ample store of everything and were not yet nearly finished with it, they got up from time to time to make sure whether there was still anything on the table and they could still expect something for themselves; K. paid no attention to them and only began to take notice when Frieda laughed at them. He covered her hand with his tenderly and asked softly why she was so indulgent to them and treated even their naughtinesses so kindly. In this way one would never get rid of them, while through a certain degree of severity, which besides was demanded by their behaviour, one could manage either to curb them or, what was both more probable and more desirable, to make their position so hot for them that they would have finally to leave. The school here didn't seem to be a very pleasant place to live in for long, well, it wouldn't last very long in any case; but they would hardly notice all the drawbacks if the assistants were once gone and they two had the quiet house to themselves; and didn't she notice, too, that the assistants were becoming more impudent every day, as if they were actually encouraged now by Frieda's presence and the hope that K. wouldn't treat them with such firmness as he would have done in other circumstances? Besides, there were probably quite simple means of getting rid of them at once, without ceremony, perhaps Frieda herself knew of these, seeing that she was so well acquainted with all the circumstances. And from all appearances one would only be doing the assistants a favour if one got rid of them in some way, for the advantage they got by staying here couldn't be great, and besides the lazy spell which they must have enjoyed till now must cease here, to a certain extent at any rate, for they would have to work while Frieda spared herself after the excitements of the last few days, and he, K., was occupied in finding a way out of their painful position. All the same, if the assistants should go away, he would be so relieved that he felt he could quite easily carry out all the school work in addition to his other duties.

Frieda, who had been listening attentively, stroked his arm and said that that was her opinion too, but that perhaps he took the assistants' mischief too seriously; they were mere lads, full of spirits and a little silly now that they were for the first time in strange service, just released from the strict discipline of the Castle, and so a little dazed and excited; and being in that state they of course committed lots of follies at which it was natural to be annoyed, but which it would be more sensible to laugh at. Often she simply couldn't keep from laughing. All the same she absolutely agreed with K. that it would be much better to send the assistants away and be by themselves, just the two of them. She pressed closer to K. and hid her face on his shoulder. And there she whispered something so low that K. had to bend his head to hear; it was that all the same she knew of no way of dealing with the assistants and she was afraid that all that K. had suggested would be of no avail. So far as she knew it was K. himself who had asked for them, and now he had them and would have to keep them. It would be best to treat them as a joke, which they certainly were; that would be the best way to put up with them.

K. was displeased by her answer: half in jest, half in earnest, he replied that she seemed actually to be in league with them, or at least to have a strong inclination in their favour; well, they were good-looking lads, but there was nobody who couldn't be got rid of if only one had the will, and he would show her that that was so in the case of the assistants.

Frieda said that she would be very grateful to him if he could manage it. And from now on she wouldn't laugh at them any more, nor have any unnecessary talk with them. Besides she didn't find anything now to laugh at, it was really no joke always to be spied on by two men, she had learned to look at the two of them with K.'s eyes. And she actually shrank a little when the assistants got up again, partly to have a look at the food that was left, partly to get at the bottom of the continued whispering.

K. employed this incident to increase Frieda's disgust for the assistants, drew her towards him, and so side by side they finished their supper. Now it was time to go to bed, for they were all very sleepy; one of the assistants had actually fallen asleep over his food; this amused the other one greatly, and he did his best to get the others to look at the vacant face of his companion, but he had no success. K. and Frieda sat on above without paying any attention. The cold was becoming so extreme that they shirked going to bed; at last K. declared that the room must be heated, otherwise it would be impossible to get to sleep. He looked round to see if he could find an axe or something. The assistants knew of one and fetched it, and now they proceeded to the wood shed. In a few minutes the flimsy door was smashed and torn open; as if they had never yet experienced anything so glorious, the assistants began to carry the wood into the classroom, hounding each other on and knocking against each other; soon there was a great pile, the stove was set going, everybody lay down round it, the assistants were given a blanket to roll themselves in – it was quite ample for them, for it was decided that one of them should always remain awake and keep the fire going – and soon it was so hot round the stove that the blankets were no longer needed, the lamps were put out, and K. and Frieda happily stretched themselves out to sleep in the warm silence.

K. was awakened during the night by some noise or other, and in his first vague sleepy state felt for Frieda; he found that, instead of Frieda, one of the assistants was lying beside him. Probably because of the exacerbation which being suddenly awakened is sufficient in itself to cause, this gave him the greatest fright that he had ever had since he first came to the village. With a cry he sat up, and not knowing what he was doing gave the assistant such a buffet that he began to cry. However the whole thing was cleared up in a moment. Frieda had been awakened – at least so it had seemed to her – by some huge animal, a cat probably, which had sprung on to her breast and then leapt away again. She had got up and was searching the whole room for the beast with a candle. One of the assistants had seized the opportunity to enjoy the sack of straw for a little, an attempt which he was now bitterly repenting. Frieda could find nothing, however; perhaps it had only been a delusion, she went back to K. and on the way she stroked the crouching and whimpering assistant over the hair to comfort him, as if she had forgotten the evening's conversation. K. said nothing, but he asked the assistant to stop putting wood on the fire, for owing to almost all the heap having been squandered the room was already too hot.

XII

NEXT morning nobody awoke until the school children were there, standing with gaping eyes round the sleepers. This was unpleasant, for on account of the intense heat, which now towards morning had given way, however, to a coldness which could be felt, they had all taken off everything but their shirts, and just as they were beginning to put on their clothes, Gisa, the lady teacher, appeared at the door, a fair, tall, beautiful, but somewhat stiff young woman. She was evidently prepared for the new janitor, and seemed also to have been given her instructions by the teacher, for as soon as she appeared at the door, she began: 'I can't put up with this. This is a fine state of affairs. You have permission to sleep in the classroom, but that's all; I am not obliged to teach in your bedroom. A janitor's family that loll in their beds far into the forenoon! Faugh!' Well, something might be said about that, particularly as far as the family and the beds were concerned, thought K., while with Frieda's help

– the assistants were of no use, lying on the floor they looked in amazement at the lady teacher and the children – he dragged across the parallel bars and the vaulting horse, threw the blanket over them, and so constructed a little room in which one could at least get on one's clothes protected from the children's gaze. He was not given a minute's peace, however, for the lady teacher began to scold because there was no fresh water in the washing basin – K. had just been thinking of fetching the basin for himself and Frieda to wash in, but he had at once given up the idea so as not to exasperate the lady teacher too much, but his renunciation was of no avail, for immediately afterwards there was a loud crash; unfortunately, it seemed, they had forgotten to clear away the remains of the supper from the teacher's table, so she sent it all flying with her ruler and everything fell on the floor; she didn't need to bother about the sardine oil and the remainder of the coffee being spilt and the coffee-pot smashed to pieces, the janitor of course could soon clear that up. Clothed once more, K. and Frieda, leaning on the parallel bars, witnessed the destruction of their few things. The assistants, who had obviously never thought of putting on their clothes, had stuck their heads through a fold of the blankets near the floor, to the great delight of the children. What grieved Frieda most was naturally the loss of the coffee-pot; only when K. to comfort her assured her that he would go immediately to the village Superintendent and demand that it should be replaced, and see that this was done, was she able to gather herself together sufficiently to run out of their stockade in her chemise and skirt and rescue the table-cover at least from being stained any more. And she managed it, though the lady teacher to frighten her kept on hammering on the table with the ruler in the most nerve-racking fashion. When K. and Frieda were quite clothed they had to compel the assistants – who seemed to be struck dumb by these events – to get their clothes on as well; had not merely to order them and push them, indeed, but actually to put some of their clothes on for them. Then, when all was ready, K. shared out the remaining work; the assistants were to bring in wood and light the fire, but in the other classrooms first, from which another and greater danger threatened, for the teacher himself was probably already there. Frieda was to scrub the floor and K. would fetch fresh water and set things to rights generally. For the time being breakfast could not be thought of. But so as to find out definitively the attitude of the lady teacher, K. decided to issue from their shelter himself first, the others were only to follow when he called them; he adopted this policy on the one hand because he did not want the position to be compromised in advance by any stupid act of the assistants, and on the other because he wanted Frieda to be spared as much as possible; for she had ambitions and he had none, she was sensitive and he was not, she only thought of the petty discomforts of the moment, while he was thinking of Barnabas and the future. Frieda followed all his instructions implicitly, and scarcely took her eyes from him. Hardly had he appeared when the lady teacher cried amid the laughter of the children, which from now on never stopped: 'Slept well?' and as K. paid no attention – seeing that after all it was not a real question – but began to clear up the washstand, she asked: 'What have you been doing to my cat?' A huge, fat old cat was lying lazily outstretched on the table, and the teacher was examining one of its paws which was evidently a little hurt. So Frieda had been right after all, this cat had not of course leapt on her, for it was past the leaping stage, but it had crawled over her, had been terrified by the presence of people in the empty house, had concealed itself hastily, and in its unaccustomed hurry had hurt itself. K. tried to explain this quietly to the lady teacher, but the only thing she had eyes for was the injury itself and she replied: 'Well, then it's your fault through coming here. Just look at this,' and she called K. over to the table, showed him the paw, and before he could get a proper look at it, gave him a whack with the tawse over the back of his hand; the tails of the tawse were blunted, it was true, but, this time without any regard for the cat, she had brought them down so sharply that they raised bloody weals. 'And now go about your business,' she said impatiently, bowing herself once more over the cat. Frieda, who had been looking on with the assistants from behind the parallel bars, cried out when she saw the blood. K. held up his hand in front of the children and said: 'Look, that's what a sly, wicked cat has done to me.' He said it, indeed, not for the children's benefit, whose shouting and laughter had become continuous, so that it needed no further occasion or incitement, and could not be pierced or influenced by any words of his. But seeing that the lady teacher, too, only acknowledged the insult by a brief side-glance, and remained still occupied with the cat, her first fury satiated by the drawing of blood, K. called Frieda and the assistants, and the work began.

When K. had carried out the pail with the dirty water, fetched fresh water, and was beginning to turn out the classroom, a boy of about twelve stepped out from his desk, touched K.'s hand, and said something which was quite lost in the general uproar. Then suddenly every sound ceased and K. turned round. The thing he had been fearing all morning had come. In the door stood the teacher; in each hand the little man held an assistant by the scruff of the neck. He had caught them, it seemed, while they were fetching wood, for in a mighty voice he began to shout, pausing after every word: 'Who has dared to break into the wood-shed? Where is the villain, so that I may annihilate him?' Then Frieda got up from the floor, which she was trying to clean near the feet of the lady teacher, looked across at K. as if she were trying to gather strength from him, and said, a little of her old superciliousness in her glance and bearing: 'I did it, Mr. Teacher. I couldn't think of any other way. If the classrooms were to be heated in time, the wood-shed had to be opened; I didn't dare to ask you for the key in the middle of the night, my fiancé was at the Herrenhof, it was possible that he might stay there all night, so I had to decide for myself. If I have done wrongly, forgive my inexperience; I've been scolded enough already by my fiancé, after he saw what had happened. Yes, he even forbade me to light the fires early, because he thought that you had shown by locking the wood-shed that you didn't want them to be put on before you came yourself. So it's his fault that the fires are not on, but mine that the shed has been broken into.' 'Who broke open the door?' asked the teacher, turning to the assistants, who were still vainly struggling to escape from his grip. 'The gentleman,' they both replied, and, so that there might be no doubt, pointed at K. Frieda laughed, and her laughter seemed to be still more conclusive than her words; then she began to wring out into the pail the rag with which she had been scrubbing the floor, as if the episode had been closed with her declaration, and the evidence of the assistants were merely a belated jest. Only when she was at work on her knees again did she add: 'Our assistants are mere children who in spite of their age should still be at their desks in school. Last evening I really did break open the door myself with the axe, it was quite easy, I didn't need the assistants to help me, they would only have been a nuisance. But when my fiancé arrived later in the night and went out to see the damage and if possible put it right, the assistants ran out after him, likely because they were afraid to stay here by themselves, and saw my fiancé working at the broken door, and that's why they say now – but they're only children –' True, the assistants kept on shaking their heads during Frieda's story, pointed again at K. and did their best by means of dumb show to deflect her from her story; but as they did not succeed they submitted at last, took Frieda's words as a command, and on being questioned anew by the teacher made no reply. 'So,' said the teacher, 'you've been lying? Or at least you've groundlessly accused the janitor?' They still remained silent, but their trembling and their apprehensive glances seemed to indicate guilt. 'Then I'll give you a sound thrashing straight away,' he said, and he

sent one of the children into the next room for his cane.
Then as he was raising it, Frieda cried: 'The assistants have
told the truth!' flung her scrubbing-cloth in despair into the
pail, so that the water splashed up on every side, and ran
behind the parallel bars, where she remained concealed. 'A
lying crew!' remarked the lady teacher, who had just finished bandaging the paw, and she took the beast into her
lap, for which it was almost too big.

'So it *was* the janitor,' said the teacher, pushing the assistants away and turning to K., who had been listening all the
time leaning on the handle of his broom: 'This fine janitor
who out of cowardice allows other people to be falsely
accused of his own villainies.' 'Well,' said K., who had not
missed the fact that Frieda's intervention had appeased the
first uncontrollable fury of the teacher, 'if the assistants had
got a little taste of the rod I shouldn't have been sorry; if
they get off ten times when they should justly be punished,
they can well afford to pay for it by being punished unjustly
for once. But besides that it would have been very welcome
to me if a direct quarrel between me and you, Mr. Teacher,
could have been avoided; perhaps you would have liked it as
well yourself too. But seeing that Frieda has sacrificed me
to the assistants now –' here K. paused, and in the silence
Frieda's sobs could be heard behind the screen – 'of course
a clean breast must be made of the whole business.' 'Scandalous!' said the lady teacher. 'I am entirely of your opinion,
Fräulein Gisa,' said the teacher. 'You, janitor, are of course
dismissed from your post for those scandalous doings. Your
further punishment I reserve meantime, but now clear
yourself and your belongings out of the house at once. It
will be a genuine relief to us, and the teaching will manage
to begin at last. Now quick about it!' 'I shan't move a foot
from here,' said K. 'You're my superior, but not the person
who engaged me for this post; it was the Superintendent
who did that, and I'll only accept notice from him. And he
certainly never gave me this post so that I and my depend-
ents should freeze here, but – as you told me yourself – to

keep me from doing anything thoughtless or desperate. To dismiss me suddenly now would therefore be absolutely against his intentions; till I hear the contrary from his own mouth I refuse to believe it. Besides it may possibly be greatly to your own advantage, too, if I don't accept your notice, given so hastily.' 'So you don't accept it?' asked the teacher. K. shook his head. 'Think it over carefully,' said the teacher, 'your decisions aren't always for the best; you should reflect, for instance, on yesterday afternoon, when you refused to be examined.' 'Why do you bring that up now?' asked K. 'Because it's my whim.' replied the teacher, 'and now I repeat for the last time, get out!' But as that too had no effect the teacher went over to the table and consulted in a whisper with Fräulein Gisa; she said something about the police, but the teacher rejected it, finally they seemed in agreement, the teacher ordered the children to go into his classroom, they would be taught there along with the other children. This change delighted everybody, the room was emptied in a moment amid laughter and shouting, the teacher and Fräulein Gisa followed last. The latter carried the class register, and on it in all its bulk the perfectly indifferent cat. The teacher would gladly have left the cat behind, but a suggestion to that effect was negatived decisively by Fräulein Gisa with a reference to K.'s inhumanity. So, in addition to all his other annoyances, the teacher blamed K. for the cat as well. And that influenced his last words to K., spoken when he reached the door: 'The lady has been driven by force to leave the room with her children, because you have rebelliously refused to accept my notice, and because nobody can ask of her, a young girl, that she should teach in the middle of your dirty household affairs. So you are left to yourself, and you can spread yourself as much as you like, undisturbed by the disapproval of respectable people. But it won't last for long, I promise you that.' With that he slammed the door.

XIII

HARDLY was everybody gone when K. said to the assistants: 'Clear out!' Disconcerted by the unexpectedness of the command, they obeyed, but when K. locked the door behind them they tried to get in again, whimpered outside and knocked on the door. 'You are dismissed,' cried K., 'never again will I take you into my service!' But that, of course, was just what they did not want, and they kept hammering on the door with their hands and feet. 'Let us back to you, sir!' they cried, as if they were being swept away by a flood and K. were dry land. But K. did not relent, he waited impatiently for the unbearable din to force the teacher to intervene. That soon happened. 'Let your confounded assistants in!' he shouted. 'I've dismissed them,' K. shouted back; it had the incidental effect of showing the teacher what it was to be strong enough not merely to give notice, but to enforce it. The teacher next tried to soothe the assistants by kindly assurances that they had only to wait quietly and K. would have to let them in sooner or later. Then he went away. And now things might have settled down if K. had not begun to shout at them again that they were finally dismissed once and for all, and had not the faintest chance of being taken back. Upon that they recommenced their din. Once more the teacher entered, but this time he no longer tried to reason with them, but drove them, apparently with his dreaded rod, out of the house.

Soon they appeared in front of the windows of the gymnasium, rapped on the panes and cried something, but their words could no longer be distinguished. They did not stay there long either, in the deep snow they could not be as active as their frenzy required. So they flew to the railings of the school garden and sprang on to the stone pediment, where, moreover, though only from a distance, they had a better view of the room; there they ran to and fro holding on to the railings, then remained standing and stretched out their clasped hands beseechingly towards K. They went on like this for a long time, without thinking of the uselessness of their efforts; they were as if obsessed, they did not even stop when K. drew down the window blinds so as to rid himself of the sight of them. In the now darkened room K. went over to the parallel bars to look for Frieda. On encountering his gaze she got up, put her hair in order, dried her tears and began in silence to prepare the coffee. Although she knew of everything, K. formally announced to her all the same that he had dismissed the assistants. She merely nodded. K. sat down at one of the desks and followed her tired movements. It had been her unfailing liveliness and decision that had given her insignificant physique its beauty; now that beauty was gone. A few days of living with K. had been enough to achieve this. Her work in the taproom had not been light, but apparently it had been more suited to her. Or was her separation from Klamm the real cause of her falling away? It was the nearness of Klamm that had made her so irrationally seductive; that was the seduction which had drawn K. to her, and now she was withering in his arms.

'Frieda,' said K. She put away the coffee-mill at once and went over to K. at his desk. 'You're angry with me?' asked she. 'No,' replied K. 'I don't think you can help yourself. You were happy in the Herrenhof. I should have let you stay there.' 'Yes,' said Frieda, gazing sadly in front of her, 'you should have let me stay there. I'm not good enough for you to live with. If you were rid of me, perhaps you would be able to achieve all that you want. Out of regard for me you've submitted yourself to the tyranny of the teacher, taken on this wretched post, and are doing your utmost to get an interview with Klamm. All for me, but I don't give you much in return.' 'No, no,' said K., putting his arm round her comfortingly. 'All these things are trifles

138

that don't hurt me, and it's not only on your account that I want to get to Klamm. And then think of all you've done for me! Before I knew you I was going about in a blind circle. Nobody took me up, and if I made up to anybody I was soon sent about my business. And when I was given the chance of a little hospitality it was with people that I always wanted to run away from, like Barnabas's family –' 'You wanted to run away from them? You did? Darling!' cried Frieda eagerly, and after a hesitating 'Yes,' from K., sank back once more into her apathy. But K. had no longer resolution enough to explain in what way everything had changed for the better for him through his connection with Frieda. He slowly took away his arm and they sat for a little in silence, until – as if his arm had given her warmth and comfort, which now she could not do without – Frieda said: 'I won't be able to stand this life here. If you want to keep me with you, we'll have to go away somewhere or other, to the south of France, or to Spain.' 'I can't go away,' replied K. 'I came here to stay. I'll stay here.' And giving utterance to a self-contradiction which he made no effort to explain, he added as if to himself: 'What could have enticed me to this desolate country except the wish to stay here?' Then he went on: 'But you want to stay here too, after all it's your own country. Only you miss Klamm and that gives you desperate ideas.' 'I miss Klamm?' said Frieda, 'I've all I want of Klamm here, too much Klamm; it's to escape from him that I want to go away. It's not Klamm that I miss, it's you. I want to go away for your sake, because I can't get enough of you, here where everything distracts me. I would gladly lose my pretty looks, I would gladly be sick and ailing, if I could be left in peace with you.' K. had only paid attention to one thing. 'Then Klamm is still in communication with you?' he asked eagerly, 'he sends for you?' 'I know nothing about Klamm,' replied Frieda, 'I was speaking just now of others, I mean the assistants.' 'Oh, the assistants,' said K. in disappointment, 'do they persecute you?' 'Why, have you never noticed it?' asked Frieda. 'No,' replied K., trying in vain to remember anything, 'they're certainly importunate and lascivious young fellows, but I hadn't noticed that they had dared to lift their eyes to you.' 'No?' said Frieda, 'did you never notice that they simply weren't to be driven out of our room in the Bridge Inn, that they jealously watched all our movements, that one of them finished up by taking my place on that sack of straw, that they gave evidence against you a minute ago so as to drive you out of this and ruin you, and so as to be left alone with me? You've never noticed all that?' K. gazed at Frieda without replying. Her accusations against the assistants were true enough, but all the same they could be interpreted far more innocently as simple effects of the ludicrously childish, irresponsible, and undisciplined characters of the two. And didn't it also speak against their guilt that they had always done their best to go with K. everywhere and not to be left with Frieda? K. half-suggested this. 'It's their deceit,' said Frieda, 'have you never seen through it? Well, why have you driven them away, if not for those reasons?' And she went to the window, drew the blind aside a little, glanced out, and then called K. over. The assistants were still clinging to the railings; tired as they must have been by now, they still gathered their strength together every now and then and stretched their arms out beseechingly towards the school. So as not to have to hold on all the time, one of them had hooked himself on to the railings behind by the tail of his coat.

'Poor things! Poor things!' said Frieda.

'You ask why I drove them away?' asked K. 'You were the sole cause of that.' 'I?' asked Frieda without taking her eyes from the assistants. 'Your much too kind treatment of the assistants,' said K., 'the way you forgave their offences and smiled at them and stroked their hair, your perpetual sympathy for them – "Poor things! Poor things!" you said just now – and finally this last thing that has happened, that you haven't scrupled even to sacrifice me to save the assistants from a beating.' 'Yes, that's just it, that's what I've been trying to tell you, that's just what makes me unhappy, what keeps me from you even though I can't think of any greater happiness than to be with you all the time, without interruption, endlessly, even though I feel that here in this world there's no undisturbed place for our love, neither in the village nor anywhere else; and I dream of a grave, deep and narrow, where we could clasp each other in our arms as with iron bars, and I would hide my face in you and you would hide your face in me, and nobody would ever see us any more. But here – look, there are the assistants! It's not you they think of when they clasp their hands, but me.' 'And it's not I who am looking at them,' said K., 'but you.' 'Certainly, me,' said Frieda almost angrily, 'that's what I've been saying all the time; why else should they be always at my heels, even if they are messengers of Klamm's?' 'Messengers of Klamm's?' repeated K. extremely astonished by this designation, though it seemed natural enough at the same time. 'Certainly, messengers of Klamm's,' said Frieda. 'Even if they are, still they're silly boys, too, who need to have more sense hammered into them. What ugly black young demons they are, and how disgusting the contrast is between their faces, which one would say belonged to grown-ups, almost to students, and their silly childish behaviour. Do you think I don't see that? It makes me feel ashamed for them. Well, that's just it, they don't repel me, but I feel ashamed for them. I can't help looking at them. When one ought to be annoyed with them, I can only laugh at them. When people want to strike them, I can only stroke their hair. And when I'm lying beside you at night I can't sleep and must always be leaning across you to look at them, one of them lying rolled up asleep in the blanket and the other kneeling before the stove door putting in wood, and I have to bend forward so far that I nearly waken you. And it wasn't the cat that frightened me – oh, I've had experience of cats and I've had experience as well of disturbed nights in the taproom – it wasn't the cat that frightened me, I'm frightened at myself. No, it didn't need that big beast of a

141

cat to waken me, I start up at the slightest noise. One minute I'm afraid you'll waken and spoil everything, and the next I spring up and light the candle to force you to waken at once and protect me.' 'I knew nothing of all this,' said K., 'it was only a vague suspicion of it that made me send them away; but now they're gone, and perhaps everything will be all right.' 'Yes, they're gone at last,' said Frieda, but her face was worried, not happy, 'only we don't know who they are. Messengers of Klamm's I call them in my mind, though not seriously, but perhaps they are really that. Their eyes – those ingenuous and yet flashing eyes – remind me somehow of Klamm's; yes, that's it, it's Klamm's glance that sometimes runs through me from their eyes. And so it's not true when I say that I'm ashamed for them. I only wish it were. I know quite well that anywhere else and in anyone else their behaviour would seem stupid and offensive, but in them it isn't. I watch their stupid tricks with respect and admiration. But if they're Klamm's messengers who'll rid us of them? and besides would it be a good thing to be rid of them? Wouldn't you have to fetch them back at once in that case and be happy if they were still willing to come?' 'You want me to bring them back again?' asked K. 'No, no!' said Frieda, 'it's the last thing I desire. The sight of them, if they were to rush in here now, their joy at seeing me again, the way they would hop round like children and stretch out their arms to me like men; no, I don't think I would be able to stand that. But all the same when I remember that if you keep on hardening your heart to them, it will keep you, perhaps, from ever getting admittance to Klamm, I want to save you by any means at all from such consequences. In that case my only wish is for you to let them in. In that case let them in now at once. Don't bother about me; what do I matter? I'll defend myself as long as I can, but if I have to surrender, then I'll surrender with the consciousness that that, too, is for your sake.' 'You only strengthen me in my decision about the assistants,' said K. 'Never will they come in with my will. The fact that I've got them out of this proves at least that in certain circumstances they can be managed, and therefore, in addition, that they have no real connection with Klamm. Only last night I received a letter from Klamm from which it was clear that Klamm was quite falsely informed about the assistants, from which again one can only draw the conclusion that he is completely indifferent to them, for if that were not so he would certainly have obtained exact information about them. And the fact that you see Klamm in them proves nothing, for you're still, unfortunately, under the landlady's influence and see Klamm everywhere. You're still Klamm's sweetheart, and not my wife yet by a long chalk. Sometimes that makes me quite dejected, I feel then as if I had lost everything, I feel as if I had only newly come to the village, yet not full of hope, as I actually came, but with the knowledge that only disappointments await me, and that I will have to swallow them down one after another to the very dregs. But that is only sometimes,' K. added smiling, when he saw Frieda's dejection at hearing his words, 'and at bottom it merely proves one good thing, that is, how much you mean to me. And if you order me now to choose between you and the assistants, that's enough to decide the assistants' fate. What an idea, to choose between you and the assistants! But now I want to be rid of them finally, in word and thought as well. Besides who knows whether the weakness that has come over us both mayn't be due to the fact that we haven't had breakfast yet?' 'That's possible,' said Frieda, smiling wearily and going about her work. K., too, grasped the broom again.

After a while there was a soft rap at the door. 'Barnabas!' cried K., throwing down the broom, and with a few steps he was at the door. Frieda stared at him, more terrified at the name than anything else. With his trembling hands K. could not turn the old lock immediately. 'I'll open in a minute,' he kept on repeating, instead of asking who was actually there. And then he had to face the fact that through the wide-open door came in, not Barnabas, but the little boy who had tried to speak to him before. But K. had no wish to be reminded of him. 'What do you want here?' he asked. 'The classes are being taught next door.' 'I've come from there,' replied the boy, looking up at K. quietly with his great brown eyes, and standing at attention, with his arms by his side. 'What do you want then? Out with it!' said K., bending a little forward, for the boy spoke in a low voice. 'Can I help you?' asked the boy. 'He wants to help us,' said K. to Frieda, and then to the boy: 'What's your name?' 'Hans Brunswick,' replied the boy, 'fourth standard, son of Otto Brunswick, master cobbler in Madeleinegasse.' 'I see, your name is Brunswick,' said K., now in a kinder tone. It came out that Hans had been so indignant at seeing the bloody weals which the lady teacher had raised on K.'s hand, that he had resolved at once to stand by K. He had boldly slipped away just now from the classroom next door at the risk of severe punishment, somewhat as a deserter goes over to the enemy. It may indeed have been chiefly some such boyish fancy that had impelled him. The seriousness which he evinced in everything he did seemed to indicate it. Shyness held him back at the beginning, but he soon got used to K. and Frieda, and when he was given a cup of good hot coffee he became lively and confidential and began to question them eagerly and insistently, as if he wanted to know the gist of the matter as quickly as possible, to enable him to come to an independent decision about what they should do. There was something imperious in his character, but it was so mingled with childish innocence that they submitted to it without resistance, half-smilingly, half in earnest. In any case he demanded all their attention for himself; work completely stopped, the breakfast lingered on unconscionably. Although Hans was sitting at one of the scholars' desks and K. in a chair on the dais with Frieda beside him, it looked as if Hans were the teacher, and as if he were examining them and passing judgment on their answers. A faint smile round his soft mouth seemed to indicate that he knew quite well that all this was only a game, but that made him only the more serious in conducting it; perhaps, too, it was not really a smile but the happiness of childhood that played round his lips. Strangely enough he only admitted quite late in the conversation that he had known K. ever since his visit to Lasemann's. K. was delighted. 'You were playing at the lady's feet?' asked K. 'Yes,' replied Hans, 'that was my mother.' And now he had to tell about his mother, but he did so hesitatingly and only after being repeatedly asked; and it was clear now that he was only a child, out of whose mouth, it is true – especially in his questions – sometimes the voice of an energetic, far-seeing man seemed to speak; but then all at once, without transition, he was only a schoolboy again who did not understand many of the questions, misconstrued others, and in childish inconsiderateness spoke too low, although he had the fault repeatedly pointed out to him, and out of stubbornness silently refused to answer some of the other questions at all, quite without embarrassment, however, as a grown-up would have been incapable of doing. He seemed to feel that he alone had the right to ask questions, and that by the questions of Frieda and K. some regulation were broken and time wasted. That made him sit silent for a long time, his body erect, his head bent, his underlip pushed out. Frieda was so charmed by his expression at these moments that she sometimes put questions to him in the hope that they would evoke it. And she succeeded several times, but K. was only annoyed. All that they found out did not amount to much. Hans's mother was slightly unwell, but what her illness was remained indefinite; the child which she had had in her lap was Hans's sister and was called Frieda (Hans was not pleased by the fact that her name was the same as the lady's who was questioning him), the family lived in the village, but not with Lasemann – they had only been there on a visit and to be bathed, seeing that Lasemann had the big tub in which the younger children, to whom Hans didn't belong, loved to bathe and splash about. Of his father Hans spoke now with respect, now with fear, but only when his mother was not occupying the conversation; compared with his mother his father evidently was of little account, but all their questions about Brunswick's family life remained, in spite of their efforts, unanswered. K. learned that the father had the biggest shoemaker's business in the place, nobody could compete with him, a fact which quite remote questions brought again and again; he actually gave out work to the other shoemakers, for example to Barnabas's father; in this last case he had done it of course as a special favour – at least Hans's proud toss of the head seemed to hint at this, a gesture which made Frieda run over and give him a kiss. The question whether he had been in the Castle yet he only answered after it had been repeated several times, and with a 'No'. The same question regarding his mother he did not answer at all. At last K. grew tired; to him, too, these questions seemed useless, he admitted that the boy was right; besides there was something humiliating in ferreting out family secrets by taking advantage of a child; doubly humiliating, however, was the fact that in spite of his effort she had learned nothing. And when to finish the matter he asked the boy what was the help he wanted to offer, he was no longer surprised to hear that Hans had only wanted to help with the work in the school, so that the teacher and his assistant might not scold K. so much. K. explained to Hans that help of that kind was not needed, scolding was part of the teacher's nature and one could scarcely hope to avoid it even by the greatest diligence, the work itself was not hard, and only because of special circumstances had it been so far behind that morning, besides scolding hadn't the same effect on K. as on a scholar, he shook it off, it was almost a matter of indifference to him, he hoped, too, to get quite clear of the teacher soon. Though Hans had only wanted to help him in dealing with the teacher, however, he thanked him sincerely, but now Hans had better return to his class, with luck he would not be punished if he went back at once. Although K. did not emphasise and only involuntarily suggested that it was simply help in dealing with the teacher which he did not require, leaving the question of other kinds of help open, Hans caught the suggestion clearly and asked whether perhaps K. needed any other assistance; he would be very glad to help him, and if he were not in a position to help him himself, he would ask his mother to do so, and then it would be sure to be all right. When his father had difficulties, he, too, asked Hans's mother for help. And his mother had already asked once about K., she herself hardly ever left the house, it had been a great exception for her to be at Lasemann's that day. But he, Hans, often went there to play with Lasemann's children, and his mother had once asked him whether the Land Surveyor had ever happened to be there again. Only his mother wasn't supposed to talk too much, seeing she was so weak and tired, and so he had simply replied that he hadn't seen the Land Surveyor there, and nothing more had been said; but when he had found K. here in the school, he had had to speak to him, so that he might tell his mother the news. For that was what pleased his mother most, when without her express command one did what she wanted. After a short pause for reflection K. said that he did not need any help, he had all that he required, but it was very good of Hans to want to help him, and he thanked him for his good intentions; it was possible that later he might be in need of something and then he would turn to Hans, he had his address. In return perhaps he, K., might be able to offer a little help; he was sorry to hear that Hans's mother was ill and that apparently nobody in the village understood her illness; if it was neglected like that a trifling malady might sometimes lead to grave consequences. Now he, K., had some medical knowledge, and, what was of still more value, experience in treating sick people. Many a case which the doctors had given up he had been able to cure. At home they had called him 'The Bitter Herb' on account of his healing powers. In any case he would be glad to see Hans's mother and speak with her. Perhaps he might be able to give her good advice, for if only for Hans's sake he would be delighted to do it. At first Hans's eyes lit up at this offer, exciting K. to greater urgency, but the outcome was unsatisfactory, for to several questions Hans replied, without showing the slightest trace of regret, that no stranger was allowed to visit his mother, she had to be guarded so carefully; although that day K. had scarcely spoken to her she had had to stay for several days in bed, a thing indeed that often happened. But his father had then been very angry with K. and he would certainly never allow K. to come to the house; he had actually wanted to seek K. out at the time to punish him for his impudence, only Hans's mother had held him back. But in any case his mother never wanted to talk with anybody whatever, and her enquiry about K. was no exception to the rule; on the contrary, seeing he had been mentioned, she could have expressed the wish to see him, but she hadn't done so, and in that had clearly made known her will. She only wanted to hear about K. but she did not want to speak to him. Besides it wasn't any real illness that she was suffering from, she knew quite well the cause of her state and often had actually indicated it; apparently it was the climate here that she could not stand, but all the same she would not leave the place, on account of her husband and children, besides, she was already better in health than she used to be. Here K. felt Hans's powers of thought visibly increasing in his attempt to protect his mother from K., from K. whom he had ostensibly wanted to help; yes, in the good cause of keeping K. away from his mother he even contradicted in several respects what he had said before, particularly in regard to his mother's illness. Nevertheless K. marked that even so Hans was still well disposed towards him, only when his mother was in question he forgot everything else; whoever was set up beside his mother was immediately at a disadvantage; just now it had been K., but it could as well be his father, for example. K. wanted to test this supposition and said that it was certainly thoughtful of Hans's father to shield his mother from any disturbance, and if he, K., had only guessed that day at this state of things, he would never have thought of venturing to speak to her, and he asked Hans to make his apologies to her now. On the other hand he could not quite understand why Hans's father, seeing that the cause of her sickness was so clearly known as Hans said, kept her back from going somewhere else to get well; one had to infer that he kept her back, for she only remained on his account and the children's, but she could take the children with her, and she need not have to go away for any long time or for any great distance, even up on the Castle Hill the air was quite different. Hans's father had no need to fear the cost of the holiday, seeing that he was the biggest shoemaker in the place, and it was pretty certain that he or she had relations or acquaintances in the Castle who would be glad to take her in. Why did he not let her go? He shouldn't underestimate an illness like this, K. had only seen Hans's mother for a minute, but it had actually been her striking pallor and weakness that had impelled him to speak to her. Even at that time he had been surprised that her husband had let her sit there in the damp steam of the washing and bathing when she was ill, and had put no restraint either on his loud talk with the others. Hans's father really did not know the actual state of things; even if her illness had improved in the last few weeks, illnesses like that had ups and downs, and in the end, if one did not fight them, they returned with redoubled strength, and then the patient was past help. Even if K. could not speak to Hans's mother, still it would perhaps be advisable if he were to speak to his father and draw his attention to all this.

Hans had listened intently, had understood most of it, and had been deeply impressed by the threat implicit in this dark advice. Nevertheless he replied that K. could not speak to his father, for his father disliked him and would probably treat him as the teacher had done. He said this with a shy smile when he was speaking of K., but sadly and bitterly when he mentioned his father. But he added that perhaps K. might be able to speak to his mother all the same, but only without his father's knowledge. Then deep in thought Hans stared in front of him for a little – just like a woman who wants to do something forbidden and seeks an opportunity to do it without being punished – and said that the day after to-morrow it might be possible, his father was going to the Herrenhof in the evening, he had a conference there; then he, Hans, would come in the evening and take K. along to his mother, of course, assuming that his mother agreed, which was however very improbable. She never did anything at all against the wishes of his father, she submitted to him in everything, even in things whose unreasonableness he, Hans, could see through.

Long before this K. had called Hans up to the dais, drawn him between his knees, and had kept on caressing him comfortingly. The nearness helped, in spite of Hans's occasional recalcitrance, to bring about an understanding. They agreed finally to the following: Hans would first tell his mother the entire truth, but, so as to make her consent easier, add that K. wanted to speak to Brunswick himself as well, not about her at all, but about his own affairs. Besides this was true; in the course of the conversation K. had remembered that Brunswick, even if he were a bad and dangerous man, could scarcely be his enemy now, if he had been, according to the information of the Superintendent, the leader of those who, even if only on political grounds, were in favour of engaging a Land Surveyor. K.'s arrival in the village must therefore have been welcomed by Brunswick. But in that case his morose greeting that first day and the dislike of which Hans spoke were almost incomprehensible – perhaps, however, Brunswick had been hurt simply because K. had not turned to him first for help, perhaps there existed some other misunderstanding which could be cleared up by a few words. But if that were done K. might very well secure in Brunswick a supporter against the teacher, yes and against the Superintendent as well; the whole official plot – for was it anything else really? – by means of which the Superintendent and the teacher were keeping him from reaching the Castle authorities and had driven him into taking a janitor's post, might be unmasked; if it came anew to a fight about K. between Brunswick and the Superintendent, Brunswick would have to include K. on his side, K. would become a guest in Brunswick's house, Brunswick's fighting resources would be put at his disposal in spite of the Superintendent; who could tell what he might not be able to achieve by those means, and in any case he would often be in the lady's company – so he played with his dreams and they with him, while Hans, thinking only of his mother, painfully watched K.'s silence, as one watches a doctor who is sunk in reflection while he tries to find the proper remedy for a grave case. With K.'s proposal to speak to Brunswick about his post as Land Surveyor Hans was in agreement, but only because by means of this his mother would be shielded from his father, and because in any case it was only a last resort which with good luck might not be needed. He merely asked further how K. was to explain to his father the lateness of the visit, and was content at last, though his face remained a little overcast, with the suggestion that K. would say that his unendurable post in the school and the teacher's humiliating treatment had made him in sudden despair forget all caution.

Now that, so far as one could see, everything had been provided for, and the possibility of success at least conceded, Hans, freed from his burden of reflection, became happier, and chatted for some time longer with K. and afterwards with Frieda – who had sat for a long time as if absorbed by quite different thoughts, and only now began to take part in the conversation again. Among other things she asked him what he wanted to become; he did not think long but said he wanted to be a man like K. When he was asked next for his reasons he really did not know how to reply, and the question whether he would like to be a janitor he answered with a decided negative. Only through further questioning did they perceive by what roundabout ways he had arrived at his wish. K.'s present condition was in no way enviable, but wretched and humiliating; even Hans saw this clearly without having to ask other people; he himself would have certainly preferred to shield his mother from K.'s slightest word, even from having to see him. In spite of this, however, he had come to K. and had begged to be allowed to help him, and had been delighted when K. agreed; he imagined, too, that other people felt the same; and, most important of all, it had been his mother herself who had mentioned K.'s name. These contradictions had engendered in him the belief that though for the moment K. was wretched and looked down on, yet in an almost unimaginable and distant future he would excel everybody. And it was just this absurdly distant future and the glorious developments which were to lead up to it that attracted Hans; that was why he was willing to accept K. even in his present state. The peculiar childish-grown-up acuteness of this wish consisted in the fact that Hans looked on K. as on a younger brother whose future would reach further than his own, the future of a very little boy. And it was with an almost troubled seriousness that, driven into a corner by Frieda's questions, he at last confessed those things. K. only cheered him up again when he said that he knew what Hans envied him for; it was for his beautiful walking-stick, which was lying on the table and with which Hans had been playing absently during the conversation. Now K. knew how to produce sticks like that, and if their plan were successful he would make Hans an even more beautiful one. It was no longer quite clear now whether Hans had not really meant merely the walking-stick, so happy was he made by K.'s promise; and he said good-bye with a glad face, not without pressing K.'s hand firmly and saying: 'The day after to-morrow, then.'

It had been high time for Hans to go, for shortly afterwards the teacher flung open the door and shouted when he saw K. and Frieda sitting idly at the table: 'Forgive my intrusion! But will you tell me when this place is to be finally put in order? We have to sit here packed like herring, so that the teaching can't go on. And there are you lolling about in the big gymnasium, and you've even sent away the assistants to give yourselves more room. At least get on to your feet now and get a move on!' Then to K.: 'Now go and bring me my lunch from the Bridge Inn.' All this was delivered in a furious shout, though the words were comparatively inoffensive. K. was quite prepared to obey, but to draw the teacher he said: 'But I've been given notice.' 'Notice or no notice, bring me my lunch,' replied the teacher. 'Notice or no notice, that's just what I want to be sure about,' said K. 'What nonsense is this?' asked the teacher. 'You know you didn't accept the notice.' 'And is that enough to make it invalid?' asked K. 'Not for me,' said the teacher, 'you can take my word for that, but for the Superintendent, it seems, though I can't understand it. But take to your heels now, or else I'll fling you out in earnest.' K. was content the teacher then had spoken with the Superintendent, or perhaps he hadn't spoken after all, but had merely thought over carefully the Superintendent's probable intentions, and these had weighed in K.'s favour. Now K. was setting out hastily to get the lunch, but the teacher called him back from the very doorway, either because he wanted by this counter order to test K.'s willingness to serve, so that he might know how far he could go in future, or because a fresh fit of imperiousness had seized him, and it gave him pleasure to make K. run to and fro like a waiter. On his side K. knew that through too great compliance he would only become the teacher's slave and scapegoat, but within certain limits he decided for the present to give way to the fellow's caprices, for even if the teacher, as had been shown, had not the power to dismiss him, yet he could certainly make the post so difficult that it could not be borne. And the post was more important in K.'s eyes now than ever before. The conversation with Hans had raised new hopes in him, improbable, he admitted, completely groundless even, but all the same not to be put out of his mind; they almost superseded Barnabas himself. If he gave himself up to them – and there was no choice – then he must husband all his strength, trouble about nothing else, food, shelter, the village authorities, no not even about Frieda – and in reality the whole thing turned only on Frieda, for everything else only gave him anxiety in relation to her. For this reason he must try to keep this post which gave Frieda a certain degree of security, and he must not complain if for this end he were made to endure more at the teacher's hands than he would have had to endure in the ordinary course. All that sort of thing could be put up with, it belonged to the ordinary continual petty annoyances of life, it was nothing compared with what K. was striving for, and he had not come here simply to lead an honoured and comfortable life.

And so, as he had been ready to run over to the inn, he showed himself now willing to obey the second order, and first set the room to rights so that the lady teacher and her children could come back to it. But it had to be done with all speed, for after that K. had to go for the lunch, and the teacher was already ravenous. K. assured him that it would all be done as he desired; for a little the teacher looked on while K. hurried up, cleared away the sack of straw, put back the gymnastic apparatus in its place, and swept the room out while Frieda washed and scrubbed the dais. Their diligence seemed to appease the teacher, he only drew their attention to the fact that there was a pile of wood for the fire outside the door – he would not allow K. further access to the shed, of course – and then went back to his class with the threat that he would return soon and inspect.

After a few minutes of silent work Frieda asked K. why he submitted so humbly to the teacher now. The question was asked in a sympathetic, anxious tone, but K., who was thinking how little Frieda had succeeded in keeping her original promise to shield him from the teacher's orders and insults, merely replied shortly that since he was the janitor he must fulfil the janitor's duties. Then there was silence again until K., reminded vividly by this short exchange of words that Frieda had been for a long time lost in anxious thought – and particularly through almost the whole conversation with Hans – asked her bluntly while he carried in the firewood what had been troubling her. Slowly turning her eyes upon him she replied that it was nothing definite, she had only been thinking of the landlady and the truth of much of what she said. Only when K. pressed her did she reply more consecutively after hesitating several times, but without looking up from her work – not that she was thinking of it, for it was making no progress, but simply so that she might not be compelled to look at K. And now she told him that during his talk with Hans she had listened quietly at first, that then she had been startled by certain words of his, then had begun to grasp the meaning of them more clearly, and that ever since she had not been able to cease reading into his words a confirmation of a warning which the landlady had once given her, and which she had always refused to believe. Exasperated by all this circumlocution, and more irritated than touched by Frieda's tearful, complaining voice – but annoyed above all because the landlady was coming into his affairs again, though only as a recollection, for in person she had had little success up till now – K. flung the wood he was carrying in his arms on to the floor, sat down on it, and in tones which were now serious demanded the whole truth. 'More than once,' began Frieda, 'yes, since the beginning, the landlady has tried to make me doubt you, she didn't hold that you were lying, on the contrary she said that you were childishly open, but your character was so different from ours, she said, that, even when you spoke frankly, it was bound to be difficult for us to believe you; and if we did not listen to good advice we would have to learn to believe you through bitter experience. Even she with her keen eye for people was almost taken in. But after her last talk with you in the Bridge Inn

– I am only repeating her own words – she woke up to your tricks, she said, and after that you couldn't deceive her even if you did your best to hide your intentions. But you hid nothing, she repeated that again and again, and then she said afterwards: Try to listen to him carefully at the first favourable opportunity, not superficially, but carefully, carefully. That was all that she had done and your own words had told her all this regarding myself: That you made up to me – she used those very words – only because I happened to be in your way, because I did not actually repel you, and because quite erroneously you considered a barmaid the destined prey of any guest who chose to stretch out his hand for her. Moreover, you wanted, as the landlady learned at the Herrenhof, for some reason or other to spend that night at the Herrenhof, and that could in no circumstances be achieved except through me. Now all that was sufficient cause for you to become my lover for one night, but something more was needed to turn it into a more serious affair. And that something more was Klamm. The landlady doesn't claim to know what you want from Klamm, she merely maintains that before you knew me you strove as eagerly to reach Klamm as you have done since. The only difference was this, that before you knew me you were without any hope, but that now you imagine that in me you have a reliable means of reaching Klamm certainly and quickly and even with advantage to yourself. How startled I was – but that was only a superficial fear without deeper cause – when you said to-day that before you knew me you had gone about here in a blind circle. These might actually be the same words that the landlady used, she, too, says that it's only since you have known me that you've become aware of your goal. That's because you believe you have secured in me a sweetheart of Klamm's, and so possess a hostage which can only be ransomed at a great price. Your one endeavour is to treat with Klamm about this hostage. As in your eyes I am nothing and the price everything, so you are ready for any concession so far as I'm concerned, but as for the price you're adamant. So it's a matter of indifference to you that I've lost my post at the Herrenhof and that I've had to leave the Bridge Inn as well, a matter of indifference that I have to endure the heavy work here in the school. You have no tenderness to spare for me, you have hardly even time for me, you leave me to the assistants, the idea of being jealous never comes into your mind, my only value for you is that I was once Klamm's sweetheart, in your ignorance you exert yourself to keep me from forgetting Klamm, so that when the decisive moment comes I should not make any resistance; yet at the same time you carry on a feud with the landlady, the only one you think capable of separating me from you, and that's why you brought your quarrel with her to a crisis, so as to have to leave the Bridge Inn with me; but that, so far as I'm concerned, I belong to you whatever happens, you haven't the slightest doubt. You think of the interview with Klamm as a business deal, a matter of hard cash. You take every possibility into account; providing that you reach your end you're ready to do anything; should Klamm want me you are prepared to give me to him, should he want you to stick to me you'll stick to me, should he want you to fling me out, you'll fling me out, but you're prepared to play a part too; if it's advantageous to you, you'll give out that you love me, you'll try to combat his indifference by emphasising your own littleness, and then shame him by the fact that you're his successor, or you'll be ready to carry him the protestations of love for him which you know I've made, and beg him to take me on again, of course on your terms; and if nothing else answers, then you'll simply go and beg from him in the name of K. and wife. But, the landlady said finally, when you see then that you have deceived yourself in everything, in your assumptions and in your hopes, in your ideas of Klamm and his relations with me, then my purgatory will begin, for then for the first time I'll be in reality the only possession you'll have to fall back on, but at the same time it will be a possession that has proved to be worthless, and you'll treat it accordingly, seeing that you have no feeling for me but the feeling of ownership.'

With his lips tightly compressed K. had listened intently, the wood he was sitting on had rolled asunder though he had not noticed it, he had almost slid on to the floor, and now at last he got up, sat down on the dais, took Frieda's hand, which she feebly tried to pull away, and said: 'In what you've said I haven't always been able to distinguish the landlady's sentiments from your own.' 'They're the landlady's sentiments purely,' said Frieda, 'I heard her out because I respected her, but it was the first time in my life that I completely and wholly refused to accept her opinion. All that she said seemed to me so pitiful, so far from any understanding of how things stood between us. There seemed actually to be more truth to me in the direct opposite of what she said. I thought of that sad morning after our first night together. You kneeling beside me with a look as if everything were lost. And how it really seemed then that in spite of all I could do, I was not helping you but hindering you. It was through me that the landlady had become your enemy, a powerful enemy, whom even now you still undervalue; it was for my sake that you had to take thought, that you had to fight for your post, that you were at a disadvantage before the Superintendent, that you had to humble yourself before the teacher and were delivered over to the assistants, but worst of all for my sake you had perhaps lost your chance with Klamm. That you still went on trying to reach Klamm was only a kind of feeble endeavour to propitiate him in some way. And I told myself that the landlady, who certainly knew far better than I, was only trying to shield me by her suggestions from bitter self-reproach. A well-meant but superfluous attempt. My love for you had helped me through everything, and would certainly help you on too, in the long run, if not here in the village, then somewhere else; it had already given a proof of its power, it had rescued you from Barnabas's family.' 'That was your opinion, then, at the time,' said K., 'and has it changed since?' 'I don't know,' replied Frieda, glancing down at K.'s hand which still held hers, 'perhaps nothing has changed; when you're so close to me and question me so calmly, then I think that nothing has changed. But in reality' – she drew her hand away from K., sat erect opposite him and wept without hiding her face: she held her tear-covered face up to him as if she were weeping not for herself and so had nothing to hide, but as if she were weeping over K.'s treachery and so the pain of seeing her tears was his due – 'But in reality everything has changed since I've listened to you talking with that boy. How innocently you began asking about the family, about this and that! To me you looked just as you did that night when you came into the taproom, impetuous and frank, trying to catch my attention with such a childlike eagerness. You were just the same as then, and all I wished was that the landlady had been here and could have listened to you, and then we should have seen whether she could still stick to her opinion. But then quite suddenly – I don't know how it happened – I noticed that you were talking to him with a hidden intention. You won his trust – and it wasn't easy to win – by sympathetic words, simply so that you might with greater ease reach your end, which I began to recognise more and more clearly. Your end was that woman. In your apparently solicitous enquiries about her I could see quite nakedly your simple preoccupation with your own affairs. You were betraying that woman even before you had won her. In your words I recognised not only my past, but my future as well, it was as if the landlady were sitting beside me and explaining everything, and with all my strength I tried to push her away, but I saw clearly the hopelessness of my attempt, and yet it was not really myself who was going to be betrayed, it was not I who was really being betrayed, but that unknown woman. And then when I collected myself and asked Hans what he wanted to be and he said he wanted to be like you, and I saw that he had fallen under your influence so completely already, well what great difference was there between him, being exploited here by you, the poor boy, and myself that time in the taproom?'

'Everything,' said K., who had regained his composure in listening. 'Everything that you say is in a certain sense justifiable, it is not untrue, it is only partisan. These are the landlady's ideas, my enemy's ideas, even if you imagine that they're your own; and that comforts me. But they're instructive, one can learn a great deal from the landlady. She didn't express them to me personally, although she did not spare my feelings in other ways; evidently she put this weapon in your hands in the hope that you would employ it at a particularly bad or decisive point for me. If I am abusing you, then she is abusing you in the same way. But, Frieda, just consider; even if everything were just as the landlady says, it would only be shameful on one supposition, that is, that you did not love me. Then, only then, would it really seem that I had won you through calculation and trickery, so as to profiteer by possessing you. In that case it might even have been part of my plan to appear before you arm-in-arm with Olga so as to evoke your pity, and the landlady has simply forgotten to mention that too in her list of my offences. But if it wasn't as bad as all that, if it wasn't a sly beast of prey that seized you that night, but you came to meet me, just as I went to meet you, and we found one another without a thought for ourselves, in that case, Frieda, tell me, how would things look? If that were really so, in acting for myself I was acting for you too, there is no distinction here, and only an enemy could draw it. And that holds in everything, even in the case of Hans. Besides, in your condemnation of my talk with Hans your sensitiveness makes you exaggerate things morbidly, for if Hans's intentions and my own don't quite coincide, still that doesn't by any means amount to an actual antagonism between them, moreover our discrepancies were not lost on Hans, if you believe that you do grave injustice to the cautious little man, and even if they should have been all lost on him, still nobody will be any the worse for it, I hope.'

'It's so difficult to see one's way, K.,' said Frieda with a sigh. 'I certainly had no doubts about you, and if I have acquired something of the kind from the landlady, I'll be only too glad to throw it off and beg you for forgiveness on my knees, as I do, believe me, all the time, even when I'm saying such horrible things. But the truth remains that you keep many things from me; you come and go, I don't know where or from where. Just now when Hans knocked you cried out Barnabas's name. I only wish you had once called out my name as lovingly as for some incomprehensible reason you called that hateful name. If you have no trust in me, how can I keep mistrust from rising? It delivers me completely to the landlady, whom you justify in appearance by your behaviour. Not in everything, I won't say that you justify her in everything, for was it not on my account alone that you sent the assistants packing? Oh, if you but knew with what passion I try to find a grain of comfort for myself in all that you do and say, even when it gives me pain.' 'Once and for all, Frieda,' said K., 'I conceal not the slightest thing from you. See how the landlady hates me, and how she does her best to get you away from me, and what despicable means she uses, and how you give in to her, Frieda, how you give in to her! Tell me, now, in what way do I hide anything from you? That I want to reach Klamm you know, that you can't help me to do it and that accordingly I must do it by my own efforts you know too; that I have not succeeded up till now you see for yourself. Am I to humiliate myself doubly, perhaps, by telling you of all the bootless attempts which have already humiliated me sufficiently? Am I to plume myself on having waited and shivered in vain all an afternoon at the door of Klamm's sledge? Only too glad not to have to think of such things any more, I hurry back to you, and I am greeted again with all those reproaches from you. And Barnabas? It's true I'm waiting for him. He's Klamm's messenger, it isn't I who made him that.' 'Barnabas again!' cried Frieda. 'I can't believe that he's a good messenger.' 'Perhaps you're right,' said K., 'but he's the only messenger that's sent to me.' 'All the worse for you,' said Frieda, 'all the more reason why you should beware of him.' 'Unfortunately he has given me no cause for that till now,' said K. smiling. 'He comes very seldom, and what messages he brings are of no importance; only the fact that they come from Klamm gives them any value.' 'But listen to me,' said Frieda, 'for it is not even Klamm that's your goal now, perhaps that disturbs me most of all; that you always longed for Klamm while you had me was bad enough, but that you seem to have stopped trying to reach Klamm now is much worse, that's something which not even the landlady foresaw. According to the landlady your happiness, a questionable and yet very real happiness, would end on the day when you finally recognised that the hopes you founded on Klamm were in vain. But now you don't wait any longer even for that day, a young lad suddenly comes in and you begin to fight with him for his mother, as if you were fighting for your very life.' 'You've understood my talk with Hans quite correctly,' said K., 'it was really so. But is your whole former life so completely wiped from your mind (all except the landlady, of course, who won't allow herself to be wiped out), that you can't remember any longer how one must fight to get to the top, especially when one begins at the bottom? How one must take advantage of everything that offers any hope whatever? And this woman comes from the Castle, she told me herself on my first day here, when I happened to stray into Lasemann's. What's more natural than to ask her for advice or even for help; if the landlady only knows the obstacles which keep one from reaching Klamm, then this woman probably knows the way to him, for she has come here by that way herself.' 'The way to Klamm?' asked Frieda. 'To Klamm, certainly, where else?' said K. Then he jumped up: 'But now it's high time I was going for the lunch.' Frieda implored him to stay, urgently, with an eagerness quite disproportionate to the occasion, as if only his staying with her would confirm all the comforting things he had told her. But K. was thinking of the teacher, he pointed towards the door, which any moment might fly open with a thunderous crash, and promised to return at once, she was not even to light the fire, he himself would see about it. Finally Frieda gave in in silence. As K. was stamping through the snow outside – the path should have been shovelled free long ago, strange how slowly the work was getting forward! – he saw one of the assistants, now dead tired, still holding to the railings. Only one, where was the other? Had K. broken the endurance of one of them, then, at least? The remaining one was certainly still zealous enough, one could see that when, animated by the sight of K., he began more feverishly than ever to stretch out his arms and roll his eyes. 'His obstinacy is really wonderful,' K. told himself, but had to add, 'he'll freeze to the railings if he keeps it up.' Outwardly, however, K. had nothing for the assistant but a threatening gesture with his fist, which prevented any nearer approach; indeed the assistant actually retreated for an appreciable distance. Just then Frieda opened one of the windows so as to air the room before putting on the fire, as she had promised K. Immediately the assistant turned his attention from K., and crept as if irresistibly attracted to the window. Her face torn between pity for the assistant and a beseeching helpless glance which she cast at K., Frieda put her hand out hesitatingly from the window, it was not clear whether it was a greeting or a command to go away, nor did the assistant let it deflect him from his resolve to come nearer. Then Frieda closed the outer window hastily, but remained standing behind it, her hand on the sash, with her head bent sidewards, her eyes wide, and a fixed smile on her face. Did she know that standing like that she was more likely to attract the assistant than repel him? But K. did not look back again, he thought he had better hurry as fast as he could and get back quickly.

XIV

AT long last, late in the afternoon, when it was already dark, K. had cleared the garden path, piled the snow high on either side, beaten it down hard, and also accomplished his work for the day. He was standing by the garden gate in the middle of a wide solitude. He had driven off the remaining assistant hours before, and chased him a long way, but the fellow had managed to hide himself somewhere between the garden and the schoolhouse and could not be found, nor had he shown himself since. Frieda was indoors either starting to wash clothes or still washing Gisa's cat; it was a sign of great confidence on Gisa's part that this task had been entrusted to Frieda, an unpleasant and uncalled-for task, indeed, which K. would not have suffered her to attempt had it not been advisable in view of their various shortcomings to seize every opportunity of securing Gisa's goodwill. Gisa had looked on approvingly while K. brought down the little children's bath from the garret, heated water, and finally helped to put the cat carefully into the bath. Then she actually left the cat entirely in charge of Frieda, for Schwarzer, K.'s acquaintance of the first evening, had arrived, had greeted K. with a mixture of embarrassment (arising out of the events of that evening) and of unmitigated contempt such as one accords to a debtor, and had vanished with Gisa into the other school-room. The two of them were still there. Schwarzer, K. had been told in the Bridge Inn, had been living in the village for some time, although he was a castellan's son, because of his love for Gisa, and through his influential connections had got himself appointed as a pupil-teacher, a position which he filled chiefly by attending all Gisa's classes, either sitting on a school bench among the children, or preferably at Gisa's feet on the teacher's dais. His presence was no longer a disturbance, the children had got quite used to it, all the more easily, perhaps, because Schwarzer neither liked nor understood children and rarely spoke to them except when he took over the gymnastic lesson from Gisa, and was content merely to breathe the same air as Gisa and bask in her warmth and nearness.

The only astonishing thing about it was that in the Bridge Inn at least Schwarzer was spoken of with a certain degree of respect, even if his actions were ridiculous rather than praiseworthy, and that Gisa was included in this respectful atmosphere. It was none the less unwarranted of Schwarzer to assume that his position as a pupil-teacher gave him a great superiority over K., for this superiority was non-existent. A school janitor was an important person to the rest of the staff – and should have been especially so to such an assistant as Schwarzer – a person not to be lightly despised, who should at least be suitably conciliated if professional considerations were not enough to prevent one from despising him. K. decided to keep this fact in mind, also that Schwarzer was still in his debt on account of their first evening, a debt which had not been lessened by the way in which events of succeeding days had seemed to justify Schwarzer's reception of him. For it must not be forgotten that this reception had perhaps determined the later course of events. Because of Schwarzer the full attention of the authorities had been most unreasonably directed to K. at the very first hour of his arrival, while he was still a complete stranger in the village without a single acquaintance or an alternative shelter; over-tired with walking as he was and quite helpless on his sack of straw, he had been at the mercy of any official action. One night later might have made all the difference, things might have gone quietly and been only half noticed. At any rate nobody would have known anything about him or have had any suspicions, there would have been no hesitation in accepting him at least for one day as a stray wanderer, his handiness and trustworthiness would have been recognised and spoken of in the neighbourhood, and probably he would soon have found accommodation somewhere as a servant. Of course the authorities would have found him out. But there would have been a big difference between having the Central Bureau, or whoever was on the telephone, disturbed on his account in the middle of the night by an insistent although ostensibly humble request for an immediate decision, made, too, by Schwarzer, who was probably not in the best odour up there, and a quiet visit by K. to the Superintendent on the next day during official hours to report himself in proper form as a wandering stranger who had already found quarters in a respectable house, and who would probably be leaving the place in another day's time unless the unlikely were to happen and he found some work in the village, only for a day or two, of course, since he did not mean to stay longer. That, or something like that, was what would have happened had it not been for Schwarzer. The authorities would have pursued the matter further, but calmly, in the ordinary course of business, unharassed by what they probably hated most, the impatience of a waiting client. Well, all that was not K.'s fault, it was Schwarzer's fault, but Schwarzer was the son of a castellan, and had behaved with outward propriety, and so the matter could only be visited on K.'s head. And what was the trivial cause of it all? Perhaps an ungracious mood of Gisa's that day, which made Schwarzer roam sleeplessly all night, and vent his annoyance on K. Of course on the other hand one could argue that Schwarzer's attitude was something K. had to be thankful for. It had been the sole precipitant of a situation K. would never by himself have achieved, nor have dared to achieve, and which the authorities themselves would hardly have allowed, namely, that from the very beginning without any dissimulation he found himself confronting the authorities face to face, in so far as that was at all possible. Still, that was a dubious gift, it spared K. indeed the necessity of lying and contriving, but it made him almost defenceless, handicapped him anyhow in the struggle, and might have driven him to despair had he not been able to remind himself that the difference in strength between the authorities and himself was so enormous that all the guile of which he was capable would hardly have served appreciably to reduce the difference in his favour. Yet that was only a reflection for his own consolation, Schwarzer was none the less in his debt, and having harmed K. then could be called upon now to help. K. would be in need of help in the quite trivial and tentative opening moves, for Barnabas seemed to have failed him again.

On Frieda's account K. had refrained all day from going to Barnabas's house to make enquiries; in order to avoid receiving Barnabas in Frieda's presence he had laboured out of doors, and when his work was done had continued to linger outside in expectation of Barnabas, but Barnabas had not come. The only thing he could do now was to visit the sisters, only for a minute or two, he would only stand at the door and ask, he would be back again soon. So he thrust the shovel into the snow and set off at a run. He arrived breathless at the house of Barnabas, and after a sharp knock flung the door open and asked, without looking to see who was inside: 'Hasn't Barnabas come back yet?' Only then did he notice that Olga was not there, that the two old people, who were again sitting at the far end of the table in a state of vacancy, had not yet realised what was happening at the door and were only now slowly turning their faces towards it, and finally that Amalia had been lying beside the stove under a blanket and in her alarm at K.'s sudden appearance had started up with her hand to her brow in an effort to recover her composure. If Olga had been there she would have answered immediately, and K. could have gone away again, but as it was he had at least to take a step or two towards Amalia, give her his hand which she pressed in silence, and beg her to keep the startled old folks from attempting to meander through the room, which she did with a few words. K. learned that Olga was chopping wood in the yard, that Amalia, exhausted – for what reason she

did not say – had had to lie down a short time before, and
that Barnabas had not yet indeed returned, but must return
very soon, for he never stayed overnight in the Castle. K.
thanked her for the information, which left him at liberty to
go, but Amalia asked if he would not wait to see Olga.
However, she added, he had already spoken to Olga during
the day. He answered with surprise that he had not, and
asked if Olga had something of particular importance to say
to him. As if faintly irritated Amalia screwed up her mouth
silently, gave him a nod, obviously in farewell, and lay down
again. From her recumbent position she let her eyes rest on
him as if she were astonished to see him still there. Her
gaze was cold, clear, and steady as usual, it was never
levelled exactly on the object she regarded but in some disturbing way always a little past it, hardly perceptibly, but
yet unquestionably past it, not from weakness, apparently,
nor from embarrassment, nor from duplicity, but from a
persistent and dominating desire for isolation, which she
herself perhaps only became conscious of in this way. K.
thought he could remember being baffled on the very first
evening by that look, probably even the whole hatefulness of
the impression so quickly made on him by this family was
traceable to that look, which in itself was not hateful but
proud and upright in its reserve. 'You are always so sad,
Amalia,' said K., 'is anything troubling you? Can't you say
what it is? I have never seen a country girl at all like you. It
never struck me before. Do you really belong to this village?
Were you born here?' Amalia nodded, as if K. had only put
the last of those questions, and then said: 'So you'll wait for
Olga?' 'I don't know why you keep on asking me that,' said
K. 'I can't stay any longer because my fiancée's waiting for
me at home.' Amalia propped herself on one elbow; she had
not heard of the engagement. K. gave Frieda's name. Amalia did not know it. She asked if Olga knew of their betrothal. K. fancied she did, for she had seen him with Frieda,
and news like that was quick to fly round in a village. Amalia assured him, however, that Olga knew nothing about it,

and that it would make her very unhappy, for she seemed to be in love with K. She had not directly said so, for she was very reserved, but love betrayed itself involuntarily. K. was convinced that Amalia was mistaken. Amalia smiled, and this smile of hers, although sad, lit up her gloomy face, made her silence eloquent, her strangeness intimate, and unlocked a mystery jealously guarded hitherto, a mystery which could indeed be concealed again, but never so completely. Amalia said that she was certainly not mistaken, she would even go further and affirm that K., too, had an inclination for Olga, and that his visits, which were ostensibly concerned with some message or other from Barnabas, were really intended for Olga. But now that Amalia knew all about it he need not be so strict with himself and could come oftener to see them. That was all she wanted to say. K. shook his head, and reminded her of his betrothal. Amalia seemed to set little store by this betrothal, the immediate impression she received from K., who was after all unaccompanied, was in her opinion decisive, she only asked when K. had made the girl's acquaintance, for he had been but a few days in the village. K. told her about his night at the Herrenhof, whereupon Amalia merely said briefly that she had been very much against his being taken to the Herrenhof.

She appealed for confirmation to Olga, who had just come in with an armful of wood, fresh and glowing from the frosty air, strong and vivid, as if transformed by the change from her usual aimless standing about inside. She threw down the wood, greeted K. frankly, and asked at once after Frieda. K. exchanged a look with Amalia, who seemed, however, not at all disconcerted. A little relieved, K. spoke of Frieda more freely than he would otherwise have done, described the difficult circumstances in which she was managing to keep house in a kind of way in the school, and in the haste of his narrative – for he wanted to go home at once – so far forgot himself when bidding them good-bye as to invite the sisters to come and pay him a visit. He began

THE CASTLE

to stammer in confusion, however, when Amalia, giving him no time to say another word, interposed with an acceptance of the invitation; then Olga was compelled to associate herself with it. But K., still harassed by the feeling that he ought to go at once, and becoming uneasy under Amalia's gaze, did not hesitate any longer to confess that the invitation had been quite unpremeditated and had sprung merely from a personal impulse, but that unfortunately he could not confirm it since there was a great hostility, to him quite incomprehensible, between Frieda and their family. 'It's not hostility,' said Amalia, getting up from her couch and flinging the blanket behind her, 'it's nothing so big as that, it's only a parrot repetition of what she hears everywhere. And now, go away, go to your young woman, I can see you're in a hurry. You needn't be afraid that we'll come, I only said it at first for fun, out of mischief. But you can come often enough to see us, there's nothing to hinder you, you can always plead Barnabas's messages as an excuse. I'll make it easier for you by telling you that Barnabas, even if he has a message from the Castle for you, can't go all the way up to the school to find you. He can't trail about so much, poor boy, he wears himself out in the service, you'll have to come yourself to get the news.' K. had never before heard Amalia utter so many consecutive sentences, and they sounded differently from her usual comments, they had a kind of dignity which obviously impressed not only K. but Olga too, although she was accustomed to her sister. She stood a little to one side, her arms folded, in her usual stolid and somewhat stooping posture once more, with her eyes fixed on Amalia, who on the other hand looked only at K. 'It's an error,' said K., 'a gross error to imagine that I'm not in earnest in looking for Barnabas, it's my most urgent wish, really my only wish, to get my business with the authorities properly settled. And Barnabas has to help me in that, most of my hopes are based on him. I grant he has disappointed me greatly once as it is, but that was more my fault than his; in the bewilderment of

170

my first hours in the village I believed that everything could be settled by a short walk in the evening, and when the impossible proved impossible I blamed him for it. That influenced me even in my opinion of your family and of you. But that is all past, I think I understand you better now, you are even –' K. tried to think of the exact word, but could not find it immediately, so contented himself with a makeshift – 'You seem to be the most good-natured people in the village so far as my experience goes. But now, Amalia, you're putting me off the track again by your depreciation – if not of your brother's service – then of the importance he has for me. Perhaps you aren't acquainted with his affairs, in which case it doesn't matter, but perhaps you are acquainted with them – and that's the impression I incline to have – in which case it's a bad thing, for that would indicate that your brother is deceiving me.' 'Calm yourself,' said Amalia, 'I'm not acquainted with them, nothing could induce me to become acquainted with them, nothing at all, not even my consideration for you, which would move me to do a great deal, for, as you say, we are good-natured people. But my brother's affairs are his own business, I know nothing about them except what I hear by chance now and then against my will. On the other hand Olga can tell you all about them, for she's in his confidence.' And Amalia went away, first to her parents, with whom she whispered, then to the kitchen; she went without taking leave of K., as if she knew that he would stay for a long time yet and that no good-bye was necessary.

XV

SEEING that with a somewhat astonished face K. remained standing where he was, Olga laughed at him and drew him towards the settle by the stove, she seemed to be really happy at the prospect of sitting there alone with him, but it was a contented happiness without a single hint of jealousy. And precisely this freedom of hers from jealousy and therefore from any kind of claim upon him did K. good, he was glad to look into her blue eyes which were not cajoling, nor hectoring, but shyly simple and frank. It was as if the warning of Frieda and the landlady had made him, not more susceptible to all those things, but more observant and more discerning. And he laughed with Olga when she expressed her wonder at his calling Amalia good-natured, of all things, for Amalia had many qualities, but good-nature was certainly not one of them. Whereupon K. explained that of course his praise had been meant for Olga, only Amalia was so masterful that she not only took to herself whatever was said in her presence, but induced other people of their own free will to include her in everything. 'That's true,' said Olga, becoming more serious, 'truer than you think. Amalia's younger than me, and younger than Barnabas, but hers is the decisive voice in the family for good or for ill, of course she bears the burden of it more than anybody, the good as well as the bad.' K. thought that an exaggeration, for Amalia had just said that she paid no attention, for instance, to her brother's affairs, while Olga knew all about them. 'How can I make it clear?' said Olga, 'Amalia bothers neither about Barnabas nor about me, she really bothers about nobody but the old people whom she tends day and night; now she has just asked them again if they want anything and has gone into the kitchen to cook them something, and for their sakes she has overcome her indisposition, for she's been ill since midday and been lying here on the settle. But although she doesn't bother about us we're as dependent on her as if she were the eldest, and if she were to advise us in our affairs we should certainly follow her advice, only she doesn't do it, she's different from us. You have experience of people, you come from a strange land, don't you think, too, that she's extraordinarily clever?' 'Extraordinarily unhappy is what she seems to me,' said K., 'but how does it go with your respect for her that Barnabas, for example, takes service as a messenger, in spite of Amalia's evident disapproval, and even her scorn?' 'If he knew what else to do he would give up being a messenger at once, for it doesn't satisfy him.' 'Isn't he an expert shoemaker?' asked K. 'Of course he is,' said Olga, 'and in his spare time he does work for Brunswick, and if he liked he could have enough work to keep him going day and night and earn a lot of money.' 'Well then,' said K., 'that would be an alternative to his service as a messenger.' 'An alternative?' asked Olga in astonishment. 'Do you think he does it for the money?' 'Maybe he does,' said K., 'but didn't you say he was discontented?' 'He's discontented, and for various reasons,' said Olga, 'but it's Castle service, anyhow a kind of Castle service, at least one would suppose so.' 'What!' said K., 'do you even doubt that?' 'Well,' said Olga, 'not really, Barnabas goes into the bureaux and is accepted by the attendants as one of themselves, he sees various officials, too, from the distance, is entrusted with relatively important letters, even with verbally delivered messages, that's a good deal, after all, and we should be proud of what he has achieved for a young man of his years.' K. nodded and no longer thought of going home. 'He has a uniform of his own, too?' he asked. 'You mean the jacket?' said Olga. 'No, Amalia made that for him long before he became a messenger. But you're touching on a sore spot now. He ought long ago to have had, not a uniform, for there aren't many in the Castle, but a suit provided by the department, and he has been promised one, but in things of that kind the Castle moves slowly, and the worst of it is that one never knows what this slowness means; it can mean that the matter's being considered, but it can also mean that it hasn't yet been taken up, that Barnabas for instance is still on probation, and in the long run it can also mean that the whole thing has been settled, that for some reason or other the promise has been cancelled, and that Barnabas will never get his suit. One can never find out exactly what is happening, or only a long time afterwards. We have a saying here, perhaps you've heard it: Official decisions are as shy as young girls.' 'That's a good observation,' said K., he took it still more seriously than Olga, 'a good observation, and the decisions may have other characteristics in common with young girls.' 'Perhaps,' said Olga. 'But as far as the official suit's concerned, that's one of Barnabas's great sorrows, and since we share all our troubles, it's one of mine too. We ask ourselves in vain why he doesn't get an official suit. But the whole affair is not just so simple as that. The officials, for instance, apparently have no official dress; so far as we know here, and so far as Barnabas tells us, the officials go about in their ordinary clothes, very fine clothes, certainly. Well, you've seen Klamm. Now, Barnabas is certainly not an official, not even one in the lowest category, and he doesn't overstep his limitations so far as to want to be one. But according to Barnabas, the higher-grade servants, whom one certainly never sees down here in the village, have no official dress; that's a kind of comfort, one might suppose, but it's a deceptive comfort, for is Barnabas a high-grade servant? Not he; however partial one might be towards him one couldn't maintain that, the fact that he comes to the village and even lives here is sufficient proof of the contrary, for the higher-grade servants are even more inaccessible than the officials, perhaps rightly so, perhaps they are even of higher rank than many an official, there's some evidence of that, they work less, and Barnabas says it's a marvellous sight to see these tall and distinguished men slowly walking through the corridors, Barnabas always give them a wide berth. Well, he might be one of the lower-grade servants, then, but these always have an official suit, at least whenever they come down into the village, it's not exactly a uniform, there are many different versions of it, but at any rate one can always tell Castle servants by their clothes, you've seen some of them in the Herrenhof. The most noticeable thing about the clothes is that they're mostly close-fitting, a peasant or a handworker couldn't do with them. Well, a suit like that hasn't been given to Barnabas and it's not merely the shame of it or the disgrace – one could put up with that – but the fact that in moments of depression – and we often have such moments, none too rarely, Barnabas and I – it makes us doubt everything. Is it really Castle service Barnabas is doing, we ask ourselves then; granted, he goes into the bureaux, but are the bureaux part of the real Castle? And even if there are bureaux actually in the Castle, are they the bureaux that Barnabas is allowed to enter?

'He's admitted into certain rooms, but they're only a part of the whole, for there are barriers behind which there are more rooms. Not that he's actually forbidden to pass the barriers, but he can't very well push past them once he has met his chiefs and been dismissed by them. Besides, everybody is watched there, at least so we believe. And even if he did push on farther what good would it be to him, if he had no official duties to carry out and were a mere intruder? And you mustn't imagine that these barriers are a definite dividing-line; Barnabas is always impressing that on me. There are barriers even at the entrance to the rooms where he's admitted, so you see there are barriers he can pass, and they're just the same as the ones he's never yet passed, which looks as if one oughtn't to suppose that behind the ultimate barriers the bureaux are any different from those Barnabas has already seen. Only that's what we do suppose in moments of depression. And the doubt doesn't stop there, we can't keep it within bounds. Barnabas sees officials, Barnabas is given messages. But who are those officials, and what are the messages? Now, so he says, he's assigned to Klamm, who gives him his instructions in person. Well, that would be a great favour, even higher-grade servants don't get so far as that, it's almost too much to believe, almost terrifying. Only think, directly assigned to Klamm, speaking with him face to face! But is it really the case? Well, suppose it is so, then why does Barnabas doubt that the official who is referred to as Klamm is really Klamm?' 'Olga,' said K., 'you surely must be joking; how can there be any doubt about Klamm's appearance, everybody knows what he looks like, even I have seen him.' 'Of course not, K.,' said Olga. 'I'm not joking at all, I'm desperately serious. Yet I'm not telling you all this simply to relieve my own feelings and burden yours, but because Amalia charged me to tell you, since you were asking for Barnabas, and because I think too that it would be useful for you to know more about it. I'm doing it for Barnabas's sake as well, so that you won't pin too many hopes upon him, and suffer disappointment, and make him suffer too because of your disappointment. He's very sensitive, for instance he didn't sleep all night because you were displeased with him yesterday evening. He took you to say that it was a bad lookout for you to have only a messenger like him. These words kept him off his sleep. I don't suppose that you noticed how upset he was, for Castle messengers must keep themselves well under control. But he hasn't an easy time, not even with you, although from your point of view you don't ask too much of him, for you have your own prior conception of a messenger's powers and make your demands accordingly. But in the Castle they have a different conception of a messenger's duties, which couldn't be reconciled with yours, even if Barnabas were to devote himself entirely to the task, which, unfortunately, he often seems inclined to do. Still, one would have to submit to that and raise no objections if it weren't for the question whether Barnabas is really a messenger or not. Before you, of course, he can't express any doubt of it whatever, to do that would be to undermine his very existence and to offend grievously against laws which he believes himself still plighted to, and even to me he doesn't speak freely, I have to cajole and kiss his doubts out of him, and even then he refuses to admit that his doubts are doubts. He has something of Amalia in him. And I'm sure that he doesn't tell me everything, although I'm his sole confidante. But we do often speak about Klamm, whom I've never seen; you know Frieda doesn't like me and has never let me look at him, still his appearance is well known in the village, some people have seen him, everybody has heard of him, and out of glimpses and rumours and through various distorting factors an image of Klamm has been constructed which is certainly true in fundamentals. But only in fundamentals. In detail it fluctuates, and yet perhaps not so much as Klamm's real appearance. For he's reported as having one appearance when he comes into the village and another on leaving it; after having his beer he looks different from what he does before it, when he's awake he's different from when he's asleep, when he's alone he's different from when he's talking to people, and – what is comprehensible after all that – he's almost another person up in the Castle. And even within the village there are considerable differences in the accounts given of him, differences as to his height, his bearing, his size, and the cut of his beard; fortunately there's one thing in which all the accounts agree, he always wears the same clothes, a black morning coat with long tails. Now of course all these differences aren't the result of magic, but can be easily explained; they depend on the mood of the observer, on the degree of his excitement, on the countless graduations of hope or despair which are possible for him when he sees Klamm, and besides, he can usually see Klamm only for a second or two. I'm telling you all this just as Barnabas has often told it to me, and, on the whole, for anyone not personally interested in the matter, it would be a sufficient explanation. Not for us, however; it's a matter of life or death for Barnabas whether it's really Klamm he speaks to or not.' 'And for me no less,' said K., and they moved nearer to each other on the settle.

All this depressing information of Olga's certainly affected K., but he regarded it as a great consolation to find other people who were at least externally much in the same situation as himself, with whom he could join forces and whom he could touch at many points, not merely at a few points as in Frieda's case. He was indeed gradually giving up all hope of achieving success through Barnabas, but the worse it went with Barnabas in the Castle the nearer he felt drawn to him down here; never would K. have believed that in the village itself such a despairing struggle could go on as Barnabas and his sister were involved in. Of course it was as yet far from being adequately explained and might turn out to be quite the reverse, one shouldn't let Olga's unquestionable innocence mislead one into taking Barnabas's uprightness for granted. 'Barnabas is familiar with all those accounts of Klamm's appearance,' went on Olga, 'he has collected and compared a great many, perhaps too many, he even saw Klamm once through a carriage window in the village, or believed he saw him, and so was sufficiently prepared to recognise him again, and yet – how can you explain this? – when he entered a bureau in the Castle and had one of several officials pointed out to him as Klamm he didn't recognise him, and for a long time afterwards couldn't accustom himself to the idea that it was Klamm. But if you ask Barnabas what was the difference between that Klamm and the usual description given of Klamm, he can't tell you, or rather he tries to tell you and describes the official of the Castle, but his description coincides exactly with the descriptions we usually hear of Klamm. Well then, Barnabas, I say to him, why do you doubt it, why do you torment yourself? Whereupon in obvious distress he begins to reckon up certain characteristics of the Castle official, but he seems to be thinking them out rather than describing them, and besides that they are so trivial – a particular way of nodding the head, for instance, or even an unbuttoned waistcoat – that one simply can't take them seriously. Much more important seems to me the way in which Klamm receives Barnabas. Barnabas has often described it to me, and even sketched the room. He's usually admitted into a large room, but the room isn't Klamm's bureau, nor even the bureau of any particular official. It's a room divided into two by a single reading-desk stretching all its length from wall to wall; one side is so narrow that two people can hardly squeeze past each other, and that's reserved for the officials, the other side is spacious, and that's where clients wait, spectators, servants, messengers. On the desk there are great books lying open, side by side, and officials stand by, most of them reading. They don't always stick to the same book, yet it isn't the books that they change but their places, and it always astounds Barnabas to see how they have to squeeze past each other when they change places, because there's so little room. In front of the desk and close to it there are small, low tables at which clerks sit ready to write from dictation, whenever the officials wish it. And the way that is done always amazes Barnabas. There's no express command given by the official, nor is the dictation given in a loud voice, one could hardly tell that it was being given at all, the official just seems to go on reading as before, only whispering as he reads, and the clerk hears the whisper. Often it's so low that the clerk can't hear it at all in his seat, and then he has to jump up, catch what's being dictated, sit down again quickly and make a note of it, then jump up once more, and so on. What a strange business! It's almost incomprehensible. Of course Barnabas has time enough to observe it all, for he's often kept standing in the big room for hours and days at a time before Klamm happens to see him. And even if Klamm sees him and he springs to attention, that needn't mean anything, for Klamm may turn away from him again to the book and forget all about him. That often happens. But what can be the use of a messenger-service so casual as that? It makes me quite doleful to hear Barnabas say in the early morning that he's going to the Castle. In all likelihood a quite useless journey, a lost day, a completely vain hope. What's the good of it all? And here's cobbler's work piled up which never gets done and which Brunswick is always asking for.' 'Oh, well,' said K., 'Barnabas has just to hang on till he gets a commission. That's understandable, the place seems to be over-staffed, and everybody can't be given a job every day, you needn't complain about that, for it must affect everybody. But in the long run even a Barnabas gets commissions, he has brought two letters already to me.' 'It's possible, of course,' answered Olga, 'that we're wrong in complaining, especially a girl like me who knows things only from hearsay and can't understand it all so well as Barnabas, who certainly keeps many things to himself. But let me tell you how the letters are given out, your letters, for example. Barnabas doesn't get these letters directly from Klamm, but from a clerk. On no particular day, at no particular hour – that's why the service, however easy it appears, is really very exhausting, for Barnabas must be always on the alert – a clerk suddenly remembers about him and gives him a sign, without any apparent instructions from Klamm, who merely goes on reading in his book. True, sometimes Klamm is polishing his glasses when Barnabas comes up, but he often does that, anyhow – however, he may take a look at Barnabas then, supposing, that is, that he can see anything at all without his glasses, which Barnabas doubts; for Klamm's eyes are almost shut, he generally seems to be sleeping and only polishing his glasses in a kind of dream. Meanwhile the clerk hunts among the piles of manuscripts and writings under his table and fishes out a letter for you, so it's not a letter newly written, indeed, by the look of the envelope, it's usually a very old letter, which has been lying there a long time. But if that is so, why do they keep Barnabas waiting like that? And you too? And the letter too, of course, for it must be long out of date. That's how they get Barnabas the reputation of being a bad and slow messenger. It's all very well for the clerk, he just gives Barnabas the letter, saying: 'From Klamm for K.' and so dismisses him. But Barnabas comes home breathless, with his hardly won letter next to his bare skin, and then we sit here on the settle like this and he tells me about it and we go into all the particulars and weigh up what he has achieved and find ultimately that it's very little, and questionable at that until Barnabas lays the letter down with no longer any inclination to deliver it, yet doesn't feel inclined to go to sleep either, and so sits cobbling on his stool all night. That's how it is,

K., and now you have all my secrets and you can't be surprised any longer at Amalia's indifference to them.' 'And what happens to the letter?' asked K. 'The letter?' said Olga. 'Oh, some time later when I've plagued Barnabas enough about it, it may be days or weeks later, he picks it up again and goes to deliver it. In such practical matters he's very dependent on me. For I can usually pull myself together after I've recovered from the first impression of what he has told me, but he can't, probably because he knows more. So I always find something or other to say to him, such as "What are you really aiming at, Barnabas? What kind of career, what ambition are you dreaming of? Are you thinking of climbing so high that you'll have to leave us, to leave me, completely behind you? Is that what you're aiming at? How can I help believing so when it's the only possible explanation why you're so dreadfully discontented with all you've done already? Only take a look round and see whether any of our neighbours has got on so well as you. I admit their situation is different from ours and they have no grounds for ambition beyond their daily work, but even without making comparisons it's easy to see that you're all right. Hindrances there may be, doubts and disappointments, but that only means, what we all knew beforehand, that you get nothing without paying for it, that you have to fight for every trivial point; all the more reason for being proud instead of downcast. And aren't you fighting for us as well? Doesn't that mean anything to you? Doesn't that put new strength into you? And the fact that I'm happy and almost conceited at having such a brother, doesn't that give you any confidence? It isn't what you've achieved in the Castle that disappoints me, but the little that I'm able to achieve with you. You're allowed into the Castle, you're a regular visitor in the bureaux, you spend whole days in the same room as Klamm, you're an officially recognised messenger, with a claim on an official suit, you're entrusted with important commissions, you have all that to your credit, and then you come down here and instead of embracing me and weeping for joy you seem to lose all heart as soon as you set eyes on me, and you doubt everything, nothing interests you but cobbling, and you leave the letter, the pledge of our future, lying in a corner." That's how I speak to him, and after I've repeated the same words day after day he picks up the letter at last with a sigh and goes off. Yet probably it's not the effect of what I say that drives him out, but a desire to go to the Castle again, which he dare not do without having delivered his message.' 'But you're absolutely right in everything you say,' said K., 'it's amazing how well you grasp it all. What an extraordinarily clear mind you have!' 'No,' said Olga, 'it takes you in, and perhaps it takes him in too. For what has he really achieved? He's allowed in to a bureau, but it doesn't seem to be even a bureau. He speaks to Klamm, but is it Klamm? Isn't it rather someone who's a little like Klamm? A secretary, perhaps, at the most, who resembles Klamm a little and takes pains to increase the resemblance and poses a little in Klamm's sleepy and dreamy style. That side of his nature is the easiest to imitate, there are many who try it on, although they have sense enough not to attempt anything more. And a man like Klamm who is so much sought after and so rarely seen is apt to take different shapes in people's imagination. For instance, Klamm has a village secretary here called Momus. You know him, do you? He keeps well in the background too, but I've seen him several times. A stoutly-built young man, isn't he? And so evidently not in the least like Klamm. And yet you'll find people in the village who swear that Momus is Klamm, he and no other. That's how people work their own confusion. Is there any reason why it should be different in the Castle? Somebody pointed out that particular official to Barnabas as Klamm, and there is actually a resemblance that Barnabas has always questioned. And everything goes to support his doubt. Are we to suppose that Klamm has to squeeze his way among other officials in a common room with a pencil behind his ear? It's wildly improbable. Barnabas often says, somewhat like a child and yet in a child's mood of trustfulness: "The official is really very like Klamm, and if he were sitting in his own office at his own desk with his name on the door I would have no more doubt at all." That's childish, but reasonable. Of course it would be still more reasonable of Barnabas when he's up there to ask a few people about the truth of things, for judging from his account there are plenty of men standing round. And even if their information were no more reliable than that of the man who pointed out Klamm of his own accord, there would be surely some common ground, some ground for comparison, in the various things they said. That's not my idea, but Barnabas's, yet he doesn't dare to follow it out, he doesn't venture to speak to anybody for fear of offending in ignorance against some unknown rule and so losing his job; you see how uncertain he feels; and this miserable uncertainty of his throws a clearer light on his position there than all his descriptions. How ambiguous and threatening everything must appear to him when he won't even risk opening his mouth to put an innocent question! When I reflect on that I blame myself for letting him go alone into those unknown rooms, which have such an effect on him that, though he's daring rather than cowardly, he apparently trembles with fright as he stands there.'

'Here I think you've touched on the essential point,' said K. 'That's it. After all you've told me, I believe I can see the matter clearly. Barnabas is too young for this task. Nothing he tells you is to be taken seriously at its face value. Since he's beside himself with fright up there, he's incapable of observing, and when you force him to give an account of what he has seen you get simply confused fabrications. That doesn't surprise me. Fear of the authorities is born in you here, and is further suggested to you all your lives in the most various ways and from every side, and you yourselves help to strengthen it as much as possible. Still, I have no fundamental objection to that; if an authority is good why should it not be feared? Only one shouldn't suddenly send an inexperienced youngster like Barnabas, who has never been farther than this village, into the Castle, and then expect a truthful account of everything from him, and interpret each single word of his as if it were a revelation, and base one's own life's happiness on the interpretation. Nothing could be more mistaken. I admit that I have let him mislead me in exactly the same way and have set hopes upon him and suffered disappointments through him, both based simply on his own words, that is to say, with almost no basis.' Olga was silent. 'It won't be easy for me,' went on K., 'to talk you out of your confidence in your brother, for I see how you love him and how much you expect from him. But I must do it, if only for the sake of that very love and expectation. For let me point out that there's always something – I don't know what it is – that hinders you from seeing clearly how much Barnabas has – I'll not say achieved – but has had bestowed on him. He's permitted to go into the bureaux, or if you prefer, into an antechamber, well let it be an antechamber, it has doors that lead on farther, barriers which can be passed if one has the courage. To me, for instance, even this antechamber is utterly inaccessible, for the present at least. Who it is that Barnabas speaks to there I have no idea, perhaps the clerk is the lowest in the whole staff, but even if he is the lowest he can put one in touch with the next man above him, and if he can't do that he can at least give the other's name, and if he can't even do that he can refer to somebody who can give the name. This so-called Klamm may not have the smallest trait in common with the real one, the resemblance may not exist except in the eyes of Barnabas, half-blinded by fear, he may be the meanest of the officials, he may not even be an official at all, but all the same he has work of some kind to perform at the desk, he reads something or other in his great book, he whispers something to the clerk, he thinks something when his eye falls on Barnabas once in a while, and even if that isn't true and he and his acts have no significance whatever he has at least been set there by somebody for some purpose. All that simply means that

184

something is there, something which Barnabas has the chance of using, something or other at the very least; and that it is Barnabas's own fault if he can't get any further than doubt and anxiety and despair. And that's only on the most unfavourable interpretation of things, which is extremely improbable. For we have the actual letters which I certainly set no great store on, but more than on what Barnabas says. Let them be worthless old letters, fished at random from a pile of other such worthless old letters, at random and with no more discrimination than the love-birds show in the fairs when they pick one's fortune out of a pile; let them be all that, still they have some bearing on my fate. They're evidently meant for me, although perhaps not for my good, and, as the Superintendent and his wife have testified, they are written in Klamm's own hand, and, again on the Superintendent's evidence, they have a significance which is only private and obscure, it is true, but still great.' 'Did the Superintendent say that?' asked Olga. 'Yes, he did,' replied K. 'I must tell Barnabas that,' said Olga quickly; 'that will encourage him greatly.' 'But he doesn't need encouragement,' said K.; 'to encourage him amounts to telling him that he's right, that he has only to go on as he is doing now, but that is just the way he will never achieve anything by. If a man has his eyes bound you can encourage him as much as you like to stare through the bandage, but he'll never see anything. He'll be able to see only when the bandage is removed. It's help Barnabas needs, not encouragement. Only think, up there you have all the inextricable complications of a great authority – I imagined that I had an approximate conception of its nature before I came here, but how childish my ideas were! – up there, then, you have the authorities and over against them Barnabas, nobody more, only Barnabas, pathetically alone, where it would be enough honour for him to spend his whole life cowering in a dark and forgotten corner of some bureau.' 'Don't imagine, K., that we underestimate the difficulties Barnabas has to face,' said Olga, 'we have reverence enough for the authorities, you said so yourself.' 'But it's a mistaken reverence,' said K., 'a reverence in the wrong place, the kind of reverence that dishonours its object. Do you call it reverence that leads Barnabas to abuse the privilege of admission to that room by spending his time there doing nothing, or makes him when he comes down again belittle and despise the men before whom he has just been trembling, or allows him because he's depressed or weary to put off delivering letters and fail in executing commissions entrusted to him? That's far from being reverence. But I have a further reproach to make, Olga; I must blame you too, I can't exempt you. Although you fancy you have some reverence for the authorities, you sent Barnabas into the Castle in all his youth and weakness and forlornness, or at least you didn't dissuade him from going.'

'This reproach that you make,' said Olga, 'is one I have made myself from the beginning. Not indeed that I sent Barnabas to the Castle, I didn't send him, he went himself, but I ought to have prevented him by all the means in my power, by force, by craft, by persuasion. I ought to have prevented him, but if I had to decide again this very day, and if I were to feel as keenly as I did then and still do the straits Barnabas is in, and our whole family, and if Barnabas, fully conscious of the responsibility and danger ahead of him, were once more to free himself from me with a smile and set off, I wouldn't hold him back even to-day, in spite of all that has happened in between, and I believe that in my place you would do exactly the same. You don't know the plight we are in, that's why you're unfair to all of us, and especially to Barnabas. At that time we had more hope than now, but even then our hope wasn't great, but our plight was great, and is so still. Hasn't Frieda told you anything about us?' 'Mere hints,' said K., 'nothing definite, but the very mention of your name exasperates her.' 'And has the landlady told you nothing either?' 'No, nothing.' 'Nor anybody else?' 'Nobody.' 'Of course; how could anybody tell you anything? Everyone knows something about us, either the truth, so far as it is accessible, or at least some exaggerated rumour, mostly invention, and everybody thinks about us more than need be, but nobody will actually speak about it, people are shy of putting these things into words. And they're quite right in that. It's difficult to speak of it even before you, K., and when you've heard it all it's possible – isn't it? – that you'll go away and not want to have anything more to do with us, however little it may seem to concern you. Then we should have lost you, and I confess that now you mean almost more to me than Barnabas's service in the Castle. But yet – and this argument has been distracting me all the evening – you must be told, otherwise you would have no insight into our situation, and, what would vex me most of all, you would go on being unfair to Barnabas. Complete accord would fail between us, and you could neither help us, nor accept our additional help. But there is still one more question: Do you really want to be told?' 'Why do you ask?' said K., 'if it's necessary, I would rather be told, but why do you ask me so particularly?' 'Superstition,' said Olga. 'You'll become involved in our affairs, innocent as you are, almost as innocent as Barnabas.' 'Tell me quickly,' said K., 'I'm not afraid. You're certainly making it much worse than it is with such womanish fussing.'

AMALIA'S SECRET

'Judge for yourself,' said Olga, 'I warn you it sounds quite simple, one can't comprehend at first why it should be of any importance. There's a great official in the Castle called Sortini.' 'I've heard of him already,' said K., 'he had something to do with bringing me here.' 'I don't think so,' said Olga, 'Sortini hardly ever comes into the open. Aren't you mistaking him for Sordini, spelt with a 'd'?' 'You're quite right,' said K., 'Sordini it was.' 'Yes,' said Olga, 'Sordini is well known, one of the most industrious of the officials, he's often mentioned; Sortini on the other hand is very retiring and quite unknown to most people. More than three years ago I saw him for the first and last time. It was on the third of July at a celebration given by the Fire Brigade, the Castle too had contributed to it and provided a new fire-engine. Sortini, who was supposed to have some hand in directing the affairs of the Fire Brigade, but perhaps he was only deputising for someone else – the officials mostly hide behind each other like that, and so it's difficult to discover what any official is actually responsible for – Sortini took part in the ceremony of handing over the fire-engine. There were of course many other people from the Castle, officials and attendants, and true to his character Sortini kept well in the background. He's a small, frail, reflective-looking gentleman, and one thing about him struck all the people who noticed him at all, the way his forehead was furrowed; all the furrows – and there were plenty of them although he's certainly not more than forty – were spread fanwise over his forehead, running towards the root of his nose, I've never seen anything like it. Well then, we had that celebration. Amalia and I had been excited about it for weeks beforehand, our Sunday clothes had been done up for the occasion and were partly new, Amalia's dress was specially fine, a white blouse foaming high in front with one row of lace after the other, our mother had taken every bit of her lace for it. I was jealous, and cried half the night before the celebration. Only when the Bridge Inn landlady came to see us in the morning –' 'The Bridge Inn landlady?' asked K. 'Yes,' said Olga, 'she was a great friend of ours, well, she came and had to admit that Amalia was the finer, so to console me she lent me her own necklace of Bohemian garnets. When we were ready to go and Amalia was standing beside me and we were all admiring her, my father said: 'To-day, mark my words, Amalia will find a husband'; then, I don't know why, I took my necklace, my great pride, and hung it round Amalia's neck, and wasn't jealous any longer. I bowed before her triumph and I felt that

188

everyone must bow before her, perhaps what amazed us so much was the difference in her appearance, for she wasn't really beautiful, but her sombre glance, and it has kept the same quality since that day, was high over our heads and involuntarily one had almost literally to bow before her. Everybody remarked on it, even Lasemann and his wife who came to fetch us.' 'Lasemann?' asked K. 'Yes, Lasemann,' said Olga, 'we were in high esteem, and the celebration couldn't well have begun without us, for my father was the third in command of the Fire Brigade.' 'Was your father still so active?' asked K. 'Father?' returned Olga, as if she did not quite comprehend, 'three years ago he was still relatively a young man, for instance, when a fire broke out at the Herrenhof he carried an official, Galater, who is a heavy man, out of the house on his back at a run. I was there myself, there was no real danger, it was only some dry wood near a stove which had begun to smoke, but Galater was terrified and cried for help out of the window, and the Fire Brigade turned out, and father had to carry him out although the fire was already extinguished. Of course Galater finds it difficult to move and has to be careful in circumstances like that. I'm telling you this only on father's account; not much more than three years have passed since then, and look at him now.' Only then did K. become aware that Amalia was again in the room, but she was a long way off at the table where her parents sat, she was feeding her mother who could not move her rheumaticky arms, and admonishing her father meanwhile to wait in patience for a little, it would soon be his turn. But her admonition was in vain, for her father, greedily desiring his soup, overcame his weakness and tried to drink it first out of the spoon and then out of the bowl, and grumbled angrily when neither attempt succeeded; the spoon was empty long before he got it to his lips, and his mouth never reached the soup, for his drooping moustache dipped into it and scattered it everywhere except into his mouth. 'And have three years done that to him?' asked K., yet he could not summon up any sympathy for the old people, and for that whole corner with the table in it he felt only repulsion. 'Three years,' replied Olga slowly, 'or, more precisely, a few hours at that celebration. The celebration was held on a meadow by the village, at the brook; there was already a large crowd there when we arrived, many people had come in from neighbouring villages, and the noise was bewildering. Of course my father took us first to look at the fire-engine, he laughed with delight when he saw it, the new fire-engine made him happy, he began to examine it and explain it to us, he wouldn't hear of any opposition or holding back, but made every one of us stoop and almost crawl under the engine if there was something there he had to show us, and he smacked Barnabas for refusing. Only Amalia paid no attention to the engine, she stood upright beside it in her fine clothes and nobody dared to say a word to her, I ran up to her sometimes and took her arm, but she said nothing. Even to-day I cannot explain how we came to stand for so long in front of the fire-engine without noticing Sortini until the very moment my father turned away, for he had obviously been leaning on a wheel behind the fire-engine all the time. Of course there was a terrific racket all round us, not only the usual kind of noise, for the Castle had presented the Fire Brigade with some trumpets as well as the engine, extraordinary instruments on which with the smallest effort – a child could do it – one could produce the wildest blasts; to hear them was enough to make one think the Turks were there, and one could not get accustomed to them, every fresh blast made one jump. And because the trumpets were new everybody wanted to try them, and because it was a celebration, everybody was allowed to try. Right at our ears, perhaps Amalia had attracted them, were some of these trumpet blowers. It was difficult to keep one's wits about one, and obeying father and attending to the fire-engine was the utmost we were capable of, and so it was that Sortini escaped our notice for such a long time, and besides we had no idea who he was. 'There is Sortini,' Lasemann whispered at last to my father – I was beside him – and father, greatly excited, made a deep bow, and signed to us to do the same. Without having met him till now father had always honoured Sortini as an authority in Fire Brigade matters, and had often spoken of him at home, so it was a very astonishing and important matter for us actually to see Sortini with our own eyes. Sortini, however, paid no attention to us, and in that he wasn't peculiar, for most of the officials hold themselves aloof in public, besides he was tired, only his official duty kept him there. It's not the worst officials who find duties like that particularly trying, and anyhow there were other officials and attendants mingling with the people. But he stayed by the fire-engine and discouraged by his silence all those who tried to approach him with some request or piece of flattery. So it happened that he didn't notice us until long after we had noticed him. Only as we bowed respectfully and father was making apologies for us did he look our way and scan us one after another wearily, as if sighing to find that there was still another and another to look at, until he let his eyes rest on Amalia, to whom he had to look up, for she was much taller than he. At the sight of her he started and leapt over the shaft to get nearer to her, we misunderstood him at first and began to approach him, father leading the way, but he held us off with uplifted hand and then waved us away. That was all. We teased Amalia a lot about having really found a husband, and in our ignorance we were very merry the whole of that afternoon. But Amalia was more silent than usual. 'She's fallen head over ears in love with Sortini,' said Brunswick, who is always rather vulgar and has no comprehension of natures like Amalia's. Yet this time we were inclined to think that he was right, we were quite mad that day, and all of us, even Amalia, were as if stupefied by the sweet Castle wine when we came home about midnight.' 'And Sortini?' asked K. 'Yes, Sortini,' said Olga, 'I saw him several times during the afternoon as I passed by, he was sitting on the engine shaft with his arms folded, and he stayed there till the Castle carriage came to fetch him. He didn't even go over to watch the fire-drill at which father, in the very hope that Sortini was watching, distinguished himself beyond all the other men of his age.' 'And did you hear nothing more from him?' asked K. 'You seem to have a great regard for Sortini.' 'Oh, yes, regard,' said Olga, 'oh, yes, and hear from him we certainly did. Next morning we were roused from our heavy sleep by a scream from Amalia; the others rolled back into their beds again, but I was completely awake and ran to her. She was standing by the window holding a letter in her hand which had just been given in through the window by a man who was still waiting for an answer. The letter was short, and Amalia had already read it, and held it in her drooping hand; how I always loved her when she was tired like that! I knelt down beside her and read the letter. Hardly had I finished it when Amalia after a brief glance at me took it back, but she couldn't bring herself to read it again, and tearing it in pieces she threw the fragments in the face of the man outside and shut the window. That was the morning which decided our fate. I say "decided", but every minute of the previous afternoon was just as decisive.' 'And what was in the letter?' asked K. 'Yes, I haven't told you that yet,' said Olga, 'the letter was from Sortini addressed to the girl with the garnet necklace. I can't repeat the contents. It was a summons to come to him at the Herrenhof, and to come at once, for in half an hour he was due to leave. The letter was couched in the vilest language, such as I have never heard, and I could only half guess its meaning from the context. Anyone who didn't know Amalia and saw this letter must have considered a girl who could be written to like that as dishonoured, even if she had never had a finger laid on her. And it wasn't a love letter, there wasn't a tender word in it, on the contrary Sortini was obviously enraged because the sight of Amalia had disturbed him and distracted him in his work. Later on we pieced it all together for ourselves; evidently Sortini had intended to go straight to the Castle that evening, but on Amalia's account had stayed in the village instead, and in the morning, being very angry because even overnight he hadn't succeeded in forgetting her, had written the letter. One couldn't but be furious on first reading a letter like that, even the most cold-blooded person might have been, but though with anybody else fear at its threatening tone would soon have got the upper hand, Amalia only felt anger, fear she doesn't know, neither for herself nor for others. And while I crept into bed again repeating to myself the closing sentence, which broke off in the middle, "See that you come at once, or else – !" Amalia remained on the window-seat looking out, as if she were expecting further messengers and were prepared to treat them all as she had done the first.' 'So that's what the officials are like,' said K. reluctantly, 'that's the kind of type one finds among them. What did your father do? I hope he protested energetically in the proper quarter, if he didn't prefer a shorter and quicker way of doing it at the Herrenhof. The worst thing about the story isn't the insult to Amalia, that could easily have been made good, I don't know why you lay such exaggerated stress upon it; why should such a letter from Sortini shame Amalia for ever? – which is what one would gather from your story, but that's a sheer impossibility, it would have been easy to make up for it to Amalia, and in a few days the whole thing might have blown over, it was himself that Sortini shamed, and not Amalia. It's Sortini that horrifies me, the possibility of such an abuse of power. The very thing that failed this one time because it came naked and undisguised and found an effective opponent in Amalia, might very well succeed completely on a thousand other occasions in circumstances just a little less favourable, and might defy detection even by its victim.' 'Hush,' said Olga, 'Amalia's looking this way.' Amalia had finished giving food to her parents and was now busy taking off her mother's clothes. She had just undone the skirt, hung her mother's arms round her neck, lifted her a little, while she drew the skirt off, and now gently set her down again. Her father, still affronted because his wife was being attended to first, which obviously only happened because she was even more helpless than he, was attempting to undress himself; perhaps, too, it was a reproach to his daughter for her imagined slowness; yet although he began with the easiest and least necessary thing, the removal of the enormous slippers in which his feet were loosely stuck, he could not get them pulled off at all, and wheezing hoarsely was forced to give up trying, and leaned back stiffly in his chair again. 'But you don't realise the really decisive thing,' said Olga, 'you may be right in all you say, but the decisive thing was Amalia's not going to the Herrenhof; her treatment of the messenger might have been excused, it could have been passed over; but it was because she didn't go that the curse was laid upon our family, and that turned her treatment of the messenger into an unpardonable offence, yes, it was even brought forward openly later as the chief offence.' 'What!' cried K. at once, lowering his voice again, as Olga raised her hands imploringly, 'do you, her sister, actually say that Amalia should have run to the Herrenhof after Sortini?' 'No,' said Olga, 'Heaven preserve me from such a suspicion, how can you believe that? I don't know anybody who's so right as Amalia in everything she does. If she had gone to the Herrenhof I should of course have upheld her just the same; but her not going was heroic. As for me, I confess it frankly, had I received a letter like that I should have gone. I shouldn't have been able to endure the fear of what might happen, only Amalia could have done that. For there were many ways of getting round it; another girl, for instance, might have decked herself up and wasted some time in doing it and then gone to the Herrenhof only to find that Sortini had left, perhaps to find that he had left immediately after sending the messenger, which is very probable, for the moods of the gentlemen are fleeting. But Amalia neither did that nor anything else, she was too deeply insulted, and answered without reserve. If she had only made some pretence of compliance, if she had but crossed the threshold of the Herrenhof at the right moment, our punishment could have been turned aside, we have very clever advocates here who can make a great deal out of a mere nothing, but in this case they hadn't even the mere nothing to go on, there was, on the contrary, the disrespect to Sortini's letter and the insult to his messenger.' 'But what is all this about punishment and advocates?' said K. 'Surely Amalia couldn't be accused or punished because of Sortini's criminal proceedings?' 'Yes,' said Olga, 'she could, not in a regular suit at law, of course; and she wasn't punished directly, but she was punished all right in other ways, she and the whole family, and how heavy the punishment has been you are surely beginning to understand. In your opinion it's unjust and monstrous, but you're the only one in the village of that opinion, it's an opinion favourable to us, and ought to comfort us, and would do that if it weren't so obviously based on error. I can easily prove that, and you must forgive me if I mention Frieda by the way, but between Frieda and Klamm, leaving aside the final outcome of the two affairs, the first preliminaries were much the same as between Amalia and Sortini, and yet, although that might have shocked you at the beginning, you accept it now as quite natural. And that's not merely because you're accustomed to it, custom alone couldn't blunt one's plain judgment, it's simply that you've freed yourself from prejudice.' 'No, Olga,' said K., 'I don't see why you drag in Frieda, her case wasn't the same, don't confuse two such different things, and now go on with your story.' 'Please don't be offended,' said Olga, 'if I persist in the comparison, it's a lingering trace of prejudice on your part, even in regard to Frieda, that makes you feel you must defend her from a comparison. She's not to be defended, but only to be praised. In comparing the two cases I don't say they're exactly alike, they stand in the same relation as black to white, and the white is Frieda. The worst thing one can do to Frieda is to laugh at her, as I did in the bar very rudely – and I was sorry for it later – but even if one laughs it's out of envy or malice, at any rate one can laugh. On the other hand, unless one is related to her by blood, one can only despise Amalia. Therefore the two cases are quite different, as you say, but yet they are alike.' 'They're not at all alike,' said K., and he shook his head stubbornly, 'leave Frieda out of it, Frieda got no such fine letter as that of Sortini's, and Frieda was really in love with Klamm, and, if you doubt that, you need only ask her, she loves him still.' 'But is that really a difference?' asked Olga. 'Do you imagine Klamm couldn't have written to Frieda in the same tone? That's what the gentlemen are like when they rise from their desks, they feel out of place in the ordinary world and in their distraction they say the most beastly things, not all of them, but many of them. The letter to Amalia may have been the thought of a moment, thrown on the paper in complete disregard for the meaning to be taken out of it. What do we know of the thoughts of these gentlemen? Haven't you heard of, or heard yourself, the tone in which Klamm spoke to Frieda? Klamm's notorious for his rudeness, he can apparently sit dumb for hours and then suddenly bring out something so brutal that it makes one shiver. Nothing of that kind is known of Sortini, but then very little is known of him. All that's really known about him is that his name is like Sordini's. If it weren't for that resemblance between the two names probably he wouldn't be known at all. Even as the Fire Brigade authority apparently he's confused with Sordini, who is the real authority, and who exploits the resemblance in name to push things on to Sortini's shoulders, especially any duties falling on him as a deputy, so that he can be left undisturbed to his work. Now when a man so unused to society as Sortini suddenly felt himself in love with a village girl, he'll naturally take it quite differently from, say, the joiner's apprentice next door. And one must remember, too, that between an official and a village cobbler's daughter there's a great gulf fixed which has to be somehow bridged over, and Sortini tried to do it in that way, where someone else might have acted differently. Of course we're all supposed to belong to the Castle, and there's supposed to be no gulf between us, and nothing to be bridged over, and that may be true enough on ordinary occasions, but we've had grim evidence that it's not true when anything really important crops up. At any rate, all that should make Sortini's methods more comprehensible to you, and less monstrous; compared with Klamm's they're comparatively reasonable, and even for those intimately affected by them much more endurable. When Klamm writes a loving letter it's much more exasperating than the most brutal letter of Sortini's. Don't mistake me, I'm not venturing to criticise Klamm, I'm only comparing the two, because you're shutting your eyes to the comparison. Klamm's a kind of tyrant over women, he orders first one and then another to come to him, puts up with none of them for long, and orders them to go just as he ordered them to come. Oh, Klamm wouldn't even give himself the trouble of writing a letter first. And in comparison with that is it so monstrous that Sortini, who's so retiring, and whose relations with women are at least unknown, should conde-scend for once to write in his beautiful official hand a letter, however abominable? And if there's no distinction here in Klamm's favour, but the reverse, how can Frieda's love for him establish one? The relation existing between the women and the officials, believe me, is very difficult, or rather very easy to determine. Love always enters into it. There's no such thing as an official's unhappy love affair. So in that respect it's no praise to say of a girl – I'm refer-ring to many others besides Frieda – that she gave herself to an official only out of love. She loved him and gave herself to him, that was all, there's nothing praiseworthy in that. But you'll object that Amalia didn't love Sortini. Well, per-haps she didn't love him, but then after all perhaps she did love him, who can decide? Not even she herself. How can she fancy she didn't love him, when she rejected him so violently, as no official has ever been rejected? Barnabas says that even yet she sometimes trembles with the violence of the effort of closing the window three years ago. That is true, and therefore one can't ask her anything; she has finished with Sortini, and that's all she knows; whether she loves him or not she does not know. But we do know that women can't help loving the officials once they give them any encouragement, yes, they even love them beforehand, let them deny it as much as they like, and Sortini not only gave Amalia encouragement, but leapt over the shaft when he saw her; although his legs were stiff from sitting at desks he leapt right over the shaft. But Amalia's an exception, you will say. Yes, that she is, that she has proved in refusing to go to Sortini, that's exception enough, but if in addition she weren't in love with Sortini, she would be too exceptional for plain human understanding. On that afternoon, I grant you, we were smitten with blindness, but the fact that in spite of our mental confusion we thought we noticed signs of Amalia's being in love, showed at least some remnants of sense. But when all that's taken into account, what difference is left between Frieda and Amalia? One thing only, that Frieda did what Amalia refused to do.' 'Maybe,' said K., 'but for me the main difference is that I'm engaged to Frieda, and only interested in Amalia because she's a sister of Barnabas's, the Castle messenger, and because her destiny may be bound up with his duties. If she had suffered such a crying injustice at the hands of an official as your tale seemed to infer at the beginning, I should have taken the matter up seriously, but more from a sense of public duty than from any personal sympathy with Amalia. But what you say has changed the aspect of the situation for me in a way I don't quite understand, but am prepared to accept, since it's you who tell me, and therefore I want to drop the whole affair; I'm no member of the Fire Brigade, Sortini means nothing to me. But Frieda means something to me, I have trusted her completely and want to go on trusting her, and it surprises me that you go out of your way, while discussing Amalia, to attack Frieda and try to shake my confidence in her. I'm not assuming that you're doing it with deliberate intent, far less with malicious intent, for in that case I should have left long ago. You're not doing it deliberately, you're betrayed into it by circumstances, impelled by your love for Amalia you want to exalt her above all other women, and since you can't find enough virtue in Amalia herself you help yourself out by belittling the others. Amalia's act was remarkable enough, but the more you say about it the less clearly can it be decided whether it was noble or petty, clever or foolish, heroic or cowardly; Amalia keeps her motives locked in her own bosom and no one will ever get at them. Frieda, on the other hand, has done nothing at all remarkable, she has only followed her own heart, for anyone who looks at her actions with goodwill that is clear, it can be substantiated, it leaves no room for slander. However, I don't want either to belittle Amalia or to defend Frieda, all I want is to let you see what my relation is to Frieda, and that every attack on Frieda is an attack on myself. I came here of my own accord, and of my own accord I have settled here, but all that has happened to me since I came, and, above all, any prospects I may have – dark as they are, they still exist – I owe entirely to Frieda, and you can't argue that away. True, I was engaged to come here as a Land Surveyor, yet that was only a pretext, they were playing with me, I was driven out of everybody's house, they're playing with me still to-day; but how much more complicated the game is now that I have, so to speak, a larger circumference – which means something, it may not be much – yet I have already a home, a position and real work to do, I have a promised wife who takes her share of my professional duties when I have other business, I'm going to marry her and become a member of the community, and besides my official connection I have also a personal connection with Klamm, although as yet I haven't been able to make use of it. That's surely quite a lot? And when I come to you, why do you make me welcome? Why do you confide the history of your family to me? Why do you hope that I might possibly help you? Certainly not because I'm the Land Surveyor whom Lasemann and Brunswick, for instance, turned out of their house a week ago, but because I'm a man with some power at my back. But that I owe to Frieda, to Frieda who is so modest that if you were to ask her about it, she wouldn't know it existed. And so, considering all this, it seems that Frieda in her innocence has achieved more than Amalia in all her pride, for may I say that I have the impression that you're seeking help for Amalia. And from whom? In the last resort from no one else but Frieda.' 'Did I really speak so abominably of Frieda?' asked Olga, 'I certainly didn't mean to, and I don't think I did, still, it's possible; we're in a bad way, our whole world is in ruins, and once we begin to complain we're carried farther than we realise. You're quite right, there's a big difference now between us and Frieda, and it's a good thing to emphasise it once in a while. Three years ago we were respectable girls and Frieda an outcast, a servant in the Bridge Inn, we used to walk past her without looking at her, I admit we were too arrogant, but that's how we were brought up. But that evening in the Herrenhof probably enlightened you about our respective positions to-day. Frieda with the whip in her hand, and I among the crowd of servants. But it's worse even than that! Frieda may despise us, her position entitles her to do so, actual circumstances compel it. But who is there who doesn't despise us? Whoever decides to despise us will find himself in good company. Do you know Frieda's successor? Pepi, she's called. I met her for the first time the night before last, she used to be a chambermaid. She certainly outdoes Frieda in her contempt for me. She saw me through the window as I was coming for beer, and ran to the door and locked it, so that I had to beg and pray for a long time and promise her the ribbon from my hair before she would let me in. But when I gave it to her she threw it into a corner. Well, I can't help it if she despises me, I'm partly dependent on her goodwill, and she's the barmaid in the Herrenhof. Only for the time being, it's true, for she certainly hasn't the qualities needed for permanent employment there. One only has to overhear how the landlord speaks to Pepi and compare it with his tone to Frieda. But that doesn't hinder Pepi from despising even Amalia, Amalia, whose glance alone would be enough to drive Pepi with all her plaits and ribbons out of the room much faster than her own fat legs would ever carry her. I had to listen again yesterday to her infuriating slanders against Amalia until the customers took my part at last, although only in the kind of way you have seen already.' 'How touchy you are,' said K. 'I only put Frieda in her right place, but I had no intention of belittling you, as you seem to think. Your family has a special interest for me, I have never denied it; but how this interest could give me cause for despising you I can't understand.' 'Oh, K.,' said Olga, 'I'm afraid that even you will understand it yet; can't you even understand that Amalia's behaviour to Sortini was the original cause of our being despised?' 'That would be strange indeed,' said K., 'one might admire or condemn Amalia for such an action, but despise her? And even if she is despised for some reason I can't comprehend, why should the contempt be extended to you others, her innocent family? For Pepi to despise you, for instance, is a piece of impudence, and I'll let her know it if ever I'm in the Herrenhof again.' 'If you set out, K.,' said Olga, 'to convert all the people who despise us you'll have your work cut out for you, for it's all engineered from the Castle. I can still remember every detail of that day following the morning I spoke of. Brunswick, who was our assistant then, had arrived as usual, taken his share of the work and gone home, and we were sitting at breakfast, all of us, even Amalia and myself, very gay, father kept on talking about the celebration and telling us his plans in connection with the Fire Brigade, for you must know that the Castle has its own Fire Brigade which had sent a deputation to the celebration, and there had been much discussion about it, the gentlemen present from the Castle had seen that performance of our

Fire Brigade, had expressed great approval, and compared the Castle Brigade unfavourably with ours, so there had been some talk of reorganising the Castle Brigade with the help of instructors from the village; there were several possible candidates, but father had hopes that he would be chosen. That was what he was discussing, and in his usual delightful way had sprawled over the table until he embraced half of it in his arms, and as he gazed through the open window at the sky his face was young and shining with hope, and that was the last time I was to see it like that. Then Amalia, with a calm conviction we had never noticed in her before, said that too much trust shouldn't be placed in what the gentlemen said, they were in the habit of saying pleasant things on such occasions, but it meant little or nothing, the words were hardly out of their mouths before they were forgotten, only of course people were always ready to be taken in again next time. Mother forbade her to say things like that, but father only laughed at her precocious air of wisdom, then he gave a start, and seemed to be looking round for something he had only just missed – but there was nothing missing – and said that Brunswick had told him some story of a messenger and a torn-up letter, did we know anything of it, who was concerned in it, and what it was all about? We kept silent; Barnabas, who was as youthful then as a spring lamb, said something particularly silly or cheeky, the subject was changed, and the whole affair forgotten.'

AMALIA'S PUNISHMENT

'But not long afterwards we were overwhelmed with questions from all sides about the story of the letter, we were visited by friends and enemies, acquaintances and complete strangers. Not one of them stayed for any length of time, and our best friends were the quickest to go. Lasemann, usually so slow and dignified, came in hastily as if only to see the size of the room, one look round it and he was gone, it was like a horrible kind of children's game when he fled, and father, shaking himself free from some other people, ran after him to the very door and then gave it up; Brunswick came and gave notice, he said quite honestly that he wanted to set up in business for himself, a shrewd man, he knew how to seize the right moment; customers came and hunted round father's storeroom for the boots they had left to be repaired, at first father tried to persuade them to change their minds – and we all backed him up as much as we could – but later he gave it up, and without saying a word helped them to find their belongings, line after line in the order-book was cancelled, the pieces of leather people had left with us were handed back, all debts owing us were paid, everything went smoothly without the slightest trouble, they asked for nothing better than to break every connection with us quickly and completely, even if they lost by it; that counted for nothing. And finally, as we might have foreseen, Seemann appeared, the Captain of the Fire Brigade; I can still see the scene before me, Seemann, tall and stout, but with a slight stoop from weakness in the lungs, a serious man who never could laugh, standing in front of my father whom he admired, whom he had promised in confidence to make a deputy Captain, and to whom he had now to say that the Brigade required his services no longer and asked for the return of his diploma. All the people who happened to be in our house left their business for the moment and crowded round the two men, Seemann found it difficult to speak and only kept on tapping father on the shoulder, as if he were trying to tap out of him the words he ought to say and couldn't find. And he kept on laughing, probably to cheer himself a little and everybody else, but since he's incapable of laughing and no one had ever heard him laugh, it didn't occur to anybody that he was really laughing. But father was too tired and desperate after the day he'd had to help anybody out, he looked even too tired to grasp what was happening. We were all in despair, too, but being young didn't believe in the completeness of our ruin, and kept on expecting that someone in the long procession of visitors would arrive and put a stop to it all and make everything swing the other way again. In our foolishness we thought that Seemann was that very man. We were all keyed up waiting for his laughter to stop, and for the decisive statement to come out at last. What could he be laughing at, if not at the stupid injustice of what had happened to us? Oh, Captain, Captain, tell them now at last, we thought, and pressed close to him, but that only made him recoil from us in the most curious way. At length, however, he did begin to speak, in response not to our secret wishes, but to the encouraging or angry cries of the crowd. Yet still we had hopes. He began with great praise for our father. Called him an ornament to the Brigade, an inimitable model to posterity, an indispensable member whose removal must reduce the Brigade almost to ruin. That was all very fine, had he stopped there. But he went on to say that since in spite of that the Brigade had decided, only as a temporary measure of course, to ask for his resignation, they would all understand the seriousness of the reason which forced the Brigade to do so. Perhaps if father had not distinguished himself so much at the celebration of the previous day it would not have been necessary to go so far, but his very superiority had drawn official attention to the Brigade, and brought it into such prominence that the spotlessness of its reputation was more than ever a matter of honour to it. And now that a messenger had been insulted, the Brigade couldn't help itself, and he, Seemann, found himself in the difficult position of having to convey its decision. He hoped that father would not make it any more difficult for him. Seemann was glad to have got it out. He was so pleased with himself that he even forgot his exaggerated tact, and pointed to the diploma hanging on the wall and made a sign with his finger. Father nodded and went to fetch it, but his hands trembled so much that he couldn't get it off the hook. I climbed on a chair and helped him. From that moment he was done for, he didn't even take the diploma out of its frame, but handed the whole thing over to Seemann. Then he sat down in a corner and neither moved nor spoke to anybody, and we had to attend to the last people there by ourselves as well as we could.' 'And where do you see in all this the influence of the Castle?' asked K. 'So far it doesn't seem to have come in. What you've told me about is simply the ordinary senseless fear of the people, malicious pleasure in hurting a neighbour, specious friendship, things that can be found anywhere, and, I must say, on the part your father – at least, so it seems to me – a certain pettiness, for what was the diploma? Merely a testimonial to his abilities, these themselves weren't taken from him, if they made him indispensable so much the better, and the one way he could have made things difficult for the Captain would have been by flinging the diploma at his feet before he had said two words. But the significant thing to me is that you haven't mentioned Amalia at all; Amalia, who was to blame for everything, apparently stood quietly in the background and watched the whole house collapse.' 'No,' said Olga, 'nobody ought to be blamed, nobody could have done anything else, all that was already due to the influence of the Castle.' 'Influence of the Castle,' repeated Amalia, who had slipped in unnoticed from the courtyard; the old people had been long in bed. 'Is it Castle gossip you're at? Still sitting with your heads together? And yet you wanted to go away immediately you came, K., and it's nearly ten now. Are you really interested in that kind of gossip? There are people in the village who live on it, they stick their heads together just like you two and entertain each other by the hour. But I didn't think you were one of them.' 'On the contrary,' said K., 'that's exactly what I am, and moreover people who don't care for such gossip and leave it all to others don't interest me particularly.' 'Indeed,' said Amalia, 'well, there are many different kinds of interest, you know; I heard once of a young man who thought of nothing but the Castle day and night, he neglected everything else and people feared for his reason, his mind was so wholly absorbed by the Castle. It turned out at length, however, that it wasn't really the Castle he was thinking of, but the daughter of a charwoman in the offices up there, so he got the girl and was all right again.' 'I think I would like that man,' said K. 'As for your liking the man, I doubt it,' said Amalia, 'it's probably his wife you would like. Well, don't let me disturb you, I've got to go to bed, and I must put out the light for the old folks' sake. They're sound asleep now, but they don't really sleep for more than an hour, and after that the smallest glimmer disturbs them. Goodnight.' And actually the light went out at once, and Amalia bedded herself somewhere on the floor near her parents. 'Who's the young man she mentioned?' asked K. 'I don't know,' said Olga, 'perhaps Brunswick although it doesn't fit him exactly, but it might have been somebody else. It's not easy to follow her, for often one can't tell whether she's speaking ironically or in earnest. Mostly she's in earnest but sounds ironical.' 'Never mind explaining,' said K. 'How have you come to be so dependent on her? Were things like that before the catastrophe? Or did it happen later? And do you never feel that you want to be independent of her? And is there any sense in your dependence? She's the youngest, and should give way to you. Innocently or not, she was the person who brought ruin on the family. And instead of begging your pardon for it anew every day she carries her head higher than anybody else, bothers herself about nothing except what she chooses to do for her parents, nothing would induce her to become acquainted with your affairs, to use her own expression, and then if she does speak to you at all she's mostly in earnest, but sounds ironical. Does she queen it over you on account of her beauty, which you've mentioned more than once? Well, you're all three very like each other, but Amalia's distinguishing mark is hardly a recommendation, and repelled me the first time I saw it, I mean her cold hard eye. And although she's the youngest she doesn't look it, she has the ageless look of women who seem not to grow any older, but seem never to have been young either. You see her every day, you don't notice the hardness of her face. That's why, on reflection, I can't take Sortini's passion for her very seriously, perhaps he sent the letter simply to punish her, but not to summon her.' 'I won't argue about Sortini,' said Olga, 'for the Castle gentlemen everything is possible, let a girl be as pretty or as ugly as you like. But in all the rest you're utterly mistaken so far as Amalia is concerned. I have no particular motive for winning you over to Amalia's side, and if I try to do it it's only for your own sake. Amalia in some way or other was the cause of our misfortunes, that's true, but not even my father, who was the hardest hit, and who was never very sparing of his tongue, particularly at home, not even my father has ever said a word of reproach to Amalia even in our very worst times. Not because he approved of her action, he was an admirer of Sortini, and how could he have approved of it? He couldn't understand it even remotely, for Sortini he would have been glad to sacrifice himself and all that was his, although hardly in the way things actually happened, as an outcome apparently of Sortini's anger. I say apparently, for we never heard another word from Sortini: if he was reticent before then, from that day on he might as well have been dead. Now, you should have seen Amalia at that time. We all knew that no definite punishment would be visited on us. We were only shunned. By the village and by the Castle. But while we couldn't help noticing the ostracism of the village, the Castle gave us no sign. Of course we had no sign of favour from the Castle in the past, so how could we notice the reverse? This blankness was the worst of all. It was far worse than the withdrawal of the people down here, for they hadn't deserted us out of conviction, perhaps they had nothing very serious against us, they didn't despise us then as they do to-day, they only did it out of fear, and were waiting to see what would happen next. And we weren't afraid of being stranded, for all our debtors had paid us, the settling-up had been entirely in our favour, and any provisions we didn't have were sent us secretly by relations, it was easy enough for us, it was harvest time – though we had no fields of our own and nobody would take us on as workers, so that for the first time in our lives we were condemned to go nearly idle. So there we sat all together with the windows shut in the heats of July and August. Nothing happened. No invitations, no news, no callers, nothing.' 'Well,' said K., 'since nothing happened and you had no definite punishment hanging over you, what was there to be afraid of? What people you are!' 'How am I to explain it?' said Olga. 'We weren't afraid of anything in the future, we were suffering under the immediate present, we were actually enduring our punishment. The others in the village were only waiting for us to come to them, for father to open his workshop again, for Amalia, who could sew the most beautiful clothes, fit for the best families, to come asking for orders again, they were all sorry to have had to act as they did; when a respected family is suddenly cut out of village life it means a loss for everybody, so when they broke with us they thought they were only doing their duty, in their place we should have done just the same. They didn't know very clearly what was the matter, except that the messenger had returned to the Herrenhof with a handful of torn paper. Frieda had seen him go out and come back, had exchanged a few words with him, and then spread what she had learned everywhere. But not in the least from enmity to us, simply from a sense of duty which anybody would have felt in the same circumstances. And, as I've said, a happy ending to the whole story would have pleased everybody else. If we had suddenly put in an appearance with the news that everything was settled, that it had only been a misunderstanding, say, which was now quite cleared up, or that there had been actually some cause for offence which had now been made good, or else – and even this would have satisfied people – that through our influence in the Castle the affair had been dropped, we should certainly have been

received again with open arms, there would have been kiss-
ings and congratulations, I have seen that kind of thing happen to others once or twice already. And it wouldn't have
been necessary to say even as much as that; if we had only
come out in the open and shown ourselves, if we had picked
up our old connections without letting fall a single word
about the affair of the letter, it would have been enough,
they would all have been glad to avoid mentioning the matter; it was the painfulness of the subject as much as their
fear that made them draw away from us, simply to avoid
hearing about it or speaking about it or thinking about it or
being affected by it in any way. When Frieda gave it away
it wasn't out of mischief but as a warning, to let the parish
know that something had happened which everybody
should be careful to keep clear of. It wasn't our family that
was taboo, it was the affair, and our family only in so far as
we were mixed up in the affair. So if we had quietly come
forward again and let bygones be bygones and shown by
our behaviour that the incident was closed, no matter in
what way, and reassured public opinion that it was never
likely to be mentioned again, whatever its nature had been,
everything would have been made all right in that way, too,
we should have found friends on all sides as before, and
even if we hadn't completely forgotten what had happened
people would have understood and helped us to forget it
completely. Instead of that we sat in the house. I don't
know what we were expecting, probably some decision from
Amalia, for on that morning she had taken the lead in the
family and she still maintained it. Without any particular
contriving or commanding or imploring, almost by her
silence alone. We others, of course, had plenty to discuss,
there was a steady whispering from morning till evening,
and sometimes father would call me to him in sudden panic
and I would have to spend half the night on the edge of his
bed. Or we would often creep away together, I and Barnabas, who knew nothing about it all at first, and was always
in a fever for some explanation, always the same, for he

realised well enough that the care-free years that others of his age looked forward to were now out of the question for him, so we used to put our heads together, K., just like we two now, and forget that it was night, and that morning had come again. Our mother was the feeblest of us all, probably because she had not only endured our common sorrows but the private sorrow of each of us, and so we were horrified to see changes in her which, as we guessed, lay in wait for all of us. Her favourite seat was the corner of the sofa, it's long since we parted with it, it stands now in Brunswick's big living-room, well, there she sat and – we couldn't tell exactly what was wrong – used to doze or carry on long conversations with herself, we guessed it from the moving of her lips. It was so natural for us to be always discussing the letter, to be always turning it over in all its known details and unknown potentialities, and to be always outdoing each other in thinking out plans for restoring our fortunes; it was natural and unavoidable, but not good, we only plunged deeper and deeper into what we wanted to escape from. And what good were these inspirations, however brilliant? None of them could be acted on without Amalia, they were all tentative, and quite useless because they stopped short of Amalia, and even if they had been put to Amalia they would have met with nothing but silence. Well, I'm glad to say I understand Amalia better now than I did then. She had more to endure than all of us, it's incomprehensible how she managed to endure it and still survive. Mother, perhaps, had to endure all our troubles, but that was because they came pouring in on her; and she didn't hold out for long; no one could say that she's holding out against them to-day, and even at that time her mind was beginning to go. But Amalia not only suffered, she had the understanding to see her suffering clearly, we saw only the effects, but she knew the cause, we hoped for some small relief or other, she knew that everything was decided, we had to whisper, she had only to be silent. She stood face to face with the truth and went on living and endured her life then as now. In all our straits we were better off than she. Of course, we had to leave our house. Brunswick took it on, and we were given this cottage, we brought our things over in several journeys with a handcart, Barnabas and I pulling and father and Amalia pushing behind, mother was already sitting here on a chest, for we had brought her here first, and she whimpered softly all the time. Yet I remember that even during those toilsome journeys – they were painful, too, for we often met harvest waggons, and the people became silent when they saw us and turned away their faces – even during those journeys Barnabas and I couldn't stop discussing our troubles and our plans, so that we often stood stock still in the middle of pulling and had to be roused by father's "Hallo" from behind. But all our talking made no difference to our life after the removal, except that we began gradually to feel the pinch of poverty as well. Our relatives stopped sending us things, our money was almost done, and that was the time when people first began to despise us in the way you can see now. They saw that we hadn't the strength to shake ourselves clear of the scandal, and they were irritated. They didn't underestimate our difficulties, although they didn't know exactly what they were, and they knew that probably they wouldn't have stood up to them any better themselves, but that made it only all the more needful to keep clear of us – if we had triumphed they would have honoured us correspondingly, but since we failed they turned what had only been a temporary measure into a final resolve, and cut us off from the community for ever. We were no longer spoken of as ordinary human beings, our very name was never mentioned, if they had to refer to us they called us Barnabas's people, for he was the least guilty; even our cottage gained an evil reputation, and you yourself must admit, if you're honest, that on your first entry into it you thought it justified its reputation; later on, when people occasionally visited us again, they used to screw up their noses at the most trivial things, for instance, because the little oil-lamp hung over the table. Where should it hang if not over the table? and yet they found it insupportable. But if we hung the lamp somewhere else they were still disgusted. Whatever we did, whatever we had, it was all despicable.'

PETITIONS

'And what did we do meanwhile? The worst thing we could have done, something much more deserving of contempt than our original offence – we betrayed Amalia, we shook off her silent restraint, we couldn't go on living like that, without hope of any kind we could not live, and we began each in his or her own fashion with prayers or blustering to beg the Castle's forgiveness. We knew, of course, that we weren't in a position to make anything good, and we knew too that the only likely connection we had with the Castle – through Sortini, who had been father's superior and had approved of him – was destroyed by what had happened, and yet we buckled down to the job. Father began it, he started making senseless petitions to the Village Superintendent, to the secretaries, the advocates, the clerks, usually he wasn't received at all, but if by guile or chance he managed to get a hearing – and how we used to exult when the news came, and rub our hands! – he was always thrown out immediately and never admitted again. Besides, it was only too easy to answer him, the Castle always has the advantage. What was it that he wanted? What had been done to him? What did he want to be forgiven for? When and by whom had so much as a finger been raised against him in the Castle? Granted he had become poor and lost his customers, etc., these were all chances of everyday life, and happened in all shops and markets; was the Castle to concern itself about things of that kind? It concerned itself about the common welfare, of course, but it couldn't simply interfere with the natural course of events for the sole purpose of serving the interest of one man. Did he expect officials to be sent out to run after his customers and force them to come back? But, father would object – we always discussed the whole interview both before and afterwards, sitting in a corner as if to avoid Amalia, who knew well enough what we were doing, but paid no attention – well, father would object, he wasn't complaining about his poverty, he could easily make up again for all he had lost, that didn't matter if only he were forgiven. But what was there to forgive? came the answer; no accusation had come in against him, at least there was none in the registers, not in those registers anyhow which were accessible to the public advocates, consequently, so far as could be established, there was neither any accusation standing against him, nor one in process of being taken up. Could he perhaps refer to some official decree that had been issued against him? Father couldn't do that. Well then, if he knew of nothing and nothing had happened, what did he want? What was there to forgive him? Nothing but the way he was aimlessly wasting official time, but that was just the unforgivable sin. Father didn't give in, he was still very strong in those days, and his enforced leisure gave him plenty of time. "I'll restore Amalia's honour, it won't take long now," he used to say to Barnabas and me several times a day, but only in a low voice in case Amalia should hear, and yet he only said it for her benefit, for in reality he wasn't hoping for the restoration of her honour, but only for forgiveness. Yet before he could be forgiven he had to prove his guilt, and that was denied in all the bureaux. He hit upon the idea – and it showed that his mind was already giving way – that his guilt was being concealed from him because he didn't pay enough; until then he had paid only the established taxes, which were at least high enough for means like ours. But now he believed that he must pay more, which was certainly a delusion, for, although our officials accept bribes simply to avoid trouble and discussion, nothing is ever achieved in that way. Still, if father had set his hopes on that idea, we didn't want them upset. We sold what we had left to sell –

nearly all things we couldn't do without – to get father the money for his efforts, and for a long time every morning brought us the satisfaction of knowing that when he went on his day's rounds he had at least a few coins to rattle in his pocket. Of course we simply starved all day, and the only thing the money really did was to keep father fairly hopeful and happy. That could hardly be called an advantage, however. He wore himself out on these rounds of his, and the money only made them drag on and on instead of coming to a quick and natural end. Since in reality nothing extra could be done for him in return for those extra payments, clerks here and there tried to make a pretence of giving something in return, promising to look the matter up, and hinting that they were on the track of something, and that purely as a favour to father, and not as a duty, they would follow it up – and father, instead of growing sceptical, only became more and more credulous. He used to bring home such obviously worthless promises as if they were great triumphs, and it was a torment to see him behind Amalia's back twisting his face in a smile and opening his eyes wide as he pointed to her and made signs to us that her salvation, which would have surprised nobody so much as herself, was coming nearer and nearer through his efforts, but that it was still a secret and we mustn't tell. Things would certainly have gone on like this for a long time if we hadn't finally been reduced to the position of having no more money to give him. Barnabas, indeed, had been taken on meanwhile by Brunswick, after endless imploring, as an assistant, on condition that he fetched his work in the dusk of the evening and brought it back again in the dark – it must be admitted that Brunswick was taking a certain risk in his business for our sake, but in exchange he paid Barnabas next to nothing, and Barnabas is a model workman – yet his wages were barely enough to keep us from downright starvation. Very gently and after much softening of the blow we told our father that he could have no more money, but he took it very quietly. He was no longer capable of understanding how hopeless were his attempts at intervention, but he was wearied out by continual disappointments. He said, indeed – and he spoke less clearly than before, he used to speak almost too clearly – that he would have needed only a very little more money, for to-morrow or that very day he would have found out everything, and now it had all gone for nothing, ruined simply for lack of money, and so on but the tone in which he said it showed that he didn't believe it all. Besides, he brought out a new plan immediately of his own accord. Since he had failed in proving his guilt, and consequently could hope for nothing more through official channels, he would have to depend on appeals alone, and would try to move the officials personally. There must certainly be some among them who had good sympathetic hearts, which they couldn't give way to in their official capacity, but out of office hours, if one caught them at the right time, they would surely listen.'

Here K., who had listened with absorption hitherto, interrupted Olga's narrative with the question: 'And don't you think he was right?' Although his question would have answered itself in the course of the narrative he wanted to know at once.

'No,' said Olga, 'there could be no question of sympathy or anything of the kind. Young and inexperienced as we were, we knew that, and father knew it too, of course, but he had forgotten it like nearly everything else. The plan he had hit on was to plant himself on the main road near the Castle, where the officials pass in their carriages, and seize any opportunity of putting up his prayer for forgiveness. To be honest, it was a wild and senseless plan, even if the impossible should have happened, and his prayer have really reached an official's ear. For how could a single official give a pardon? That could only be done at best by the whole authority, and apparently even the authority can only condemn and not pardon. And in any case even if an official stepped out of his carriage and was willing to take up the matter, how could he get any clear idea of the affair

from the mumblings of a poor, tired, ageing man like
father? Officials are highly educated, but one-sided; in his
own department an official can grasp whole trains of
thought from a single word, but let him have something
from another department explained to him by the hour, he
may nod politely, but he won't understand a word of it.
That's quite natural, take even the small official affairs that
concern the ordinary person – trifling things that an official
disposes of with a shrug – and try to understand one of
them through and through, and you'll waste a whole lifetime on it without result. But even if father had chanced on
a responsible official, no official can settle anything without
the necessary documents, and certainly not on the main
road; he can't pardon anything, he can only settle it officially, and he would simply refer to the official procedure,
which had already been a complete failure for father. What
a pass father must have been in to think of insisting on such
a plan! If there were even the faintest possibility of getting
anything in that way, that part of the road would be packed
with petitioners; but since it's a sheer impossibility, patent
to the youngest schoolboy, the road is absolutely empty. But
maybe even that strengthened father in his hopes, he found
food for them everywhere. He had great need to find it, for
a sound mind wouldn't have had to make such complicated
calculations, it would have realised from external evidence
that the thing was impossible. When officials travel to the
village or back to the Castle it's not for pleasure, but
because there's work waiting for them in the village or in
the Castle, and so they travel at a great pace. It's not likely
to occur to them to look out of the carriage windows in
search of petitioners, for the carriages are crammed with
papers which they study on the way.'

'But,' said K., 'I've seen the inside of an official sledge in
which there weren't any papers.' Olga's story was opening
for him such a great and almost incredible world that he
could not help trying to put his own small experiences in

relation to it, as much to convince himself of its reality as of his own existence.

'That's possible,' said Olga, 'but in that case it's even worse, for that means that the official's business is so important that the papers are too precious or too numerous to be taken with him, and those officials go at a gallop. In any case, none of them can spare time for father. And besides, there are several roads to the Castle. Now one of them is in fashion, and most carriages go by that, now it's another and everything drives pell-mell there. And what governs this change of fashion has never yet been found out. At eight o'clock one morning they'll all be on another road, ten minutes later on a third, and half an hour after that on the first road again, and then they may stick to that road all day, but every minute there's the possibility of a change. Of course all the roads join up near the village, but by that time all the carriages are racing like mad, while nearer the Castle the pace isn't quite so fast. And the amount of traffic varies just as widely and incomprehensively as the choice of roads. There are often days when there's not a carriage to be seen, and others when they travel in crowds. Now, just think of all that in relation to father. In his best suit, which soon becomes his only suit, off he goes every morning from the house with our best wishes. He takes with him a small Fire Brigade badge, which he has really no business to keep, to stick in his coat once he's out of the village, for in the village itself he's afraid to let it be seen, although it's so small that it can hardly be seen two paces away, but father insists that it's just the thing to draw a passing official's attention. Not far from the Castle entrance there's a market garden, belonging to a man called Bertuch who sells vegetables to the Castle, and there on the narrow stone ledge at the foot of the garden fence father took up his post. Bertuch made no objection because he used to be very friendly with father and had been one of his most faithful customers – you see, he has a lame foot, and he thought that nobody but father could make him a boot to fit it. Well, there sat father day after day, it was a wet and stormy autumn, but the weather meant nothing to him. In the morning at his regular hour he had his hand on the latch and waved us good-bye, in the evening he came back soaked to the skin, every day, it seemed, a little more bent, and flung himself down in a corner. At first he used to tell us all his little adventures, such as how Bertuch for sympathy and old friendship's sake had thrown him a blanket over the fence, or that in one of the passing carriages he thought he had recognised this or the other official, or that this or the other coachman had recognised him again and playfully flicked him with his whip. But later he stopped telling us these things, evidently he had given up all hope of ever achieving anything there, and looked on it only as his duty, his dreary job, to go there and spend the whole day. That was when his rheumatic pains began, winter was coming on, snow fell early, the winter begins very early here; well, so there he sat sometimes on wet stones and at other times in the snow. In the night he groaned with pain, and in the morning he was many a time uncertain whether to go or not, but always overcame his reluctance and went. Mother clung to him and didn't want to let him go, so he, apparently grown timid because his limbs wouldn't obey him, allowed her to go with him, and so mother began to get pains too. We often went out to them, to take them food, or merely to visit them, or to try to persuade them to come back home; how often we found them crouching together, leaning against each other on their narrow seat, huddled up under a thin blanket which scarcely covered them, and round about them nothing but the grey of snow and mist, and far and wide for days at a time not a soul to be seen, not a carriage; a sight that was, K., a sight to be seen! Until one morning father couldn't move his stiff legs out of bed at all, he wasn't to be comforted, in a slight delirium he thought he could see an official stopping his carriage beside Bertuch's just at that moment, hunting all along the fence for him and then climbing angrily into his carriage again with a shake of his head. At that father shrieked so loudly that it was as if he wanted to make the official hear him at all that distance, and to explain how blameless his absence was. And it became a long absence, he never went back again, and for weeks he never left his bed. Amalia took over the nursing, the attending, the treatment, did everything he needed, and with a few intervals has kept it up to this day. She knows healing herbs to soothe his pain, she needs hardly any sleep, she's never alarmed, never afraid, never impatient, she does everything for the old folks; while we were fluttering round uneasily without being able to help in anything she remained cool and quiet whatever happened. Then when the worst was past and father was able again to struggle cautiously out of bed with one of us supporting him on each side, Amalia withdrew into the background again and left him to us.'

OLGA'S PLANS

'Now it was necessary again to find some occupation for father that he was still fit for, something that at least would make him believe that he was helping to remove the burden of guilt from our family. Something of the kind was not hard to find, anything at all in fact would have been as useful for the purpose as sitting in Bertuch's garden, but I found something that actually gave me a little hope. Whenever there had been any talk of our guilt among officials or clerks or anybody else, it was only the insult to Sortini's messenger that had always been brought up, further than that nobody dared to go. Now, I said to myself, since public opinion, even if only ostensibly, recognised nothing but the insult to the messenger, then, even if it were still only ostensibly, everything might be put right if one could propitiate the messenger. No charge had actually been made, we were told, no department therefore had taken up the affair yet, and so the messenger was at liberty, as far as he was concerned – and there was no question of anything more – to forgive the offence. All that of course couldn't have any decisive importance, was mere semblance and couldn't produce in turn anything but semblance, but all the same it would cheer up my father and might help to harass the swarm of clerks who had been tormenting him, and that would be a satisfaction. First of course one had to find the messenger. When I told father of my plan, at first he was very annoyed, for to tell the truth he had become terribly self-willed; for one thing he was convinced – this happened during his illness – that we had always held him back from final success, first by stopping his allowance and then by keeping him in his bed; and for another he was no longer capable of completely understanding any new idea. My plan was turned down even before I had finished telling him about it, he was convinced that his job was to go on waiting in Bertuch's garden, and as he was in no state now to go there every day himself, we should have to push him there in a hand-barrow. But I didn't give in, and gradually he became reconciled to the idea, the only thing that disturbed him was that in this matter he was quite dependent on me, for I had been the only one who had seen the messenger, he did not know him. Actually one messenger is very like another, and I myself was not quite certain that I would know this one again. Presently we began to go to the Herrenhof and look round among the servants. The messenger of course had been in Sortini's service and Sortini had stopped coming to the village, but the gentlemen are continually changing their servants, one might easily find our man among the servants of another gentleman, and even if he himself was not to be found, still one might perhaps get news of him from the other servants. For this purpose it was of course necessary to be in the Herrenhof every evening, and people weren't very pleased to see us anywhere, far less in a place like that; and we couldn't appear either as paying customers. But it turned out that they could put us to some use all the same. You know what a trial the servants were to Frieda, at bottom they are mostly quiet people, but pampered and made lazy by too little work – "May you be as well off as a servant" is a favourite toast among the officials – and really, as far as an easy life goes, the servants seem to be the real masters in the Castle, they know their own dignity too, and in the Castle, where they have to behave in accordance with their regulations, they're quiet and dignified, several times I've been assured of that, and one can find even among the servants down here some faint signs of that, but only faint signs, for usually, seeing that the Castle regulations aren't fully binding on them in the village, they seem quite changed; a wild unmanageable lot, ruled by their insatiable impulses instead of by their regulations. Their scandalous behaviour knows no limits, it's lucky for the village that they can't leave the Herrenhof without permission, but in the Herrenhof itself one must try to get on with them somehow; Frieda, for instance, felt that very hard to do and so she was very glad to employ me to quieten the servants. For more than two years, at least twice a week, I've spent the night with the servants in the stalls. Earlier, when father was still able to go to the Herrenhof with me, he slept somewhere in the taproom, and in that way waited for the news that I would bring in the morning. There wasn't much to bring. We've never found the messenger to this day, he must be still with Sortini who values him very highly, and he must have followed Sortini when Sortini retired to a more remote bureau. Most of the servants haven't seen him since we saw him last ourselves, and when one or other claims to have seen him it's probably a mistake. So my plan might have actually failed, and yet it hasn't failed completely; it's true we haven't found the messenger, and going to the Herrenhof and spending the night there – perhaps his pity for me, too, any pity that he's still capable of – has unfortunately ruined my father, and for two years now he has been in the state you've seen him in, and yet things are perhaps better with him than with my mother, for we're waiting daily for her death; it has only been put off thanks to Amalia's superhuman efforts. But what I've achieved in the Herrenhof is a certain connection with the Castle; don't despise me when I say that I don't repent what I've done. What conceivable sort of a connection with the Castle can this be, you'll no doubt be thinking; and you're right, it's not much of a connection. I know a great many of the servants now, of course, almost all the gentlemen's servants who have come to the village during the last two years, and if I should ever get into the Castle I shan't be a stranger there. Of course they're servants only in the village, in the Castle they're quite different, and probably wouldn't know me or anybody else there that they've had dealings with in the village, that's quite certain, even if they have sworn a hundred times in the stall that they would be delighted to see me again in the Castle. Besides, I've already had experience of how little all these promises are worth. But still that's not the really important thing. It isn't only through the servants themselves that I have a connection with the Castle, for apart from that I hope and trust that what I'm doing is being noticed by someone up there – and the management of the staff of servants is really an extremely important and laborious official function – and that finally whoever is noticing me may perhaps arrive at a more favourable opinion of me than the others, that he may recognise that I'm fighting for my family and carrying on my father's efforts, no matter in how poor a way. If he should see it like that, perhaps he'll forgive me too for accepting money from the servants and using it for our family. And I've achieved something more yet, which even you, I'm afraid, will blame me for. I learned a great deal from the servants about the ways in which one can get into the Castle service without going through the difficult preliminaries of official appointment lasting sometimes for years; in that case, it's true, one doesn't become an actual official employee, but only a private and semi-official one, one has neither rights nor duties – and the worst is not to have any duties – but one advantage one does have, that one is on the spot, one can watch for favourable opportunities and take advantage of them, one may not be an employee, but by good luck some work may come one's way, perhaps no real employee is handy, there's a call, one flies to answer it, and one has become the very thing that one wasn't a minute before, an employee. Only, when is one likely to get a chance like that? Sometimes at once, one has hardly arrived, one has hardly had time to look round before the chance is there, and many a one hasn't even the presence of mind, being quite new to the job, to seize the opportunity; but in another case one may have to wait for even more years than the official employees, and after being a semi-official servant for so long one can never be lawfully taken on afterwards as an official employee. So there's enough here to make one pause, but it sinks to nothing when one takes into account that the test for the official appointments is very stringent and that a member of any doubtful family is turned down in advance; let us say someone like that goes in for the examination, for years he waits in fear and trembling for the result, from the very first day everybody asks him in amazement how he could have dared to do anything so wild, but he still goes on hoping – how else could he keep alive? – then after years and years, perhaps as an old man, he learns that he has been rejected, learns that everything is lost and that all his life has been in vain. Here, too, of course there are exceptions, that's how one is so easily tempted. It happens sometimes that really shady customers are actually appointed, there are officials who, literally in spite of themselves, are attracted by those outlaws; at the entrance examinations they can't help sniffing the air, smacking their lips, and rolling their eyes towards an entrant like that, who seems in some way to be terribly appetising to them, and they have to stick close to their books of regulations so as to withstand him. Sometimes, however, that doesn't help the entrant to an appointment, but only leads to an endless postponement of the preliminary proceedings,

which are never terminated, but only broken off by the
death of the poor man. So official appointment no less than
the other kind is full of obvious and concealed difficulties,
and before one goes in for anything of the kind it's highly
advisable to weigh everything carefully. Now, we didn't fail
to do that, Barnabas and I. Every time that I came back
from the Herrenhof we sat down together and I told the
latest news that I had gathered, for days we talked it over,
and Barnabas's work lay idle for longer spells than was good
for it. And here I may be to blame in your opinion. I knew
quite well that much reliance was not to be put on the
servants' stories. I knew that they never had much inclination to tell me things about the Castle, that they always
changed the subject, and that every word had to be dragged
out of them, and then, when they were well started, that
they let themselves go, talked nonsense, bragged, tried to
surpass one another in inventing improbable lies, so that in
the continuous shouting in the dark stalls, one servant
beginning where the other left off, it was clear that at best
only a few scanty scraps of truth could be picked up. But I
repeated everything to Barnabas again just as I had heard it,
though he still had no capacity whatever to distinguish
between what was true and what was false, and on account
of the family's position was almost famishing to hear all
these things; and he drank in everything and burned with
eagerness for more. And as a matter of fact the cornerstone
of my new plan was Barnabas. Nothing more could be done
through the servants. Sortini's messenger was not to be
found and would never be found, Sortini and his messenger
with him seemed to be receding farther and farther, by
many people their appearance and names were already
forgotten, and often I had to describe them at length and in
spite of that learn nothing more than that the servant I was
speaking to could remember them with an effort, but except
for that could tell nothing about them. And as for my
conduct with the servants, of course I had no power to
decide how it might be looked on and could only hope that

the Castle would judge it in the spirit I did it in, and that in return a little of the guilt of our family would be taken away, but I've received no outward sign of that. Still I stuck to it, for so far as I was concerned I saw no other chance of getting anything done for us in the Castle. But for Barnabas I saw another possibility. From the tales of the servants – if I had the inclination, and I had only too much inclination – I could draw the conclusion that anyone who was taken into the Castle service could do a great deal for his family. But then what was there that was worthy of belief in these tales? It was impossible to make certain of that, but that there was very little was clear. For when, say, a servant that I would never see again, or that I would hardly recognise even were I to see him again, solemnly promised me to help to get my brother a post in the Castle, or at least, if Barnabas should come to the Castle on other business, to support him, or at least to back him up – for according to the servants' stories it sometimes happens that candidates for posts become unconscious or deranged during the protracted waiting and then they're lost if some friend doesn't look after them – when things like that and a great many more were told to me, they were probably justified as warnings, but the promises that accompanied them were quite baseless. But not to Barnabas; it's true I warned him not to believe them, but my mere telling of them was enough to enlist him for my plan. The reasons I advanced for it myself impressed him less, the thing that chiefly influenced him was the servants' stories. And so in reality I was completely thrown back upon myself, Amalia was the only one who could make herself understood to my parents, and the more I followed, in my own way, the original plans of father, the more Amalia shut herself off from me, before you or anybody else she talks to me, but not when we're alone; to the servants in the Herrenhof I was a plaything which in their fury they did their best to wreck, not one intimate word have I spoken with any of them during those two years, I've had only cunning or lying or silly words from them, so only Barnabas remained for me, and Barnabas was still very young. When I saw the light in his eyes as I told him those things, a light which has remained in them ever since, I felt terrified and yet I didn't stop, the things at stake seemed too great. I admit I hadn't my father's great though empty plans, I hadn't the resolution that men have, I confined myself to making good the insult to the messenger, and only asked that the actual modesty of my attempt should be put to my credit. But what I had failed to do by myself I wanted now to achieve in a different way and with certainty through Barnabas. We had insulted a messenger and driven him into a more remote bureau; what was more natural than for us to offer a new messenger in the person of Barnabas, so that the other messenger's work might be carried on by him, and the other messenger might remain quietly in retirement as long as he liked, for as long a time as he needed to forget the insult? I was quite aware, of course, that in spite of all its modesty there was a hint of presumption in my plan, that it might give rise to the impression that we wanted to dictate to the authorities how they should decide a personal question, or that we doubted their ability to make the best arrangements, which they might have made long before we had struck upon the idea that something could be done. But then, I thought again that it was impossible that the authorities should misunderstand me so grossly, or if they should, that they should do so intentionally, than in other words all that I did should be turned down in advance without further examination. So I did not give in and Barnabas's ambition kept him from giving in. In this term of preparation Barnabas became so uppish that he found that cobbling was far too menial work for him, a future bureau employee, yes, he even dared to contradict Amalia, and flatly, on the few occasions that she spoke to him about it. I didn't grudge him this brief happiness, for with the first day that he went to the Castle his happiness and his arrogance would be gone, a thing easy enough to foresee. And now began that parody of service of which I've told you already. It was amazing with what little difficulty Barnabas got into the Castle that first time, or more correctly into the bureau which in a manner of speaking has become his workroom. This success drove me almost frantic at the time, when Barnabas whispered the news to me in the evening after he came home. I ran to Amalia, seized her, drew her into a corner, and kissed her so wildly that she cried with pain and terror. I could explain nothing for excitement, and then it had been so long since we had spoken to each other, so I put off telling her until next day or the day after. For the next few days, however, there was really nothing more to tell. After the first quick success nothing more happened. For two long years Barnabas led this heart-breaking life. The servants failed us completely, I gave Barnabas a short note to take with him recommending him to their consideration, reminding them at the same time of their promises, and Barnabas, as often as he saw a servant, drew out the note and held it up, and even if he sometimes may have presented it to someone who didn't know me, and even if those who did know me were irritated by his way of holding out the note in silence – for he didn't dare to speak up there – yet all the same it was a shame that nobody helped him, and it was a relief – which we could have secured, I must admit, by our own action and much earlier – when a servant who had probably been pestered several times already by the note, crushed it up and flung it into the wastepaper basket. Almost as if he had said: "That's just what you yourselves do with letters," it occurred to me. But barren of results as all this time was in other ways, it had a good effect on Barnabas, if one can call it a good thing that he grew prematurely old, became a man before his time, yes, even in some ways more grave and sensible than most men. Often it makes me sad to look at him and compare him with the boy that he was only two years ago. And with it all I'm quite without the comfort and support that, being a man, he could surely give me. Without me he could hardly have got into the Castle, but since he is there, he's independent of me. I'm his only intimate friend, but I'm certain that he only tells me a small part of what he has on his mind. He tells me a great many things about the Castle, but from his stories, from the trifling details that he gives, one can't understand in the least how those things could have changed him so much. In particular I can't understand how the daring he had as a boy – it actually caused us anxiety – how he can have lost it so completely up there now that he's a man. Of course all that useless standing about and waiting all day, and day after day, and going on and on without any prospect of a change, must break a man down and make him unsure of himself and in the end actually incapable of anything else but this hopeless standing about. But why didn't he put up a fight even at the beginning? Especially seeing that he soon recognised that I had been right and that there was no opportunity there for his ambition, though there might be some hope perhaps for the betterment of our family's condition. For up there, in spite of the servants' whims, everything goes on very soberly, ambition seeks its sole satisfaction in work, and as in this way the work itself gains the ascendancy, ambition ceases to have any place at all, for childish desires there's no room up there. Nevertheless Barnabas fancied, so he has told me, that he could clearly see how great the power and knowledge even of those very questionable officials were into whose bureau he is allowed. How fast they dictated, with half-shut eyes and brief gestures, merely by raising a finger quelling the surly servants, and making them smile with happiness even when they were checked; or perhaps finding an important passage in one of the books and becoming quite absorbed in it, while the others would crowd round as near as the cramped space would allow them, and crane their necks to see it. These things and other things of the same kind gave Barnabas a great idea of those men, and he had the feeling that if he could get the length of being noticed by them and could venture to address a few words to them, not as a stranger, but as a colleague – true a very subordinate colleague – in the bureau, incalculable things might be achieved for our family. But things have never got that length yet, and Barnabas can't venture to do anything that might help towards it, although he's well aware that, young as he is, he's been raised to the difficult and responsible position of chief breadwinner in our family on account of this whole unfortunate affair. And now for the final confession: it was a week after your arrival. I heard somebody mentioning it in the Herrenhof, but didn't pay much attention; a Land Surveyor had come and I didn't even know what a Land Surveyor was. But next evening Barnabas – at an agreed hour I usually set out to go a part of the way to meet him – came home earlier than usual, saw Amalia in the sitting-room, drew me out into the street, laid his head on my shoulder, and cried for several minutes. He was again the little boy he used to be. Something had happened to him that he hadn't been prepared for. It was as if a whole new world had suddenly opened to him, and he could not bear the joy and the anxieties of all this newness. And yet the only thing that had happened was that he had been given a letter for delivery to you. But it was actually the first letter, the first commission, that he had ever been given.'

Olga stopped. Everything was still except for the heavy, occasionally disturbed breathing of the old people. K. merely said casually, as if to round off Olga's story: 'You've all been playing with me. Barnabas brought me the letter with the air of an old and much occupied messenger, and you as well as Amalia – who for that time must have been in with you – behaved as if carrying messages and the letter itself were matters of indifference.' 'You must distinguish between us,' said Olga. 'Barnabas had been made a happy boy again by the letter, in spite of all the doubts that he had about his capability. He confined those doubts to himself and me, but he felt it a point of honour to look like a real messenger, as according to his ideas real messengers looked. So although his hopes were now rising to an official uniform I had to alter his trousers, and in two hours, so that they would have some resemblance at least to the close-fitting trews of the official uniform, and he might appear in them before you, knowing, of course, that on this point you could be easily taken in. So much for Barnabas. But Amalia really despises his work as a messenger, and now that he seemed to have had a little success – as she could easily guess from Barnabas and myself and our talking and whispering together – she despised it more than ever. So she was speaking the truth, don't deceive yourself about that. But if I, K., have seemed to slight Barnabas's work, it hasn't been with any intention to deceive you, but from anxiety. These two letters that have gone through Barnabas's hands are the first signs of grace, questionable as they are, that our family has received for three years. This change, if it is a change and not deception – deceptions are more frequent than changes – is connected with your arrival here, our fate has become in a certain sense dependent on you, perhaps these two letters are only a beginning, and Barnabas's abilities will be used for other things than these two letters concerning you – we must hope that as long as we can – for the time being, however, everything centres on you. Now up in the Castle we must rest content with whatever our lot happens to be, but down here we can, it may be, do something ourselves, that is, make sure of your goodwill, or at least save ourselves from your dislike, or, what's more important, protect you as far as our strength and experience go, so that your connection with the Castle – by which we might perhaps be helped too – might not be lost. Now what was our best way of bringing that about? To prevent you from having any suspicion of us when we approached you – for you're a stranger here and because of that certain to be full of suspicion, full of justifiable suspicion. And, besides, we're despised by everybody and you must be influenced by the general opinion, particularly through your fiancée, so how could we put ourselves forward without quite unintentionally setting ourselves up

against your fiancée, and so offending you? And the messages, which I had read before you got them – Barnabas
didn't read them, as a messenger he couldn't allow himself
to do that – seemed at the first glance obsolete and not of
much importance, yet took on the utmost importance in as
much as they referred you to the Superintendent. Now in
these circumstances how were we to conduct ourselves
towards you? If we emphasised the letters' importance, we
laid ourselves under suspicion by overestimating what was
obviously unimportant, and in pluming ourselves as the
vehicle of these messages we should be suspected of seeking
our own ends, not yours; more, in doing that we might
depreciate the value of the letter itself in your eyes and so
disappoint you sore against our will. But if we didn't lay
much stress on the letters we should lay ourselves equally
under suspicion, for why in that case should we have taken
the trouble of delivering such an unimportant letter, why
should our actions and our words be in such clear contradiction, why should we in this way disappoint not only you,
the addressee, but also the sender of the letter, who certainly hadn't handed the letter to us so that we should
belittle it to the addressee by our explanations? And to hold
the mean, without exaggeration on either side, in other
words to estimate the just value of those letters, is
impossible, they themselves change in value perpetually, the
reflections they give rise to are endless, and chance deter-
mines where one stops reflecting, and so even our estimate
of them is a matter of chance. And when on the top of that
there came anxiety about you, everything became confused,
and you mustn't judge whatever I said too severely. When,
for example – as once happened – Barnabas arrived with the
news that you were dissatisfied with his work, and in his
first distress – his professional vanity was wounded too I
must admit – resolved to retire from the service altogether,
then to make good the mistake I was certainly ready to
deceive, to lie, to betray, to do anything, no matter how
wicked, if it would only help. But even then I would have

been doing it, at least in my opinion, as much for your sake as for ours.'

There was a knock. Olga ran to the door and unfastened it. A strip of light from a dark lantern fell across the threshold. The late visitor put questions in a whisper and was answered in the same way, but was not satisfied and tried to force his way into the room. Olga found herself unable to hold him back any longer and called to Amalia, obviously hoping that to keep the old people from being disturbed in their sleep Amalia would do anything to eject the visitor. And indeed she hurried over at once, pushed Olga aside, and stepped into the street and closed the door behind her. She only remained there for a moment, almost at once she came back again, so quickly had she achieved what had proved impossible for Olga.

K. then learned from Olga that the visit was intended for him. It had been one of the assistants, who was looking for him at Frieda's command. Olga had wanted to shield K. from the assistant; if K. should confess his visit here to Frieda later, he could, but it must not be discovered through the assistant; K. agreed. But Olga's invitation to spend the night there and wait for Barnabas he declined, for himself he might perhaps have accepted for it was already late in the night and it seemed to him that now, whether he wanted it or not, he was bound to this family in such a way that a bed for the night here, though for many reasons painful, nevertheless, when one considered this common bond, was the most suitable for him in the village; all the same he declined it, the assistant's visit had alarmed him, it was incomprehensible to him how Frieda, who knew his wishes quite well, and the assistants, who had learned to fear him, had come together again like this, so that Frieda didn't scruple to send an assistant for him, only one of them, too, while the other had probably remained to keep her company. He asked Olga whether she had a whip, she hadn't one, but she had a good hazel switch, and he took it; then he asked whether there was any other way out of the house, there was one through the yard, only one had to clamber over the wall of the neighbouring garden and walk through it before one reached the street. K. decided to do this. While Olga was conducting him through the yard, K. tried hastily to reassure her fears, told her that he wasn't in the least angry at the small artifices she had told him about, but understood them very well, thanked her for the confidence she had shown in him in telling him her story, and asked her to send Barnabas to the school as soon as he arrived, even if it were during the night. It was true, the messages which Barnabas brought were not his only hope, otherwise things would be bad indeed with him, but he didn't by any means leave them out of account, he would hold to them and not forget Olga either, for still more important to him than the messages themselves was Olga, her bravery, her prudence, if he had to choose between Olga and Amalia it wouldn't cost him much reflection. And he pressed her hand cordially once more as he swung himself on to the wall of the neighbouring garden.

XVI

WHEN he reached the street he saw indistinctly in the darkness that a little farther along the assistant was still walking up and down before Barnabas's house; sometimes he stopped and tried to peep into the room through the drawn blinds. K. called to him; without appearing visibly startled he gave up his spying on the house and came towards K. 'Who are you looking for?' asked K., testing the suppleness of the hazel switch on his leg. 'You,' replied the assistant as he came nearer. 'But who are you?' asked K. suddenly, for this did not appear to be the assistant. He seemed older, wearier, more wrinkled, but fuller in the face, his walk too was quite different from the brisk walk of the assistants, which gave an impression as if their joints were charged

with electricity; it was slow, a little halting, elegantly vale-
tudinarian. 'You don't recognise me?' asked the man, 'Jeremiah, your old assistant.' 'I see,' said K. tentatively
producing the hazel switch again, which he had concealed
behind his back. 'But you look quite different.' 'It's because
I'm by myself,' said Jeremiah. 'When I'm by myself then all
my youthful spirits are gone.' 'But where is Arthur?' asked
K. 'Arthur?' said Jeremiah. 'The little dear? He has left the
service. You were rather hard and rough on us, you know,
and the gentle soul couldn't stand it. He's gone back to the
Castle to put in a complaint.' 'And you?' asked K. 'I'm able
to stay here,' said Jeremiah, 'Arthur is putting in a complaint for me too.' 'What have you to complain about,
then?' asked K. 'That you can't understand a joke. What
have we done? Jested a little, laughed a little, teased your
fiancée a little. And all according to our instructions, too.
When Galater sent us to you –' 'Galater?' asked K. 'Yes,
Galater,' replied Jeremiah, 'he was deputising for Klamm
himself at the time. When he sent us to you he said – I took
a good note of it, for that's our business: You're to go down
there as assistants to the Land Surveyor. We replied: But we
don't know anything about the work. Thereupon he replied:
That's not the main point: if it's necessary, he'll teach you
it. The main thing is to cheer him up a little. According to
the reports I've received he takes everything too seriously.
He has just got to the village, and starts off thinking that a
great experience, whereas in reality it's nothing at all. You
must make him see that.' 'Well?' said K., 'was Galater right,
and have you carried out your task?' 'That I don't know,'
replied Jeremiah. 'In such a short time it was hardly
possible. I only know that you were very rough on us, and
that's what we're complaining of. I can't understand how
you, an employee yourself and not even a Castle employee,
aren't able to see that a job like that is very hard work, and
that it's very wrong to make the work harder for the poor
workers, and wantonly, almost childishly, as you have done.
Your total lack of consideration in letting us freeze at the

railings, and almost felling Arthur with your fist on the straw sack – Arthur, a man who feels a single cross word for days – and in chasing me up and down in the snow all afternoon, so that it was an hour before I could recover from it! And I'm no longer young!' 'My dear Jeremiah,' said K., 'you're quite right about all this, only it's Galater you should complain to. He sent you here of his own accord, I didn't beg him to send you. And as I hadn't asked for you it was at my discretion to send you back again, and like you, I would much rather have done it peacefully than with violence, but evidently you wouldn't have it any other way. Besides, why didn't you speak to me when you came first as frankly as you've done just now?' 'Because I was in the service,' said Jeremiah, 'surely that's obvious.' 'And now you're in the service no longer?' asked K. 'That's so,' said Jeremiah, 'Arthur has given notice in the Castle that we're giving up the job, or at least proceedings have been set going that will finally set us free from it.' 'But you're still looking for me just as if you were in the service,' said K. 'No,' replied Jeremiah, 'I was only looking for you to reassure Frieda. When you forsook her for Barnabas's sister she was very unhappy, not so much because of the loss, as because of your treachery, besides she had seen it coming for a long time and had suffered a great deal already on that account. I only went up to the schoolwindow for one more look to see if you mightn't have become more reasonable. But you weren't there. Frieda was sitting by herself on a bench crying. So then I went to her and we came to an agreement. Everything's settled. I'm to be waiter in the Herrenhof, at least until my business is settled in the Castle, and Frieda is back in the taproom again. It's better for Frieda. There was no sense in her becoming your wife. And you haven't known how to value the sacrifice that she was prepared to make for you either. But the good soul had still some scruples left, perhaps she was doing you an injustice, she thought, perhaps, you weren't with the Barnabas girl after all. Although of course there could be no doubt where you were, I went all the same so as to make sure of it once and for all; for after all this worry Frieda deserved to sleep peacefully for once, not to mention myself. So I went and not only found you there, but was able to see incidentally as well that you had the girls on a string. The black one especially – a real wild-cat – she's set her cap at you. Well, every one to his taste. But all the same it wasn't necessary for you to take the roundabout way through the next-door garden, I know that way.'

So now the thing had come after all which he had been able to foresee, but not to prevent. Frieda had left him. It could not be final, it was not so bad as that, Frieda could be won back, it was easy for any stranger to influence her, even for those assistants who considered Frieda's position much the same as their own, and now that they had given notice had prompted Frieda to do the same, but K. would only have to show himself and remind her of all that spoke in his favour, and she would rue it and come back to him, especially if he should be in a position to justify his visit to those girls by some success due entirely to them. Yet in spite of those reflections, by which he sought to reassure himself on Frieda's account, he was not reassured. Only a few minutes ago he had been praising Frieda up to Olga and calling her his only support; well, that support was not of the firmest, no intervention of the mighty ones had been needed to rob K. of Frieda – even this not very savoury assistant had been enough – this puppet which sometimes gave one the impression of not being properly alive.

Jeremiah had already begun to disappear. K. called him back. 'Jeremiah,' he said, 'I want to be quite frank with you; answer one question of mine too in the same spirit. We're no longer in the position of master and servant, a matter of congratulation not only to you but to me too; we have no grounds, then, for deceiving each other. Here before your eyes I snap this switch which was intended for you, for it wasn't for fear of you that I chose the back way out, but so as to surprise you and lay it across your shoulders a few times. But don't take it badly, all that is over; if you hadn't been forced on me as a servant by the bureau, but had been simply an acquaintance, we would certainly have got on splendidly, even if your appearance might have disturbed me occasionally. And we can make up now for what we have missed in that way.' 'Do you think so?' asked the assistant, yawning and closing his eyes wearily. 'I could of course explain the matter more at length, but I have no time, I must go to Frieda, the poor child is waiting for me, she hasn't started on her job yet, at my request the landlord has given her a few hours' grace – she wanted to fling herself into the work at once probably to help her to forget – and we want to spend that little time at least together. As for your proposal, I have no cause, certainly, to deceive you, but I have just as little to confide anything to you. My case, in other words, is different from yours. So long as my relation to you was that of a servant, you were naturally a very important person in my eyes, not because of your own qualities, but because of my office, and I would have done anything for you that you wanted, but now you're of no importance to me. Even your breaking the switch doesn't affect me, it only reminds me what a rough master I had, it's not calculated to prejudice me in your favour.' 'You talk to me,' said K., 'as if it were quite certain that you'll never have to fear anything from me again. But that isn't really so. From all appearances you're not free from me, things aren't settled here so quickly as that –' 'Sometimes even more quickly,' Jeremiah threw in. 'Sometimes,' said K., 'but nothing points to the fact that it's so this time, at least neither you nor I have anything that we can show in black and white. The proceedings are only started, it seems, and I haven't used my influence yet to intervene, but I will. If the affair turns out badly for you, you'll find that you haven't exactly endeared yourself to your master, and perhaps it was superfluous after all to break the hazel switch. And then you have abducted Frieda, and that has given you an inflated notion of yourself, but with all the respect that I have for your person, even if you have none for me any longer, a few words from me to Frieda will be enough – I know it – to smash up the lies that you've caught her with. And only lies could have estranged Frieda from me.' 'These threats don't frighten me,' replied Jeremiah, 'you don't in the least want me as an assistant, you were afraid of me even as an assistant, you're afraid of assistants in any case, it was only fear that made you strike poor Arthur.' 'Perhaps,' said K., 'but did it hurt the less for that? Perhaps I'll be able to show my fear of you in that way many times yet. Once I see that you haven't much joy in an assistant's work, it'll give me great satisfaction again, in spite of all my fear, to keep you at it. And moreover I'll do my best next time to see that you come by yourself, without Arthur, I'll be able then to devote more attention to you.' 'Do you think,' asked Jeremiah, 'that I have even the slightest fear of all this?' 'I do think so,' said K., 'you're a little afraid, that's certain, and if you're wise, very much afraid. If that isn't so why didn't you go straight back to Frieda? Tell me, are you in love with her, then?' 'In love!' said Jeremiah. 'She's a nice clever girl, a former sweetheart of Klamm's, so respectable in any case. And as she kept on imploring me to save her from you why shouldn't I do her the favour, particularly as I wasn't doing you any harm, seeing that you've consoled yourself with these damned Barnabas girls?' 'Now I can see how frightened you are,' said K., 'frightened out of your wits; you're trying to catch me with lies. All that Frieda asked for was to be saved from those filthy swine of assistants, who were getting past bounds, but unfortunately I hadn't time to fulfil her wish completely, and now this is the result of my negligence.'

'Land Surveyor, Land Surveyor!' someone shouted down the street. It was Barnabas. He came up breathless with running, but did not forget to greet K. with a bow. 'It's done!' he said. 'What's done?' asked K. 'You've laid my request before Klamm?' 'That didn't come off,' said Barnabas, 'I did my best, but it was impossible, I was urgent, stood there all day without being asked and so close to the desk that once a clerk actually pushed me away, for I was standing in his light, I reported myself when Klamm looked up – and that's forbidden – by lifting my hand, I was the last in the bureau, was left alone there with only the servants, but had the luck all the same to see Klamm coming back again, but it was not on my account, he only wanted to have another hasty glance at something in a book and went away immediately; finally, as I still made no move, the servants almost swept me out of the door with the broom. I tell you all this so that you need never complain of my efforts again.' 'What good is all your zeal to me, Barnabas,' said K., 'when it hasn't the slightest success?' 'But I have had success!' replied Barnabas. 'As I was leaving my bureau – I call it my bureau – I saw a gentleman coming slowly towards me along one of the passages; which were quite empty except for him. By that time in fact it was very late. I decided to wait for him. It was a good pretext to wait longer, indeed I would much rather have waited in any case, so as not to have to bring you news of failure. But apart from that it was worth while waiting, for it was Erlanger. You don't know him? He's one of Klamm's chief secretaries. A weakly little gentleman, he limps a little. He recognised me at once, he's famous for his splendid memory and his knowledge of people, he just draws his brows together and that's enough for him to recognise anybody, often people even that he's never seen before, that he's only heard of or read about; for instance, he could hardly ever have seen me. But although he recognises everybody immediately, he always asks first as if he weren't quite sure. Aren't you Barnabas? he asked me. And then he went on: You know the Land Surveyor, don't you? And then he said: That's very lucky. I'm just going to the Herrenhof. The Land Surveyor is to report to me there. I'll be in room Number 15. But he must come at once. I've only a few things to settle there and I leave again for the Castle at 5 o'clock in the morning. Tell him that it's very important that I should speak to him.'

Suddenly Jeremiah set off at a run. In his excitement Barnabas had scarcely noticed his presence till now and asked: 'Where's Jeremiah going?' 'To forestall me with Erlanger,' said K., and set off after Jeremiah, caught him up, hung on to his arm, and said: 'Is it a sudden desire for Frieda that's seized you? I've got it as well, so we'll go together side by side.'

XVII

BEFORE the dark Herrenhof a little group of men were standing, two or three had lanterns with them, so that a face here and there could be distinguished. K. recognised only one acquaintance, Gerstäcker the carrier. Gerstäcker greeted him with the enquiry: 'You're still in the village?' 'Yes,' replied K. 'I've come here for good.' 'That doesn't matter to me,' said Gerstäcker, breaking out into a fit of coughing and turning away to the others.

It turned out that they were all waiting for Erlanger. Erlanger had already arrived, but he was consulting first with Momus before he admitted his clients. They were all complaining at not being allowed to wait inside and having to stand out there in the snow. The weather wasn't very cold, but still it showed a lack of consideration to keep them standing there in front of the house in the darkness, perhaps for hours. It was certainly not the fault of Erlanger, who was always very accommodating, knew nothing about it, and would certainly be very annoyed if it were reported to him. It was the fault of the Herrenhof landlady, who in her positively morbid determination to be refined, wouldn't suffer a lot of people to come into the Herrenhof at the same time. 'If it absolutely must be and they must come,' she used to say, 'then in Heaven's name let them come one at a time.'

And she had managed to arrange that the clients, who at first had waited simply in a passage, later on the stairs, then in the hall, and finally in the taproom, were at last pushed out into the street. But even that had not satisfied her. It was unendurable for her to be always 'besieged', as she expressed herself, in her own house. It was incomprehensible to her why there should need to be clients waiting at all. 'To dirty the front-door steps,' an official had once told her, obviously in annoyance, but to her this pronouncement had seemed very illuminating, and she was never tired of quoting it. She tried her best – and she had the approval in this case of the clients too – to get a building set up opposite the Herrenhof where the clients could wait. She would have liked best of all if the interviews and examinations could have taken place outside the Herrenhof altogether, but the officials opposed that, and when the officials opposed her seriously the land-lady naturally enough was unable to gainsay them, though in lesser matters she exercised a kind of petty tyranny, thanks to her indefatigable, yet femininely insinuating zeal. And the landlady would probably have to endure those interviews and examinations in the Herrenhof in perpetuity, for the gentlemen from the Castle refused to budge from the place whenever they had official business in the village. They were always in a hurry, they came to the village much against their will, they had not the slightest intention of prolonging their stay beyond the time absolutely necessary, and so they could not be asked, simply for the sake of making things more pleasant in the Herrenhof, to waste time by transferring themselves with all their papers to some other house. The officials preferred indeed to get through their business in the taproom or in their rooms, if possible while they were at their food, or in bed before retiring for the night, or in the morning when they were too weary to get up and wanted to stretch themselves for a little longer. Yet the question of the erection of a waiting-room outside seemed to be nearing a favourable solution; but it was really a sharp blow for the landlady – people laughed a little over it – that this matter of a waiting-room should itself make innumerable interviews necessary, so that the lobbies of the house were hardly ever empty.

The waiting group passed the time by talking in half-whispers about those things. K. was struck by the fact that, though their discontent was general, nobody saw any objection to Erlanger's summoning his clients in the middle of the night. He asked why this was so and got the answer that they should be only too thankful to Erlanger. It was only his goodwill and his high conception of his office that induced him to come to the village at all, he could easily if he wished – and it would probably be more in accordance with the regulations too – he could easily send an under-secretary and let him draw up statements. Still, he usually refused to do this, he wanted to see and hear everything for himself, but for this purpose he had to sacrifice his nights, for in his official time-table there was no time allowed for journeys to the village. K. objected that even Klamm came to the village during the day and even stayed for several days; was Erlanger, then, a mere secretary, more indispensable up there? One or two laughed good humouredly, others maintained an embarrassed silence, the latter gained the ascendancy, and K. received hardly any reply. Only one man replied hesitatingly, that of course Klamm was indispensable, in the Castle as in the village.

Then the front door opened and Momus appeared between two attendants carrying lamps. 'The first who will be admitted to Herr Erlanger,' he said, 'are Gerstäcker and K. Are these two men here?' They reported themselves, but before they could step forward Jeremiah slipped in with a 'I'm a waiter here,' and, greeted by Momus with a smiling slap on the shoulder, disappeared inside. 'I'll have to keep a sharper eye on Jeremiah,' K. told himself, though he was quite aware at the same time that Jeremiah was probably far less dangerous than Arthur who was working against him in the Castle. Perhaps it would actually have been wiser to let himself be annoyed by them as assistants, than to have them prowling about without supervision and allow them to carry on their intrigues in freedom, intrigues for which they seemed to have special facilities.

As K. was passing Momus the latter started as if only now did he recognise in him the Land Surveyor. 'Ah, the Land Surveyor?' he said. 'The man who was so unwilling to be examined and now is in a hurry to be examined. It would have been simpler to let me do it that time. Well, really it's difficult to choose the right time for a hearing.' Since at these words K. made to stop, Momus went on: 'Go in, go in! I needed your answers then, I don't now.' Nevertheless K. replied, provoked by Momus's tone: 'You only think of yourselves. I would never and will never answer merely because of someone's office, neither then nor now.' Momus replied: 'Of whom, then, should we think? Who else is there here? Look for yourself!'

In the hall they were met by an attendant who led them the old way, already known to K., across the courtyard, then into the entry and through the low, somewhat downward sloping passage. The upper storeys were evidently reserved only for higher officials, the secretaries, on the other hand, had their rooms in this passage, even Erlanger himself, although he was one of the highest among them. The servant put out his lantern, for here it was brilliant with electric light. Everything was on a small scale, but elegantly finished. The space was utilised to the best advantage. The passage was just high enough for one to walk without bending one's head. Along both sides the doors almost touched each other. The walls did not quite reach to the ceiling, probably for reasons of ventilation, for here in the low cellar-like passage the tiny rooms could hardly have windows. The disadvantage of those incomplete walls was that the passage, and necessarily the rooms as well, were noisy. Many of the rooms seemed to be occupied, in most the people were still awake, one could hear voices, hammering, the clink of glasses. But the impression was not one of particular gaiety. The voices were muffled, only a word here and there could be indistinctly made out, it did not seem to be conversation either, probably someone was only dictating something or reading something aloud; and precisely from the rooms where there was a clinking of glasses and plates no word was to be heard, and the hammering reminded K. that he had been told some time or other that certain of the officials occupied themselves occasionally with carpentry, model engines, and so forth, to recuperate from the continual strain of mental work. The passage itself was empty except for a pallid, tall, thin gentleman in a fur coat, under which his night clothes could be seen, who was sitting before one of the doors. Probably it had become too stuffy for him in the room, so he had sat down outside and was reading a newspaper, but not very carefully; often he yawned and left off reading, then bent forward and glanced along the passage, perhaps he was waiting for a client whom he had invited and who had omitted to come. When they had passed him the servant said to Gerstäcker: 'That's Pinzgauer.' Gerstäcker nodded: 'He hasn't been down here for a long time now,' he said. 'Not for a long time now,' the servant agreed.

At last they stopped before a door which was not in any way different from the others, and yet behind which, so the servant informed them, was Erlanger. The servant got K. to lift him on to his shoulders and had a look into the room through the open slit. 'He's lying down,' said the servant climbing down, 'on the bed, in his clothes, it's true, but I fancy all the same that he's asleep. Often he's overcome with weariness like that, here in the village, what with the change in his habits. We'll have to wait. When he wakes up he'll ring. Besides, it has happened before this for him to sleep away all his stay in the village, and then when he woke to have to leave again immediately for the Castle. It's voluntary, of course, the work he does here.' 'Then it would be better if he just slept on,' said Gerstäcker, 'for when he has a little time left for his work after he wakes, he's very vexed at having fallen asleep, and tries to get everything settled in

a hurry, so that one can hardly get a word in.' 'You've come
on account of the contract for the carting for the new building?' asked the servant. Gerstäcker nodded, drew the servant aside and talked to him in a low voice, but the servant
hardly listened, gazed away over Gerstäcker, whom he over-
topped by more than a head, and stroked his hair slowly
and seriously.

XVIII

THEN, as he was looking round aimlessly, K. saw Frieda far
away at a turn of the passage; she behaved as if she did not
recognise him and only stared at him expressionlessly; she
was carrying a tray with some empty dishes in her hand. He
said to the servant, who, however, paid no attention whatever to him – the more one talked to the servant the more
absent-minded he seemed to become – that he would be
back in a moment, and ran off to Frieda. Reaching her he
took her by the shoulders as if he were seizing his own
property again, and asked her a few unimportant questions
with his eyes holding hers. But her rigid bearing hardly as
much as softened, to hide her confusion she tried to rear-
range the dishes on the tray and said: 'What do you want
from me? Go back to the others – oh, you know whom I
mean, you've just come from them, I can see it.' K.
changed his tactics immediately; the explanation mustn't
come so suddenly, and mustn't begin with the worst point,
the point most unfavourable to himself. 'I thought you were
in the taproom,' he said. Frieda looked at him in amazement and then softly passed her free hand over his brow
and cheeks. It was as if she had forgotten what he looked
like and were trying to recall it to mind again, even her eyes
had the veiled look of one who was painfully trying to
remember. 'I've been taken on in the taproom again,' she
said slowly at last, as if it did not matter what she said, but

245

as if beneath her words she were carrying on another conversation with K. which was more important – 'this work
here is not for me, anybody at all could do it; anybody who
can make beds and look good-natured and doesn't mind the
advances of the boarders, but actually likes them; anybody
who can do that can be a chamber-maid. But in the tap-
room, that's quite different. I've been taken on straight
away for the taproom again, in spite of that fact that I didn't
leave it with any great distinction, but, of course, I had a
word put in for me. But the landlord was delighted that I
had a word put in for me to make it easy for him to take me
on again. It actually ended by them having to press me to
take on the post; when you reflect what the taproom
reminds me of you'll understand that. Finally I decided to
take it on. I'm only here temporarily. Pepi begged us not to
put her to the shame of having to leave the taproom at once,
and seeing that she has been willing and has done everything to the best of her ability, we have given her a twenty-
four hours' extension.' 'That's all very nicely arranged,' said
K., 'but once you left the taproom for my sake, and now
that we're soon to be married are you going back to it
again?' 'There will be no marriage,' said Frieda. 'Because
I've been unfaithful to you?' asked K. Frieda nodded.
'Now, look here, Frieda,' said K., 'we've often talked
already about this alleged unfaithfulness of mine, and every
time you've had to recognise finally that your suspicions
were unjust. And since then nothing has changed on my
side, all I've done has remained as innocent as it was at first
and as it must always remain. So something must have
changed on your side, through the suggestions of strangers
or in some way or other. You do me an injustice in any
case, for just listen to how I stand with those two girls. The
one, the dark one – I'm almost ashamed to defend myself on
particular points like this, but you give me no choice – the
dark one, then, is probably just as displeasing to me as to
you; I keep my distance with her in every way I can, and
she makes it easy, too, no one could be more retiring than

she is.' 'Yes,' cried Frieda, the words slipped out as if against her will, K. was delighted to see her attention diverted, she was not saying what she had intended – 'Yes, you may look upon her as retiring, you tell me that the most shameless creature of them all is retiring, and incredible as it is, you mean it honestly, you're not shamming, I know. The Bridge Inn landlady once said of you: "I can't abide him, but I can't let him alone either, one simply can't control oneself when one sees a child that can hardly walk trying to go too far for it, one simply has to interfere." ' 'Pay attention to her advice for this once,' said K. smiling, 'but that girl – whether she's retiring or shameless doesn't matter – I don't want to hear any more about her.' 'But why do you call her retiring?' asked Frieda obdurately – K. considered this interest of hers a favourable sign – 'have you found her so, or are you simply casting a reflection on somebody else?' 'Neither the one nor the other,' said K., 'I call her that out of gratitude, because she makes it easy for me to ignore her, and because if she said even a word or two to me I couldn't bring myself to go back again, which would be a great loss to me, for I must go there for the sake of both our futures, as you know. And it's simply for that reason that I have to talk with the other girl, whom I respect, I must admit, for her capability, prudence, and unselfishness, but whom nobody could say was seductive.' 'The servants are of a different opinion,' said Frieda. 'On that as on lots of other subjects,' said K. 'Are you going to deduce my unfaithfulness from the tastes of the servants?' Frieda remained silent and suffered K. to take the tray from her, set it on the floor, put his arm through hers, and walk her slowly up and down in the corner of the passage. 'You don't know what fidelity is,' she said, his nearness putting her a little on the defensive, 'what your relations with the girl may be isn't the most important point; the fact that you go to that house at all and come back with the smell of their kitchen on your clothes is itself an unendurable humiliation for me. And then you rush out of the school without saying a word. And stay with them, too, the half of the night. And when you're asked for, you let those girls deny that you're there, deny it passionately, especially the wonderfully retiring one. And creep out of the house by a secret way, perhaps actually to save the good name of the girls, the good name of those girls. No, don't let us talk about it any more.' 'Yes, don't let us talk of this,' said K., 'but of something else, Frieda. Besides, there's nothing more to be said about it. You know why I have to go there. It isn't easy for me, but I overcome my feelings. You shouldn't make it any harder for me than it is. To-night I only thought of dropping in there for a minute to see whether Barnabas had come at last, for he had an important message which he should have brought long before. He hadn't come, but he was bound to come very soon, so I was assured, and it seemed very probable too. I didn't want to let him come after me, for you to be insulted by his presence. The hours passed and unfortunately he didn't come. But another came all right, a man whom I hate. I had no intention of letting myself be spied on by him, so I left through the neighbour's garden, but I didn't want to hide from him either, and I went up to him frankly when I reached the street, with a very good and supple hazel switch, I admit. That is all, so there's nothing more to be said about it; but there's plenty to say about something else. What about the assistants, the very mention of whose name is as repulsive to me as that family is to you? Compare your relations with them with my relations with that family. I understand your antipathy to Barnabas's family and I can share it. It's only for the sake of my affairs that I go to see them, sometimes it almost seems to me that I'm abusing and exploiting them. But you and the assistants! You've never denied that they persecute you, and you've admitted that you're attracted by them. I wasn't angry with you for that, I recognised that powers were at work which you weren't equal to, I was glad enough to see that you put up a resistance at least, I helped to defend you, and just because I left off for a few hours, trusting in your constancy, trusting also, I must admit, in the hope that the house was securely locked and the assistants finally put to flight – I still underestimate them, I'm afraid – just because I left off for a few hours and this Jeremiah – who is, when you look at him closely, a rather unhealthy elderly creature – had the impudence to go up to the window; just for this, Frieda, I must lose you and get for a greeting: "There will be no marriage." Shouldn't I be the one to cast reproaches? But I don't. I have never done so.' And once more it seemed advisable to K. to distract Frieda's mind a little, and he begged her to bring him something to eat for he had had nothing since midday. Obviously relieved by the request, Frieda nodded and ran to fetch something, not farther along the passage, however, where K. conjectured the kitchen was, but down a few steps to the left. In a little she brought a plate with slices of meat and a bottle of wine, but they were clearly only the remains of a meal, the scraps of meat had been hastily ranged out anew so as to hide the fact, yet whole sausage skins had been overlooked, and the bottle was three-quarters empty. However, K. said nothing and fell on the food with a good appetite. 'You were in the kitchen?' he asked. 'No, in my own room,' she said. 'I have a room down there.' 'You might surely have taken me with you,' said K. 'I'll go down now, so as to sit down for a little while I'm eating.' 'I'll bring you a chair,' said Frieda already making to go. 'Thanks,' replied K. holding her back, 'I'm neither going down there, nor do I need a chair any longer.' Frieda endured his hand on her arm defiantly, bowed her head and bit her lip. 'Well, then, he is down there,' she said, 'did you expect anything else? He's lying on my bed, he got a cold out there, he's shivering, he's hardly had any food. At bottom it's all your fault, if you hadn't driven the assistants away and run after those people, we might be sitting comfortably in the school now. You alone have destroyed our happiness. Do you think that Jeremiah, so long as he was in service, would have dared to take me away? Then you entirely misunderstood the way things are ordered here. He wanted me, he tormented himself, he lay in watch for me, but that was only a game, like the play of a hungry dog who nevertheless wouldn't dare to leap up on the table. And just the same with me. I was drawn to him, he was a playmate of mine in my childhood – we played together on the slope of the Castle Hill, a lovely time, you've never asked me anything about my past – but all that wasn't decisive as long as Jeremiah was held back by his service, for I knew my duty as your future wife. But then you drove the assistants away and plumed yourself on it besides, as if you had done something for me by it; well, in a certain sense it was true. Your plan has succeeded as far as Arthur is concerned, but only for the moment, he's delicate, he hasn't Jeremiah's passion that nothing can daunt, besides you almost shattered his health for him by the buffet you gave him that night – it was a blow at my happiness as well – he fled to the Castle to complain, and even if he comes back soon, he's gone now all the same. But Jeremiah stayed. When he's in service he fears the slightest look of his master, but when he's not in service there's nothing he's afraid of. He came and took me; forsaken by you, commanded by him, my old friend, I couldn't resist. I didn't unlock the school door. He smashed the window and lifted me out. We flew here, the landlord looks up to him, nothing could be more welcome to the guests, either, than to have such a waiter, so we were taken on, he isn't living with me, but we are staying in the same room.' 'In spite of everything,' said K., 'I don't regret having driven the assistants from our service. If things stood as you say, and your faithfulness was only determined by the assistants being in the position of servants, then it was a good thing that it came to an end. The happiness of a married life spent with two beasts of prey, who could only be kept under by the whip, wouldn't have been very great. In that case I'm even thankful to this family who have unintentionally had some part in separating us.' They became silent and began to walk backwards and forwards again side by side, though neither this time could have told who had made the first move. Close beside him, Frieda seemed annoyed that K. did not take her arm again. 'And so everything seems in order,' K. went on, 'and we might as well say good-bye, and you go to your Jeremiah, who must have had this chill, it seems, ever since I chased him through the garden, and whom you've already left by himself too long in that case, and I to the empty school, or, seeing that there's no place for me there without you, anywhere else where they'll take me in. If I hesitate still in spite of this, it's because I have still a little doubt about what you've told me, and with good reason. I have a different impression of Jeremiah. So long as he was in service he was always at your heels and I don't believe that his position would have held him back permanently from making a serious attempt on you. But now that he considers that he's absolved from service, it's a different case. Forgive me if I have to explain myself in this way: Since you're no longer his master's fiancée, you're by no means such a temptation for him as you used to be. You may be the friend of his childhood, but – I only got to know him really from a short talk to-night – in my opinion he doesn't lay much weight on such sentimental considerations. I don't know why he should seem a passionate person in your eyes. His mind seems to me on the contrary to be particularly cold. He received from Galater certain instructions relating to me, instructions probably not very much in my favour, he exerted himself to carry them out, with a certain passion for service, I'll admit – it's not so uncommon here – one of them was that he should wreck our relationship; probably he tried to do it by several means, one of them was to tempt you by his evil languishing glances, another – here the landlady supported him – was to invent fables about my unfaithfulness; his attempt succeeded, some memory or other of Klamm that clung to him may have helped, he has lost his position, it is true, but probably just at the moment when he no longer needed it, then he reaped the fruit of his labours and lifted you out through the school window, with that his task was finished, and his passion for service having left him now, he'll feel bored, he would rather be in Arthur's shoes, who isn't really complaining up there at all, but earning praise and new commissions, but someone had to stay behind to follow the further developments of the affair. It's rather a burdensome task to him to have to look after you. Of love for you he hasn't a trace, he frankly admitted it to me; as one of Klamm's sweethearts he of course respects you, and to insinuate himself into your bedroom and feel himself for once a little Klamm certainly gives him pleasure, but that is all, you yourself mean nothing to him now, his finding a place for you here is only a supplementary part of his main job; so as not to disquieten you he has remained here himself too, but only for the time being, as long as he doesn't get further news from the Castle and his cooling feelings towards you aren't quite cured.' 'How you slander him!' said Frieda, striking her little fists together. 'Slander?' said K., 'no, I don't wish to slander him. But I may quite well perhaps be doing him an injustice, that is certainly possible. What I've said about him doesn't lie on the surface for anybody to see, and it may be looked at differently too. But slander? Slander could only have one object, to combat your love for him. If that were necessary and if slander were the most fitting means, I wouldn't hesitate to slander him. Nobody could condemn me for it, his position puts him at such an advantage as compared with me that, thrown back solely on my own resources, I could even allow myself a little slander. It would be a comparatively innocent, but in the last resort a powerless, means of defence. So put down your fists.' And K. took Frieda's hand in his ; Frieda tried to draw it away, but smilingly and not with any great earnestness. 'But I don't need slander,' said K., 'for you don't love him, you only think you do, and you'll be thankful to me for ridding you of your illusion. For think, if anybody wanted to take you away from me, without violence, but with the most careful calculation, he could only do it through the two assistants. In appearance good, childish, merry, irresponsible youths, fallen from the sky, from the Castle, a dash of childhood's memories with them too; all that of course must have seemed very nice, especially when I was the antithesis of it all, and was always running after affairs moreover which were scarcely comprehensible, which were exasperating to you, and which threw me together with people whom you considered deserving of your hate – something of which you carried over to me too, in spite of all my innocence. The whole thing was simply a wicked but very clever exploitation of the failings in our relationship. Everybody's relations have their blemishes, even ours, we came together from two very different worlds, and since we have known each other the life of each of us has had to be quite different, we still feel insecure, it's all too new. I don't speak of myself, I don't matter so much, in reality I've been enriched from the very first moment that you looked on me, and to accustom oneself to one's riches isn't very difficult. But – not to speak of anything else – you were torn away from Klamm, I can't calculate how much that must have meant, but a vague idea of it I've managed to arrive at gradually, you stumbled, you couldn't find yourself, and even if I was always ready to help you, still I wasn't always there, and when I was there you were held captive by your dreams or by something more palpable, the landlady, say – in short there were times when you turned away from me, longed, poor child, for vague inexpressible things, and at those periods any passable man had only to come within your range of vision and you lost yourself to him, succumbing to the illusion that mere fancies of the moment, ghosts, old memories, things of the past and things receding ever more into the past, life that had once been lived – that all this was your actual present-day life. A mistake, Frieda, nothing more than the last and, properly regarded, contemptible difficulties attendant on our final reconciliation. Come to yourself, gather yourself together; even if you thought that the assistants were sent by Klamm – it's quite untrue, they come from Galater – and even if they did manage by the help of this illusion to charm you so completely that even in their disreputable tricks and their lewdness you thought you found traces of Klamm, just as one fancies one catches a glimpse of some precious stone that one has lost in a dung-heap, while in reality one wouldn't be able to find it even if it were there – all the same they're only hobbledehoys like the servants in the stall, except that they're not healthy like them, and a little fresh air makes them ill and compels them to take to their beds, which I must say that they know how to snuffle out with a servant's true cunning.' Frieda had let her head fall on K.'s shoulder; their arms round each other, they walked silently up and down. 'If we had only,' said Frieda after a while, slowly, quietly, almost serenely, as if she knew that only a quite short respite of peace on K.'s shoulder were reserved for her, and she wanted to enjoy it to the utmost, 'if we had only gone away somewhere at once that night, we might be in peace now, always together, your hand always near enough for mine to grasp; oh, how much I need your companionship, how lost I have felt without it ever since I've known you, to have your company, believe me, is the only dream that I've had, that and nothing else.'

Then someone called from the side passage, it was Jeremiah, he was standing there on the lowest step, he was in his shirt, but had thrown a wrap of Frieda's round him. As he stood there, his hair rumpled, his thin beard lank as if dripping with wet, his eyes painfully beseeching and wide with reproach, his sallow cheeks flushed, but yet flaccid, his naked legs trembling so violently with cold that the long fringes of the wrap quivered as well, he was like a patient who had escaped from hospital, and whose appearance could only suggest one thought, that of getting him back in bed again. This in fact was the effect that he had on Frieda, she disengaged herself from K., and was down beside Jeremiah in a second. Her nearness, the solicitude with which she drew the wrap closer round him, the haste with which she tried to force him back into the room, seemed to give him new strength, it was as if he only recognised K. now.

'Ah, the Land Surveyor!' he said, stroking Frieda's cheek to propitiate her, for she did not want to let him talk any further, 'forgive the interruption. But I'm not at all well, that must be my excuse. I think I'm feverish, I must drink some tea and get a sweat. Those damned railings in the school garden, they'll give me something to think about yet, and then, already chilled to the bone, I had to run about all night afterwards. One sacrifices one's health for things not really worth it, without noticing it at the time. But you, Land Surveyor, mustn't let yourself be disturbed by me, come into the room here with us, pay me a sick visit, and at the same time tell Frieda whatever you have still to say to her. When two who are accustomed to one another say good-bye, naturally they have a great deal to say to each other at the last minute which a third party, even if he's lying in bed waiting for his tea to come, can't possibly understand. But do come in, I'll be perfectly quiet.' 'That's enough, enough!' said Frieda pulling at his arm. 'He's feverish and doesn't know what he's saying. But you, K., don't you come in here, I beg you not to. It's my room and Jeremiah's, or rather it's my room and mine alone, I forbid you to come in with us. You always persecute me; oh, K., why do you always persecute me? Never, never will I go back to you, I shudder when I think of the very possibility. Go back to your girls; they sit beside you before the fire in nothing but their shifts, I've been told, and when anybody comes to fetch you they spit at him. You must feel at home there, since the place attracts you so much. I've always tried to keep you from going there, with little success, but all the same I've tried; all that's past now, you are free. You've a lovely life in front of you; for the one you'll perhaps have to squabble a little with the servants, but as for the other, there's nobody in heaven or earth that will grudge you her. The union is blessed beforehand. Don't deny it, I know you can disprove anything, but in the end nothing is disproved. Only think, Jeremiah, he has disproved everything!' They nodded with a smile of mutual understanding. 'But,' Frieda went on, 'even if everything were disproved, what would be gained by that, what would it matter to me? What happens in that house is purely their business and his business, not mine. Mine is to nurse you till you're well again, as you were at one time, before K. tormented you for my sake.' 'So you're not coming in after all, Land Surveyor?' asked Jeremiah, but was now definitely dragged away by Frieda, who did not even turn to look at K. again. There was a little door down there, still lower than the doors in the passage – not Jeremiah only, even Frieda had to stoop on entering – within it seemed to be bright and warm, a few whispers were audible, probably loving cajolements to get Jeremiah to bed, then the door was closed.

Here the text of the first German edition of THE CASTLE *ends. It has been translated by*

WILLA AND EDWIN MUIR.

What follows is the continuation of the text together with additional material (different versions, fragments, passages deleted by the author, etc.) as found among Kafka's papers after the publication of the first edition and included by the editor, Max Brod, in the definitive German edition. The translation is by

EITHNE WILKINS AND ERNST KAISER

Only now did K. notice how quiet it had become in the passage, not only here in this part of the passage where he had been with Frieda, and which seemed to belong to the public rooms of the inn, but also in the long passage with the rooms that had earlier been so full of bustle. So the gentlemen had gone to sleep at last after all. K. too was very tired, perhaps it was from fatigue that he had not stood up to Jeremiah as he should have. It would perhaps have been more prudent to take his cue from Jeremiah, who was obviously exaggerating how bad his chill was – his woefulness was not caused by his having a chill, it was congenital and could not be relieved by any herbal tea – to take his cue entirely from Jeremiah, make a similar display of his own really great fatigue, sink down here in the passage, which would in itself afford much relief, sleep a little, and then perhaps be nursed a little too. Only it would not have worked out as favourably as with Jeremiah, who would certainly have won this competition for sympathy, and rightly so, probably, and obviously every other fight too. K. was so tired that he wondered whether he might not try to go into one of these rooms, some of which were sure to be empty, and have a good sleep in a luxurious bed. In his view this might turn out to be recompense for many things. He also had a night-cap handy. On the tray that Frieda had left on the floor there had been a small decanter of rum. K. did not shrink from the exertion of making his way back, and he drained the little bottle to the dregs.

Now he at least felt strong enough to go before Erlanger. He looked for the door of Erlanger's room, but since the servant and Gerstäcker were no longer to be seen and all the doors looked alike, he could not find it. Yet he believed he remembered more or less in what part of the passage the door had been, and decided to open a door that in his opinion was probably the one he was looking for. The experiment could not be so very dangerous; if it was Erlanger's room Erlanger would doubtless receive him, if it was somebody else's room it would still be possible to apologise and go away again, and if the inmate was asleep, which was what was probable, then K.'s visit would not be noticed at all; it could turn out badly only if the room was empty, for then K. would scarcely be able to resist the temptation to get into the bed and sleep for ages. He once more glanced along the passage to right and to left, to see whether after all there might not be somebody coming who would be able to give him some information and make the venture unnecessary, but the long passage was quiet and empty. Then K. listened at the door. Here too was no inmate. He knocked so quietly that it could not have wakened a sleeper, and when even now nothing happened he opened the door very cautiously indeed. But now he was met with a faint scream. It was a small room, more than half filled by a wide bed, on the night-table the electric lamp was burning, beside it was a travelling handbag. In the bed, but completely hidden under the quilt, someone stirred uneasily and whispered through a gap between quilt and sheet: 'Who is it?' Now K. could not withdraw again so easily, discontentedly he surveyed the voluptuous but unfortunately not empty bed, then remembered the question and gave his name. This seemed to have a good effect, the man in the bed pulled the quilt a little off his face, anxiously ready, however, to cover himself up again completely if something was not quite all right out there. But then he flung back the quilt without qualms and sat up. It was certainly not Erlanger. It was a small, well-looking gentleman whose face had a certain contradictoriness in it in that the cheeks were chubby as a child's and the eyes merry as a child's, but that the high forehead, the pointed nose, the narrow mouth, the lips of which would scarcely remain closed, the almost vanishing chin, were not like a child's at all, but revealed superior intellect. It was doubtless his satisfaction with this, his satisfaction with himself, that had preserved in him a marked residue of something healthily childlike. 'Do you know Friedrich?' he asked. K. said he did not. 'But he knows you,' the gentleman said, smiling. K. nodded, there was no lack of people who knew him, this was indeed one of the main obstacles in his way. 'I am his secretary,' the gentleman said, 'my name is Bürgel.' 'Excuse me,' K. said, reaching for the door-handle, 'I am sorry, I mistook your door for another. The fact is I have been summoned to Secretary Erlanger.' 'What a pity,' Bürgel said. 'Not that you are summoned elsewhere, but that you made a mistake about the doors. The fact is once I am wakened I am quite certain not to go to sleep again. Still, that need not sadden you so much, it's my personal misfortune. Why, anyway, can't these doors be locked, eh? There's a reason for that, of course. Because, according to an old saying, the secretaries' doors should always be open. But that, again, need not be taken quite so literally.' Bürgel looked queryingly and merrily at K., in contrast to his lament he seemed thoroughly well rested; Bürgel had doubtless never in his life been as tired as K. was now. 'Where do you think of going now?' Bürgel asked. 'It's four o'clock. Anyone to whom you might think of going you would have to wake, not everybody is as used to being disturbed as I am, not everyone will put up with it as tolerantly, the secretaries are a nervous species. So stay for a little while. Round about five o'clock people here begin to get up, then you will be best able to answer your summons. So please do let go of the door-handle now and sit down somewhere, granted there isn't overmuch room here, it will be best if you sit here on the edge of the bed. You are surprised that I should have neither chair nor table here? Well, I had the choice of getting either a completely furnished room with a narrow hotel bed, or this big bed and nothing else except the washstand. I chose the big bed, after all, in a bedroom the bed is undoubtedly the main thing! Ah, for anyone who could stretch out and sleep soundly, for a sound sleeper, this bed would surely be truly delicious. But even for me, perpetually tired as I am without being able to sleep, it is a blessing, I spend a large part of the day in it, deal with all my correspondence in it, here conduct all the interviews with applicants. It works quite well. Of course the applicants have nowhere to sit, but they get over that, and after all it's more agreeable for them too if they stand and the recorder is at ease than if they sit comfortably and get barked at. So the only place I have to offer is this here on the edge of the bed, but that is not an official place and is only intended for nocturnal conversations. But you are so quiet, Land Surveyor?' 'I am very tired,' said K., who on receiving the invitation had instantly, rudely, without respect, sat down on the bed and leaned against the post. 'Of course,' Bürgel said, laughing, 'everybody is tired here. The work, for instance, that I got through yesterday and have already got through even to-day is no small matter. It's completely out of the question of course that I should go to sleep now, but if this most utterly improbable thing should happen after all and I should go to sleep while you are still here, then please stay quiet and don't open the door, either. But don't worry, I shall certainly not go to sleep or at best only for a few minutes. The way it is with me is that probably because I am so very used to dealing with applicants I do actually find it easiest to go to sleep when I have company.' 'Do go to sleep, please do, Mr. Secretary,' K. said, pleased at this announcement, 'I shall then, with your permission, sleep a little too.' 'No, no,' Bürgel said, laughing again, 'unfortunately I can't go to sleep merely on being invited to do so, it's only in the course of conversation that the opportunity may arise, it's most likely to be a conversation that puts me to sleep. Yes, one's nerves suffer in our business. I, for instance, am a liaison secretary. You don't know what that is? Well, I constitute the strongest liaison' – here he hastily rubbed his hands in involuntary merriment – 'between Friedrich and the village, I constitute the liaison between his Castle and village secretaries, am mostly in the village, but not permanently; at every moment I must be prepared to drive up to the Castle. You see the travelling-bag – a restless life, not suitable for everyone. On the other hand it is true that now I could not do without this kind of work, all other work would seem insipid to me. And how do things stand with the land-surveying?' 'I am not doing any such work, I am not being employed as a Land Surveyor,' K. said, he was not really giving his mind to the matter, actually he was only yearning for Bürgel to fall asleep, but even this was only out of a certain sense of duty towards himself, in his heart of hearts he was sure that the moment when Bürgel

would go to sleep was still infinitely remote. 'That is amazing,' Bürgel said with a lively jerk of his head, and pulled a
note-pad out from under the quilt in order to make a note.
'You are a Land Surveyor and have no land-surveying to
do.' K. nodded mechanically, he had stretched out his left
arm along the top of the bed-post and laid his head on it, he
had already tried various ways of making himself comfortable, but this position was the most comfortable of all, and
now, too, he could attend a little better to what Bürgel was
saying. 'I am prepared,' Bürgel continued, 'to follow up this
matter further. With us here things are quite certainly not
in such a way that an expert employee should be left
unused. And it must after all be painful to you too. Doesn't
it cause you distress?' 'It causes me distress,' K. said slowly
and smiled to himself, for just now it was not distressing
him in the least. Besides, Bürgel's offer made little impression on him. It was utterly dilettante. Without knowing anything of the circumstances under which K.'s appointment
had come about, of the difficulties that it encountered in the
community and at the Castle, of the complications that had
already occurred during K.'s sojourn here or had been fore-
shadowed, without knowing anything of all this, indeed
without even showing, what should have been expected of a
secretary as a matter of course, that he had at least an inkling of it all, he offered to settle the whole affair up there in
no time at all with the aid of his little note-pad. 'You seem
to have had some disappointments,' Bürgel said, by this
remark showing that he had after all some knowledge of
human nature, and indeed, since entering the room, K. had
from time to time reminded himself not to underestimate
Bürgel, but in his state it was difficult to form a fair judgment of anything but his own weariness. 'No,' Bürgel said,
as if he were answering a thought of K.'s and were con-
siderately trying to save him the effort of formulating it
aloud. 'You must not let yourself be frightened off by disappointments. Much here does seem to be arranged in such
a way as to frighten people off, and when one is newly

arrived here the obstacles do appear to be completely unsurmountable. I don't want to enquire into what all this really amounts to, perhaps the appearance does really correspond to the reality, in my position I lack the right detachment to come to a conclusion about that, but pay attention, there are sometimes after all opportunities that are almost not in accord with the general situation, opportunities in which by means of a word, a glance, a sign of trust, more can be achieved than by means of lifelong exhausting efforts. Indeed, that is how it is. But, then again, of course, these opportunities are in accord with the general situation in so far as they are never made use of. But why then are they never made use of? I ask time and again.' K. did not know why; he did certainly realise that what Bürgel was talking about probably concerned him closely, but he now felt a great dislike of everything that concerned him, he shifted his head a little to one side as though in this manner he were making way for Bürgel's questions and could no longer be touched by them. 'It is,' Bürgel continued, stretching his arms and yawning, which was in bewildering contradiction to the gravity of his words, 'it is a constant complaint of the secretaries that they are compelled to carry out most of the village interrogations by night. But why do they complain of this? Because it is too strenuous for them? Because they would rather spend the night sleeping? No, that is certainly not what they complain of. Among the secretaries there are of course those who are hard-working and those who are less hard-working, as everywhere; but none of them complains of excessive exertion, and least of all in public. That is simply not our way. In this respect we make no distinction between ordinary time and working-time. Such distinctions are alien to us. But what then have the secretaries got against the night interrogations? Is it perhaps consideration for the applicants? No, no, it is not that either. Where the applicants are concerned the secretaries are ruthless, admittedly not a jot more ruthless than towards themselves, but merely precisely as ruthless. Actually this ruthlessness is, when you come to think of it, nothing but a rigid obedience to and execution of their duty, the greatest consideration that the applicants can really wish for. And this is at bottom – granted, a superficial observer does not notice this – completely recognised; indeed, it is, for instance in this case, precisely the night interrogations that are welcomed by the applicants, no objections in principle come in regarding the night interrogations. Why then nevertheless the secretaries' dislike?' This K. did not know either, he knew so little, he could not even distinguish where Bürgel was seriously or only apparently expecting an answer. 'If you let me lie down in your bed,' he thought, 'I shall answer all your questions for you at noon to-morrow or, better still, to-morrow evening.' But Bürgel did not seem to be paying any attention to him, he was far too much occupied with the question that he had put to himself: 'So far as I can see and so far as my own experience takes me, the secretaries have the following qualms regarding the night interrogations: the night is less suitable for negotiations with applicants for the reason that by night it is difficult or positively impossible completely to preserve the official character of the negotiations. This is not a matter of externals, the forms can of course, if desired, be just as strictly observed by night as by day. So it is not that, on the other hand the official power of judgment suffers at night. One tends involuntarily to judge things from a more private point of view at night, the allegations of the applicants take on more weight than is due to them, the judgment of the case becomes adulterated with quite irrelevant considerations of the rest of the applicants' situation, their sufferings and anxieties, the necessary barrier between the applicants and the officials, even though externally it may be impeccably maintained, weakens, and where otherwise, as is proper, only questions and answers are exchanged, what sometimes seems to take place is an odd, wholly unsuitable changing of places between the persons. This at least is what the secretaries say, and they are of course the people who, through their vocation, are endowed with a quite extraordinary subtlety of feeling in such matters. But even they – and this has often been discussed in our circles – notice little of those unfavourable influences during the night interrogations; on the contrary, they exert themselves right from the beginning to counteract them and end up by believing they have achieved quite particularly good results. If, however, one reads the records through afterwards one is often amazed at their obvious and glaring weaknesses. And these are defects, and, what is more, ever and again mean half-unjustified gains for the applicants, which at least according to our regulations cannot be repaired by the usual direct method. Quite certainly they will at some later time be corrected by a control-office, but this will only profit the law, but will not be able to damage that applicant any more. Are the complaints of the secretaries under such circumstances not thoroughly justified?' K. had already spent a little while sunk in half-sleep, but now he was roused again. 'Why all this? Why all this?' he wondered, and from under lowered eyelids considered Bürgel not like an official discussing difficult questions with him, but only like something that was preventing him from sleeping and whose further meaning he could not discover. But Bürgel, wholly abandoned to the pursuit of his thoughts, smiled, as though he had just succeeded in misleading K. a little. Yet he was prepared to bring him back on to the right road immediately. 'Well,' he said, 'on the other hand one cannot simply go and call these complaints quite justified, either. The night interrogations are, indeed, nowhere actually prescribed by the regulations, so one is not offending against any regulation if one tries to avoid them, but conditions, the excess of work, the way the officials are occupied in the Castle, how indispensable they are, the regulation that the interrogation of applicants is to take place only after the final conclusion of all the rest of the investigation, but then instantly, all this and much else has after all made the night interrogations an indispensable necessity. But if now they have become a necessity – this is what I say – this is nevertheless also, at least indirectly, a result of the regulations, and to find fault with the nature of the night interrogations would then almost mean – I am, of course, exaggerating a little, and only since it is an exaggeration can I utter it, as such – would then indeed mean finding fault with the regulations.

'On the other hand it may be conceded to the secretaries that they should try as best they can to safeguard themselves, within the terms of the regulations, against the night interrogations and their perhaps only apparent disadvantages. This is in fact what they do, and indeed to the greatest extent. They permit only subjects of negotiation from which there is in every sense as little as possible to be feared, test themselves closely prior to negotiations and, if the result of the test demands it, even at the very last moment cancel all examinations, strengthen their hand by summoning an applicant often as many as ten times before really dealing with him, have a liking for sending along to deputise for them colleagues who are not competent to deal with the given case and who can, therefore, handle it with greater ease, schedule the negotiations at least for the beginning or the end of the night, avoiding the middle hours, there are many more such measures, the secretaries are not the people to let anyone get the better of them so easily, they are almost as resilient as they are vulnerable.' K. was asleep, it was not real sleep, he could hear Bürgel's words perhaps better than during his former dead-tired state of waking, word after word struck his ear, but the tiresome consciousness had gone, he felt free, it was no longer Bürgel who held him, only he still sometimes groped towards Bürgel, he was not yet in the depths of sleep, but immersed in it he certainly was. No one should deprive him of that now. And it seemed to him as though with this he had achieved a great victory and already there was a party of people there to celebrate it, and he or perhaps someone else raised the champagne glass in honour of this victory. And so that all should know what it was all about the fight and the victory were repeated once again or perhaps not repeated at all, but only took place now and had already been celebrated earlier and there was no leaving off celebrating it, because fortunately the outcome was certain. A secretary, naked, very like the statue of a Greek god, was hard pressed by K. in the fight. It was very funny and K. in his sleep smiled gently about how the secretary was time and again startled out of his proud attitude by K.'s assaults and would hastily have to use his raised arm and clenched fist to cover unguarded parts of his body and yet was always too slow in doing so. The fight did not last long step for step, and they were very big steps, K. advanced. Was it a fight at all? There was no serious obstacle, only now and then a squeak from the secretary. This Greek god squeaked like a girl being tickled. And finally he was gone, K. was alone in a large room, ready for battle he turned round, looking for his opponent; but there was no longer anyone there, the company had also scattered, only the champagne glass lay broken on the floor. K. trampled it to smithereens. But the splinters pricked him, with a start he woke once again, he felt sick, like a small child being waked up. Nevertheless, at the sight of Bürgel's bare chest a thought that was part of his dream brushed his awareness: Here you have your Greek god! Go on, haul him out of bed! 'There is, however,' Bürgel said, his face thoughtfully tilted towards the ceiling, as though he were searching his memory for examples, but without being able to find any, 'there is, however, nevertheless, in spite of all precautionary measures, a way in which it is possible for the applicants to exploit this nocturnal weakness of the secretaries – always assuming that it is a weakness – to their own advantage. Admittedly, a very rare possibility, or, rather, one that almost never occurs. It consists in the applicant's coming unannounced in the middle of the night. You marvel, perhaps, that this, although it seems to be so obvious, should happen so very seldom. Well, yes, you are not familiar with conditions here. But even you must, I suppose, have been struck by the foolproofness of the official organisation. Now from this foolproofness it does result that everyone who has any petition or who must be interrogated in any matter for other reasons, instantly, without delay, usually indeed even before he has worked the matter out for himself, more, indeed, even before he himself knows of it, has already received the summons. He is not yet questioned this time, usually not yet questioned, the matter has usually not yet reached that stage, but he has the summons, he can no longer come unannounced, at best he can come at the wrong time, well, then all that happens is that his attention is drawn to the date and the hour of the summons, and if he then comes back at the right time he is as a rule sent away, that no longer causes any difficulty; having the summons in the applicant's hand and the case noted in the files are, it is true, not always adequate, but, nevertheless, powerful defensive weapons for the secretaries. This refers admittedly only to the secretary in whose competence the matter happens to lie; it would still, of course, be open to everyone to approach the others in the night, taking them by surprise. Yet this is something scarcely anyone will do, it is almost senseless. First of all it would mean greatly annoying the competent secretary. We secretaries are, it is true, by no means jealous of each other with regard to work, as everyone carries far too great a burden of work, a burden that is piled on him truly without stint, but in dealing with the applicants we simply must not tolerate any interference with our sphere of competence. Many a one before now has lost the game because, thinking he was not making progress with the competent authority, he tried to slip through by approaching some other, one not competent. Such attempts must, besides, fail also because of the fact that a non-competent secretary, even when he is taken unawares at dead of night and has the best will to help, precisely as a consequence of his non-competence can scarcely intervene any more effectively than the next best lawyer, indeed at bottom much less so, for what he lacks, of course – even if otherwise he could do something, since after all he knows the secret paths of the law better than all these legal gentry –

concerning things with regard to which he is not competent, what he lacks is quite simply time, he hasn't a moment to spare for it. So who then, the prospects being such, would spend his nights playing the non-competent secretary? Indeed, the applicants are in any case fully occupied if, besides carrying out their normal duties, they wish to respond to the summonses and hints from the competent authorities, "fully occupied" that is to say in the sense in which it concerns the applicants, which is, of course, far from being the same as "fully occupied" in the sense in which it concerns the secretaries.' K. nodded, smiling, he believed he now understood everything perfectly; not because it concerned him, but because he was now convinced he would fall fast asleep in the next few minutes, this time without dreaming or being disturbed; between the competent secretaries on the one hand and the non-competent on the other, and confronted with the crowd of fully occupied applicants, he would sink into deep sleep and in this way escape everything. Bürgel's quiet, self-satisfied voice, which was obviously doing its best to put its owner to sleep, was something he had now become so used to that it would do more to put him to sleep than to disturb him. 'Clatter, mill, clatter on and on,' he thought, 'you clatter just for me.' 'Where then, now,' Bürgel said, fidgeting at his underlip with two fingers, with widened eyes, craning neck, rather as though after a strenuous long walk he were approaching a delightful view, 'where then, now, is that previously mentioned, rare possibility that almost never occurs? The secret lies in the regulations regarding competence. The fact is things are not so constituted, and in such a large living organisation cannot be so constituted, that there is only one definite secretary competent to deal with each case. It is rather that one is competent above all others, but many others are in certain respects, even though to a smaller degree, also competent. Who, even if he were the hardest of workers, could keep together on his desk, single-handed, all the aspects of even the most minor incident? Even what I have been saying about the competence above all others is saying too much. For is not the whole competence contained even in the smallest? Is not what is decisive here the passion with which the case is tackled? And is this not always the same, always present in full intensity? In all things there may be distinctions among the secretaries, and there are countless such distinctions, but not in the passion; none of them will be able to restrain himself if it is demanded of him that he shall concern himself with a case in regard to which he is competent if only in the smallest degree. Outwardly, indeed, an orderly mode of negotiation must be established, and so it comes about that a particular secretary comes into the foreground for each applicant, one they have, officially, to keep to. This, however, does not even need to be the one who is in the highest degree competent in regard to the case, what is decisive here is the organisation and its particular needs of the moment. That is the general situation. And now, Land Surveyor, consider the possibility that through some circumstances or other, in spite of the obstacles already described to you, which are in general quite sufficient, an applicant does nevertheless, in the middle of the night, surprise a secretary who has a certain degree of competence with regard to the given case. I dare say you have never thought of such a possibility? I am quite prepared to believe it. Nor is it at all necessary to think of it, for it does, after all, practically never occur. What sort of oddly and quite specially constituted, small, skilful grain would such an applicant have to be in order to slip through the incomparable sieve? You think it cannot happen at all? You are right, it cannot happen at all. But some night – for who can vouch for everything? – it *does* happen. Admittedly, I don't know anyone among my acquaintances to whom it has ever happened, well, it is true that proves very little, the circle of my acquaintances is restricted in comparison to the number involved here, and besides it is by no means certain that a secretary to whom such a thing has happened will admit it, since it is, after all, a very personal affair and one that in a sense gravely touches the official sense of shame. Nevertheless my experience does perhaps prove that what we are concerned with is a matter so rare, actually only existing by way of rumour, not confirmed by anything else at all, that there is, therefore, really no need to be afraid of it. Even if it were really to happen, one can – one would think – positively render it harmless by proving to it, which is very easy, that there is no room for it in this world. In any case it is morbid to be so afraid of it that one hides, say, under the quilt and does not dare to peep out. And even if this perfect improbability should suddenly have taken on shape, is then everything lost? On the contrary. That everything should be lost is yet more improbable than the most improbable thing itself. Granted, if the applicant is actually in the room things are in a very bad way. It constricts the heart. "How long will you be able to put up resistance?" one wonders. But it will be no resistance at all, one knows that. You must only picture the situation correctly. The never-beheld, always-expected applicant, truly thirstingly expected and always reasonably regarded as out of reach – there this applicant sits. By his mute presence, if by nothing else, he constitutes an invitation to penetrate into his poor life, to look around there as in one's own property and there to suffer with him under the weight of his futile demands. This invitation in the silent night is beguiling. One gives way to it, and now one has actually ceased to function in one's official capacity. It is a situation in which it very soon becomes impossible to refuse to do a favour. To put it precisely, one is desperate; to put it still more precisely, one is very happy. Desperate, for the defenceless position in which one sits here waiting for the applicant to utter his plea and knowing that once it is uttered one must grant it, even if, at least in so far as one has oneself a general view of the situation, it positively tears the official organisation to shreds: this is, I suppose, the worst thing that can happen to one in the fulfilment of one's duties. Above all – apart from everything else – because it is also a promotion, one surpassing all conceptions, that one here for the moment usurps. For it is inherent in our position that we are not empowered to grant pleas such as that with which we are here concerned, yet through the proximity of this nocturnal applicant our official powers do in a manner of speaking grow, we pledge ourselves to do things that are outside our scope; indeed, we shall even fulfil our pledges. The applicant wrings from us in the night, as the robber does in the forest, sacrifices of which we should otherwise never be capable; well, all right, that is the way it is now when the applicant is still there, strengthening us and compelling us and spurring us on, and while everything is still half unconsciously under way; but how it will be afterwards, when it is all over, when, sated and carefree, the applicant leaves us and there we are, alone, defenceless in the face of our misuse of official power – that does not bear thinking of! Nevertheless, we are happy. How suicidal happiness can be! We might, of course, exert ourselves to conceal the true position from the applicant. He himself will scarcely notice anything of his own accord. He has, after all, in his own opinion probably only for some indifferent, accidental reasons – being overtired, disappointed, ruthless and indifferent from over-fatigue and disappointment – pushed his way into a room other than the one he wanted to enter, he sits there in ignorance, occupied with his thoughts, if he is occupied at all, with his mistake or with his fatigue. Could one not leave him in that situation? One cannot. With the loquacity of those who are happy one has to explain everything to him. Without being able to spare oneself in the slightest one must show him in detail what has happened and for what reasons this has happened, how extraordinarily rare and how uniquely great the opportunity is, one must show how the applicant, though he has stumbled into this opportunity in utter helplessness such as no other being is capable of than precisely an applicant, can, however, now, if he wants to, Land Surveyor, dominate everything and to that end has to do nothing but in some way or other put forward his plea, for which fulfilment is already waiting, which indeed it is already coming to meet, all this one must show; it is the official's hour of travail. But when one has done even that, then, Land Surveyor, all that is essential has been done, then one must resign oneself and wait.'

K. was asleep, impervious to all that was happening. His head, which had at first been lying on his left arm on top of the bedpost, had slid down as he slept and now hung unsupported, slowly drooping lower; the support of the arm above was no longer sufficient; involuntarily K. provided himself with new support by planting his right hand firmly against the quilt, whereby he accidentally took hold of Bür-gel's foot, which happened to be sticking up under the quilt. Bürgel looked down and abandoned the foot to him, tiresome though this might be.

Now there came some vigorous knocking on the partition wall. K. started up and looked at the wall. 'Isn't the Land Surveyor there?' a voice asked. 'Yes,' Bürgel said, freed his foot from K.'s hold and suddenly stretched wildly and wantonly like a little boy. 'Then tell him it's high time for him to come over here,' the voice continued; there was no consideration shown for Bürgel or for whether he might still require K.'s presence. 'It's Erlanger,' Bürgel said in a whisper, seeming not at all surprised that Erlanger was in the next room. 'Go to him at once, he's already annoyed, try to conciliate him. He's a sound sleeper; but still, we have been talking too loudly; one cannot control oneself and one's voice when one is speaking of certain things. Well, go along now, you don't seem able to shake yourself out of your sleep. Go along, what are you still doing here? No, you don't need to apologise for being sleepy, why should you? One's physical energies last only to a certain limit. Who can help the fact that precisely this limit is significant in other ways too? No, nobody can help it. That is how the world itself corrects the deviations in its course and maintains the balance. This is indeed an excellent, time and again unimaginably excellent arrangement, even if in other respects dismal and cheerless. Well, go along, I don't know why you look at me like that. If you delay much longer Erlanger will be down on me, and that is something I should very much like to avoid. Go along now. Who knows what awaits you over there? Everything here is full of opportunities, after all. Only there are, of course, opportunities that are, in a manner of speaking, too great to be made use of, there are things that are wrecked on nothing but themselves. Yes, that is astonishing. For the rest, I hope I shall now be able to get to sleep for a while after all. Of course, it is five o'clock by now and the noise will soon be beginning. If you would only go!'

Stunned by being suddenly waked up out of deep sleep, still boundlessly in need of sleep, his body aching all over from having been in such an uncomfortable position, K. could for a long time not bring himself to stand up, but held his forehead and looked down at his lap. Even Bürgel's continual dismissals would not have been able to make him go, it was only a sense of the utter uselessness of staying any longer in this room that slowly brought him to it. How indescribably dreary this room seemed to him. Whether it had become so or had been so all the time, he did not know. Here he would not even succeed in going to sleep again. This conviction was indeed the decisive factor; smiling a little at this, he rose, supporting himself wherever he found any support, on the bed, on the wall, on the door, and, as though he had long ago taken leave of Bürgel, left without saying goodbye.

XIX

PROBABLY he would have walked past Erlanger's room just as indifferently if Erlanger had not been standing in the open door, beckoning to him. One short sign with the forefinger. Erlanger was already completely dressed to go out, he wore a black fur coat with a tight collar buttoned up high. A servant was just handing him his gloves and was still holding a fur cap. 'You should have come long ago,' Erlanger said. K. tried to apologise. Wearily shutting his eyes, Erlanger indicated that he was not interested in hearing apologies. 'The matter is as follows,' he said. 'Formerly a certain Frieda was employed in the tap-room; I only know her name, I don't know the girl herself, she is no concern of mine. This Frieda sometimes served Klamm with beer. Now there seems to be another girl there. Well, this change is, of course, probably of no importance to anyone, and quite certainly of none to Klamm. But the bigger a job is, and Klamm's job is, of course, the biggest, the less strength is left over for protecting oneself against the external world, and as a result any unimportant alteration in the most unimportant things can be a serious disturbance. The smallest alteration on the writing-desk, the removal of a dirty spot that has been there ever since anyone can remember, all this can be disturbing, and so, in the same way, can a new bar-maid. Well, of course, all of this, even if it would disturb anyone else and in any given job, does not disturb Klamm; that is quite out of the question. Nevertheless we are obliged to keep such a watch over Klamm's comfort that we remove even disturbances that are not such for him – and probably there are none whatsoever for him – if they strike us as being possible disturbances. It is not for his sake, it is not for the sake of his work, that we remove these disturbances, but for our sake, for the sake of our conscience and our peace of mind. For this reason this Frieda must at once return to the tap-room. Perhaps she will be disturbing precisely through the fact of her return; well, then we shall send her away again, but, for the time being, she must return. You are living with her, as I am told, therefore arrange immediately for her return. In this no consideration can be given to personal feelings, that goes without saying, of course, hence I shall not enter into the least further discussion of the matter. I am already doing much more than is necessary if I mention that if you show yourself reliable in this trivial affair it may on some occasion be of use to you in improving your prospects. That is all I have to say to you.' He gave K. a nod of dismissal, put on the fur cap handed to him by the servant, and, followed by the servant, went down the passage, rapidly, but limping a little.

Sometimes orders that were given here were very easy to carry out, but this case did not please K. Not only because the order affected Frieda and, though intended as an order, sounded to K. like scornful laughter, but above all because what it confronted K. was with the futility of all his endeavours. The orders, the unfavourable and the favourable, disregarded him, and even the most favourable probably had an ultimate unfavourable core, but in any case they all disregarded him, and he was in much too lowly a position to be able to intervene or, far less, to silence them and to gain a hearing for his own voice. If Erlanger waves you off, what are you going to do? And if he were not to wave you off, what could you say to him? True, K. remained aware that his weariness had to-day done him more harm than all the unfavourableness of circumstances, but why could he, who had believed he could rely on his body and who would never have started out on his way without that conviction, why could he not endure a few bad nights and one sleepless night, why did he become so unmanageably tired precisely here where nobody was tired or, rather, where everyone was tired all the time, without this, however, doing any damage to the work, indeed, even seeming to promote it? The conclusion to be drawn from this was that this was in its way a quite different sort of fatigue from K.'s. Here it was doubtless fatigue amid happy work, something that outwardly looked like fatigue and was actually indestructible repose, indestructible peace. If one is a little tired at noon, that is part of the happy natural course of the day. 'For the gentlemen here it is always noon,' K. said to himself.

And it was very much in keeping with this that now, at five o'clock, things were beginning to stir everywhere on each side of the passage. This babel of voices in the rooms had something extremely merry about it. Once it sounded like the jubilation of children getting ready for a picnic, another time like daybreak in a hen-roost, like the joy of being in complete accord with the awakening day. Somewhere indeed a gentleman imitated the crowing of a cock. Though the passage itself was still empty, the doors were already in motion, time and again one would be opened a little and quickly shut again, the passage buzzed with this opening and shutting of doors, now and then, too, in the space above the partition walls, which did not quite reach to the ceiling, K. saw towsled early-morning heads appear and instantly vanish again. From far off there slowly came a little barrow pushed by a servant, containing files. A second servant walked beside it, with a catalogue in his hand, obviously comparing the numbers on the doors with those on the files. The little barrow stopped outside most of the doors, usually then, too, the door would open and the appropriate files, sometimes, however, only a small sheet of paper – in such cases a little conversation came about between the room and the passage, probably the servant was being reproached – would be handed into the room. If the door remained shut, the files were carefully piled up on the threshold. In such cases it seemed to K. as though the movement of the doors round about did not diminish, even though there the files had already been distributed, but as though it were on the contrary increasing. Perhaps the others were yearningly peering out at the files incomprehensibly left lying on the threshold, they could not understand how anyone should only need to open the door in order to gain possession of his files and yet should not do so; perhaps it was even possible that files that were never picked up at all might later be distributed among the other gentlemen, who were even now seeking to make sure, by frequent peering out, whether the files were still lying on the threshold and whether there was thus still hope for them. Incidentally, these files that remained lying were for the most part particularly big bundles; and K. assumed that they had been temporarily left lying out of a certain desire to boast or out of malice or even out of a justifiable pride that would be stimulating to colleagues. What strengthened him in this assumption was the fact that sometimes, always when he happened not to be looking, the bag, having been exposed to view for long enough, was suddenly and hastily pulled into the room and the door then remained as motionless as before, the doors round about then also became quiet again, disappointed or, it might be, content that this object of constant provocation had at last been removed, but then, however, they gradually came into motion again.

K. considered all this not only with curiosity but also with sympathy. He almost enjoyed the feeling of being in the midst of this bustle, looked this way and that, following – even though at an appropriate distance – the servants, who, admittedly, had already more than once turned towards him with a severe glance, with lowered head and pursed lips, while he watched their work of distribution. The further it progressed the less smoothly it went, either the catalogue was not quite correct, or the files were not always clearly identifiable for the servants, or the gentlemen were raising objections for other reasons; at any rate it would happen that some of the distributions had to be withdrawn, then the little barrow moved back, and through the chink of the door negotiations were conducted about the return of files. These negotiations in themselves caused great difficulties, but it happened frequently enough that if it was a matter of return precisely those doors that had earlier on been in the most lively motion now remained inexorably shut, as though they did not wish to know anything more about the matter at all. Only then did the actual difficulties begin. He who believed he had a claim to the files became extremely impatient, made a great din inside his room, clapping his hands, stamping his feet, ever and again shouting a particular file-number out into the passage through the chink of the door. Then the little barrow was often left quite unattended. The one servant was busy trying to appease the impatient official, the other was outside the shut door battling for the return. Both had a hard time of it. The impatient official was often made still more impatient by the attempts to appease him, he could no longer endure listening to the servant's empty words, he did not want consolation, he wanted files; such a gentleman once poured the contents of a whole wash-basin through the gap at the top, on to the servant. But the other servant, obviously the higher in rank, was having a much harder time of it. If the gentleman concerned at all deigned to enter into negotiations, there were matter-of-fact discussions during which the servant referred to his catalogue, the gentleman to his notes and to precisely those files that he was supposed to return, which for the time being, however, he clutched tightly in his hand, so that scarcely a corner of them remained visible to the servant's longing eyes. Then, too, the servant would have to run back for fresh evidence to the little barrow, which had by itself rolled a little further along the slightly sloping passage, or he would have to go to the gentleman claiming the files and there report the objections raised by the gentleman now in possession, receiving in return fresh counter-objections. Such negotiations lasted a very long time, sometimes agreement was reached, the gentleman would perhaps hand over part of the files or get other files as compensation, since all that had happened was that a mistake had been made; but it also happened sometimes that someone simply had to abandon all the files demanded, either because he had been driven into a corner by the servant's evidence or because he was tired of the prolonged bargaining, but then he did not give the files to the servant, but with sudden resolution flung them out into the passage, so that the strings came undone and the papers flew about and the servants had a great deal of trouble getting everything straight again. But all this was still relatively simple compared with what happened when the servant got no answer at all to his pleading for the return of the files. Then he would stand outside the closed door, begging, imploring, citing his catalogue, referring to regulations, all in vain, no sound came from inside the room, and to go in without permission was obviously something the servant had no right to do. Then even this excellent servant would sometimes lose his self-control, he would go to his barrow, sit down on the files, wipe the sweat from his brow and for a little while do nothing at all but sit there helplessly swinging his feet. All round there was very great interest in the affair, everywhere there was whispering going on, scarcely any door was quiet, and up above at the top of the partition wall faces queerly masked almost to the eyes with scarves and kerchiefs, though for the rest never for an instant remaining quiet in one place, watched all that was going on. In the midst of this unrest K. had been struck by the fact that Bürgel's door had remained shut the whole time and that the servant had already passed along this part of the passage, but no files had been allotted to Bürgel. Perhaps he was still asleep, which would indeed, in all this din, have indicated that he was a very sound sleeper, but why had he not received any files? Only very few rooms, and these probably unoccupied ones, had been passed over in this manner. On the other hand there was already a new and particularly restless occupant of Erlanger's room, Erlanger must positively have been driven out in the night by him, this was not much in keeping with Erlanger's cool, distant nature, but the fact that he had had to wait on the threshold for K. did after all indicate that it was so.

Ever and again K. would then soon return from all distracting observations to watching the servant; truly, what K. had otherwise been told about servants in general, about their slackness, their easy life, their arrogance, did not apply to this servant, there were doubtless exceptions among the servants too or, what was more probable, various groups among them, for here, as K. noticed, there were many nuances of which he had up to now scarcely had as much as a glimpse. What he particularly liked was this servant's inexorability. In his struggle with these stubborn little rooms – to K. it often seemed to be a struggle with the rooms, since he scarcely ever caught sight of the occupants – the servant never gave up. His strength did sometimes fail – whose strength would not have failed? – but he soon recovered, slipped down from the little barrow and, holding himself straight, clenching his teeth, returned to the attack against the door that had to be conquered. And it would happen that he would be beaten back twice or three times, and that in a very simple way, solely by means of that confounded silence, and nevertheless was still not defeated. Seeing that he could not achieve anything by frontal assault, he would try another method, for instance, if K. understood rightly, cunning. He would then seemingly abandon the door, so to speak allowing it to exhaust its own taciturnity, turned his attention to other doors, after a while returned, called the other servant, all this ostentatiously and noisily, and began piling up files on the threshold of the shut door, as though he had changed his mind, and as though there were no justification for taking anything away from this gentleman, but, on the contrary, something to be allotted to him. Then he would walk on, still, however, keeping an eye on the door, and then when the gentleman, as usually happened, soon cautiously opened the door in order to pull the files inside, in a few leaps the servant was there, thrust his foot between the door and the doorpost, so forcing the gentleman at least to negotiate with him face to face, which then usually led after all to a more or less satisfactory result. And if this method was not successful or if at one door this seemed to him not the right approach, he would try another method. He would then transfer his attention to the gentleman who was claiming the files. Then he pushed aside the other servant, who worked always only in a mechanical way, a fairly useless assistant to him, and himself began talking persuasively to the gentleman, whisperingly, furtively, pushing his head right round the door, probably making promises to him and assuring him that at the next distribution the other gentleman would be appropriately punished, at any rate he would often point towards the opponent's door and laugh, in as far as his fatigue allowed. Then, however, there were cases, one or two, when he did abandon all attempts, but even here K. believed that it was only an apparent abandonment or at least an abandonment for justifiable reasons, for he quietly walked on, tolerating, without glancing round, the din made by the wronged gentleman, only an occasional, more prolonged closing of the eyes indicating that the din was painful to him. Yet then the gentleman would gradually quiet down, and just as a child's ceaseless crying gradually passes into ever less frequent single sobs, so it was also with his outcry; but even after it had become quite quiet there, there would, nevertheless, sometimes be a single cry or a rapid opening and slamming of that door. In any case it became apparent that here, too, the servant had probably acted in exactly the right way. Finally there remained only one gentleman who would not quiet down, he would be silent for a long period, but only in order to gather strength, then he would burst out again, no less furiously than before. It was not quite clear why he shouted and complained in this way, perhaps it was not about the distribution of files at all. Meanwhile the servant had finished his work; only one single file, actually only a little piece of paper, a leaf from a note-pad, was left in the little barrow, through his helper's fault, and now they did not know whom to allot it to. 'That might very well be my file,' it flashed through K.'s mind. The Mayor had, after all, constantly spoken of this smallest of small cases. And, arbitrary and ridiculous though he himself at bottom regarded his assumption as being, K. tried to get closer to the servant, who was thoughtfully glancing over the little piece of paper; this was not altogether easy, for the servant ill repaid K.'s sympathy, even in the midst of his most strenuous work he had always still found time to look round at

K., angrily or impatiently, with nervous jerks of his head. Only now, after finishing the distribution, did he seem to have somewhat forgotten K., as indeed he had altogether become more indifferent, this being understandable as a result of his great exhaustion, nor did he give himself much trouble with the little piece of paper, perhaps not even reading it through, only pretending to do so, and although here in the passage he would probably have delighted any occupant of a room by allotting this piece of paper to him, he decided otherwise, he was now sick and tired of distributing things, with his forefinger on his lips he gave his companion a sign to be silent, tore – K. was still far from having reached his side – the piece of paper into shreds and put the pieces into his pocket. It was probably the first irregularity that K. had seen in the working of the administration here, admittedly it was possible that he had misunderstood this too. And even if it was an irregularity, it was pardonable; under the conditions prevailing here the servant could not work unerringly, some time the accumulated annoyance, the accumulated uneasiness, must break out, and if it manifested itself only in the tearing up of a little piece of paper it was still comparatively innocent. For the yells of the gentleman who could not be quieted by any method were still resounding through the passage, and his colleagues, who in other respects did not adopt a very friendly attitude to each other, seemed to be wholly of one mind with respect to this uproar; it gradually began to seem as if the gentleman had taken on the task of making a noise for all those who simply by calling out to him and nodding their heads encouraged him to keep it up. But now the servant was no longer paying any further attention to the matter, he had finished his job, he pointed to the handle of the little barrow, indicating that the other servant should take hold of it, and so they went away again as they had come, only more contentedly and so quickly that the little barrow bounced along ahead of them. Only once did they start and glance back again, when the gentleman who was ceaselessly

screaming and shouting, and outside whose door K. was
now hanging about because he would have liked to discover
what it really was that the gentleman wanted, evidently
found shouting no longer adequate, probably had discovered
the button of an electric bell and, doubtless enraptured at
being relieved in this way, instead of shouting now began an
uninterrupted ringing of the bell. Hereupon a great muttering began in the other rooms, which seemed to indicate
approval, the gentleman seemed to be doing something that
all would have liked to do long ago and only for some
unknown reason had had to leave undone. Was it perhaps
attendance, perhaps Frieda, for whom the gentleman was
ringing? If that was so, he could go on ringing for a long
time. For Frieda was busy wrapping Jeremiah up in wet
sheets, and even supposing he were well again by now, she
had no time, for then she was in his arms. But the ringing
of the bell did instantly have an effect. Even now the landlord of the Herrenhof himself came hastening along from
far off, dressed in black and buttoned up as always; but it
was as though he were forgetful of his dignity, he was in
such a hurry; his arms were half outspread, just as if he had
been called on account of some great disaster and were
coming in order to take hold of it and instantly smother it
against his chest, and at every little irregularity in the ringing he seemed briefly to leap into the air and hurry on faster
still. Now his wife also appeared, a considerable distance
behind him, she too running with outspread arms, but her
steps were short and affected, and K. thought to himself
that she would come too late, the landlord would in the
meantime have done all that was necessary. And in order to
make room for the landlord as he ran K. stood close back
against the wall. But the landlord stopped straight in front
of K., as though K. were his goal, and the next instant the
landlady was there too, and both overwhelmed him with
reproaches, which in the suddenness and surprise of it he
did not understand, especially since the ringing of the
gentleman's bell was also mixed up with it and other bells

also began ringing, now no longer indicating a state of emergency, but only for fun and in excess of delight. Because he was very much concerned to understand exactly what his fault was, K. was entirely in agreement with the landlord's taking him by the arm and walking away with him out of this uproar, which was continually increasing, for behind them – K. did not turn round at all, because the landlord, and even more, on the other side, the landlady, was talking to him urgently – the doors were now opening wide, the passage was becoming animated, traffic seemed to be beginning there as in a lively narrow little alley, the doors ahead of them were evidently waiting impatiently for K. to go past them at long last so that they could release the gentlemen, and in the midst of all this, pressed again and again, the bells kept on ringing as though celebrating a victory. Now at last – they were by now again in the quiet white courtyard, where some sledges were waiting – K. gradually learnt what it was all about. Neither the landlord nor the landlady could understand how K. could have dared to do such a thing. But what had he done? K. asked time and again, but for a long time could not get any answer because his guilt was all too much a matter of course to the two of them and hence it simply did not occur to them that he asked in good faith. Only very slowly did K. realise how everything stood. He had had no right to be in the passage; in general it was at best the tap-room, and this only by way of privilege and subject to revocation, to which he had entry. If he was summoned by one of the gentlemen, he had, of course, to appear in the place to which he was summoned, but had to remain always aware – surely he at least had some ordinary common sense? – that he was in a place where he actually did not belong, a place whither he had only been summoned by one of the gentlemen, and that with extreme reluctance and only because it was necessitated by official business. It was up to him, therefore, to appear quickly, to submit to the interrogation, then, however, to disappear again, if possible even more quickly. Had

he then not had any feeling at all of the grave impropriety
of being there in the passage? But if he had had it, how had
he brought himself to roam about there like cattle at pas-
ture? Had he not been summoned to attend a night interrogation and did he not know why the night interrogations
had been introduced? The night interrogations – and here K.
was given a new explanation of their meaning – had after all
only the purpose of examining applicants the sight of whom
by day would be unendurable to the gentlemen, and this
quickly, at night, by artificial light, with the possibility of,
immediately after the interrogation, forgetting all the ugli-
ness of it in sleep. K.'s behaviour, however, had been a
mockery of precautionary measures. Even ghosts vanish towards morning, but K. had remained there, his hands in his
pockets, as though he were expecting that, since he did not
take himself off, the whole passage with all the rooms and
gentlemen would take itself off. And this – he could be sure
of it – would quite certainly have happened if it had been in
any way possible, for the delicacy of the gentlemen was
limitless. None of them would drive K. away, or even say,
what went after all without saying, that he should at long
last go away; none of them would do that, although during
the period of K.'s presence they were probably trembling
with agitation and the morning, their favourite time, was
being ruined for them. Instead of taking any steps against
K., they preferred to suffer, in which, indeed, a certain part
was probably played by the hope that K. would not be able
to help gradually, at long last, coming to realise what was so
glaringly obvious and, in accord with the gentlemen's
anguish, would himself begin to suffer, to the point of
unendurability, from his own standing there in the passage
in the morning, visible to all, in that horribly unfitting manner. A vain hope. They did not know or in their kindness
and condescension did not want to admit there also existed
hearts that were insensitive, hard, and not to be softened by
any feeling of reverence. Does not even the nocturnal moth,
the poor creature, when day comes seek out a quiet cranny,

flatten itself out there, only wishing it could vanish and being unhappy because it cannot? K. on the other hand planted himself precisely where he was most visible, and if by doing so he had been able to prevent day from breaking, he would have done so. He could not prevent it, but, alas, he could delay it and make it more difficult. Had he not watched the distribution of the files? Something that nobody was allowed to watch except the people most closely involved. Something that neither the landlord nor his wife had been allowed to see in their own house. Something of which they had only heard tell and in allusions, as for instance to-day from the servants. Had he then not noticed under what difficulties the distribution of files had proceeded, something in itself incomprehensible, since after all each of the gentlemen served only the cause, never thinking of his personal advantage and hence being obliged to exert all his powers to seeing that the distribution of the files, this important, fundamental, preliminary work, should proceed quickly and easily and without any mistakes? And had K. then not been even remotely struck by the notion that the main cause of all the difficulties was the fact that the distribution had had to be carried out with the doors almost quite shut, without any chance of direct dealings between the gentlemen, who among each other naturally could come to an understanding in a twinkling, while the mediation through the servants inevitably dragged on almost for hours, never could function smoothly, was a lasting torment to the gentlemen and the servants and would probably have damaging consequences in the later work? And why could the gentlemen not deal with each other? Well, did K. *still* not understand? The like of it had never occurred in the experience of the landlady – and the landlord for his part confirmed this – and they had, after all, had to deal with many sorts of difficult people. Things that in general one would not dare to mention in so many words one had to tell him frankly, for otherwise he would not understand the most essential things. Well, then, since it had to be said: it was on his account, solely and exclusively on his account, that the gentlemen had not been able to come forth out of their rooms, since in the morning, so soon after having been asleep, they were too bashful, too vulnerable, to be able to expose themselves to the gaze of strangers; they literally felt, however completely dressed they might be, too naked to show themselves. It was admittedly difficult to say why they felt this shame, perhaps these everlasting workers felt shame merely because they had been asleep. But what perhaps made them feel even acuter shame than showing themselves was seeing strangers; what they had successfully disposed of by means of the night interrogations, namely the sight of the applicants they found so hard to endure, they did not want now in the morning to have suddenly, without warning, in all its truth to nature, obtruding itself upon them all over again. That was something they simply could not face. What sort of person must it be who failed to respect that! Well, yes, it must be a person like K. Someone who rode roughshod over everything, both over the law and over the most ordinary human consideration, with this callous indifference and sleepiness, someone who simply did not care that he was making the distribution of the files almost impossible and damaging the reputation of the house and who brought about something that had never happened before, that the gentlemen, driven to desperation, had begun to defend themselves, and, after an overcoming of their own feelings unimaginable for ordinary people, had reached for the bell and called for help to expel this person on whom nothing else could make any impression! They, the gentlemen, calling for help! Would not the landlord and his wife and their entire staff have come dashing along ages before that if they had only dared to appear before the gentlemen, all unsummoned, in the morning, even if it was only in order to bring help and then disappear again at once? Quivering with indignation about K., inconsolable about their own helplessness, they had waited there at the end of the passage, and the ringing of the bell, which they had never really expected to hear at all, had been a god-send to them. Well, now the worst was over! If you could cast a glance into the merry bustle among the gentlemen now at long last liberated from K.! For K., of course, it was not yet over and done with; he would certainly have to answer for the trouble he had caused here.

Meanwhile they had entered the tap-room; why the landlord, despite all his anger, had nevertheless brought K. along here, was not quite clear, perhaps he had after all realised that K.'s state of fatigue for the present made it impossible for him to leave the house. Without waiting to be asked to sit down, K. the next moment simply collapsed on one of the barrels. There in the dark he felt all right. In the large room there was only one dim electric bulb burning over the beer-taps. Outside, too, there was still deep dark-ness, there seemed to be snow blowing on the wind. Being here in the warmth was something to be thankful for and one had to take precautions against being driven out. The landlord and his wife were still standing before him as though even now he still constituted a certain menace, as though in view of his utter unreliability it were not quite impossible that he might here suddenly start up and try to invade the passage once again. Besides, they themselves were tired after the shock they had had in the night and getting up earlier than usual, especially the landlady, who was wearing a silkily rustling, wide-skirted, brown dress, buttoned and tied up in a somewhat slovenly way – where had she pulled it out from in her haste? – and stood with her head resting, like a drooping flower, on her husband's shoulder, dabbing at her eyes with a fine cambric handker-chief, now and then casting childishly malevolent glances at K. In order to reassure the couple, K. said that everything they had told him now was entirely new to him, but that in spite of his ignorance of these facts he would not have remained so long in the passage, where he really had had no business to be and where he had certainly not wanted to upset anyone, but that all this had only happened because he had been excessively tired. He thanked them for having put an end to the distressing scene, if he should be taken to task about the matter it would be very welcome to him, for only in this way could he prevent a general misinterpretation of his behaviour. Fatigue, and nothing else, was to blame for it. This fatigue, however, originated in the fact that he was not yet used to the strenuous nature of the interrogations. After all, he had not yet been here long. As soon as he was more experienced in these matters, it would become impossible for anything of this sort to happen again. Perhaps he was taking the interrogations too seriously, but that in itself was, after all, probably no disadvantage. He had had to go through two interrogations, one following quickly on the other, one with Bürgel and the second with Erlanger, and the first in particular had greatly exhausted him, though the second one had not lasted long, Erlanger having only asked him for a favour, but both together had been more than he could stand at one go, and perhaps a thing like that would be too much for other people too, for instance for the landlord. By the time he was done with the second interrogation he had really been walking in a sort of swoon. It had been almost like being drunk; after all, he had seen and heard the two gentlemen for the first time and had also had to answer their questions, into the bargain. Everything, so far as he knew, had worked out pretty well, but then that misfortune had occurred, which, after what had gone before, he could scarcely be blamed for. Unfortunately only Erlanger and Bürgel had realised what a condition he was in and they would certainly have looked after him and so prevented all the rest, but Erlanger had had to go away immediately after the interrogation, evidently in order to drive up to the Castle, and Bürgel, probably himself tired after that interrogation – and how then should K. have been able to come out of it with his strength unimpaired? – had gone to sleep and had indeed slept through the whole distribution of files. If K. had had a similar chance he would have been delighted to take it and would gladly have done without all the prohibited insight into what was going on there, and this all the more lightheartedly since in reality he had been quite incapable of seeing anything, for which reason even the most sensitive gentlemen could have shown themselves before him without embarrassment.

The mention of the two interrogations – particularly of that with Erlanger – and the respect with which K. spoke of the gentlemen inclined the landlord favourably towards him. He seemed to be prepared to grant K.'s request to be allowed to lay a board across the barrels and sleep there at least till dawn, but the landlady was markedly against it, twitching ineffectively here and there at her dress, the slovenly state of which she seemed only now to have noticed, she kept on shaking her head; a quarrel obviously of long standing with regard to the orderliness of the house was on the point of breaking out afresh. For K. in his fatigued state the talk between the couple took on exaggeratedly great significance. To be driven out from here again seemed to him to be a misfortune surpassing all that had happened to him hitherto. This must not be allowed to happen, even if the landlord and the landlady should unite against him. Crumpled up on the barrel, he looked in eager expectance at the two of them until the landlady, with her abnormal touchiness, which had long ago struck K., suddenly stepped aside and – probably she had by now been discussing other things with the landlord – exclaimed: 'How he stares at me! Do send him away now!' But K., seizing the opportunity and now utterly, almost to the point of indifference, convinced that he would stay, said: 'I'm not looking at you, only at your dress.' 'Why my dress?' the landlady asked agitatedly. K. shrugged his shoulders. 'Come on!' the land-lady said to the landlord. 'Don't you see he's drunk, the lout? Leave him here to sleep it off!' and she even ordered Pepi, who on being called by her emerged out of the dark, towsled, tired, idly holding a broom in her hand, to throw K. some sort of a cushion.

XX

WHEN K. woke up he at first thought he had hardly slept
at all; the room was as empty and warm as before, all the
walls in darkness, the one bulb over the beer-taps extinguished, and outside the windows was the night. But when
he stretched, and the cushion fell down and the bed and the
barrels creaked, Pepi instantly appeared, and now he learnt
that it was already evening and that he had slept for well
over twelve hours. The landlady had asked after him several
times during the day, and so had Gerstäcker, who had been
waiting here in the dark, by the beer, while K. had been
talking to the landlady in the morning, but then he had not
dared to disturb K., had been here once in the meantime to
see how K. was getting on, and finally, so at least it was
alleged, Frieda had also come and had stood for a moment
beside K., yet she had scarcely come on K.'s account, but
because she had had various things to make ready here, for
in the evening she was to resume her old duties after all. 'I
suppose she doesn't like you any more?' Pepi asked, bringing coffee and cakes. But she no longer asked it maliciously,
in her old way, but sadly, as though in the meantime she
had come to know the malice of the world, compared with
which all one's own malice fails and becomes senseless; she
spoke to K. as to a fellow sufferer, and when he tasted the
coffee and she thought she saw that it was not sweet enough
for him, she ran and brought him the full sugar-bowl. Her
sadness had, indeed, not prevented her from tricking herself
out to-day if anything even more than the last time; she
wore an abundance of bows and ribbons plaited into her
hair, along her forehead and on her temples the hair had
been carefully curled with the tongs, and round her neck
she had a little chain that hung down into the low-cut opening of her blouse. When, in his contentment at having at

last slept his fill and now being permitted to drink a good cup of coffee, K. furtively stretched his hand out towards one of the bows and tried to untie it, Pepi said wearily: 'Do leave me alone,' and sat down beside him on a barrel. And K. did not even need to ask her what was the matter, she at once began telling the story herself, rigidly staring into K.'s coffee-mug, as though she needed some distraction, even while she was talking, as though she could not quite abandon herself to her suffering even when she was discussing it, as that would be beyond her powers. First of all K. learnt that actually he was to blame for Pepi's misfortunes, but that she did not bear him any grudge. And she nodded eagerly as she talked, in order to prevent K. from raising any objection. First he had taken Frieda away from the tap-room and thus made Pepi's rise possible. There was nothing else that could be imagined that could have brought Frieda to give up her situation, she sat tight there in the tap-room like a spider in its web, with all the threads under her control, threads of which no one knew but she; it would have been quite impossible to winkle her out against her will, only love for some lowly person, that is to say, something that was not in keeping with her position, could drive her from her place. And Pepi? Had *she* ever thought of getting the situation for herself? She was a chamber-maid, she had an insignificant situation with few prospects, she had dreams of a great future like any other girl, one can't stop oneself from having dreams, but she had never seriously thought of getting on in the world, she had resigned herself to staying in the job she had. And now Frieda suddenly vanished from the tap-room, it had happened so suddenly that the landlord had not had a suitable substitute on hand at the moment, he had looked round and his glance had fallen on Pepi, who had, admittedly, pushed herself forward in such a way as to be noticed. At that time she had loved K. as she had never loved anyone before; month after month she had been down there in her tiny dark room, prepared to spend years there, or, if the worst came to the worst, to spend her whole life here, ignored by everyone, and now suddenly K. had appeared, a hero, a rescuer of maidens in distress, and had opened up the way upstairs for her. Admittedly he did not know anything about her, he had not done it for her sake, but that did not diminish her gratitude, in the night preceding her appointment – the appointment was not yet definite, but still, it was now very probable – she spent hours talking to him, whispering her thanks in his ear. And in her eyes it exalted what he had done still more that it should have been Frieda, of all people, with whom he had burdened himself; there was something incomprehensibly selfless in his making Frieda his mistress in order to pave the way for Pepi – Frieda, a plain, oldish, skinny girl with short, thin hair, a deceitful girl, into the bargain, always having some sort of secrets, which was probably connected, after all, with her appearance; if her wretchedness was glaringly obvious in her face and figure, she must at least have other secrets that nobody could enquire into, for instance her alleged affair with Klamm. And even thoughts like the following had occurred to Pepi at that time: is it possible that K. really loves Frieda, isn't he deceiving himself or is he perhaps deceiving only Frieda, and will perhaps the sole outcome of the whole thing after all be nothing but Pepi's rise in the world, and will K. then notice the mistake, or not want to cover it up any more, and no longer see Frieda, but only Pepi, which need not even be a crazy piece of conceit on Pepi's part, for so far as Frieda was concerned she was a match for her, one girl against another, which nobody would deny, and it had, after all, been primarily Frieda's position and the glory that Frieda had been able to invest it with that had dazzled K. at the moment. And so then Pepi had dreamed that when she had the position K. would come to her, pleading, and she would then have the choice of either granting K.'s plea and losing her situation or of rejecting him and rising further. And she had worked out for herself that she would renounce everything and lower herself to him and teach him what true love was, which he would never be able to learn from Frieda and which was independent of all positions of honour in the world. But then everything turned out differently. And what was to blame for this? Above all, K., and then, of course, Frieda's artfulness. Above all, K. For what was he after, what sort of strange person was he? What was he trying to get, what were these important things that kept him busy and made him forget what was nearest of all, best of all, most beautiful of all? Pepi was the sacrifice and everything was stupid and everything was lost; and anyone who had the strength to set fire to the whole Herrenhof and burn it down, burn it to the ground, so that not a trace of it was left, burn it up like a piece of paper in the stove, *he* would to-day be Pepi's chosen love. Well, so Pepi came into the tap-room, four days ago to-day, shortly before lunch-time. The work here was far from easy, it was almost killingly hard work, but there was a good deal to be got out of it too. Even previously Pepi had not lived only for the day, and even if she would never have aspired to this situation even in her wildest dreams, still, she had made plenty of observations, she knew what this situation involved, she had not taken on the situation without being prepared. One could not take it on without being prepared, otherwise one lost it in the first few hours. Particularly if one were to behave here the way the chamber-maids did! As a chamber-maid one did in time come to feel one was quite lost and forgotten; it was like working down a mine, at least that was the way it was in the secretaries' passage, for days on end there; except for a few daytime applicants who flitted in and out without daring to look up one didn't see a soul but two or three other chamber-maids, and they were just as embittered. In the morning one wasn't allowed to leave the room at all, that was when the secretaries wished to be alone among themselves, their meals were brought to them from the kitchen by the men-servants, the chamber-maids usually had nothing to do with that, and during meal-times, too, one was not allowed to show oneself in the passage. It was only while the gentlemen were working that the chamber-maids were allowed to do the rooms, but naturally not those that were occupied, only those that happened to be empty at the time, and the work had to be done quite quietly so that the gentlemen were not disturbed at their work. But how was it possible to do the cleaning quietly when the gentlemen occupied their rooms for several days on end, and the men-servants, dirty lot that they were, pottered about there into the bargain, and when the chamber-maid was finally allowed to go into the room, it was in such a state that not even the Flood could wash it clean? Truly, they were exalted gentlemen, but one had to make a great effort to overcome one's disgust so as to be able to clean up after them. It wasn't that the chamber-maids had such a great amount of work, but it was pretty tough. And never a kind word, never anything but reproaches, in particularly the following, which was the most tormenting and the most frequent: that files had got lost during the doing of the rooms. In reality nothing ever got lost, every scrap of paper was handed over to the landlord, but in fact of course files did get lost, only it happened not to be the fault of the maids. And then commissions came, and the maids had to leave their room, and the members of commission rummaged through the beds, the girls had no possessions, of course, their few things could be put in a basket, but still, the commission searched for hours all the same. Naturally they found nothing. How should files come to be there? What did the maids care about files? But the outcome was always the same, abuse and threats uttered by the disappointed commission and passed on by the landlord. And never any peace, neither by day nor by night, noise going on half through the night and noise again at the crack of dawn. If at least one didn't have to live in, but one had to, for it was the chamber-maids' job to bring snacks from the kitchen as they might be ordered, in between times, particularly at night. Always suddenly the fist thumping on the chamber-maids' door, the order being dictated, the running down to the kitchen, shaking the sleeping scullery-lads, the setting down of the tray with the things ordered outside the chamber-maids' door, from where the men-servants fetched it – how sad all that was. But that was not the worst. The worst was when no order came, that was to say, when, at dead of night, when everyone ought to be asleep and most of them really were asleep at last, sometimes a tiptoeing around began outside the chamber-maids' door. Then the girls got out of bed – the bunks were on top of each other, for there was very little space there, the whole room the maids had being actually nothing more than a large cupboard with three shelves in it – listened at the door, knelt down, put their arms round each other in fear. And whoever was tiptoeing outside the door could be heard all the time. They would all be thankful if only he would come right in and be done with it, but nothing happened, nobody came in. And at the same time one had to admit to oneself that it need not necessarily be some danger threatening, perhaps it was only someone walking up and down outside the door, trying to make up his mind to order something, and then not being able to bring himself to it after all. Perhaps that was all it was, but perhaps it was something quite different. For really one didn't know the gentlemen at all, one had hardly set eyes on them. Anyway, inside the room the maids were fainting in terror, and when at last it was quiet again outside they leant against the wall and had not enough strength left to get back into bed. This was the life that was waiting for Pepi to return to it, this very evening she was to move back to her place in the maids' room. And why? Because of K. and Frieda. Back again into that life she had scarcely escaped from, which she escaped from, it is true, with K.'s help, but also, of course, through very great exertions of her own. For in that service there the girls neglected themselves, even those who were otherwise the most careful and tidy. For whom should they smarten themselves? Nobody saw them, at best the staff in the kitchen; anyone for whom that was enough was welcome to smarten herself. But for the rest they were always in their little room or in the gentlemen's rooms, which it was madness and a waste so much as to set foot in with clean clothes on. And always by artificial light and in that stuffy air – with the heating always on – and actually always tired. The one free afternoon in the week was best spent sleeping quietly and without fear in one of the cubby-holes in the kitchen. So what should one smarten oneself up for? Yes, one scarcely bothered to dress at all. And now Pepi had suddenly been transferred to the tap-room, where, if one wanted to maintain one's position there, exactly the opposite was necessary, where one was always in full view of people, and among them very observant gentlemen, used to the best of everything, and where one therefore always had to look as smart and pleasant as possible. Well, that was a change. And Pepi could say of herself that she had not failed to rise to the occasion. Pepi was not worrying about how things would turn out later. She knew she had the abilities necessary in this situation, she was quite certain of it, she had this conviction even now and nobody could take it away from her, not even to-day, on the day of her defeat. The only difficulty was how she was to stand the test in the very beginning, because she was, after all, only a poor chamber-maid, with nothing to wear and no jewellery, and because the gentlemen had not the patience to wait and see how one would develop, but instantly, without transition, wanted a bar-maid of the proper kind, or else they turned away. One would think they didn't expect so very much since, after all, Frieda could satisfy them. But that was not right. Pepi had often thought about this, she had, after all, often been together with Frieda and had for a time even slept together with her. It wasn't easy to find Frieda out, and anyone who was not very much on the look-out – and which of the gentlemen was very much on the look-out, after all? – was at once misled by her. No one knew better than Frieda herself how miserable her looks were, for instance when one saw her for the first time with her hair down, one clasped one's hands in pity, by rights a girl like that shouldn't even be a chamber-maid; and she knew it, too, and many a night she had spent crying about it, pressing tight against Pepi and laying Pepi's hair round her own head. But when she was on duty all her doubts vanished, she thought herself better-looking than anyone, and she had the knack of getting everyone to think the same. She knew what people were like, and really that was where her art lay. And she was quick with a lie, and cheated, so that people didn't have time to get a closer look at her. Naturally that wouldn't do in the long run, people had eyes in their heads and sooner or later their eyes would tell them what to think. But the moment she noticed the danger of that she was ready with another method, recently, for instance, her affair with Klamm. Her affair with Klamm! If you don't believe it, you can go and get proof; go to Klamm and ask him. How cunning, how cunning. And if you don't happen to dare to go to Klamm with an enquiry like that, and perhaps wouldn't be admitted to him with infinitely more important enquiries, and Klamm is, in fact, completely inaccessible to you – only to you and your sort, for Frieda, for instance, pops in to see him whenever she likes – if that's how it is, you can still get proof of the thing, you only need to wait. After all, Klamm won't be able to tolerate such a false rumour for long, he's certain to be very keen to know what stories go round about him in the tap-room and in the public rooms, all this is of the greatest importance to him, and if it's wrong he will refute it at once. But he doesn't refute it; well, then there is nothing to be refuted and it is sheer truth. What one sees, indeed, is only that Frieda takes the beer into Klamm's room and comes out again with the money; but what one doesn't see Frieda tells one about, and one has to believe her. And she doesn't even tell it, after all, she's not going to let such secrets out; no, the secrets let themselves out wherever she goes and, since they have been let out once and for all, she herself, it is true, no longer shrinks from talking about them herself, but modestly,

without asserting anything, only referring to what is generally known anyway. Not to everything. One thing, for
instance, she does not speak of, namely that since she has
been in the tap-room Klamm drinks less beer than formerly,
not much less, but still perceptibly less beer, and there may
indeed be various reasons for this, it may be that a period
has come when Klamm has less taste for beer or that it is
Frieda who causes him to forget about beer-drinking. Anyway, however amazing it may be, Frieda is Klamm's mistress. But how should the others not also admire what is
good enough for Klamm? And so, before anyone knows
what is happening, Frieda has turned into a great beauty, a
girl of exactly the kind that the tap-room needs; indeed,
almost too beautiful, too powerful, even now the tap-room
is hardly good enough for her any more. And, in fact, it
does strike people as odd that she is still in the tap-room;
being a bar-maid is a great deal, and from that point of view
the liaison with Klamm seems very credible, but if the tap-
room girl has once become Klamm's mistress, why does he
leave her in the tap-room, and so long? Why does he not
take her up higher? One can tell people a thousand times
that there is no contradiction here, that Klamm has definite
reasons for acting as he does, or that some day, perhaps
even at any moment now, Frieda's elevation will suddenly
come about; all this does not make much impression; people
have definite notions and in the long run will not let themselves be distracted from them by any talk, however
ingenious. Nobody any longer doubted that Frieda was
Klamm's mistress, even those who obviously knew better
were by now too tired to doubt it. 'Be Klamm's mistress,
and to hell with it,' they thought, 'but if you *are*, we want
to see signs of it in your getting on, too.' But one saw no
signs of it, and Frieda stayed in the tap-room as before and
secretly was thoroughly glad that things remained the way
they were. But she lost prestige with people, that, of course,
she could not fail to notice, indeed she usually noticed
things even before they existed. A really beautiful, lovable

girl, once she has settled down in the tap-room, does not need to display any arts; as long as she is beautiful, she will remain tap-room maid, unless some particularly unfortunate accident occurs. But a girl like Frieda must be continually worried about her situation, naturally she has enough sense not to show it, on the contrary, she is in the habit of complaining and cursing the situation. But in secret she keeps a weather-eye open all the time. And so she saw how people were becoming indifferent, Frieda's appearance on the scene was no longer anything that made it worth anyone's while even to glance up, not even the men-servants bothered about her any more, they had enough sense to stick to Olga and girls of that sort, from the landlord's behaviour, too, she noticed that she was becoming less and less indispensable, one could not go on for ever inventing new stories about Klamm, everything has its limits, and so dear Frieda decided to try something new. If anyone had only been capable of seeing through it immediately! Pepi had sensed it, but unfortunately she had not seen through it. Frieda decided to cause a scandal, she, Klamm's mistress, throws herself away on the first comer, if possible on the lowest of the low. That will make a stir, that will keep people talking for a long time, and at last, at last, people will remember what it means to be Klamm's mistress and what it means to throw away this honour in the rapture of a new love. The only difficulty was to find the suitable man with whom the clever game could be played. It must not be an acquaintance of Frieda's, not even one of the men-servants, for he would probably have looked at her askance and have walked on, above all he would not have remained serious enough about it and for all her ready tongue it would have been impossible to spread the story that she, Frieda, had been attacked by him, had not been able to defend herself against him and in an hour when she did not know what she was doing had submitted to him. And although it had to be one of the lowest of the low, it nevertheless had to be one of whom it could be made credible that in spite of his crude, coarse nature he longed for nobody but Frieda herself and had no loftier desire than – heavens above! – to marry Frieda. But although it had to be a common man, if possible even lower than a servant, much lower than a servant, yet it must be one on whose account one would not be laughed to scorn by every girl, one in whom another girl, a girl of sound judgment, might also at some time find something attractive. But where does one find such a man? Another girl would probably have spent her whole life looking for him. Frieda's luck brought the Land Surveyor into the tap-room to her, perhaps on the very evening when the plan had come into her mind for the first time. The Land Surveyor! Yes, what was K. thinking of? What special things had he in mind? Was he going to achieve something special? A good appointment, a distinction? Was he after something of that sort? Well, then he ought to have set about things differently from the very beginning. After all, he was a nonentity, it was heart-rending to see his situation. He was a Land Surveyor, that was perhaps something, so he had learnt something, but if one didn't know what to do with it, then again it was nothing after all. And at the same time he made demands, without having the slightest backing, made demands not outright, but one noticed that he was making some sort of demands, and that was, after all, infuriating. Did he know that even a chamber-maid was lowering herself if she talked to him for any length of time? And with all these special demands he tumbled headlong into the most obvious trap on the very first evening. Wasn't he ashamed of himself? What was it about Frieda that he found so alluring? Could she really appeal to him, that skinny, sallow thing? Ah no, he didn't even look at her, she only had to tell him she was Klamm's mistress, for him that was still a novelty, and so he was lost! But now she had to move out, now, of course, there was no longer any room for her in the Herrenhof. Pepi saw her the very same morning before she moved out, the staff all came running up, after all, everyone was curious to see the sight. And so great was her power even then that she was pitied, she was pitied by everyone, even by her enemies; so correct did her calculations prove to be from the very start; having thrown herself away on such a man seemed incomprehensible to everyone and a blow of fate, the little kitchen-maids, who, of course, admire every bar-maid, were inconsolable. Even Pepi was touched, not even she could remain quite unmoved, even though her attention was actually focussed on something else. She was struck by how little sad Frieda actually was. After all it was at bottom a dreadful misfortune that had come upon her, and indeed she was behaving as though she were very unhappy, but it was not enough, this acting could not deceive Pepi. So what was it that was keeping her going? Perhaps the happiness of her new love? Well, this possibility could not be considered. But what else could it be? What gave her the strength to be as coolly pleasant as ever even to Pepi, who was already regarded as her successor? Pepi had not then had the time to think about it, she had too much to do getting ready for the new job. She was probably to start on the job in a few hours and still had not had her hair done nicely, had no smart dress, no fine underclothes, no decent shoes. All this had to be procured in a few hours; if one could not equip oneself properly, then it was better to give up all thought of the situation, for then one was sure of losing it in the very first half-hour. Well, she succeeded partly. She had a special gift for hair-dressing, once, indeed, the landlady had sent for her to do *her* hair, it was a matter of having a specially light hand, and she had it, of course, her abundant hair was the sort you could do anything you like with. There was help forthcoming in the matter of the dress too. Her two colleagues kept faith with her, it was after all a sort of honour for them, too, if a girl out of their own group was chosen to be bar-maid, and then later on, when she had come to power, Pepi would have been able to provide them with many advantages. One of the girls had for a long time been keeping some expensive material, it was her treasure, she had often let the others admire it, doubtless dreaming of how some day she would make magnificent use of it and – this had been really very nice of her – now, when Pepi needed it, she sacrificed it. And both girls had very willingly helped her with the sewing, if they had been sewing it for themselves they could not have been keener. That was indeed a very merry, happy job of work. They sat, each on her bunk, one over the other, sewing and singing, and handed each other the finished parts and the accessories, up and down. When Pepi thought of it, it made her heart ever heavier to think that it was all in vain and that she was going back to her friends with empty hands! What a misfortune and how frivolously brought about, above all by K.! How pleased they had all been with the dress at that time, it seemed a pledge of success and when at the last moment it turned out that there was still room for another ribbon, the last doubt vanished. And was it not really beautiful, this dress? It was crumpled now and showed some spots, the fact was, Pepi had no second dress, had to wear this one day and night, but it could still be seen how beautiful it was, not even that accursed Barnabas woman could produce a better one. And that one could pull it tight and loosen it again as one liked, on top and at the bottom, so that although it was only one dress, it was so changeable – this was a particular advantage and was actually her invention. Of course it wasn't difficult to make clothes for her, Pepi didn't boast of it, there it was – everything suited young, healthy girls. It was much harder to get hold of underclothing and boots, and here was where the failure actually began. Here, too, her girl friends helped out as best they could, but they could not do much. It was, after all, only coarse underclothing that they got together and patched up, and instead of high-heeled little boots she had to make do with slippers, of a kind one would rather hide than show. They comforted Pepi: after all, Frieda was not dressed so very beautifully either, and sometimes she went round looking so sluttish that the guests preferred to be served by the cellarmen rather than by her. This was in fact

so, but Frieda could afford to do that, she already enjoyed
favour and prestige; when a lady for once makes an appearance looking besmirched and carelessly dressed, that is all
the more alluring – but in the case of a novice like Pepi?
And besides, Frieda could not dress well at all, she was
simply devoid of all taste; if a person happened to have a
sallow skin, then, of course, she must put up with it, but
she needn't go around, like Frieda, wearing a low-cut cream
blouse to go with it, so that one's eyes were dazzled by all
that yellow. And even if it hadn't been for that, she was too
mean to dress well; everything she earned, she hung on to,
nobody knew what for. She didn't need any money in her
job, she managed by means of lying and trickery, this was
an example Pepi did not want to and could not imitate, and
that was why it was justifiable that she should smarten herself up like this in order to get herself thoroughly noticed
right at the beginning. Had she only been able to do it by
stronger means, she would, in spite of all Frieda's cunning,
in spite of all K.'s foolishness, have been victorious. After
all, it started very well. The few tricks of the trade and
things it was necessary to know she had found out about
well beforehand. She was no sooner in the tap-room than
she was thoroughly at home there. Nobody missed Frieda at
the job. It was only on the second day that some guests
enquired what had become of Frieda. No mistake was
made, the landlord was satisfied, on the first day he had
been so anxious that he spent all the time in the taproom,
later he only came in now and then, finally, since the money
in the till was correct – the takings were on the average even
a little higher than in Frieda's time – he left everything to
Pepi. She introduced innovations. Frieda had even super-
vised the men-servants, at least partly, particularly when
anyone was looking, and this not out of keenness on the
work, but out of meanness, out of a desire to dominate, out
of fear of letting anyone else invade her rights, Pepi on
the other hand allotted this job entirely to the cellarmen,
who, after all, are much better at it. In this way she had

more time left for the private rooms, the guests got quick service; nevertheless she was able to chat for a moment with everyone, not like Frieda, who allegedly reserved herself entirely for Klamm and regarded every word, every approach, on the part of anyone else as an insult to Klamm. This was, of course, quite clever of her, for, if for once she did allow anyone to get near her, it was an unheard-of favour. Pepi, however, hated such arts, and anyway they were no use at the beginning. Pepi was kind to everyone and everyone requited her with kindness. All were visibly glad of the change; when the gentlemen, tired after their work, were at last free to sit down to their beer for a little while, one could positively transform them by a word, by a glance, by a shrug of the shoulders. So eagerly did all hands stroke Pepi's curls that she had to do her hair again quite ten times a day, no one could resist the temptation offered by these curls and bows, not even K., who was otherwise so absent-minded. So exciting days flew past, full of work, but successful. If only they had not flown past so quickly, if only there had been a little more of them! Four days were too little even if one exerted oneself to the point of exhaustion, perhaps the fifth day would have been enough, but four days were too little. Pepi had, admittedly, gained wellwishers and friends even in four days, if she had been able to trust all the glances she caught, when she came along with the beer-mugs, she positively swam in a sea of friendliness, a clerk by the name of Bartmeier was crazy about her, gave her this little chain and locket, putting his picture into the locket, which was, of course, brazen of him; this and other things had happened, but it had only been four days, in four days, if Pepi set about it, Frieda could be almost, but still not quite, forgotten; and yet she would have been forgotten, perhaps even sooner, had she not seen to it by means of her great scandal that she kept herself talked about, in this way she had become new to people, they might have liked to see her again simply for the sake of curiosity; what they had come to find boring to the point of disgust had, and this was the doing of the otherwise entirely uninteresting K., come to have charm for them again, of course they would not have given up Pepi as long as she was there in front of them and exerting influence by her presence, but they were mostly elderly gentlemen, slow and heavy in their habits, it took some time for them to get used to a new bar-maid, and however advantageous the exchange might be, it still took a few days, took a few days against the gentlemen's own will, only five days perhaps, but four days were not enough, in spite of everything Pepi still counted only as the temporary bar-maid. And then what was perhaps the greatest misfortune: in these four days, although he had been in the village during the first two, Klamm did not come down into the saloon. Had he come, that would have been Pepi's most decisive test, a test, incidentally, that she was least afraid of, one to which she was more inclined to look forward. She would – though it is, of course, best not to touch on such things in words at all – not have become Klamm's mistress, nor would she have promoted herself to that position by telling lies, but she would have been able to put the beer-glass on the table at least as nicely as Frieda, have said good-day and goodbye prettily without Frieda's officiousness, and if Klamm did look for anything in any girl's eyes at all, he would have found it to his entire satisfaction in Pepi's eyes. But why did he not come? Was it chance? That was what Pepi had thought at the time, too. All those two days she had expected him at any moment, and in the night she waited too. 'Now Klamm is coming,' she kept on thinking, and dashed to and fro for no other reason than the restlessness of expectation and the desire to be the first to see him, immediately on his entry. This continual disappointment made her very tired; perhaps that was why she did not get so much as she could have got done. Whenever she had a little time she crept up into the passage that the staff was strictly forbidden to enter, there she would squeeze into a recess and wait. 'If only Klamm would come now,' she thought, 'if only I could take the gentleman out of his room and carry him down into the saloon on my arms. I should not collapse under that burden, however great it might be.' But he did not come. In that passage upstairs it was so quiet that one simply couldn't imagine it if one hadn't been there. It was so quiet that one couldn't stand being there for very long, the quietness drove one away. But over and over again: driven away ten times, ten times again Pepi went up there. It was senseless, of course. If Klamm wanted to come, he would come, but if he did not want to come, Pepi would not lure him out, even if the beating of her heart half suffocated her there in the recess. It was senseless, but if he did not come, almost everything was senseless. And he did not come. To-day Pepi knew why Klamm did not come. Frieda would have found it wonderfully amusing if she had been able to see Pepi up there in the passage, in the recess, both hands on her heart. Klamm did not come down because Frieda did not allow it. It was not by means of her pleading that she brought this about, her pleading did not penetrate to Klamm. But – spider that she was – she had connections of which nobody knew. If Pepi said something to a guest, she said it openly, the next table could hear it too. Frieda had nothing to say, she put the beer on the table and went; there was only the rustling of her silk petticoat, the only thing on which she spent money. But if she did for once say something, then not openly, then she whispered it to the guest, bending low so that people at the next table pricked up their ears. What she said was probably quite trivial, but still, not always, she had connections, she supported the ones by means of the others, and if most of them failed – who would keep on bothering about Frieda? – still, here and there one did hold firm. These connections she now began to exploit. K. gave her the chance to do this; instead of sitting with her and keeping a watch on her, he hardly stayed at home at all, wandering, having discussions here and there, paying attention to everything, only not to Frieda, and finally, in order to give her still more freedom, he moved out of the Bridge Inn into the empty school. A very nice beginning for a honeymoon all this was. Well, Pepi was certainly the last person to reproach K. for not having been able to stand living with Frieda; nobody *could* stand living with her. But why then did he not leave her entirely, why did he time and again return to her, why did he cause the impression, by his roaming about, that he was fighting for her cause? It really looked as though it were only through his contact with Frieda that he had discovered what a nonentity he in fact was, that he wished to make himself worthy of Frieda, wished to make his way up somehow, and for that reason was for the time being sacrificing her company in order to be able later to compensate himself at leisure for these hardships. Meanwhile Frieda was not wasting her time, she sat tight in the school, where she had probably led K., and kept the Herrenhof and K. under observation. She had excellent messengers at her disposal: K.'s assistants, whom – one couldn't understand it, even if one knew K. one couldn't understand it – K. left entirely to her. She sent them to her old friends, reminded people of her existence, complained that she was kept a prisoner by a man like K., incited people against Pepi, announced her imminent arrival, begged for help, implored them to betray nothing to Klamm, behaved as if Klamm's feelings had to be spared and as if for this reason he must on no account be allowed to come down into the tap-room. What she represented to one as a way of sparing Klamm's feelings she successfully turned to account where the landlord was concerned, drawing attention to the fact that Klamm did not come any more. How could he come when downstairs there was only a Pepi serving? True, it wasn't the landlord's fault, this Pepi was after all the best substitute that could be found, only the substitute wasn't good enough, not even for a few days. All this activity of Frieda's was something of which K. knew nothing, when he was not roaming about he was lying at her feet, without an inkling of it, while she counted the hours still keeping her from the tap-room. But this running of errands was not the only thing the assistants did, they also served to make K. jealous, to keep him interested! Frieda had known the assistants since her childhood, they certainly had no secrets from each other now, but in K.'s honour they were beginning to have a yearning for each other, and for K. there arose the danger that it would turn out to be a great love. And K. did everything Frieda wanted, even what was contradictory and senseless, he let himself be made jealous by the assistants, at the same time allowing all three to remain together while he went on his wanderings alone. It was almost as though he were Frieda's third assistant. And so, on the basis of her observations, Frieda at last decided to make her great *coup*: she made up her mind to return. And it was really high time, it was admirable how Frieda, the cunning creature, recognised and exploited this fact; this power of observation and this power of decision were Frieda's inimitable art; if Pepi had it, how different the course of her life would be. If Frieda had stayed one or two days longer in the school, it would no longer be possible to drive Pepi out, she would be barmaid once and for all, loved and supported by all, having earned enough money to replenish her scanty wardrobe in the most dazzling style, only one or two more days and Klamm could not be kept out of the saloon by any intrigues any longer, would come, drink, feel comfortable and, if he noticed Frieda's absence at all, would be highly satisfied with the change, only one or two more days and Frieda, with her scandal, with her connections, with the assistants, with everything, would be utterly and completely forgotten, never would she come out into the open again. Then perhaps she would be able to cling all the more tightly to K. and, assuming that she were capable of it, would really learn to love him? No, not that either. For it didn't take even K. more than one day to get tired of her, to recognise how infamously she was deceiving him, with everything, with her alleged beauty, her alleged constancy, and most of all with Klamm's alleged love, it would only take him one day more, and no longer, to chase her out of the house, and together with her the whole dirty set-up with the assistants; just think, it wouldn't take even K. any longer than that. And now, between these two dangers, when the grave was positively beginning to close over her – K. in his simplicity was still keeping the last narrow road open for her – she suddenly bolted. Suddenly – hardly anyone expected such a thing, it was against nature – suddenly it was she who drove away K., the man who still loved her and kept on pursuing her, and, aided by the pressure of her friends and the assistants, appeared to the landlord as the rescuer, as a result of the scandal associated with her much more alluring than formerly, demonstrably desired by the lowest as by the highest, yet having fallen a prey to the lowest only for a moment, soon rejecting him as was proper, and again inaccessible to him and to all others, as formerly; only that formerly all this was quite properly doubted, whereas now everyone was again convinced. So she came back, the landlord, with a sidelong glance at Pepi, hesitated – should he sacrifice her, after she had proved her worth so well? – but he was soon talked over, there was too much to be said for Frieda, and above all, of course, she would bring Klamm back to the saloon again. That is where we stand, this evening. Pepi is not going to wait till Frieda comes and makes a triumph out of taking over the job. She has already handed over the till to the landlady, she can go now. The bunk downstairs in the maids' room is waiting for her, she will come in, welcomed by the weeping girls, her friends, will tear the dress from her body, the ribbons from her hair, and stuff it all into a corner where it will be thoroughly hidden and won't be an unnecessary reminder of times better forgotten. Then she will take the big pail and the broom, clench her teeth, and set to work. In the meantime, however, she had to tell K. everything so that he, who would not have realised this even now without help, might for once see clearly how horridly he had treated Pepi and how unhappy he had made her. Admittedly, he, too, had only been made use of and misused in all this.

Pepi had finished. Taking a long breath, she wiped a few tears from her eyes and cheeks and then looked at K., nodding, as if meaning to say that at bottom what mattered was not her misfortune at all, she would bear it all right, for that she needed neither help nor comfort from anyone at all, and least of all from K., even though she was so young she knew something about life, and her misfortune was only a confirmation of what she knew already, but what mattered was K., she had wanted to show him what he himself was like, even after the collapse of all her hopes she had thought it necessary to do that.

'What a wild imagination you have, Pepi,' K. said. 'For it isn't true at all that you have discovered all these things only now; all this is, of course, nothing but dreams out of that dark, narrow room you chamber-maids have downstairs, dreams that are in their place there, but which look odd here in the freedom of the tap-room. You couldn't maintain your position here with such ideas, that goes without saying. Even your dress and your way of doing your hair, which you make such a boast of, are only freaks born of that darkness and those bunks in your room, there they are very beautiful, I am sure, but here everyone laughs at them, secretly or openly. And the rest of your story? So I have been misused and deceived, have I? No, my dear Pepi, I have not been misused and deceived any more than you have. It is true, Frieda has left me for the present or has, as you put it, run away with one of the assistants, you do see a glimmer of the truth, and it is really very improbable that she will ever become my wife, but it is utterly and completely untrue that I have grown tired of her and still less that I drove her out the very next day or that she deceived me, as other women perhaps deceive a man. You chamber-maids are used to spying through keyholes, and from that you set this way of thinking, of drawing conclusions, as grand as they are false, about the whole situation from some little thing you really see. The consequence of this is that I, for instance, in this case know much less than you. I cannot explain by any means as exactly as you can why Frieda left me. The most probable explanation seems to me to be that you have touched on but not elaborated, which is that I neglected her. That is unfortunately true, I did neglect her, but there were special reasons for that, which have nothing to do with this discussion; I should be happy if she were to come back to me, but I should at once begin to neglect her all over again. This is how it is. While she was with me I was continually out on those wanderings that you make such a mock of; now that she is gone I am almost unemployed, am tired, have a yearning for a state of even more complete unemployment. Have you no advice to give me, Pepi?' 'Oh yes, I have,' Pepi said, suddenly becoming animated and seizing K. by the shoulders, 'we have both been deceived, let us stick together. Come downstairs with me to the maids!' 'So long as you complain about being deceived,' K. said, 'I cannot come to an understanding with you. You are always claiming to have been deceived because you find it flattering and touching. But the truth is that you are not fitted for this job. How obvious your unfittedness must be when even I, who in your view know less about things than anyone, can see that. You are a good girl, Pepi; but it is not altogether easy to realise that, I for instance at first took you to be cruel and haughty, but you are not so, it is only this job that confuses you because you are not fitted for it. I am not going to say that the job is too grand for you; it is, after all, not a very splendid job, perhaps, if one regards it closely, it is somewhat more honourable than your previous job, on the whole, however, the difference is not great, both are indeed so similar one can hardly distinguish between them; indeed, one might almost assert that being a chamber-maid is preferable to the tap-room, for there one is always among secretaries, here, on the other hand, even though one is allowed to serve the secretaries' chiefs in the private rooms, still, one also has to have a lot to do with quite common people, for instance with me; actually I am not really supposed to sit about anywhere but right here in the tap-room – and is it such a great and glorious honour to associate with me? Well, it seems so to you, and perhaps you have your reasons for thinking so. But precisely that makes you unfitted. It is a job like any other, but for you it is heaven, consequently you set about everything with exaggerated eagerness, trick yourself out as in your opinion the angels are tricked out – but in reality they are different – tremble for the job, feel you are constantly being persecuted, try by means of being excessively pleasant to win over everyone who in your opinion might be a support to you, but in this way bother them and repel them, for what they want at the inn is peace and quiet and not the bar-maids' worries on top of their own. It is just possible that after Frieda left none of the exalted guests really noticed the occurrence, but to-day they know of it and are really longing for Frieda, for Frieda doubtless did manage everything quite differently. Whatever she may be like otherwise and however much she valued her job, in her work she was greatly experienced, cool and composed, you yourself stress that, though admittedly without learning anything from it. Did you ever notice the way she looked at things? That was not merely a bar-maid's way of looking at things, it was almost the way a landlady looks around. She saw everything, and every individual person into the bargain, and the glance that was left for each individual person was still intense enough to subdue him. What did it matter that she was perhaps a little skinny, a little oldish, that one could imagine cleaner hair? – those are trifles compared with what she really had, and anyone whom these deficiencies disturbed would only have shown that he lacked any appreciation of greater things. One can certainly not charge Klamm with that, and it is only the wrong point of view of a young, inexperienced girl that makes you unable to believe in Klamm's love for Frieda. Klamm seems to you – and this rightly – to be out of reach, and that is why you believe Frieda could not have got near to him either. You are wrong. I should take Frieda's own word for this, even if I had not infallible evidence for it. However incredible it seems to you and however little you can reconcile it with your notions of the world and official-dom and gentility and the effect a woman's beauty has, still, it is true, just as we are sitting here beside each other and I take your hand between my hands, so too, I dare say, and as though it were the most natural thing in the world, did Klamm and Frieda sit beside each other, and he came down of his own free will, indeed he came hurrying down, nobody was lurking in the passage waiting for him and neglecting the rest of the work, Klamm had to bestir him-self and come downstairs, and the faults in Frieda's way of dressing, which would have horrified you, did not disturb him at all. You won't believe her! And you don't know how you give yourself away by this, how precisely in this you show your lack of experience! Even someone who knew nothing at all about the affair with Klamm could not fail to see from her bearing that someone had moulded her, some-one who was more than you and I and all the people in the village and that their conversations went beyond the jokes that are usual between customers and waitresses and which seem to be your aim in life. But I am doing you an injus-tice. You can see Frieda's merits very well for yourself, you notice her power of observation, her resolution, her influence on people, only you do, of course, interpret it all wrongly, believing she turns everything self-seekingly to account only for her own benefit and for evil purposes, or even as a weapon against you. No, Pepi, even if she had such arrows, she could not shoot them at such short range. And self-seeking? One might rather say that by sacrificing what she had and what she was entitled to expect she has given us both the opportunity to prove our worth in higher positions, but that we have both disappointed her and are positively forcing her to return here. I do not know whether it is like this, and my own guilt is by no means clear to me, only when I compare myself with you something of this

kind dawns on me: it is as if we had both striven too inten-
sely, too noisily, too childishly, with too little experience, to
get something that for instance with Frieda's calm and
Frieda's matter-of-factness can be got easily and without
much ado. We have tried to get it by crying, by scratching,
by tugging – just as a child tugs at the tablecloth, gaining
nothing, but only bringing all the splendid things down on
the floor and putting them out of its reach for ever. I don't
know whether it is like that, but what I am sure of is that it
is more likely to be so than the way you describe it as
being.' 'Oh well,' Pepi said, 'you are in love with Frieda
because she's run away from you, it isn't hard to be in love
with her when she's not there. But let it be as you like, and
even if you are right in everything, even in making me
ridiculous, what are you going to do now? Frieda has left
you, neither according to my explanation nor according to
your own have you any hope of her coming back to you,
and even if she were to come back, you have to stay somewhere in the meantime, it is cold, and you have neither
work nor a bed, come to us, you will like my girl friends, we
shall make you comfortable, you will help us with our work,
which is really too hard for girls to do all by themselves, we
girls will not have to rely only on ourselves and won't be
frightened any more in the night! Come to us! My girl
friends also know Frieda, we shall tell you stories about her
till you are sick and tired of it. Do come! We have pictures
of Frieda too and we'll show them to you. At that time Frieda was more modest than she is to-day, you will scarcely
recognise her, only perhaps by her eyes, which even then
had a suspicious, watchful expression. Well now, are you
coming?' 'But is it permitted? Only yesterday there was that
great scandal because I was caught in your passage.' 'Because
you were caught, but when you are with us you won't be
caught. Nobody will know about you, only the three of us.
Oh, it will be jolly. Even now life there seems much more
bearable to me than only a little while ago. Perhaps now I
shall not lose so very much by having to go away from here.

Listen, even with only the three of us we were not bored, one has to sweeten the bitterness of one's life, it's made bitter for us when we're still young, well, the three of us stick together, we live as nicely as is possible there, you'll like Henriette particularly, but you'll like Emilie too, I've told them about you, there one listens to such tales without believing them, as though outside the room nothing could really happen, it's warm and snug and tight there, and we press together still more tightly; no, although we have only each other to rely on, we have not become tired of each other; on the contrary, when I think of my girl friends, I am almost glad that I am going back. Why should I get on better than they do? For that was just what held us together, the fact that the future was barred to all three of us in the same way, and now I have broken through after all and was separated from them. Of course, I have not forgotten them, and my first concern was how I could do something for them; my own position was still insecure – how insecure it was, I did not even realise – and I was already talking to the landlord about Henriette and Emilie. So far as Henriette was concerned the landlord was not quite unrelenting, but for Emilie, it must be confessed, who is much older than we are, she's about as old as Frieda, he gave me no hope. But only think, they don't *want* to go away, they know it's a miserable life they lead there, but they have resigned themselves to it, good souls, I think their tears as we said goodbye were mostly because they were sad about my having to leave our common room, going out into the cold – to us there everything seems cold that is outside the room – and having to make my way in the big strange rooms with big strange people, for no other purpose than to earn a living, which after all I had managed to do up to now in the life we led together. They probably won't be at all surprised when now I come back, and only in order to indulge me they will weep a little and bemoan my fate. But then they will see you and notice that it was a good thing after all that I went away. It will make them happy that now we have a man as a helper and protector, and they will be absolutely delighted that it must all be kept a secret and that through this secret we shall be still more tightly linked with each other than before. Come, oh please come to us! No obligation will arise so far as you are concerned, you will not be bound to our room for ever, as we are. When the spring comes and you find a lodging somewhere else and if you don't like being with us any more, then you can go if you want to; only, of course, you must keep the secret even then and not go and betray us, for that would mean our last hour in the Herrenhof had come, and in other respects too, naturally, you must be careful when you are with us, not showing yourself anywhere unless we regard it as safe, and altogether take our advice; that is the only thing that ties you, and this must count just as much with you as with us, but otherwise you are completely free, the work we shall share out to you will not be too hard, you needn't be afraid of that. Well then, are you coming?' 'How much longer is it till spring?' K. asked. 'Till spring?' Pepi repeated. 'Winter is long here, a very long winter, and monotonous. But we don't complain about that down there, we are safe from the winter. Well yes, some day spring comes too, and summer, and there's a time for that too, I suppose; but in memory, now, spring and summer seem as short as though they didn't last much longer than two days, and even on those days, even during the most beautiful day, even then sometimes snow falls.'

At this moment the door opened. Pepi started, in her thoughts she had gone too far away from the tap-room, but it was not Frieda, it was the landlady. She pretended to be amazed at finding K. still here. K. excused himself by saying that he had been waiting for her, and at the same time he expressed his thanks for having been allowed to stay here overnight. The landlady could not understand why K. had been waiting for her. K. said he had had the impression that she wanted to speak to him again, he apologised if that had been a mistake, and for the rest he must go now anyway, he had left the school, where he was care-taker, to itself much too long, yesterday's summons was to blame for everything, he still had too little experience of these matters, it would certainly not happen again that he would cause the landlady such inconvenience and bother as yesterday. And he bowed, on the point of going. The land-lady looked at him as though she were dreaming. This gaze kept K. longer than was his intention. Now she smiled a little, and it was only the amazement on K.'s face that, as it were, woke her up; it was as though she had been expecting an answer to her smile and only now, since none came, did she wake up. 'Yesterday, I think, you had the impudence to say something about my dress.' K. could not remember. 'You can't remember? Then it's not only impudence, but afterwards cowardice into the bargain.' By way of excuse K. spoke of his fatigue of the previous day, saying it was quite possible that he had talked some nonsense, in any case he could not remember now. And what could he have said about the landlady's clothes? That they were more beautiful than any he had ever seen in his life. At least he had never seen any landlady at her work in such clothes. 'That's enough of these remarks!' the landlady said swiftly. 'I don't want to hear another word from you about clothes. My clothes are none of your business. Once and for all, I forbid you to talk about them.' K. bowed again and went to the door. 'What do you mean,' the landlady shouted after him, 'by saying you've never before seen any landlady at work in such clothes? What do you mean by making such senseless remarks? It's simply quite senseless. What do you mean by it?' K. turned round and begged the landlady not to get excited. Of course the remark was senseless. After all, he knew nothing at all about clothes. In his situation any dress that happened to be clean and not patched seemed luxuri-ous. He had only been amazed at the landlady's appearing there, in the passage, at night, among all those scantily dressed men, in such a beautiful evening-dress, that was all. 'Well now,' the landlady said, 'at last you seem to have remembered the remark you made yesterday, after all. And you put the finishing-touch to it by some more nonsense. It's quite true you don't know anything about clothes. But then kindly refrain – this is a serious request I make to you – from setting yourself up as a judge of what are luxurious dresses or unsuitable evening-dresses, and the like. . . . And let me tell you' – here it seemed as if a cold shudder went through her – 'you've no business to interfere with my clothes in any way at all, do you hear?' And as K. was about to turn away again in silence, she asked: 'Where did you get your knowledge of clothes, anyway?' K. shrugged his shoulders, saying he had no knowledge. 'You have none,' the landlady said. 'Very well then, don't set up to have any, either. Come over to the office, I'll show you something, then I hope you'll stop your impudent remarks for good.' She went through the door ahead of him; Pepi rushed forward to K., on the pretext of settling the bill: they quickly made their plans, it was very easy, since K. knew the courtyard with the gate opening into the side-street, beside the gate there was a little door behind which Pepi would stand in about an hour and open it on hearing a three-fold knock.

The private office was opposite the tap-room, they only had to cross the hall, the landlady was already standing in the lighted office and impatiently looking towards K. But there was yet another disturbance. Gerstäcker had been waiting in the hall and wanted to talk to K. It was not easy to shake him off, the landlady also joined in and rebuked Gerstäcker for his intrusiveness. 'Where are you going? Where are you going?' Gerstäcker could still be heard calling out even after the door was shut, and the words were unpleasantly interspersed with sighs and coughs.

It was a small, over-heated room. Against the end-walls were a standing-desk and an iron safe, against the side-walls were a wardrobe and an ottoman. It was the wardrobe that took up most room; not only did it occupy the whole of the longer wall, its depth also made the room very narrow, it had three sliding-doors by which it could be opened completely. The landlady pointed to the ottoman, indicating that K. should sit down, she herself sat down on the revolving chair at the desk. 'Didn't you once learn tailoring?' the landlady asked. 'No, never,' K. said. 'What actually is it you are?' 'Land Surveyor.' 'What *is* that?' K. explained, the explanation made her yawn. 'You're not telling the truth. Why won't you tell the truth?' 'You don't tell the truth either.' 'I? So now you're beginning your impudent remarks again? And if I didn't tell the truth – do I have to answer for it to you? And in what way don't I tell the truth then?' 'You are not only a landlady, as you pretend.' 'Just listen to that! All the things you discover! What else am I then? But I must say, your impudence is getting thoroughly out of hand.' 'I don't know what else you are. I only see that you are a landlady and also wear clothes that are not suitable for a landlady and of a kind that to the best of my knowledge nobody else wears here in the village.' 'Well, now we're getting to the point. The fact is you can't keep it to yourself, perhaps you aren't impudent at all, you're only like a child that knows some silly thing or other and which simply can't, by any means, be made to keep it to itself. Well, speak up! What is so special about these clothes?' 'You'll be angry if I say.' 'No, I shall laugh about it, it'll be some childish chatter. What sort of clothes are they then?' 'You insist on hearing. Well, they're made of good material, pretty expensive, but they are old-fashioned, fussy, often renovated, worn, and not suitable either for your age or for your figure or for your position. I was struck by them the very first time I saw you, it was about a week ago, here in the hall.' 'So there now we have it! They are old-fashioned, fussy, and what else did you say? And what enables you to judge all this?' 'I can see for myself, one doesn't need any training for that.' 'You can see it without more ado. You don't have to enquire anywhere, you know at once what is required by fashion. So you're going to be quite indispensable to me, for I must admit I have a weakness for beautiful clothes. And what will you say when I tell you that this wardrobe is full of dresses?' She pushed the sliding doors open, one dress could be seen tightly packed against the next, filling up the whole length and breadth of the wardrobe, they were mostly dark, grey, brown, black dresses, all carefully hung up and spread out. 'These are my dresses, all old-fashioned, fussy, as you think. But they are only the dresses for which I have no room upstairs in my room, there I have two more wardrobes full, two wardrobes, each of them almost as big as this one. Are you amazed?' 'No, I was expecting something of the sort; didn't I say you're not only a landlady, you're aiming at something else.' 'I am only aiming at dressing beautifully, and you are either a fool or a child or a very wicked, dangerous person. Go, go away now!' K. was already in the hall and Gerstäcker was clutching at his sleeve again, when the landlady shouted after him: 'I am getting a new dress to-morrow, perhaps I shall send for you.'

APPENDIX

1
CONTINUATION OF THE MANUSCRIPT

2
ANOTHER VERSION OF THE OPENING PARAGRAPHS

3
FRAGMENTS

4
TWO ADDITIONAL PASSAGES INCLUDED IN THE TEXT OF THE DEFINITIVE GERMAN EDITION

5
THE PASSAGES DELETED BY THE AUTHOR

APPENDIX

1

CONTINUATION OF THE MANUSCRIPT

Gerstäcker, angrily gesticulating, as if trying from a distance to silence the landlady, who was disturbing him, asked K. to go with him. At first he would not give any further explanation. He took hardly any notice of K.'s objection that he must now go back to the school. Only when K. protested at being hauled away by him did Gerstäcker tell him there was nothing to worry about, he would get everything he needed at *his* house, he could give up the job as janitor at the school, only he was to come along without further delay, he had been waiting for him all day, his mother had no idea where he was. Slowly giving way to him, K. asked what, then, he was going to provide board and lodging for. Gerstäcker answered only vaguely that he needed K. to help with the horses, for he himself had other business to attend to, but now K. was to stop resisting like this and making unnecessary difficulties for him. If he wanted wages, he would give him wages too. But now K. stopped, in spite of all the tugging. He said he did not know anything at all about horses. Nor was it necessary that he should, Gerstäcker said impatiently and clasped his hands in annoyance, in order to induce K. to come on. 'I know why you want to take me with you,' K. said at length. Gerstäcker did not know what K. knew. 'Because you think I can do something for you with Erlanger.' 'Certainly,' Gerstäcker said, 'what interest should I have in you otherwise?' K. laughed, linked arms with Gerstäcker and let himself be led through the darkness by him.

The room in Gerstäcker's hovel was only dimly lit by the fire in the hearth and by a stub of candle, by the light of which someone hunched up in a recess under the slanting rafters, which overhung there, was reading a book. It was Gerstäcker's mother. She held out a tremulous hand to K. and made him sit down beside her, she spoke with an effort, it was difficult to understand her, but what she said,

ANOTHER VERSION

Now Gerstäcker thought his time had come at last. Despite the fact that he had all the time been trying to gain a hearing with K., he began, he obviously could not help it, rather roughly. 'Have you got a job?' he asked. 'Yes,' K. said, 'a very good one.' 'Where?' 'At the school.' 'But you're a Land Surveyor, aren't you?' 'Yes, but it's only a temporary job, I'm only staying on there till I get the certificate of my appointment as Land Surveyor. Do you understand?' 'Yes, and will that take much longer?' 'No, no, it may come at any moment, I was talking to Erlanger about it yesterday.' 'To Erlanger?' 'You know I was. Don't be tiresome. Go away. Leave me alone.' 'Well yes, you've spoken to Erlanger. I thought it was a secret.' 'I wouldn't share my secrets with you. After all, you're the fellow who snarled at me when I got stuck in the snow outside your door.' 'Yes, but then I drove you to the Bridge Inn, didn't I?' 'That's true, and I didn't pay you your fare. How much do you want?' 'Have you any money to spare? Do you get good wages at the school?' 'Enough to live on.' 'I could tell you of a job where you'd get better pay.' 'With you, I suppose, with the horses? No thanks.' 'Who told you?' 'You've been hanging about since last night, trying to get hold of me.' 'You're very much mistaken there.' 'If I'm mistaken, so much the better.' 'Only now, seeing you in your desperate situation, you, a Land Surveyor, an educated man, in dirty, ragged clothes, without a fur coat, so down and out that it's quite heart-rending, hand-in-glove with that little wretch Pepi, who's probably supporting you, only now I've remembered what my mother once said: "This man shouldn't be let go to the dogs".' 'A good saying. That's the very reason why I'm not coming to you.'

2

ANOTHER VERSION OF THE OPENING PARAGRAPHS

The landlord welcomed the guest. A room on the first floor had been got ready. 'The royal apartment,' the land-lord said. It was a large room with two windows and a glass door between them, it was distressingly large in its bareness. The few pieces of furniture that stood about in it had strangely thin legs, one might have thought they were made of iron, but they were made of wood. 'Kindly do not step out on the balcony,' the landlord said, when the guest, after he had looked out of one of the windows, into the night, approached the glass door. 'The beam is slightly rotten.' The chamber-maid came in and busied herself at the wash-stand, at the same time asking whether the room was warm enough. The guest nodded. But although he had up to now found no fault with the room, he was still walking up and down fully dressed, in his overcoat, with his stick and hat in his hand, as though it were not yet settled whether he would stay here. The landlord was standing beside the chamber-maid. Suddenly the guest stepped up behind the two of them and exclaimed: 'Why are you whispering?' Frightened, the landlord said: 'I was only giving the maid instructions about the bedclothes. The room is unfortunately, as I only now see, not so carefully prepared as I should have wished. But everything will be done in a moment.' 'That's not the point,' the guest said, 'I expected nothing but a filthy hovel and a repulsive bed. Don't try to distract my attention. There's only one thing I want to know: who informed you in advance of my arrival?' 'Nobody, sir,' the landlord said. 'You were expecting me.' 'I am an innkeeper and expect guests.' 'The room was prepared.' 'As always.' 'Very well then, you knew nothing, but I am not going to stay here.' And he pushed a window open and shouted out of it: 'Don't unharness, we're driving on!' But as he hurried to the door, the chamber-maid stepped in his way, a weakly, in fact far too young, frail girl, and said with lowered head: 'Don't go away; yes, we were expecting you, it was only because we are clumsy at answering, uncertain of your wishes, that we concealed it.' The girl's appearance touched the guest; her words seemed to him suspicious. 'Leave me alone with the girl,' he said to the landlord. The landlord hesitated, then he went. 'Come,' the guest said to the girl, and they sat down at the table. 'What is your name?' the guest asked, reaching across the table and taking the girl's hand. 'Elisabeth,' she said. 'Elisabeth,' he said, 'listen to me carefully. I have a difficult task ahead of me and have dedicated my whole life to it. I do it joyfully and ask for nobody's pity. But because it is all I have, the task I mean, I ruthlessly suppress everything that might disturb me in carrying it out. I tell you, I can be mad in my ruthlessness.' He pressed her hand, she gazed at him and nodded. 'Well, so you have understood that,' he said, 'now explain to me how you people learnt of my arrival. That is all I want to know, I am not asking what views you hold. I am here to fight, certainly, but I don't want to be attacked before my arrival. Well, what happened before I came?' 'The whole village knows of your arrival, I can't explain it, everyone has known for weeks, I suppose it comes from the Castle, I don't know any more than that.' 'Someone from the Castle was here and announced I was coming?' 'No, nobody was here, the gentlemen from the Castle don't associate with us, but the servants up there may have talked of it, people from the village may have heard it, so it got around perhaps. So few strangers come here, after all, people talk a lot about a stranger.' 'Few strangers?' the guest asked. 'Alas,' the girl said and smiled – she looked both confiding and aloof – 'nobody comes, it is as though the world had forgotten us.'

'Why should anyone come here anyway,' the guest said, 'after all, is there anything worth seeing here?' The girl slowly withdrew her hand and said: 'You still don't trust me.' 'And rightly,' the guest said and stood up. 'You are all a crowd of villains, but you are even more dangerous than the landlord. You have been specially sent from the Castle to wait on me.' 'Sent from the Castle?' the girl said. 'How little you know conditions here! It is out of mistrust you are going away, for I suppose you are going away now.' 'No,' the guest said, tore off his overcoat and threw it on a chair. 'I am not going, you have not succeeded even in that, in driving me away.' But suddenly he swayed, staggered a few steps further and then fell across the bed. The girl hurried over to him. 'What's the matter?' she whispered, and now she ran to the wash-basin and fetched water and knelt down beside him and washed his face. 'Why do you people torment me like this?' he said with an effort. 'But we are not tormenting you,' the girl said, 'you want something from us and we don't know what. Speak to me frankly and I shall answer you frankly.'

FRAGMENTS

Yesterday K. told us of the experience that he had had with Bürgel. It's too funny that it had to be with Bürgel of all people. You all know, Bürgel is secretary to the Castle official Friedrich, and Friedrich's glory has greatly declined in recent years. Why that is so is another story; I could tell you a few things about that too. What is certain, at any rate, is that Friedrich's agenda is to-day one of the most unimportant far and wide, and what that means to Bürgel, who is not even Friedrich's first secretary, but one rather far down the list, anyone, of course, can see for himself. Anyone, that is, but K. He's been living here among us in the village long enough, after all, but he's as strange here as though he'd only arrived yesterday and is capable of getting lost in the three streets there are in the village. Yet he makes a strenuous effort to be very observant, and he follows up his own affairs like a hound on the trail, but he hasn't the knack of making himself at home here. One day for instance I tell him about Bürgel, he listens eagerly, after all, everything he's told about the Castle officials concerns him very closely, he asks expert questions, he has an excellent grasp of the whole thing, not only apparently, but really; but believe it or not, the next day he doesn't know a thing about it. Or rather, he does know, he doesn't forget anything, but it's too much for him, the great number of the officials bewilders him, he has forgotten nothing of all he has ever heard, and he has heard a great deal, for he makes use of every opportunity to increase his knowledge, and perhaps he has a better theoretical understanding of the officials and official workings than we have, in this he's admirable; but when it comes to applying his knowledge, he somehow gets moving in a wrong way, he turns round as though in a kaleidoscope, he can't apply it, it mocks him. Finally, I suppose, it can all be reduced to the fact that he doesn't belong here. That's probably why he doesn't make any progress in his cause either. You all know, don't you, he maintains he was appointed by our Count to be Land Surveyor here; in its details it's a quite fantastic story, which I am not going to touch upon now, in short, he was appointed Land Surveyor and insists on being it here too. The gigantic exertions that he has made on account of this little matter, up to now entirely without success, are of course known to you all, at least by hearsay. Another person would have surveyed ten countries in this time, *he* is still here in the village dangling to and fro between the secretaries, he no longer dares to approach the officials at all, and he probably never had any hope of being admitted into the Castle chanceries. He contents himself with the secretaries, when they come down from the Castle to the Herrenhof, now he has to undergo day interrogations, now night interrogations, and he's always prowling around the Herrenhof, like the foxes round the hen-house, only that in reality the secretaries are the foxes and he is the hen. But that is only by the way, I was going to tell you about Bürgel. Well then, last night K. was summoned to the Herrenhof once again in connection with his affair, to see Secretary Erlanger, with whom he mainly has to do. He's always in raptures over such a summons, in this respect disappointments have no effect on him – if only one could learn that from him! Each new summons reinforces, not his old disappointments, but only his old hope. Lent wings by this summons, then, he hurries to the Herrenhof. Admittedly he is not in a good state, he was not expecting the summons, hence he had gone on various errands in the village with regard to his cause, you know by this time he has more connections here than families that have been living here for centuries, all these connections are meant solely to serve this land-surveyor affair of his and, since they are the result of hard fighting and have to be fought for over and over again, an eye must be kept on them all the time. You must get a proper picture of this, all these connections are positively lying in wait for a chance to slip away from him. And so he constantly has his hands full, looking after them. And yet he finds the time to have long discussions with me or anyone else about quite irrelevant things, but this only for the reason that nothing is so irrelevant that in his opinion it is not connected with his affair. So he is always at work; actually it never struck me that he sleeps too. Yet this is the case, sleep does in fact play the main part in the affair with Bürgel. The fact is that when he hurried into the Herrenhof to see Erlanger, he was already immeasurably tired, after all he had not been prepared for the summons and had frivolously wasted his energy, not having slept at all the night before, and the two previous nights each only two or three hours. For this reason, though Erlanger's summons, made out for midnight, made him happy, as any such slip of paper does, at the same time it made him worried about the condition he was in, which might prevent him from being as much of a match for the strain of the interview as he would otherwise have been. So he arrives at the Herrenhof, goes into the passage where the secretaries have their rooms and there, to his misfortune, meets a chamber-maid he knows. He has no lack of affairs with women, you know, and all for the good of his cause. This girl had something to tell him about another girl he also knew, drew him into her little room, he followed – it was not yet midnight – for it is his principle never to miss any opportunity of learning anything new. This, indeed, besides its advantages, sometimes, and perhaps very often, produces great disadvantages too, as it did this time, for instance, for, when he got away from the gossiping girl, half-demented with sleepiness, and was out in the passage again, it was four o'clock. He could think of nothing but not missing the appointment with Erlanger. He fortified himself a little, perhaps indeed too much, from a decanter of rum that he found on a tray forgotten in a corner, tiptoed along the long passage, at other times so full of bustle and now as quiet as a path through a cemetery, till he came to the door that he took to be Erlanger's door, didn't knock, in order not to wake Erlanger, supposing he were asleep, but opened the door at once, though with extreme caution. And now I am going to tell you the story as well as I can word for word, and as much in detail as K. told it to me yesterday with all the signs of mortal despair. I hope he has meanwhile been consoled by a new summons. But the story itself is really too funny, just listen: what is actually so funny about it is, of course, his own painstakingly detailed account, and a good deal of that will get lost in my re-telling of it. If I could really bring it out, it would give you a full-length picture of K. himself, though of Bürgel hardly a trace. If I could bring it out – that is the pre-condition. For otherwise the story may equally well turn out to be very boring, it contains that element too. But let us risk it.

. . . shaking hands, saying goodbye, 'but I was very glad to have this talk with you, it is positively a weight off my mind. Perhaps I shall see you again before long.'

'I dare say it will be necessary for me to come,' K. said and bowed over Mizzi's hand, he wanted to get the better of his feelings and kiss it, but Mizzi pulled it away with a little scream of fright and hid it under the pillow. 'Mizzi, Mizzi, my pet,' the Mayor said indulgently and affectionately, stroking her back.

'You are always welcome,' he said, perhaps in order to help K. to overlook Mizzi's behaviour, but then he added: 'Particularly now, as long as I am ill. When I am able to get back to my desk, of course, I shall be quite taken up with official work.' 'Do you intend to convey by that,' K. asked, 'that even you were not speaking to me officially to-day?'

'Certainly,' the Mayor said, 'I have never spoken to you officially, one may perhaps call it semi-officially. You underrate the non-official element, as I said before, but you also underrate the official element. An official decision is, after all, not just something like, for instance, this medicine bottle, standing here on this little table. One reaches out for it and has it. A real official decision is preceded by innumerable little investigations and considerations, it requires years of work by the best officials, even in a case when these officials happen to know from the very beginning what the final decision is. And is there then any such thing as a final decision? The control offices are there, of course, to prevent it from arising.'

'Well, yes,' K. said, 'it's all excellently organised, who still doubts that? But you have expounded it to me in general far too alluringly for me not to exert myself now, with all my strength, to get to know it in detail.'

Bows were exchanged, and K. left. The assistants remained behind to take a special farewell, with whispering and laughter, but soon followed.

At the inn K. found his room beautified to the point of being unrecognisable. This was all the doing of Frieda, who

332

received him with a kiss on the threshold. The room had been thoroughly aired, the stove well stoked up, the floor washed, the bed tidied, the maids' things, including their pictures, had all gone, there was only one new photograph now hanging on the wall over the bed. K. went nearer, pictures . . .

* * *

. . . on the contrary, wherever I wanted, and with the passionate enthusiasm of children, into the bargain. In this hasty walking to and fro I found myself for the moment beside Amalia, gently took the knitting out of her hand and threw it on the table, at which the rest of the family was already sitting. 'What are you doing?' Olga exclaimed. 'Oh,' I said, half angrily, half smiling, 'you all annoy me.' And I sat down in the chimney-corner, taking on my lap a little black cat that had been sleeping there. How much a stranger and yet how much at home I was there, I had not yet shaken hands with the two old people, had scarcely spoken to the girls any more than I had to this new Barnabas, as he here seemed to me to be, and yet I was sitting here in the warmth, unheeded, because I had already quarrelled a little with the girls, and the friendly cat scrambled up my chest on to my shoulder. And even if I had been disappointed here, too, still, it was from here, too, that new hopes came. Barnabas had not gone to the Castle now, but he would go in the morning, and even if that girl from the Castle did not come here, another one would.

* * *

Frieda also waits, but not for K.; she watches the Herrenhof and watches K.; she has no need to worry, her situation is more favourable than she herself expected, she can look on without envy at how Pepi exerts herself, at how Pepi's reputation grows, she will, of course, put a stop to it when the time comes, she can also afford to look on calmly, watching K. knocking about, away from her, she will see to it that he doesn't leave her for good.

4

TWO ADDITIONAL PASSAGES INCLUDED IN THE TEXT OF THE DEFINITIVE GERMAN EDITION

(1). Reference: Fischer edition, p. 197, l. 16, to end of paragraph (over), English, Muir translation, p. 150, l. 15, after 'he, Hans, could see through.'

In fact Hans was now seeking K.'s aid against his father; it was as if he had been deluding himself in believing he wanted to help K., when in reality he had been wanting to discover whether, since nobody in his old surroundings had been able to help, this sudden newcomer, who had now even been mentioned by his mother, might perhaps be capable of doing so. How unconsciously secretive, almost underhand, this boy was. Hitherto it had scarcely been possible to gather this from his appearance and his speech; one observed it only in the confessions wormed out of him as it were after the event, by chance or by deliberation. And now, in long discussions with K., he considered the difficulties that would have to be overcome. With the best of good will on Hans's part, they remained almost insurmountable difficulties; lost in thought and at the same time groping for help, he kept gazing at K. with restlessly blinking eyes. He could not say anything to his mother before his father left, otherwise his father would come to hear of it and the whole plan would be scotched, and so he could only mention it later; but even then, out of consideration for his mother, it could not be mentioned suddenly and startlingly, but must be said slowly and when a suitable opportunity occured; only then could he beg his mother to agree, only then could he fetch K. But would it not be too late by that time, would there not be danger of his father's returning by then? No, it was impossible after all. K., on the contrary, proved that it was not impossible. One need not be afraid that there would not be enough time, a short conversation, a short meeting, would be sufficient, and Hans would not need to fetch K. K. would be in hiding somewhere near the house and would come at once on getting a sign from Hans. No, Hans said, K. must not wait near the house – again it was sensitiveness on his mother's account that dictated his reaction – K. must not start without his mother's knowledge, Hans must not enter into such a secret agreement with K., deceiving his mother; he must fetch K. from the school, and this not before his mother knew of it and gave permission. All right, K. said, then it was really dangerous after all, and then it was possible that Hans's father would catch him in the house; and if this must not happen, then for fear of it Hans's mother would not let K. come at all, and so the whole plan would be frustrated because of his father after all. To this Hans had another objection to make, and so the argument went on and on

(2). Reference: Fischer edition, p. 217, l. 15, to end of paragraph (over), English, Muir translation, p. 165, l. 7, after 'bask in her wrath and nearness.'

His greatest pleasure was to sit beside Gisa, correcting exercises. To-day, again, they were occupied in this way, Schwarzer had brought a great pile of copy-books, the teacher always gave them his as well, and so long as daylight lasted K. had seen the two of them working at a little table in the window, their heads close together, motionless; now all there was to be seen there was the flickering of two candles. It was a solemn, taciturn love that united them; it was indeed Gisa who set the tone, for though her slow-blooded temperament sometimes went wild and broke through all barriers, at other times she would never have tolerated anything of the sort in others; so even the vivacious Schwarzer had to knuckle under, walking slowly, speaking slowly, and often remaining silent; but it was plain that he was richly rewarded for all this by Gisa's mere quiet presence. And yet it was possible that Gisa did not love him at all; at any rate, her round, grey, quite unblinking eyes, in which only the pupils seemed to revolve, gave no answer to such questions; all that could be seen was that she put up with Schwarzer uncomplainingly, but it was certain that she did not appreciate what an honour it was to be loved by a castellan's son, and she bore her plump, voluptuous body in unruffled calm, regardless of whether Schwarzer was following her with his gaze or not. Schwarzer, on the other hand, made a permanent sacrifice for her sake by remaining in the village; messengers from his father, who frequently came to fetch him home, he sent about their business as indignantly as if even the brief reminder of the Castle and of his duty as a son that they constituted were a grave and irreparable injury to his happiness. And yet he actually had plenty of time on his hands, for Gisa generally condescended to see him only during school hours and while correcting exercises, not, it must be admitted, out of calculation, but because what she loved more than anything was being comfortable, which meant being alone, and she was probably happiest when at home she could stretch out on the sofa, entirely at her ease, beside her the cat, which did not disturb her because, indeed, it was scarcely capable of moving any more at all. So Schwarzer spent a large part of the day drifting round without anything to do, but even this suited him, for it meant that he always had the chance, which he very often took, of going down Lion Street, where Gisa lived, going upstairs to her little attic, listening at the ever-locked door, and then hurriedly retreating, after he had every time observed that the most complete and baffling silence reigned within the room. Nevertheless, even in him the consequences of such a mode of life made themselves apparent, sometimes – though never in Gisa's presence – in ludicrous outbursts of a momentarily re-awakened official arrogance, which certainly ill accorded with his present situation; and then, to be sure, things did not usually turn out very well, as K. had seen for himself.

5

THE PASSAGES DELETED BY THE AUTHOR

P. 12, l. 12.

But was it acquaintances he was making? Did he get even a single frank, cordial word? As was indeed necessary. For it was clear to him that wasting only a few days here would make him incapable of ever acting decisively. Nevertheless he must not do anything hasty.

P. 23, l. 5.

But after a moment he regained his composure and said: 'My master wishes to know when he is to come to the Castle to-morrow.' The answer: 'Tell your master, but do not forget a single word of the message: Even if he sends ten assistants to ask when he is to come he will always get the answer: Neither to-morrow nor at any other time.' K. would have best liked to put the receiver down instantly. A conversation like this could not get him anywhere. He must set about it in some other way, this was clear to him, in some way quite different from, for instance, a conversation like this. In this way he was not fighting the others, but only himself. Of course, he had arrived yesterday, and the Castle had been here since ancient times.

P. 30, l. 10.

As K. always had notions with regard to this man that even to him did not seem to be in accordance with reality, as though it were not one man but two, and only K., and not reality, were capable of keeping them distinct from each other, so he now believed that it was not his cunning, but his worried, faintly hopeful face, which he must have recognised

337

even in the night, had induced him to take him along with him. On this his hope was based.

P. 33, l. 14.

K. turned round in order to find his coat, he wanted to put it on, wet as it was, and return to the inn, difficult as it might be. He thought it necessary to confess frankly that he had let himself be deceived, and only returning to the inn seemed to him a sufficient confession of this. Above all, however, he did not want to let any uncertainty arise in his own mind, did not want to lose himself in an enterprise that after such great initial hopes had turned out to be without prospects. He shook off a hand tugging at his sleeve, without looking to see whose hand it was.

Then he heard the old man saying to Barnabas: 'The girl from the Castle was here.' After that they talked together in low voices. K. had by now become so mistrustful that he watched them for a little while in order to make sure whether this remark had not been intentionally made for his benefit. But this was doubtless not the case, the talkative father, now and then supported by the mother, had all sorts of things to tell Barnabas; Barnabas had bent down to him and while listening he smiled across at K., as though he were meant to join him in his delight over his father. Now this K. did not do, but all the same he did look at this smile for a moment in astonishment. Then he turned to the girls and asked: 'Do you know her?' They did not know what he meant, and they were a little disconcerted, too, because he had, without meaning it, uttered his question quickly and sternly. He explained to them that he meant the girl from the Castle. Olga, the more gentle of the two – she even showed a trace of maidenly embarrassment, whereas Amalia looked at him with a serious, straight, unwavering, perhaps even slightly dull gaze – answered: 'The girl from the Castle? Of course we know her. She was here to-day. Do you know her too? I thought you arrived only yesterday.' 'Yesterday, that's right. But I met her to-day, we exchanged a few words, but then we were interrupted. I should like to see her again.' To diminish the effect of what he said, K. added: 'She wanted some advice about something.' But now he found Amalia's gaze irritating, and he said: 'What's the matter with you? Please don't keep on looking at me like that.' But instead of apologising, Amalia only shrugged her shoulders and moved away, went to the table, took up a stocking she was knitting, and took no more notice of K. Olga, in an effort to make up, on her side, for Amalia's bad manners, said: 'She'll probably be coming to see us again to-morrow, then you can talk to her.' 'All right,' K. said, 'so I shall spend the night here; it is true I could also speak to her at Cobbler Lasemann's, but I prefer to stay with you people.' 'At Lasemann's?' 'Yes, that's where I met her.' 'But then it's a misunderstanding, I meant another girl, not the one who was at Lasemann's.' 'If only you'd said so at once!' K. exclaimed and began walking up and down the room, inconsiderately crossing it from one side to the other. A strange mixture these people's behaviour seemed to be: in spite of occasional friendliness they were cold, reserved, and even suspicious, they sometimes turned up treacherously in the name of unknown masters, but all this was at least partially counterbalanced – one could, admittedly, also say made more acute, but K. did not regard it in this way, that was not in keeping with his nature – by awkwardness, by childishly slow and childishly timid thinking, even indeed by a certain docility. If one succeeded in making use of what was obliging in their character and avoiding what was hostile – something, indeed, that required more than ingenuity and for which one probably, alas, needed help even from them – then they would no longer be an obstacle, then they would not thrust K. back any more, as had happened to him all the time up to now, then they would bear him along.

P. 43, l. 20.

K. was thinking more of Klamm than of her. The conquest of Frieda meant making a change in his plans; here he

339

gained a means to power that might make the whole period of work in the village unnecessary.

P. 43, l. 28.

. . . lay then, almost undressed, for each of them had torn open the other's clothes with hands and teeth, in the little puddles of beer.

P. 60, l. 31.

He was, after all, by now well able to play on this departmental machinery, this delicate instrument always tuned for some compromise or other. The art of it lay essentially in doing nothing, leaving the machinery to work by itself and forcing it to work by the mere fact of oneself being there, irremovable in one's ponderous mortality.

P. 66, l. 25. (variant reading).

'Allow me, Mr. Mayor, to interrupt you with a question,' K. said, leaning back comfortably in his chair, but no longer feeling so much at ease as he had previously; the Mayor's mania for imparting information, which he himself had constantly been endeavouring to stimulate, was now too much for him, 'did you not a little while ago mention a Control Authority? . . .'

P. 69, l. 4.

Now I can't go rushing along to the Town Council with every letter from the authorities, but Sordini didn't know of that letter, you know, he denied its existence, and so, of course, I seemed to be put in the wrong.

P. 73, l. 21.

My interpretation is different, I shall stick to it even though I also have quite different weapons, and shall do all I can to get it acknowledged.

P. 87, l. 17.

'In a manner of speaking he was asked,' the landlady said, 'the marriage-certificate bears his signature; by accident, it must be admitted, for he was at that time deputising for the head of another department, that's why it says: "Acting Head of Department, Klamm." I remember how I ran home from the Registrar's office with the document, didn't even take off my wedding-dress, sat down at the table, spread out the document, read that dear name again and again, and with the childish eagerness of my seventeen years tried to imitate the signature, tried very hard, covering whole sheets of paper with writing, and never noticed that Hans was standing behind my chair, not daring to disturb me, and watching me at my work. Unfortunately then, when the document had been signed by everyone concerned, it had to be handed in to the Municipality.'

'Well,' K. said, 'I didn't mean an enquiry like that, indeed nothing official at all, it is not Klamm the official one must speak to, but the private person. The official aspect of things here is mostly wrong, you see; for instance, if to-day you had only seen the Municipal Records on the floor, as I did! And among them, perhaps, your beloved certificate, always assuming that it is not kept in the barn where the rats are – I think you would have agreed with me.'

P. 87, l. 37.

Perhaps it is also a legend, besides, but then it is certainly one that is invented only by those who have been abandoned, as a consolation for their life.

P. 88, l. 30.

'Gladly,' K. said. 'And so here now is what I am going to say. I could put it more or less like this: "We, Frieda and I, love each other and want to marry as soon as possible. Yet Frieda loves not only me, but you too, though admittedly in quite a different way, it is not my fault that language is so poor that it has only one word for both. Frieda herself does

341

not understand how it comes about that there is room in her heart for me too, and she can only think that it became possible solely by your will. After everything I have heard from Frieda, I can only associate myself with her view. However, it is only an assumption, apart from which the only thing I can think of is that I, a stranger, a nonentity, as the landlady calls me, have pushed my way in between Frieda and you. In order to have certainty on this point I take the liberty of asking you how the matter stands in reality." That, then, would be the first question; I think it would be respectful enough.'

The landlady sighed. 'Oh, what a person you are,' she said, 'seemingly clever enough, but at the same time abysmally ignorant. You think you can negotiate with Klamm as if he were your fiancée's father, more or less as if you had fallen in love with Olga – unfortunately you haven't – you would have spoken to old Barnabas. What a wise disposition of things it is that you will never have a chance to talk to Klamm.'

'This interpolation,' K. said, 'I should not have heard during my conversation with him, which in any case would have to be conducted *tête-à-tête*, and therefore I should not have had to let myself be influenced by it. As regards his answer, however, there are three possibilities. Either he will say: "It was not my will," or: "It was my will," or he will say nothing. The first possibility I am provisionally excluding from my speculations, partly, I must say, out of consideration for you; his saying nothing, however, I should interpret as agreement.'

'There are yet other possibilities, and very much more plausible ones,' the landlady said, 'if I do enter into your fairy-story idea of such a meeting at all, for instance, the possibility that he goes off and leaves you standing there.'

'That would change nothing,' K. said. 'I should step in his way and compel him to hear me.'

'Compel him to hear you!' the landlady said. 'Compel the lion to eat straw! What deeds of heroism!'

'Always so irritable, Landlady,' K. said. 'But I am only answering your questions, I am not forcing confidences on you. In any case, we are not talking about a lion at all, we are talking about the head of a department, and if I take the lion's lioness away from him and marry her, I suppose I shall at any rate have so much significance in his eyes that he will at least listen to me.'

P. 88, l. 30.

'You are lost, here among us, Land Surveyor,' the landlady said, 'everything you say is full of misconceptions. Perhaps Frieda, as your wife, will be able to support you here, but it is almost too hard a task for that frail little thing. And she knows it, too; when she thinks there is nobody watching her, she sighs and her eyes are full of tears. True, my husband is a burden to me too, but after all, he doesn't try to take the helm, and even if he did try, he might do something stupid, I dare say, but, as a native, nothing, after all, that would be ruinous; but you are full of very dangerous misconceptions and you will never lose them. Klamm as a private person. Who has ever seen Klamm as a private person? Who can imagine him as a private person? You can, you will object, but there you are, that's precisely the misfortune. You can do it because you can't imagine him as an official, because you simply can't imagine him at all. Because Frieda was Klamm's mistress, you think she saw him as a private person, because we love him, you think we love him as a private person. Now, one cannot say of a real official that he is sometimes more and sometimes less of an official, for he is always an official, to full capacity. But in order at least to give you a clue to understanding I shall this time disregard it, and then I can say: Never was he more of an official than then at the time of my happiness, and I and Frieda are unanimous in this: we love no one but the official Klamm, the high, the exceedingly high, official.'

343

P. 102, l. 33.

And yet, when K. saw her sitting there, on Frieda's chair, beside the room . . . perhaps still harboured Klamm to-day, her little fat feet on the floor on which he had lain with Frieda, here in the Herrenhof, in the house of these gentlemen, the officials, he could not but say to himself that if he had met Pepi here instead of Frieda and supposed her to have some kind of connections with the Castle – and probably she too had such connections – he would have tried to clutch the secret to himself with the same embraces by means of which he had had to do it in Frieda's case. In spite of her childish mind etc.

P. 104, l. 23.

Now he had nothing to do but wait here. Klamm had to come past here; he would perhaps be a little taken aback to see K. here, but he would be all the more likely to listen to him, perhaps even to answer him. One needn't take the prohibitions here too seriously. This, then, was the point K. had reached. True, he was only allowed to enter the tap-room, but nevertheless here he was, right in the courtyard, standing only a pace away from Klamm's sledge, soon to be face to face with him, and was enjoying his food better than anywhere else.

Suddenly light came on everywhere, the electric light was burning indoors in the passage and on the stairs, out-side over all the entrances, and the expanse of snow made it seem more brilliant still. All this was disagreeable to K., he stood there, as it were exposed, on the spot that had up to now been so peacefully dark, but on the other hand this seemed to signify that now Klamm would appear, of course it could have been assumed all along that he could not grope his way down the stairs in the dark in order to make K.'s task easier. Unfortunately it was not Klamm who came first, but the landlord, followed by the landlady, they came, slightly stooping, out of the depths of the passage, they too could have been expected, of course they put in an appearance in order to take leave of such a guest. This, however, made it necessary for K. to withdraw a little into the shadow, so giving up the good view he had had of the staircase.

P. 108, l. 22.

K. saw no reason to do that, let them abandon him, there almost arose new hope; the fact that the horses were being unyoked was, admittedly, a sad sign, but the gate was still there, open, could not be locked, was a perpetual promise and a perpetual expectation. Then he heard someone on the stairs again, cautiously and hastily he stepped forward, setting one foot inside the hall, instantly prepared to step back, and looked up. To his amazement it was the landlady from the Bridge Inn. She came down thoughtfully but calmly, regularly lifting her hand from the banisters and putting it down again. She said good-evening to him pleasantly when she arrived at the bottom; here on alien territory the old quarrel apparently did not have to be kept up.

What did K. care for the gentleman! Let him go away, the faster the better; it was a victory for K., only unfortunately one that could not be exploited, when at the same time the sledge went away, which he sadly watched going. 'If,' he exclaimed, turning round to the gentleman with sudden resolution, 'if I go away from here now, instantly, is the sledge permitted to come back?' While he was saying this K. did not believe he was giving way to a compulsion – otherwise he would not have done it – but felt as if he were renouncing something in favour of a weaker person and as if he were entitled to be slightly pleased about his own good deed. True, from the gentleman's hectoring answer he did at once realise in what a state of emotional confusion he must be, if he believed he was acting of his own free will; of his own free will, since he was at this moment, after all, invoking the gentleman's injunction. 'The sledge is permitted to come back,' the gentleman said, 'but only if you come along with me instantly, without delay, without making any conditions, without going back on it. Well, how about it? I ask for the last time. I assure you, it is not really my function to keep order here in the courtyard.' 'I am going,' K. said, 'but not with you; I am going through the gate here' – he pointed to the big gate of the courtyard – 'into the street!' 'Very well,' the gentleman said, again with that tormenting mixture of indulgence and harshness, 'then I shall go that way too. But now look sharp.'

The gentleman came back to K., they walked side by side across the middle of the courtyard, over the untrodden snow; looking back for a moment, the gentleman made a sign to the driver, who once more drove up to the entrance, once more climbed up on to the box, and doubtless resumed his waiting. But so, to the gentleman's annoyance, did K., for scarcely was he outside the courtyard than he stopped again. 'You are insufferably obstinate,' the gentleman said. But K., who, the further away he was from the sledge, the witness of his crime, felt more and more at ease, more and more firmly linked with his goal, more nearly the gentleman's equal, indeed even in a certain sense superior to him, turned right round to face him and said: 'Is that true? Aren't you trying to deceive me? Insufferably obstinate? I wish for nothing better.'

At this moment K. felt a faint tickling at the back of his neck, tried to brush off whatever caused it, struck out backwards with his hand, and turned round. The sledge! K. must have been still in the courtyard and already the sledge had driven off, soundless in the deep snow, without bells, without lights, had now skimmed past K., and the driver had for fun flicked K. with the whip. The horses – noble beasts that he had not been able to appreciate properly while they stood waiting – were already turning in the direction of the Castle, wheeling sharply, with a great yet easy tightening of all their muscles and without slowing up; no sooner had one become aware of what was happening than it had all disappeared in the darkness.

The gentleman pulled out his watch and said reproachfully: 'And that makes two hours Klamm has had to wait.'

'On my account?' K. asked. 'Well, yes, of course,' the gentleman said. 'You mean he can't endure the sight of me?' K. asked. 'Yes,' the gentleman said, 'it is something he cannot endure. But now I am going home,' he added. 'You simply cannot imagine how much work I have waiting for me there; I am, you see, Klamm's local secretary. Momus is my name. Klamm is a tremendous worker, and those who are in close contact with him have to emulate him, in accordance with their powers.' The gentleman had become very talkative, indeed he would probably have enjoyed answering all sorts of questions from K., but K. remained dumb, he only seemed to be closely scrutinising the secretary's face, as though he were trying to discover a law according to which a face had to be formed so that Klamm could endure it. But he found nothing and turned away, taking no notice of the secretary's farewell and pausing only to watch him elbowing his way into the courtyard through a cavalcade of people who were coming out, evidently Klamm's servants. These people were walking in twos, but otherwise without keeping in rank or in step, chatting and now and then putting their heads together as they passed K. The gate was slowly closed after them. K. felt a great need of warmth, of light, of a friendly word, and probably all this was waiting for him at the school, but he could not help feeling that he would not find the way home in his present condition, quite apart from the fact that he was now standing in a street he did not know. Besides, his goal was not sufficiently alluring; when he pictured to himself in the fairest colours everything that he would find on his arrival home, he realised that to-day it would not suffice him. Well, he could not stay here, and so he pressed on again.

P. 118, l. 36.

K. was not afraid of the landlady's threats. The hopes with which she was trying to ensnare him meant little to him, but the protocol was now beginning to be alluring to him, after all. Yet the protocol was not without significance;

not in the sense in which she meant it, but in a general sense, the landlady was right in saying that K. must not give up anything. That had always been K.'s opinion too, whenever he had not happened to be weakened by disappointment, as he had been to-day after his experience in the afternoon. But now he was gradually recovering, the landlady's attacks were giving him new strength, for even though she kept on ceaselessly talking about his ignorance and unteachability, the mere fact of her agitation proved how important it was to her to teach him, him of all people; and even though she tried to humiliate him by the manner in which she answered him, nevertheless, the blind zeal with which she did so was evidence of the power that his little questions had over her. Was he to give up this influence? And his influence on Momus was perhaps still stronger; true, Momus talked little, and when he did talk, he liked to shout, but was this taciturnity not caution, did he not wish, say, to be sparing with his authority, was it not for this purpose that he had brought the landlady with him, the lady who, since she had no official responsibility to bear, was not tied, and, her attitude being conditioned only by whatever K.'s attitude happened to be, would try, now with sweet, now with bitter, words to lure him into the snares of the record? And what were the facts of the situation where this protocol was concerned? Certainly it did not extend as far as Klamm, but was there no work for K. before Klamm, on the way to Klamm? Was not precisely this afternoon proof of the fact that anyone who believed he could, say, reach Klamm by taking a leap in the dark was after all seriously underestimating the distance separating him from Klamm? If it was at all possible to reach Klamm, then only step by step, and admittedly on this way there were also to be found, for instance, Momus and the landlady; was it not only these two, after all, at least outwardly, who had to-day kept K. from Klamm? First the landlady, who had announced K.'s arrival, and then Momus, who had looked out of the window to make sure it was K. coming and who had instantly issued the necessary orders so that even the driver was informed that the departure could not take place before K. had gone and who had therefore, at that time incomprehensibly to K., reproachfully complained that to judge by all appearances it might yet be a very long time before K. went away. In this way, then, everything had been arranged, although, as the landlady had almost had to admit, it was not Klamm's sensitiveness, about which people enjoyed spreading stories, that could be an obstacle to K.'s being admitted to his presence. Who knows what would have happened if the landlady and Momus had not been K.'s antagonists or at least had not dared to show that antagonism? It was possible and probable that even then K. would not have got to Klamm, new obstacles would have appeared, there was perhaps an inexhaustible supply of them, but K. would have had the satisfaction of having organised everything properly to the best of his knowledge, whereas to-day he should have been on his guard against the landlady's interference and yet had done nothing to protect himself from it. But K. only knew of the mistakes he had made; how they might have been avoided he did not know. His first intention, when confronted with Klamm's letter, that of becoming an ordinary, unnoticed workman in the village, had been very sensible. But he had necessarily had to abandon it when Barnabas's deceptive appearance had caused him to believe he could get into the Castle as easily as one can get to the top of a hill, say, on a little Sunday walk, more indeed, that he was positively being encouraged to do so by the smile, by the look in the eyes, of that messenger. And then immediately, before there was any time to think, Frieda had come, and with her the belief, which it was impossible to give up entirely even to-day, that through her mediation an almost physical relationship to Klamm, a relationship so close that it amounted almost to a whispering form of communication, had come about, of which for the present only K. knew, which however needed only a little intervention, a word, a glance, in order to reveal itself primarily to Klamm, but then too to everyone, as something admittedly incredible which was nevertheless, through the compulsion of life, the compulsion of the loving embrace, a matter of course. Well, it had not been so simple and, instead of temporarily contenting himself with being a workman, K. had for a long time been groping about and was still groping about, impatiently and vainly, for Klamm. But nevertheless, almost without his doing anything about it, other possibilities had presented themselves: at home the small position as janitor of the school – perhaps it was not the right job, regarded in the light of K.'s own wishes, being too closely modelled on K.'s particular circumstances, too striking, too provisional, too much dependent on the graciousness of many superiors, above all on that of the teacher, but it was nevertheless a solid starting-point, and, besides, the deficiencies of the position were being much improved through the imminent marriage, which K. had hitherto scarcely touched on in his thoughts, but the whole importance of which now became surprisingly clear to him for the first time. What, after all, was he without Frieda? A nonentity, staggering along after silkily shining will-o'-the-wisps of the sort that Barnabas was, or that girl from the Castle. With Frieda's love, admittedly, he was still not conquering Klamm as by a *coup-de-main*, only in a state of delusion had he believed that or almost known it, and even though these expectations were still present, as though no refutation by facts could make any difference to them, nevertheless he no longer meant to count on them in his plans. Nor did he need them any more; by the marriage he was gaining another, better kind of security – member of the community – rights and duties – no longer a stranger –, then he only needed to beware of the complacency of all these people, an easy matter with the Castle before his eyes. What was more difficult was knuckling under, humble work among humble people; he wanted to begin by submitting to the taking of the statement. Then he changed the subject, perhaps he could get at the truth from another side; as though there had not yet been any difference of opinion, he asked calmly: 'All that has been written about the afternoon? All these papers are concerned with that?' 'All of them,' Momus said pleasantly, as though he had been waiting for this question, 'it is my work.' If one has the strength to look at things unceasingly, so to speak without blinking, one sees a great deal; but if one falters only once and shuts one's eyes, everything instantly slips away into darkness. 'Couldn't I have a look into them?' K. asked. Momus began leafing through the papers as if he were looking to see whether there was anything that could be shown to K., then he said: 'No, I'm afraid it's not possible.' 'The impression this makes on me,' K. said, 'is that there must be things there that I could refute.' 'Things you could make great endeavours to refute,' Momus said. 'Yes, there are such things there.' And he took up a blue pencil and, smiling, heavily underlined several lines. 'I am not curious,' K. said. 'Just go on underlining things, Mr. Secretary, as long as you like. No matter what hideous things you have written down about me, at your leisure, all unchecked. What is filed in the records does not bother me. I was only thinking that there might be a number of things there that would be instructive for me, which would show me how an experienced official of long standing arrives at a critical view of me, honestly and in detail. That is something I should have liked to read, for I always like to learn, I do not like making mistakes, I do not like causing annoyance.' 'And I like playing the innocent,' the landlady said. 'You just do what the Secretary tells you and your wishes will be partly granted. From the questions you will at least indirectly learn something of what is in the protocol and through your answers you will be able to influence the spirit of the whole protocol.' 'I have too much respect for the Secretary,' K. said, 'to be able to believe that he would reveal to me against his will, through his questions, whatever he has once decided to conceal from me. Besides, I have no desire to provide a certain, even though perhaps only formal, substantiation of points that are perhaps incorrect, accusing me incorrectly, by answering at all and allowing my answers to be incorporated into the hostile text.'

Momus glanced up reflectively at the landlady. 'Well then, let's pack up our papers,' he said. 'We have delayed long enough, the Land Surveyor cannot complain of our being impatient. What was it the Land Surveyor said? "I have too much respect for the Secretary, and so on." So the excessively great respect that he has for me renders him speechless. Could I diminish it, I should get the answers. Unfortunately, however, I must increase it by confessing that these files do not require his answers, since they are not in need either of supplementation or of emendation, but that he himself is very much in need of the protocol, and indeed both of the questions and of the answers and that if I tried to persuade him to give his answers this was only in his own interest. Now, however, when I leave this room, the protocol also passes out of his reach for ever and will never be opened before him again.' The landlady nodded slowly to K., and said: 'I knew this of course, but I was only permitted to hint at it, and did do my best to hint at it, but you did not understand me. There in the courtyard you waited in vain for Klamm, and here in the protocol you have made Klamm wait in vain. How muddled, how muddled you are!' The landlady had tears in her eyes. 'Well,' K. said, influenced above all by these tears, 'for the moment, after all, the Secretary is still here, and so is the protocol.' 'But I am going now,' the secretary said, stuffing the papers into the brief-case and standing up. 'Are you going to answer now, at last, Land Surveyor?' the landlady asked. 'Too late,' the secretary said, 'it's high time for Pepi to open the gate, it's long past the hour for the servants.' For a long time now there had been a knocking at the gate, Pepi was standing there with her hand on the bolt, waiting only for the end of the interview with K., in order then to open it immediately. 'All right, open the gate, my dear!' the secretary said, and through the gate there came pushing, and elbowing each other aside, men of the sort K. already knew, in their earth-coloured uniform. They looked angry because they had had to wait for so long, they took no notice of K., the landlady, and the secretary, pushing past them as though they were only customers like themselves, it was fortunate that the secretary already had the papers in the brief-case under his arm, for the little table was knocked over the moment the crowd came in and it had not yet been stood up again, the men keeping on stepping over it, solemnly, as though it must be like this. Only the secretary's beer-glass had instantly been saved, one of them had appropriated it, with a jubilant, gurgling cry, and had hurried with it to Pepi, who, however, had already quite vanished in the crowd of men. All that could be seen was how around Pepi upstretched arms were pointing at the clock on the wall, it was being conveyed to her what a great wrong she had done these people by opening so late. But although she was not to blame for the delay, for which actually K. was to blame, even though not of his own will, Pepi did not seem to be capable of justifying herself to them, it was really difficult for one of her youth and inexperience to cope with these people in a more or less rational way. How Frieda, in Pepi's place, would have lashed out and shaken them all off! But Pepi did not emerge from among them at all; this, however, did not exactly suit the people, who above all wanted to be served with beer. But the crowd could not control itself and deprived itself of the very pleasure for which all of them were so greedy. Always the throng, heaving this way and that, kept pushing the slight girl about with it, and though Pepi held out bravely, in that she did not scream, there was nothing to be seen or heard of her. And always more people kept coming in through the gate of the courtyard, the room was now packed, the secretary could not go away, he could not get either to the door into the hall or to the door into the courtyard, the three of them stood jammed up close together, the landlady holding the secretary's arm, K. opposite them and pressed up against the secretary in such a way that their faces were almost touching. But neither the secretary nor the landlady was surprised or annoyed about the crowd, they accepted it like an ordinary natural phenomenon, trying only to guard themselves from being pushed about all too violently, leaning back into the crowd or yielding to the current when need be, bowing their heads when it was necessary in order to escape from the puffing and blowing of the men who were all the time discontentedly surging about, but apart from that they looked calm and a little abstracted. Being as near as he now was to the secretary and the landlady and being allied with them, in one group, over against the other people in the room, even though they did not seem to acknowledge this, K.'s whole relation to them in his own mind was changed, all the official, the personal element, the element of social distinctions, between them, seemed to him to be removed or at least for the present suspended. Nor could the protocol now be in any way out of K.'s reach. 'Now you can't get out anyway,' K. said to the secretary. 'No, not for the moment,' the latter replied. 'And how about the protocol?' K. asked. 'That stays in the brief-case,' Momus said. 'I should like to have a bit of a look at it,' K. said, involuntarily reaching out for the case and even getting hold of one end of it. 'No, no,' the secretary said and pulled it away from him. 'What on earth are you doing?' the landlady said and gave K.'s hand a little slap. 'You don't think, surely, you could get back by force what you have once lost through frivolity and arrogance? Wicked, dreadful man! Do you really suppose the protocol would still have any value once it was in your hands? It would be a flower plucked in the meadow.' 'But it would be destroyed,' K. said. 'How would it be if now, when I am no longer allowed to make a voluntary statement for incorporation in the protocol, I were to set out at least to destroy the protocol? I have a strong inclination to do so,' and he now resolutely pulled the case from under the secretary's arm and took possession of it. The secretary let him have it without more ado;

354

indeed, he loosened his hold so quickly that the case would have fallen to the floor if K. had not instantly reached out with his other hand. 'Why only now?' the secretary asked. 'You could have taken it by force at once.' 'It is force against force,' K. said. 'You have no justification for now refusing me the interrogation you previously offered, or at least to let me have a look into the papers. I have taken the case only in order to insist on one or the other of these things.' 'But as a pledge,' the secretary said smilingly. And the landlady said: 'Taking pledges is something he's pretty good at. You've already proved that in the files, Mr. Secretary. Couldn't he be shown just that one page?' 'Certainly,' Momus said, 'now he can be shown it.' K. held out the case, the landlady rummaged about in it, but evidently could not find the page. She stopped searching, saying, in exhaustion, only that it must be page ten. Now K. looked for it and found it at once, the landlady took it in order to make sure that it was the right one; yes, it was the right one. She glanced through it once for her own amusement, the secretary, leaning on her arm, reading at the same time. Then she handed it to K., who read: 'The Land Surveyor K. first of all had to endeavour to establish himself in the village. This was not easy, since no one needed his work. Nobody, except the landlord of the Bridge Inn, whom he had taken unawares, wanted to take him in, nobody bothered about him – apart from some jokes on the part of the officials. So he roamed about in a seemingly aimless way, doing nothing but disturb the peace of the place. In reality however he was very busy; he was on the look-out for an opportunity to get a foothold, and soon found one. Frieda, the young barmaid in the tap-room at the Herrenhof, believed in his promises and let herself be seduced by him. It is not easy to prove the guilt of Land Surveyor K. The fact is that one can only see what tricks he is up to if one forces oneself, however distressing it may be, to follow his train of thought exactly. In doing so one must not let oneself be misled if one finds oneself brought face to face

355

with what looks, on the surface, like a piece of unbelievable wickedness, on the contrary, if one has reached that stage, then one can be sure of not having gone astray, only then has one arrived at the right point. Let us take for instance the case of Frieda. It is clear that the Land Surveyor does not love Frieda and is not marrying her for love, he knows perfectly well that she is a plain, insignificant, overbearing girl, with a disreputable past into the bargain, and he treats her accordingly and roams around without bothering about her. That is a statement of the position. This now could be interpreted in various ways, to make K. appear a weak or a stupid or a noble or an infamous person. But none of this is in fact so. One can arrive at the truth only by exactly following in his footsteps, which we have traced here, starting with his arrival and continuing up to his affair with Frieda. Once the hair-raising truth has been discovered, it admittedly still remains necessary to accustom oneself to believing it, but there is no other choice.

'It was out of calculation of the lowest sort that K. attached himself to Frieda, and he will not let her go as long as he still has any hope at all that his calculations are correct. The fact is he believed that in her he had made the conquest of a mistress of the head of the department, and that he is therefore in possession of a pledge for which he can demand the highest price. His sole endeavour now is to negotiate about this price with the head of the department. Since he is not in the least interested in Frieda, and exclusively interested in the price, he is prepared to make any sort of concession with regard to Frieda herself, whereas he is certain to be stubborn with regard to the price. Though for the present he is, apart from the repulsiveness of his assumptions and his offers, quite harmless, when he realises how gravely he has been mistaken and how he has exposed himself he may even become extremely unpleasant, of course within the limits set by his insignificance.'

Here the page ended. The only other thing was, in the margin, a childishly scrawled drawing, a man with a girl in his arms. The girl's face was buried in the man's chest, but the man, who was much the taller, was looking over the girl's shoulder at a sheet of paper he had in his hands and on which he was joyfully inscribing some figures. When K. glanced up from this page he was standing in the middle of the room alone with the landlady and the secretary. The landlord had come and had evidently restored order meanwhile. With his hands raised appeasingly, in his usual urbane manner, he walked along the walls, where the men had already settled down, as well as they could, each of them with his beer, on the barrels or on the floor beside them. Now too it could be seen that there were not so overwhelmingly many of them as it had at first seemed; it had only seemed so bad because they had all been scrambling around Pepi. There was a small, wild group of men who had not yet been served still standing round Pepi; Pepi must have achieved superhuman feats in the most difficult circumstances, true, there were still tears coursing down her cheeks, her beautiful plait had come undone and was tousled, her dress was actually torn open at the bodice, so that her shift showed, but, unconcerned about herself, probably influenced, too, by the landlord's presence, she worked away untiringly at the beer-taps. At the touching sight of it K. forgave her all the annoyance she had caused him. 'Yes, the page,' he said then, put it back into the case and handed the case to the secretary. 'Excuse the hastiness with which I took the case from you. It was partly the crowd and also the excitement that were to blame. Well, I am sure you do excuse it. Apart from that, both you and the landlady here have a special capacity for arousing my curiosity, as I must frankly confess. But the page has disappointed me. It is really a very ordinary meadow-flower, as the landlady said. Well, regarded as work, it may of course have a certain official value, but for me it is merely gossip, trumped-up, empty, sad, womanish gossip, indeed, the writer of it must have had a woman to help him. Well, I assume there is at any rate still enough justice here for me to be able to lodge a complaint about this piece of handiwork with some department or other, but I shall not do that; not only because it is too pitiable, but because I am grateful to you. You contrived to make the protocol seem a little queer to me, but now it has completely lost its queerness. All that still strikes me as queer is the fact that such things should ever have been meant to be made the basis of an interrogation and that even Klamm's name should have been misused for that purpose.' 'If I were your enemy,' the landlady said, 'I could not have wished for anything better than that you should take such a view of this page.' 'Ah yes,' K. said, 'you are not my enemy. For my sake you even let Frieda be slandered.' 'You don't really mean to say you believe that what it says there is my opinion of Frieda!' the landlady exclaimed. 'It's your own opinion of her. That is simply the way you look down on the poor child.' To this K. made no reply, for this now was nothing but abuse. The secretary did his best to conceal his delight at having the brief-case restored to him, but could not do so; he gazed at the case, smiling, as though it were not his own but a new one that he had just been presented with and which he could not gaze his fill of. As though it radiated some special, beneficial warmth, he held it clutched to his chest. He even took out the page K. had read, on the pretext of putting it back more tidily, and read it once again. Only this reading, during which he hailed each word with the happy air of one greeting a dear long-lost friend surprisingly encountered, seemed to assure him that he had really regained possession of the protocol for good. He would really have liked to show it to the landlady too so that she could also read it again. K. left the two of them to each other, he scarcely glanced at them, there was far too great a discrepancy between the importance they had up till now had for him and their present insignificance. How they stood there together, those two collaborators, each helping the other with their miserable secrets!

P. 136, l. 32.

'I know,' Frieda said suddenly, 'it would be better for you if I left you. But it would break my heart if I had to do it. And yet I would do it, if it were possible, but it is not possible, and I am glad of it, at any rate it is not possible here in the village. Just as the assistants can't go away either. It's no use your hoping you've driven them away for good!' 'Frankly, that's what I do hope,' K. said, without taking any notice of Frieda's other remarks, some feeling of uncertainty prevented him from doing so, the weak hands and wrists now slowly working at the coffee-mill seemed to him more sad than ever. 'The assistants aren't coming back any more. And what are these impossibilities you're talking about?'

Frieda had stopped working. She looked at K. with a gaze blurred by tears. 'Dearest,' she said, 'understand me rightly. It is not I who have ordained all these things, I am explaining it to you only because you insist and because in this way too I can justify a number of things about my own behaviour that you cannot otherwise understand and cannot reconcile with my love for you. As a stranger you have no right to anything here, perhaps here we are particularly strict or unjust towards strangers, I don't know, but there it is, you have no right to anything. A local person, for instance, when he needs assistants, takes such people on, and when he is grown up and wants to marry, he takes himself a wife. The authorities have a great deal of influence in these matters too, but in the main everyone is free to decide for himself. But you, as a stranger, have to make do with what you are given; if it pleases the authorities to do so, they give you assistants, if it pleases them to do so, they give you a wife. Even this, of course, is not merely arbitrary, but it is a matter solely for the authorities to decide, and this means that the reasons for the decision remain hidden. Now you can perhaps refuse what you are given, I don't know for sure, perhaps you can refuse; but if you have once accepted it, then upon it and consequently upon you too there weighs the pressure of the authorities; only if the authorities so will can it be taken from you again, and in no other manner. So I have been told by the landlady, from whom I have all this, she said she must open my eyes for me about various things before I marry. And she particularly emphasised the fact that everyone who knows about such things advises the stranger to put up with such presents once they have been accepted, since one can never succeed in shaking them off; the only thing one can achieve, she said, is to turn the things given, which at the very worst do still have a trace of friendliness about them, into life-long enemies that can never be shaken off. That is what the landlady told me, I am only repeating what she said; the landlady knows everything, and she must be believed.'

'Some things she says can be believed,' K. said.

P. 141, l. 35.

'It isn't the cat that frightens me, but my bad conscience. And if the cat drops on me, I feel as if someone had poked me in the chest, as a sign that I've been seen through.' Frieda let go of the curtain, shut the inner window, and pleadingly drew K. towards the sack of straw. 'And it isn't the cat I go looking for then with the candle, but it's you I want to wake quickly. That's how it is, darling, darling.' 'They are messengers of Klamm's,' K. said, drawing Frieda closer to him and kissing her on the nape of her neck, so that a tremor ran through her and she leapt up, throwing herself on him, and both then slid to the floor and fumbled at each other hastily, breathlessly, anxiously, as though each were trying to hide in the other, as though the pleasure they were experiencing belonged to some third person whom they were depriving of it. 'Shall I open the door?' K. asked. 'Will you run to them?' 'No!' Frieda screamed, clutching his arm. 'I don't want to go to them, I want to stay with you. Protect me, keep me with you.' 'But,' K. said, 'if they are messengers of Klamm's, as you say they are, what help can doors be, what help can my protection be, and if they

360

could be of help, would such help really be a good thing?'
'I don't know who they are,' Frieda said. 'I call them messengers because after all Klamm is your superior and the
department sent the assistants to you; that's all I know,
nothing else. Dearest, take them back again, don't sin
against him who perhaps sent them.' K. freed himself from
Frieda's grip and said: 'The assistants are going to stay outside, I don't want them in my proximity any more. What?
You suggest those two have the capacity to lead me to
Klamm? I doubt that. And if they could, I should not have
the capacity to follow them; indeed, the mere fact of their
proximity would rob me of the capacity to find my way
about here. They confuse me and, as I now discover, you
too, unfortunately. I have given you the choice between
myself and them, you have chosen me, now leave everything else to me. This very day I hope to receive decisive
news. They began it all by drawing you away from me,
whether guiltily or innocently makes no difference to me.
Do you really think, Frieda, I should have opened the door
for you, making the way free for you?'

P. 164, l. 16.
Incidentally, it had looked as though the work were a
pleasure to Frieda, as though she especially enjoyed any sort
of dirty and strenuous work, any work that taxed her
strength to the utmost, keeping her from thinking and
dreaming.

P. 165, l. 6 (immediately after passage now first printed,
pp. 335-337).
Now the candles were extinguished indoors, and at the
same instant Gisa appeared at the front door; evidently she
had left the room while there was still light there, for she
attached much importance to respectability. Schwarzer soon
followed, and now they set out on their way, which to their
pleased surprise was clear of snow. When they reached K.,
Schwarzer slapped him on the back. 'If you keep things tidy

in the house here,' he said, 'you can count on me. But I have heard grave complaints about you, on account of your behaviour this morning.' 'He's improving,' Gisa said, without glancing at K. or stopping at all. 'I must say, the fellow certainly needs to,' Schwarzer said and hurried on in order not to lose contact with Gisa.

P. 183, l. 24.

'Now I don't understand you, Olga,' K. said. 'I only know that I envy Barnabas for all these things that strike you as so terrible. I admit it would be better still if everything he has were established beyond doubt, but even if he is in the most worthless of all the ante-chambers of the offices, still, he is at least there in that ante-chamber; how far beneath him he has left, for instance, the chimney-corner in which we are sitting. It surprises me that though you can pretend to appreciate this, in order to comfort Barnabas, you don't really seem to understand it in your own mind. At the same time – and this makes it even more difficult for me to understand you – you seem to be the one who spurs Barnabas on in all his endeavours, something, by the way, that I should never even have dreamt of supposing after that first evening when we met.' 'You misjudge me,' Olga said, 'I don't do any spurring, oh no; if what Barnabas does were not necessary I should be the first who would try to hold him back and keep him here always. For isn't it time for him to marry and set up house for himself? And instead of that he is frittering his powers away between his handicraft and being a messenger, standing in front of the desk up there, on the look-out for a glance from the official who looks like Klamm, and in the end gets an old dusty letter that is no good to anyone and only causes confusion in the world.' 'But that is yet another and quite different question,' K. said. 'The fact that the errands on which Barnabas is sent are worthless or harmful may be grounds for a charge against the department and may, furthermore, be a very bad thing for those to whom such messages are sent, as, for instance, for me, but after all it does no harm to Barnabas, he merely carries the messages to and fro according to orders, often not even knowing what is in them, himself remaining beyond reproach as an official messenger, just as it is the wish of you all.' 'Well, yes,' Olga said, 'perhaps it is like that. Sometimes when I sit here alone – Barnabas at the Castle, Amalia in the kitchen, our poor parents dozing over there, I take up Barnabas's cobbling work and set about it with my extremely inexpert hands, then I lay it down again and begin thinking, helpless, because I am alone and I am very far from having the understanding to cope with these things – then everything merges with everything else in my mind, not even the fear and the worries remain distinct.' 'And why then do they despise you all?' K. asked and remembered the ugly impression this stocky, broad-backed family had made on him the very first evening, all gathered round the table by the light of the little oil-lamp, one back beside the other and the two old people with their little heads almost drooping into the soup, waiting to be fed. How revolting all that had been, and all the more revolting because this impression could not be explained by details, for though one listed the details in order to have something to hold on to, they were not bad, it was something else about it all that one could not put a name to. Only after K. had discovered various things here in the village that had made him cautious about first impressions, and not only about first impressions either, but about second and even later impressions, and only after the entity this family was had for him dissolved into separate persons whom he could partially understand but with whom, above all, he could feel, as with friends, such as he had otherwise not found anywhere here in this village – only now did that old revulsion begin to fade, but it had not yet completely gone. The parents in their corner, the little oil-lamp, the room itself – it was not easy to endure all this calmly, and one needed to get some gift in return, such as Olga's story was, in order to reconcile oneself to it a little, and then only seemingly and only provisionally. And thinking of this he added: 'I am now convinced that you are all being done an injustice, I may as well say that at once. But, though I don't know the reason, it must be difficult not to do you an injustice. One must be a stranger in my special situation in order to remain free of this prejudice. And I myself was for a long time influenced by it, so much influenced by it that the mood prevailing where you are concerned – it is not only contempt, there is fear mixed with it too – seemed a matter of course to me, I did not think about it, I did not enquire into the causes, I did not in the least try to defend you all, indeed the whole thing had nothing to do with me. Now however I see it quite differently. Now I believe that the people who despise you are not merely hushing up the causes, but really do not know them; one has to get to know you all, particularly you, Olga, in order to free oneself from the prevailing delusion. What is held against you is obviously nothing but the fact that you are aiming higher than others; the fact that Barnabas has become a Castle messenger, or is trying to become one, is something for which people bear you a grudge; in order to avoid having to admire you, they despise you, and they do it with such intensity that even you yourselves are defeated by it. For what else are your worries, your timidity, your doubts, but the consequence of that universal contempt?' Olga smiled, and she gazed at K. in a way that was so shrewd and bright-eyed that he was almost disconcerted, it was as though he had said something wildly mistaken and as though Olga must now begin arguing with him and clearing up the mistakes and as though she were very happy about this task. And the question why everyone was against this family seemed to K. to be again unsolved and to be very much in need of a clear answer. 'No,' Olga said, 'that is not the way it is, our situation is not so favourable, you are trying to make up for having hitherto not defended us against Frieda and now you are defending us far too much. We do not aim higher than the rest. Do you think that wanting to be a

Castle messenger is a high aim? Anyone who can run about and memorise a few words of a message has the capacity to become a Castle messenger. Nor is it a paid job. The request to be taken on as a Castle messenger seems to be regarded much like the begging of little children who have nothing to do, who pester the grown-ups to give them some errand or other, to let them do some job or other, everything only for the honour of it and for the sake of the job itself. So it is here too, only with the difference that there are not many who push themselves forward and that he who is really or apparently taken on is not treated kindly, as a child would be, but is tormented. No, for that, you see, nobody envies us, people are rather more inclined to pity us because of it, for in spite of all hostility there is still a spark of pity to be found here and there. Perhaps in your heart too – for what else could draw you to us? Solely Barnabas's messages? I can't believe that. I don't suppose you have ever really attached much importance to them, you have insisted on them merely out of pity for Barnabas or at least to a very great extent for that reason. And you have not been unsuccessful in this aim. True, Barnabas suffers as a result of your sublime, unfulfillable demands, but at the same time they give him a little pride, a little confidence, the continual doubts from which he cannot free himself up there in the Castle are to some slight extent refuted by your trust, by your continual sympathy. Since you have been in the village things go better with him. And something of this trust is passed on to the rest of us too; it would be even more if you came to see us more often. You hold back, on Frieda's account, I can understand that, I said as much to Amalia. But Amalia is so restless, for some time now I have sometimes hardly dared to talk to her even about the most necessary things. She doesn't even seem to listen when one speaks to her, and if she does listen she does not seem to understand what is said to her, and if she does understand it, she seems to despise it. But all this, after all, she does not do on purpose, and one must not be cross with her; the more aloof she is, the more gently one must treat her. She is as weak as she seems to be strong. Yesterday for instance Barnabas said that you would be coming to-day; knowing Amalia as he does he added, as a precaution, that it was only a possibility that you would come, it was not yet definite. But nevertheless Amalia was waiting for you all day, incapable of doing anything else, and only in the evening she could not keep on her feet any longer and had to lie down.' 'Now I understand,' K. said, 'why I mean something to you all, actually without any merit of my own. We are tied to each other, just as the messenger is to him to whom the message is addressed, but no more than that, you people must not exaggerate; I attach too much importance to your friendship, especially to yours, Olga, to tolerate its being endangered by exaggerated expectations; I mean in the way that you were all almost estranged from me through the fact that I hoped for too much from you. If a game is being played with you, it is not less so with me, then it is simply one single game, a game that is amazingly all of one piece. From the stories you tell me I have even gathered the impression that the two messages Barnabas brought me are the only ones with which he has been entrusted up to now.' Olga nodded. 'I was ashamed to confess it,' she said with lowered eyes, 'or I was afraid that then the messages would seem to you even more worthless than before.' 'But you two,' K. said, 'you and Amalia, are always doing your utmost to make me have less and less confidence in the messages.' 'Yes,' Olga said, 'Amalia does so, and I imitate her. It is this hopelessness that has us all in its grip. We believe the worthlessness of the message is so obvious that we cannot spoil anything by pointing out what is so obvious, that, on the contrary, we shall gain more trust and mercy from your side, which is in fact the only thing for which, at bottom, we hope. Do you understand me? That is the way our minds work. The messages are worthless, there is no strength to be gained from them directly, you are too shrewd to let yourself be deceived in this respect, and even if we could deceive you, Barnabas would be only a false messenger, and from falsehoods no salvation could come.' 'And so you are not frank with me,' K. said, 'not even you are frank with me.' 'You still don't understand our extremity,' Olga said and gazed at K. anxiously, 'it is probably our fault, being unaccustomed to associating with people we perhaps repel you, precisely through our desperate attempts to attract you. I am not frank, you say? Nobody can be more frank than I am towards you. If I keep anything from you, it is only from fear of you, and this fear is something I do not hide from you, but show quite openly. Take this fear from me and you have me utterly and completely.' 'What fear do you mean?' K. asked. 'The fear of losing you,' Olga said, 'just reflect, for three years Barnabas has been fighting for his appointment, for three years we have been waiting and watching for some success in his endeavours, all in vain, not the slightest success, only disgrace, torment, time wasted, threats as to the future, and then one evening he comes with a letter, a letter to you. "A Land Surveyor has arrived, he seems to have come for our sake. I am to carry all communications between him and the Castle," Barnabas said. "There seem to be important things involved," he said. "Of course," I said, "a Land Surveyor! He will carry out many jobs, many messages will have to be carried to and fro. Now you are a real messenger, soon you will be given the official uniform." "It is possible," Barnabas said; even he, this boy who has become such a self-tormentor, said: "It is possible." That evening we were happy, even Amalia shared in it, in her own way, true, she didn't listen to us, but she pulled her stool, on which she sat knitting, nearer to us and sometimes glanced over at us, as we sat laughing and whispering. Our happiness did not last long, it came to an end that same evening. Admittedly, it even seemed to increase when Barnabas unexpectedly came with you. But even then the doubts began, it was an honour for us, of course, that you had come, but from the very beginning it was also disturbing. What did you want, we

wondered. Why did you come? Were you really the great
man for whom we had taken you, if you cared to come into
our poor parlour? Why did you not stay in your own place,
waiting for the messenger to come up to you, as it became
your dignity, sending him away instantly? Did you not take
away something of the importance of Barnabas's appointment as a messenger, by the fact that you had come?
Besides, though you were foreign in your dress, you were
poorly dressed, and sadly I turned this way and that the wet
coat that I took off you that time. Was it that we were to
have bad luck with the first recipient of messages, for whom
we had yearned for so long? Then, admittedly, we could see
that you did not lower yourself to our level, you remained
by the window, and nothing could bring you to our table.
We did not turn round towards you, but we thought of
nothing else. Had you come only to test us? To see from
what sort of family your messenger came? Had you suspicions of us even on the second evening after your arrival?
And was the result of the test unfavourable for us, that you
remained so taciturn, spoke no word to us, and were in a
hurry to get away from us again? Your going away was for
us a proof that you despised not only us but, what was
much worse, Barnabas's messages too. We alone were not
capable of recognising their true significance, that could be
done only by you, whom they directly concerned and to
whose profession they referred. And so it was actually you
who taught us to doubt; from that evening on Barnabas
began to make his sad observations up there in the office.
And whatever questions were left open that evening were
finally answered in the morning, when I came out of the
stable and watched you moving out of the Herrenhof with
Frieda and the assistants, realising that you no longer set
any hopes in us and had abandoned us. Of course I did not
say anything to Barnabas about it, he is heavily enough
burdened with his own worries.' 'And am I not here again?'
K. said, 'keeping Frieda waiting and listening to stories
about your misery as though it were my own?' 'Yes, you are

here,' Olga said, 'and we are glad of it. The hope that you brought us was beginning to grow fainter; we were already greatly in need of your coming again.' 'For me too,' K. said, 'it was necessary to come, I see that.'

P. 186, l. 15.

'And Amalia, of course, did not interfere at all, although according to your hints she knows more about the Castle than you do; well, perhaps she is most to blame for everything.' 'You have an amazing grasp of the whole situation,' Olga said, 'sometimes you help me with one word, probably it is because you come from abroad. We, on the other hand, with our sad experiences and fears, can't help being frightened by every creak of the floorboards, without being able to help ourselves, and if one takes fright, the next one instantly takes fright too and even without knowing the proper reason for it. In such a manner one can never arrive at a proper judgment. Even if one had once had the ability to think everything out – and we women have never had it – one would lose it under these conditions. What good luck it is for us that you have come.' It was the first time that K. heard such an unreserved welcome here in the village, but however much he had felt the want of it hitherto and however trustworthy Olga seemed to him, he did not like hearing it. He had not come to bring luck to anyone; he was at liberty to help of his own free will, if things turned out that way, but nobody was to hail him as a bringer of luck, anyone who did that was confusing his paths, claiming him for matters for which he, being thus compelled, was never at their disposal, with the greatest good will on his part he could not do that. Yet Olga repaired her blunder when she continued: 'However, whenever I think I could cast aside all my worries, for you would find the explanation for everything and the way out, you suddenly say something entirely, something painfully, wrong, such as for instance this: that Amalia knows more than anyone else, does not interfere and is most to blame. No, K., we can never get near to Amalia,

369

and least of all by means of reproaches! What helps you to judge everything else, your friendliness and your courage, makes it impossible for you to form a judgment about Amalia. Before we could dare to reproach her we should first of all have to have an inkling of how she suffers. Just lately she has been so restless, has been concealing so much – and at bottom I am sure concealing nothing but her own suffering – that I scarcely dare to talk to her even about what is most necessary. When I came in and saw you in quiet conversation with her, I was startled; in reality one cannot talk to her now, then again times come when she is quieter, or perhaps not quieter but only more tired, but now it is once again at its worst. She doesn't even seem to listen when one speaks to her, and if she does listen she does not seem to understand what is said to her, and if she does understand it, she seems to despise it. But all this, after all, she does not do on purpose, and one must not be cross with her; the more aloof she is, the more gently one must treat her. She is as weak as she seems to be strong. Yesterday, for instance, Barnabas said that you would be coming to-day; knowing Amalia as he does he added, as a precaution, that it was only a possibility that you would come, it was not yet definite. But, nevertheless, Amalia was waiting for you all day, incapable of doing anything else, and only in the evening she could not keep on her feet any longer and had to lie down.' Again what K. heard in all this was above all the demands that this family was making on him. One could easily go completely wrong about this family if one was not careful. He was only very sorry that he should be having such impossible ideas about Olga of all people, thus disturbing the intimacy that Olga had been the first to evoke, which was very comforting to him, which was primarily what kept him here and for the sake of which he would have liked best to put off his departure indefinitely. 'We shall find it difficult to agree,' K. said, 'I see that already. As yet we have hardly touched on what really matters and even now there are contradictions here and there. If the two of us were alone, it would not be difficult to agree, I should soon be of one mind with you, you are unselfish and intelligent; only we are not alone; indeed we are not even the main persons, your family is there, about which we shall scarcely manage to agree, and about Amalia we shall certainly not.' 'You condemn Amalia entirely?' Olga asked. 'Without knowing her, you condemn her?' 'I do not condemn her,' K. said, 'nor am I blind to her merits, I even admit that I may be doing her injustice, but it is very difficult not to do her injustice, for she is haughty and reserved and domineering into the bargain; if she were not also sad and obviously unhappy, one could not reconcile oneself to her at all.' 'Is that all you have against her?' Olga asked, and now she herself had become sad. 'I suppose it's enough,' K. said and saw only now that Amalia was back in the room again, but far away from them, at the parents' table. 'There she is,' K. said, and against his will there was in his tone the abhorrence of that supper and all who were partaking of it. 'You are prejudiced against Amalia,' Olga said. 'I am,' K. said. 'Why am I? Tell me, if you know. You are frank, I appreciate that very much, but you are frank only where you yourself are concerned, you believe you have to protect your brother and sister by keeping silence. That is wrong, I can't support Barnabas if I don't know everything that concerns him and, since Amalia is involved in everything to do with your family, everything that concerns Amalia too. Surely you don't want me to undertake something and, as a consequence of insufficiently detailed knowledge of the circumstances and for that reason only, to ruin everything and damage you and myself in a way that is beyond repair.' 'No, K.,' Olga said after a pause, 'I don't want that and therefore it would be better if everything could be left as it was.' 'I don't think,' K. said, 'that that is better, I don't think that it is better for Barnabas to go on leading this shadowy existence as an alleged messenger and for you all to share this life with him, grown-up people feeding on baby-food, I don't think that that is better than if Barnabas allies himself

with me, lets me think out the best ways and means here at
my leisure, and then, trustfully, no longer relying only on
himself, under constant observation, carries out everything
himself, and to his own profit and to mine also penetrates
further into the bureaux or perhaps does not make any
headway, but learns to understand and turn to account
everything in the room where he already is. I don't think
that that would be bad and not worth a good deal of sacrifice. Yet it is, of course, also possible that I am wrong and
that precisely what you are keeping back is what puts you in
the right. Then we shall remain good friends in spite of
everything, I couldn't manage here at all without your
friendship, but then it is unnecessary for me to spend the
whole evening here and keep Frieda waiting, only Barnabas's important affair, which cannot be postponed, could
have justified that.' K. was about to get up, Olga kept him
back. 'Did Frieda tell you anything about us?' she asked.
'Nothing definite.' 'Nor the landlady?' 'No, nothing.' 'That
was what I expected,' Olga said, 'you won't learn anything
definite about us from anyone in the village, on the other
hand, everyone – whether he knows what it is all about or
whether he knows nothing and only believes rumours going
around or invented by himself – everyone will somehow try
to show in a general way that he despises us, obviously he
would have to despise himself if he did not do so. That is
how it is with Frieda and with everyone, but this contempt
is only generally and broadly directed against us, against the
family, and the barb is aimed only at Amalia. Especially for
this reason too I am grateful to you, K., for despising
neither us nor Amalia, although you are under the general
influence. Only you are prejudiced, at least against Barnabas
and Amalia, the fact is nobody can completely escape the
influence of the world; but that you are capable of it to such
an extent is a great deal, and my hope is to a large extent
based on this.' 'I am not interested in other people's opinions,' K. said, 'and I am not curious to know their reasons.
Perhaps – it would be a bad thing, but it is possible – per-

haps that is a way in which I shall change when I marry and settle down here, but for the present I am free, it will not be easy for me to keep this visit of mine to you concealed from Frieda or to justify it to her, but I am still free, I can still, if something seems to me as important as Barnabas's affair, occupy myself with it as exhaustively as I want to, without grave qualms. Now, however, you will understand why I urge a very quick decision: I am still with you, but only, as it were, till further notice, at any moment someone may come and fetch me, and then I don't know when I shall be able to come again.' 'But Barnabas isn't here,' Olga said, 'what can be decided without him?' 'I don't need him for the time being,' K. said, 'for the time being I need other things. But before I go into that I beg you, don't let yourself be deceived if what I say sounds domineering, I am no more domineering than I am inquisitive, I do not want either to subdue you all or to rob you of your secrets, all I want is to treat you the way I should like to be treated myself.' 'How like a stranger you are speaking now,' Olga said, 'you were much nearer to us before, were you not? Your reservations are entirely unnecessary, I have never doubted you and shall not do so, so don't you do it with regard to me either.' 'If I speak differently from before,' K. said, 'that is because I want to be even nearer to you all than before, I want to be at home among you, either I shall attach myself to you in this way or not at all, either we shall make entirely common cause with regard to Barnabas or we shall avoid even every fleeting, objectively unnecessary contact that would compromise me and perhaps all of you too. To this alliance, as I wish it to be, this alliance with the Castle in mind, there exists, admittedly, one grave obstacle: Amalia. And that is why I ask you first of all: Can you speak for Amalia, answer for her, vouch for her?' 'I can partly speak for her, partly answer for her, but I cannot vouch for her.' 'Won't you call her?' 'That would be the end. You would learn less from her than from me. She would reject any sort of alliance and would not tolerate any

373

condition, she would forbid even me to answer; with a skill
and inexorability that you still have no idea that she pos-
sesses, she would force you to break off the discussions and
to go and then, then, to be sure, when you were outside, she
would perhaps collapse in a faint. That is what she is like.'
'But without her everything is hopeless,' K. said, 'without
her we remain half-way, in uncertainty.' 'Perhaps,' Olga
said, 'you will now be able to estimate Barnabas's work better after all, we two, he and I, work alone; without Amalia
it is as if we were building a house without foundations.'

P. 207, l. 24.
'Had he perhaps after all been officially punished on
account of the affair with the letter?' K. asked. 'Because he
completely disappeared?' Olga asked. 'On the contrary. This
complete disappearance is a reward that the officials
allegedly do their utmost to get; after all, dealing with applicants is what is so tormenting for them.' 'But Sortini had
scarcely had any of that sort of work even previously,' K.
said. 'Or was that letter perhaps also part of that dealing
with applicants which so tormented him?' 'Please, K., don't
ask in that manner,' Olga said. 'Since Amalia has been here,
you have been different. What good can such questions do?
Whether you ask them seriously or jokingly, no one can
answer them. They remind me of Amalia at the beginning
of these years of misfortune. She hardly talked at all, but
paid attention to everything that happened, she was much
more attentive than she is now, and sometimes she would
break her silence after all, and then it was with some such
question, which perhaps would shame the questioner, at any
rate the person questioned, and mostly certainly Sortini
too.'

P. 208, l. 11. (continuation of K.'s speech).
'The Castle in itself is infinitely more powerful than you
are, nevertheless there might still be some doubt whether it
will win, yet you don't turn that to account, but it is as

though all your endeavours were aimed at establishing the victory of the Castle beyond any doubt, that is why suddenly in the midst of the fight you begin to be afraid without any cause, thus increasing your own helplessness.'

P. 274, l. 1. (After first sentence of Chapter XIX.)

'Sit down somewhere,' Erlanger said; he himself sat down at the desk and put some files, which, after a fleeting glance at the covers, he first rearranged, into a small attaché-case, similar to the one Bürgel had, but which turned out to be almost too small for the files. Erlanger had to take out the files that he had already put in and try to pack them again differently. 'You ought to have come long ago,' he said; he had been unfriendly even before, but now he was probably transferring his annoyance with the obstinate files to K. K., startled out of his weariness by the new surroundings and Erlanger's brusque manner, which, allowing for the due difference in dignity, was a little reminiscent of the schoolmaster – outwardly, too, there were little points of resemblance, and he himself was sitting here on the chair like a schoolboy all of whose schoolmates to right and to left were absent that day – answered as carefully as possible, beginning by mentioning the fact that Erlanger had been asleep, told him that in order not to disturb him he had gone away, then, of course, passed over in silence what he had been doing in the meantime, resuming his account only with the incident of his confusing the doors, and concluded by referring to his extraordinary fatigue, which he asked should be taken into consideration. Erlanger at once discovered the weak point in this answer. 'Queer,' he said, 'I sleep in order to be rested for my work, but during the same time you are roaming about I don't know where, only to make excuses about being tired when the interrogation is supposed to begin.' K. was about to answer, but Erlanger stopped him with a gesture. 'Your fatigue does not seem to diminish your garrulity,' he said. 'Nor was the muttering going on for hours in the next room exactly the best way of showing consideration for my sleep, to which you allegedly attach so much importance.' Once again K. was about to answer, and once again Erlanger prevented him. 'Anyway, I shall not take up much of your time,' Erlanger said, 'I only want to ask a favour of you.' Suddenly, however, he remembered something, it now became apparent that he had all the time been vaguely thinking of something that was distracting him and that the severity with which he had spoken to K. had perhaps only been superficial and actually produced only by his inattentiveness, and he pressed the button of an electric bell on the desk. Through a side-door – so Erlanger and his suite occupied several rooms – a servant instantly appeared. He was obviously a beadle, one of those of whom Olga had told him, he himself had never seen such a person before. He was a fairly small but very broad man, his face was also broad and open, and in it the eyes, never wide open, seemed all the smaller. His suit was reminiscent of Klamm's suit, though it was worn and fitted badly, this was particularly striking in the case of the sleeves, which were too short, for the servant had fairly short arms to begin with, the suit had obviously been meant for a still smaller man, probably the servants wore the officials' cast-off clothing. That might also contribute to the proverbial pride of all the servants; this one, too, seemed to think that by answering the bell he had done all the work that could be expected of him, and gazed at K. with an expression as severe as if he had been sent for to order K. about. Erlanger, on the other hand, waited in silence for the servant to carry out some job or other, for which he had summoned him, as a customary one to be done without any further specific order. Since however, this did not happen, the servant only continuing to gaze at K. angrily or reproachfully, Erlanger stamped irritably and almost drove K. – once again K. had to bear the consequences of annoyance for which he was not to blame – out of the room, telling him to wait outside for a moment, he would be let in again instantly. When he was then called back in a markedly more amiable tone, the servant had already gone, the only change that K. noticed in the room lay in the fact that now a wooden screen concealed the bed, wash-stand, and wardrobe. 'One has a great deal of trouble with the servants,' Erlanger said, and, coming from his lips, this could be taken as an astonishingly confidential remark, if, of course, it was not merely soliloquy. 'And indeed plenty of trouble and worry on all sides,' he continued, leaning back in his chair, holding his clenched fists far away from himself on the table. 'Klamm, my chief, has been a little uneasy during the last few days, at least it seems so to us who live in his proximity and try to work out and interpret every one of his utterances. It seems so to us, that does not mean he is uneasy – how should uneasiness touch him? – but we are uneasy, we round about him are uneasy and can hardly conceal it from him any more in our work. This is, of course, a state of affairs that, if it is not to cause the greatest damage – to everyone, including you – must, if possible, not be allowed to last a moment longer! We have been searching for the reasons and have discovered various things that might possibly be to blame for it. There are among them the most ridiculous things, which is not so very astonishing, for the extremely ridiculous and the extremely serious are not far removed from each other. Office life, in particular, is so exhausting that it can only be done if all the smallest subsidiary circumstances are carefully watched and if possible no change is permitted in this respect. The circumstance, for instance, that an ink-well has been shifted a hand's-breadth from its usual place may endanger the most important work. To keep a watch over all this should really be the servants' job, but unfortunately they are so little to be depended on that a large part of this work has to be done by us, not least by me, who am reputed to have a particularly sharp eye for these things. Now, as it happens, this is a very delicate, intimate job that could be done in a twinkling by the insensitive hands of servants, but which causes me a great deal of trouble, is very remote from the rest of my work and, by the shifting to and fro that it occasions, might very well completely ruin nerves only a little weaker than mine are. You understand me?'

ANTON CHEKHOV
The Complete Short Novels
My Life and Other Stories
The Steppe and Other Stories

KATE CHOPIN
The Awakening

CARL VON CLAUSEWITZ
On War

S. T. COLERIDGE
Poems

WILKIE COLLINS
The Moonstone
The Woman in White

CONFUCIUS
The Analects

JOSEPH CONRAD
Heart of Darkness
Lord Jim
Nostromo
The Secret Agent
Typhoon and Other Stories
Under Western Eyes
Victory

THOMAS CRANMER
The Book of Common Prayer
(UK only)

ROALD DAHL
Collected Stories

DANTE ALIGHIERI
The Divine Comedy

CHARLES DARWIN
The Origin of Species
The Voyage of the Beagle
(in 1 vol.)

DANIEL DEFOE
Moll Flanders
Robinson Crusoe

CHARLES DICKENS
Barnaby Rudge
Bleak House
David Copperfield
Dombey and Son
Great Expectations
Hard Times
Little Dorrit
Martin Chuzzlewit
The Mystery of Edwin Drood
Nicholas Nickleby

CHARLES DICKENS *cont.*
The Old Curiosity Shop
Oliver Twist
Our Mutual Friend
The Pickwick Papers
A Tale of Two Cities

DENIS DIDEROT
Memoirs of a Nun

JOAN DIDION
We Tell Ourselves Stories in Order
to Live (US only)

JOHN DONNE
The Complete English Poems

FYODOR DOSTOEVSKY
The Adolescent
The Brothers Karamazov
Crime and Punishment
Demons
The Double and The Gambler
The Idiot
Notes from Underground

W. E. B. DU BOIS
The Souls of Black Folk
(US only)

UMBERTO ECO
The Name of the Rose

GEORGE ELIOT
Adam Bede
Daniel Deronda
Middlemarch
The Mill on the Floss
Silas Marner

JOHN EVELYN
The Diary of John Evelyn
(UK only)

WILLIAM FAULKNER
The Sound and the Fury
(UK only)

HENRY FIELDING
Joseph Andrews and Shamela
(UK only)
Tom Jones

F. SCOTT FITZGERALD
The Great Gatsby
This Side of Paradise
(UK only)

This book is set in EHRHARDT. The precise origin
of the typeface is unclear. Most of the founts were
probably cut by the Hungarian punch-cutter
Nicholas Kis for the Ehrhardt foundry
in Leipzig, where they were left
for sale in 1689. In 1938 the
Monotype foundry pro-
duced the modern
version.